Praise for Maya Linnell an...

'A sparkling entry into the rural romance arena.' *Canberra Weekly*

'You'll devour this rural read in one go.' *New Idea*

'Very authentic rural flavour, a surprise fast-paced ending, shows you can't deny what's in your heart.' Australian Romance Readers Association

'I lost myself in *Wildflower Ridge*. A beautiful novel, full of love, fun, excitement, cooking and country flair.' Kym, Good Reads

'My favourite romance of 2019. A masterful and moving tale . . . her writing is flawless and very believable. Can't wait to see what's next!' SHE Society

'Idyllic . . . Maya Linnell tells a good yarn.' *Ruth* magazine— Queensland CWA

'To say it was a great read is an understatement! For a debut novelist I was so impressed with her style of writing and felt totally invested in the characters within. I'm so pleased another quality Australian author has arrived!' Janine, librarian and Good Reads reviewer

'Beautifully written with strong characters and a true depiction of life on a farm with all its trials, tribulations . . . love, family

and laughter. I loved this book and didn't want it to end.'
Beauty & Lace

'*Wildflower Ridge* made excellent beach reading, and would be the perfect companion to curl up with by the fire for some cosy winter reading too. I'm looking forward to seeing what Maya's got in store for us (and the McIntyre girls!) next!'
Bookish Bron (blog)

'Five stars—a great addition to the rural family fiction with a dash of romance, a sophisticated plot, very convincing characters . . . a book you can't pass up.' Happy Valley Books

'I'm only new to Australian rural romance, but I don't know why! All the eucalyptus, the scones and "raiding the tucker tent" I loved it! I can't wait for the next Maya Linnell novel.'
Anna's Bookstore

'Rural fiction at its finest and most immersive. A ripper of a yarn, and a bloody good debut.' Alyce, Good Reads

'What a fabulous debut. Moving and heartfelt . . . this one was a page turner. Five stars.' Helen, Family Saga Blogspot

'A book of love, life, friendship, community and hard yakka . . . told with plenty of heart and lashings of authenticity.' Mrs B's Book Reviews

'Sit out on the deck with a cup of tea, baked goods at the ready, and enjoy every moment of this remarkable novel. Rural fiction at its best.' DelBookGirl

'Familiar, comforting and warm—perfect for a winter's day read in front of the fire.' Blue Wolf Reviews

Maya Linnell was recently shortlisted as the ARRA 2019 Favourite Australian Romance Author for her rural romance debut *Wildflower Ridge*. Her new novel *Bottlebrush Creek* will be released in June 2020, with both stories gathering inspiration from her rural upbringing and the small communities she has always lived in and loved. A former country journalist and PR writer, Maya now prefers the world of fiction over fact and blogs for Romance Writers Australia. She loves baking up a storm, tending to her rambling garden, and raising three little bookworms. Maya lives on a small property in country Victoria with her family, her menagerie of farm animals and the odd snake or two. Find her online at www.mayalinnell.com.

MAYA LINNELL

Wildflower Ridge

ALLEN&UNWIN
SYDNEY · MELBOURNE · AUCKLAND · LONDON

Allen & Unwin
83 Alexander Street
Crows Nest NSW 2065
Australia
Phone:(61 2) 8425 0100
Email:info@allenandunwin.com
Web:www.allenandunwin.com

A catalogue record for this book is available from the National Library of Australia

ISBN 978 1 76087 755 2

Set in Sabon LT Pro by Bookhouse, Sydney

Printed in Australia by SOS Print + Media Group

10 9 8 7 6 5 4

MIX
Paper from responsible sources
FSC® C001695

The paper in this book is FSC® certified. FSC® promotes environmentally responsible, socially beneficial and economically viable management of the world's forests.

For Mum and Dad, my lifelong cheerleaders.
Thank you for thrusting books into my hands from a
young age, always encouraging me to write
and giving me the confidence to dream big.

One

Penny McIntyre stirred before the hall lights were turned up to full strength, hours before the first stream of visitors came marching down the hallways with flowers and chocolates. The night nurses had only roused her once last night for monitoring, much better than the three-hourly checks done on the first and second nights. *Hopefully, they'll give me the all clear to head home today. Surely there's someone else who needs this bed more than me.*

She stretched carefully so the wires and drip wouldn't catch or yank at the cannula on the back of her freckled hand. The starched nightgown scratched at her skin, and a wave of fatigue made her wince, crushing her as if it were one of the steamrollers working around the clock to repair the Melbourne roads twenty or so storeys below. Penny blinked the sleep from her eyes. *Okay, maybe not home today*, she conceded silently. *But soon.* She looked out the window, at the skyline peppered with lights and streams of commuters heading into the city. Commuters that didn't include her, travelling to offices just like the one she had collapsed in three days ago.

Penny's jewellery sparkled under the hospital lights as she pushed aside a bouquet of 'get well soon' flowers and reached for her mobile. She pressed the phone screen, but it remained lifeless. *Flat as a tack.* Her strawberry-blond hair fell across her face as she wriggled closer to the other bedside table, the one containing four more floral arrangements and her phone charger. Her head and body throbbed in protest as she stretched further and plugged her phone into the charger—the most activity she had undertaken in days. She flopped back onto the pillows, a triumphant smile spreading across her pale face. *Couldn't manage that yesterday. I must be on the road to recovery already.* The smile stayed on Penny's lips as she closed her eyes and allowed the pain relief to drag her back to the darkness.

Bright daylight peeked around the edges of the window when Penny woke again. A young nurse padded into the room and swept open the curtains with unreserved efficiency.

'Beautiful day out there, Miss McIntyre. How about that lovely sunshine? You'd pay a mint for that natural light in a city apartment.' Her voice echoed off the industrial-grey walls, her smile as radiant as the streams of golden light pouring through the glass.

Penny was usually the first to comment on the sunshine and appreciate beauty in all its forms, but from her vantage point in the hospital bed, she couldn't quite muster up the same enthusiasm.

'It's lovely, though I have to admit I'd rather be in my office. I've got loads to do. Do you think I'll be out tomorrow?' Penny's enthusiastic question was met with an amused look from the nurse.

'Return to work tomorrow? Miss McIntyre, you'll be back here within a week if you return to work or any physical activity in the immediate future. Ross River fever is not to be underestimated. You need bed rest and lots of it, if you want to shake this nasty virus.' The nurse bustled around the room, checking the drip and cannula.

'Resting's not exactly in my DNA,' Penny admitted. 'If a mosquito hadn't hijacked my body, I'd be sealing the deal for a multi-million-dollar advertising campaign right now instead of lounging around in a hospital bed.'

The nurse laughed again as she straightened Penny's pillows, scribbled on the observation chart and checked the pain relief levels.

'It's not lounging around, it's recovering. Try your luck with the doctor when he does his rounds, but I can't imagine his answer will be any different from mine. I guess that's the risk you take when you sign up for those mud runs, right?'

Penny sank into the freshly plumped pillows for a second then sprang back up, receiving a sharp reprimand from her aching joints. She turned, more carefully this time, and fossicked in her handbag for a hairbrush. Lacking the luxury of a mirror or the phone camera on selfie mode, she tamed the bird's nest of shoulder-length hair into what she hoped was a slightly less frightening style. Her enthusiasm didn't carry as far as make-up, but she reasoned something was better than nothing. A clatter of footsteps neared her door. She shoved the hairbrush back into her bag as a bevy of white coats filed into her room.

'You're looking perkier this morning, Miss McIntyre,' said the doctor, reaching for her chart. 'And awfully modest. Young Belinda here showed me your double-page spread in last week's *Good Weekend* magazine. Melbourne's hottest corporate couple, eh? I was thinking of bringing it in for an autograph, but maybe I should wait until you and your boyfriend are both here.' He smiled. The mousy-brown intern behind him flushed.

Penny grinned. The novelty of being recognised from a magazine brought a spark to her grey–green eyes.

'Thank you, it was good coverage for Boutique Media,' she said. *Hope they take that into consideration while dealing with the fallout from this week's drama.*

'How are you feeling?'

'Much better,' she hedged. It wasn't a complete lie—the IV drip and pain relief had controlled the fever and helped mute what the doctor had yesterday labelled as polyarthritis. 'I'm pretty sure I'm right to check out soon.' She beamed at him, confident that a man of his standing would have more of an appreciation for career matters than the nurse.

With a wistful smile, he shook his head.

'It's not a hotel and you won't be going anywhere for a few days, Miss McIntyre. Usually, our patients are begging for sick certificates to get more time off, not less. It must be some job if you're hankering to return after collapsing on the boardroom floor.' The doctor made a note on the observation chart and nodded politely. 'I'll see you in a day or two.'

The tribe of interns scurried out the door behind him.

Penny's earlier optimism wilted at the mention of the board-room floor. She recalled the sweat dripping from her brow as she began her pitch to the company's most lucrative clients. The overhead lights that dazzled her, making her feel even hotter. The burning in her bones that contrasted against the shivery feeling on her back. The surprised squeak escaping from her mouth as she fainted from a dangerously high temperature, crumpling to the boardroom floor. Her disorientated vision of chairs scraping on carpet, people rushing to her aid before everything went dark.

Penny blinked away the memory, focusing on the flowers that had arrived from her employer the same afternoon she had been ambulanced to the hospital. Flowers that should be sitting on her office desk with a card that read: 'Congratulations on your promotion' instead of: 'Get well soon'.

Two

Georgie Morton's hair was neatly bobbed as always. Not a hint of white regrowth dared sneak into her side part, and her heavy application of make-up was set off with trademark crimson lipstick. As the executive manager for Melbourne's most prestigious PR firm, she subscribed to a holy trinity of wool, silk and linen. Today was no exception, with her linen shift dress, silk scarf and finely tailored jacket bringing a distinct flamboyance to the drab room. Penny sat in her hospital bed. With only a hastily applied veil of make-up and a cashmere cardigan over her nighty, she felt distinctly vulnerable. The conversation wasn't going quite as she'd planned. She regrouped and tried a different tack.

'Please, just let me come back, Georgie? You know I'm the best marketing executive on staff. I'll do everything in my power to fix this ... this ... this mess I've made. Surely our clients will understand. They're in the pharmaceuticals industry, maybe they'll take me on as a trial project.' Penny laughed feebly, hoping the joke would cover the hint of alarm that had crept into her voice.

Georgie kept her hands clasped neatly in her lap, though her gaze darted around the room, glancing from Penny's IV line to her cheap, standard-issue hospital nightgown, and then down to the lifeless, utilitarian bedding.

'That's precisely why I'm insisting you take a break, Penny. I can't force you, of course, but I strongly recommend it. The Whitfield Pharmaceuticals ship has sailed. Those vultures at Yarra PR were just waiting in the wings, ready to swoop in and steal them from under our noses. All it took was one hiccup and they were gone. Doesn't anyone believe in loyalty these days?'

Penny winced as she calculated the loss of income that must have followed her ambulance stretcher out the door. The commission from the Whitfield Pharmaceuticals contract alone would have paid for a fortnight in the Whitsundays.

'Surely I can woo them back when I'm better? A week, maybe ten days and I'll be fighting fit again,' she said.

Georgie sniffed and pushed her horn-rimmed glasses a millimetre up her perfectly sculpted nose. She tapped a lacquered fingernail against her lips.

'I heard on the grapevine Yarra PR reeled them in with a three-year exclusive. No enticing them back to Boutique Media in the short term. I'll pull a few strings to keep your promotion open, but you've got to be 100 per cent healthy upon your return.'

Penny opened her mouth but closed it as Georgie held up a hand. Her voice held an edge of steel.

'I won't stand for lies, either. I found Dr Atwood's medical certificate in your office. If you'd taken leave as she advised a fortnight ago, neither of us would be here right now. What were you thinking, Penny? This makes me look terrible. It makes our company look terrible, as if we're overworking our employees.'

Shame prickled at Penny's skin, though she knew as well as Georgie that both of them fell into the overworked category. Her fingers fumbled for the top button of her cardigan, brushing the swollen lymph glands under her jaw.

'I'm sorry, Georgie. I thought I could push through it.' And she truly had. Each time she'd swallowed a painkiller and masked her fever and aching joints, she'd been positive the poorly timed flu, or whatever it was, would blow over.

'Get well, Penny. That's all I ask. Ten weeks' leave should do it, starting today,' said the older woman.

Penny's stomach dropped. Georgie made a show of brushing imaginary lint from her jacket as she stood to leave.

'Ten weeks? TEN. WEEKS. I didn't want to take one week's sick leave, let alone ten. Please don't do this to me, Georgie.'

Georgie furrowed her brow and pressed her lips into a thin, red line as she turned in the doorway.

'It's not up for discussion, I'm afraid. And it sounds like a hiatus is just what the doctor ordered.' The suggestion rolled uncomfortably off Georgie's tongue, as if it were something she felt obliged to recommend but would never self-prescribe.

A sudden weariness washed over Penny. She knew Georgie well enough to read the set of her chin and the stiff back. Determined to salvage her dignity, she swallowed the lump in her throat and tried for an upbeat tone.

'Even if I'm out of the office, I won't stop thinking about work. CC me into all the emails, I'll make sure I keep my phone charged.' She watched her boss and mentor stalk down the hospital corridor, wafting a trail of Chanel perfume in her wake.

Georgie paused at the industrial-sized antibacterial gel dispenser, just as Penny had known she would. But instead of rubbing her hands and continuing on, Georgie reapplied the gel a second time. As she reached for a third dose of gel and then a fourth, Penny stifled the uncomfortable feeling that Georgie was trying her best to wash her hands of the whole situation.

Tim Patterson let the conversation and country music roll around him as he collected crockery from the farmhouse dining table. Almost every spot was filled with three generations of the McIntyre clan.

'Leave the dishes, Tim. We'll sort them out when we get back from Wildflower Ridge,' said Angus McIntyre, wiping his mouth with a handkerchief.

Tim smiled at his boss—not only the head of the McIntyre Park Merino Stud but the family patriarch—as he moved across to the sink.

'Not a chance. It's the least I can do after that feast. Get going before you miss the sunset.'

Quiet chatter followed the family out the house, as they eased into workboots, gumboots and enough jackets and scarves to ward off the unseasonably cold autumn night.

Tim cradled the treasured plates in his callused hands, determined to return the delicate porcelain to the china hutch in pristine condition. He often admired the matching set when he came in for smoko and knew it would sit behind the glass doors for another 364 days before being returned to service.

He fished around in the hot soapy water, catching the dishcloth as it snagged on the new collection of cuts and blisters on his fingers. It had been another productive week at McIntyre Park, busy enough to keep Angus's mind off the anniversary of his wife's death, but not too busy that he'd had to shelve his weekly volunteer session at the local school. Like Angus, Tim was happier buried in sheep work, paddock maintenance and a few community ventures than sitting around dwelling on his own problems.

Lara McIntyre jogged back up the verandah steps and plucked a hat from the laundry coat rack.

'Help yourself to more dessert, Tim. Or take a piece home for Stella,' she offered as she slipped the knitted beanie over her head.

'Not sure if Stella will be around tonight, and I'm already as full as a fat lady's undies.' His phrase elicited a rare grin from the austere woman, just as he'd hoped. 'But it was top notch as always—thanks, anyway,' he added.

A procession of McIntyres trailed past the kitchen window, their annual pilgrimage underway. Their destination was just visible in the blue mountain range that spanned the horizon. Diana McIntyre's three eldest boys tore across the yard, encouraging the resident rooster with loud hoots and hollers. They weaved in and out of the standard roses, sending flutters of petals into the air like confetti, before scrambling onto the back of the old farm ute. The fair-haired baby boy in Diana's arms flailed his hands, as if counting down the days until he too could ride on the back of the ute with his big brothers. Encouraged by the ruckus, the fledgling rooster joined in with another round of crowing that travelled through the farmhouse's weatherboard walls and into the kitchen.

Damn fool still hasn't worked out dawn from dusk. Tim scrubbed a dirty bowl, grinning as the oldest McIntyre daughter eyed the chicken coop. He wouldn't be surprised to turn up to work tomorrow and hear that the young cockerel was bubbling away in a stockpot on top of Diana's AGA, some five kilometres down the road. She might not live on her father's farm anymore, but she was still pretty handy with a meat cleaver.

Dark clouds rolled in from the west, casting deep shadows over the shearing shed. By the time they trekked up to Wildflower Ridge and back, it would be almost dark. A quad bike pulled up in front of the procession. Tim watched Angus shuffle back in the seat and gesture to his eldest grandchild and only granddaughter, Evie. Within seconds, the girl had jumped down off the ute tray, launched onto the front of the four-wheeler and guided it forward, leading the convoy towards the Grampians mountain range.

Tim returned his attention to the task at hand, gently wiping the dainty crockery's gold banding.

'Help, Tim?'

Tim shook his head at Eddie Patterson, keen to keep his brother as far away from the delicate china as possible.

'She's right, Ed. I've got this covered. But do us a favour and toss some wood on the fire, so it's all toasty warm when the McIntyres get back? Then we'll head home.'

Eddie grinned, his left cheek dimpling just like Tim's as he gave his brother a thumbs up. He hurried to collect the wood from a well-stocked wheelbarrow at the back door and raced across the kitchen, tiny pieces of loose kindling dropping behind him. Tim quietly picked them up and watched Eddie load the fire from the corner of his eye. Eddie's tongue poked out the corner of his mouth, his wide, almond-shaped eyes fixed with concentration.

The phone rang, cutting through the kitchen radio. Tim dried his hands, silenced the music and reached for the house phone.

'Y'ello, McIntyre Park.'

An unfamiliar voice came down the line. Smooth. Confident. City.

'Hello, is this Angus McIntyre?'

Tim leaned back against the kitchen bench, keeping an eye on the lounge room as he spoke. *Sounds like the salesman*

Angus described this morning. The nerve of the guy, hassling farmers all hours of the day.

'He's not in at the moment, but we've already told you, mate. We're happy with our local tractor dealer. Weren't you supposed to scrub this number off your call list?'

There was a pause. Tim exhaled quietly as Eddie finished loading the fire without incident and gave him another thumbs up. For most twenty-one-year-olds, such a task would be a non-event, but for a boy with Down's syndrome, each successful fire-related accomplishment was an achievement. The man's voice came down the phone again, laced with irritation.

'I've got no idea who you think you're talking to, but I'm not calling about farm machinery. I'm calling about Penny. And I'm assuming you're not her father?'

Tim looked up sharply, his grey eyes fixing on the family portrait from the late nineties. Of the four McIntyre daughters, Penny looked the most like her late mother, Annabel, with the same light-red hair, pale skin and captivating smile.

'Sorry, mate, I thought you were someone else. Can I take a message?' He reached for the notepad beside the phone and swallowed down the questions that jumped into his mind, reminding himself he had no grounds to quiz this man about the country girl who had stolen his heart and thrown it away without a backward glance.

Three

Penny woke with a start. Her eyes shot open at the strange tapping noise, and she rolled onto her side. A sleepy smile tugged at her lips as she spotted the man sitting in the corner, a laptop spread across his knees. His large frame dwarfed the plastic hospital chair, his perfectly knotted tie as precise as his haircut and professionally tailored suit, his shirt even whiter than the hospital linen. She didn't need to look at the wall clock to know it was evening—the level of stubble on Vince Callas's jaw was evidence enough. A sense of calm descended over Penny as he set aside his computer and reached for her hand. Penny squeezed it, the warmth and familiarity almost making tears well up again.

He leaned in to kiss her.

'How are you feeling, babe?'

Penny breathed in his scent; the same smell of coffee, pepper and lime that permeated their St Kilda apartment. Her aching muscles loosened a little.

'Terrible. A bit shell-shocked, really. I can't believe Georgie would do that to me.'

'Everyone in the office is gutted for you, Pen. But it's an HR thing, nothing personal.'

'Ten weeks, though? It's career suicide. I've never taken more than a fortnight off at a time, not even on our European jaunts,' she said. She grinned sleepily, trying to search for a silver lining. A glass-half-full attitude was a habit she had inherited from her late mother, Annabel, and shared with two of her three sisters. 'But at least I'll have you at my beck and call during my convalescence. Maybe we should get a bell and I can ring it when I need a fresh coffee or clean negligee.'

Vince looked away, and she squeezed his hand again.

'Relax, I'm joking. The doctor has only ordered bed rest for the first few weeks, then I'll be able to potter around quietly as long as I promise to outsource the domestics. I could always ask one of my sisters to come up for a few days, ease the strain,' she said, hoping her suggestion would lighten the mood.

Her sisters' lives were already oversubscribed with family and calling in to visit their father at the farm. But the joke fell flat. Vince didn't know the first thing about her sisters. She doubted he'd even be able to spot them in a police line-up.

'About that, Pen . . . I've got to head back to the office in a minute. We're going to pull a late-nighter to nail the quarterly budgets, but I wanted to talk to you first.'

Something about his tone set her alert system into overdrive. She was pretty sure he wasn't about to get down on bended knee and snap open the ring box she'd seen hiding in his underwear drawer the previous month. Not that she'd been snooping, of course, but before she knew it, the little aqua box with its signature white ribbon had been lying on the floor and the diamond had momentarily glittered on her left hand for all of a minute, before Vince's key had turned in the apartment door and she'd hastily stuffed it back into its hiding spot. *No*, she thought, taking in his strained expression, *this was not that moment.*

'I'm taking the Sydney secondment, Pen.'

Penny searched his blue eyes as a tight knot formed in her stomach.

'You can't be serious? Now?'

'It's bad timing, but I'd be mad not to take it.' He squeezed her hand, trying to catch her eye.

Penny wrenched her arm away. Although her energy was flagging fast, she felt like whacking him over the head with one of the bunches of flowers he'd had couriered to the hospital yesterday, when he was caught in a meeting. *Probably too busy arranging his secondment*, she realised, scrambling up into a sitting position. The cannula in her hand tugged sharply.

'What am I supposed to do? Book into a hotel and live on room service? You weren't even interested in the Sydney secondment last week.'

Vince looked away, fidgeting with the lapel of his Italian wool blazer.

'I've left a message for your father. He'll collect you from the hospital, take you back to the farm. They'll look after you much better than me, babe.'

'The farm?' Penny felt like a parrot, mimicking Vince's words. For such a confident public speaker, who regularly outlined intricate marketing plans and headed up a team of six junior staff, she was frustrated by her own inability to string a sentence together. She gaped at him, alternating between fury, hurt and confusion. *How can he spring this on me now?*

'It's a huge opportunity for me, Pen, and I'm not really the Florence Nightingale type.' He looked around the hospital room helplessly, gesturing to the cords tethering her body to the medical paraphernalia. She watched him shiver as the automatic medication dosage machine delivered its hourly top-up with an unceremonious glug.

She turned away, biting her lip to stop the tears that threatened, and tugged her hospital gown closer around her body. This new betrayal was even harder to handle than Georgie's. *What was it Georgie said about loyalty?*

'We'll be fine, babe. Plenty of couples manage long-distance relationships. We'll chat all the time.'

Penny took a deep breath and tried to assess the situation objectively. *What if Vince broke his leg on the eve of the Paris marketing conference? Would I give up the trip for him?* She bit her lip, aware that her own hesitation held the answer. For the very first time Penny cursed the mutual ambition that formed the cornerstone of their relationship.

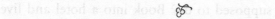

The scent of flowers and the sound of a telephone imprinted on Penny's senses before she was fully awake. For a moment she thought she was back in her office, sitting at the shiny white desk that was always adorned with fresh flowers, fielding calls from clients and media outlets. She blinked and fumbled for the phone, hoping it would be Vince or Georgie calling to explain that today had been a horrible joke. She squeezed her eyes shut against the too-bright screen and put the phone to her ear.

'Penny McIntyre speaking?'

Her youngest sister's voice rang out through the quiet hospital room.

'Are you okay? Why didn't you tell us you were ill?'

Penny winced and stabbed at the volume button as her sister Angie rushed on, barely drawing breath.

'I've been wanting to call you all evening, ever since Vince called Tim Patterson,' said Angie.

Penny squinted as she switched on the overhead light. She glanced at the clock. Almost 9 p.m. After Angie's comment, she wouldn't have been surprised to see the clock hands twirling backward. The parallel universe in which her current boyfriend would be calling her ex-boyfriend was just too strange to imagine.

'I must have hit my head harder than I realised, Angie. For a minute there, I thought you said Vince called Tim Patterson.'

'I did. Tim's our new farmhand. He was at the farmhouse when Vince called, while we were visiting Mum's memorial rock. I can't believe you missed her anniversary dinner, by the way. So, are you really coming back?'

Penny took a moment to follow Angie's excited trail of conversation. Suddenly her aches and pains receded into the background, replaced by a wave of guilt. *Mum's anniversary. Shit. Shit. Shit.* She couldn't even tell herself it was because she was away from her desk and the calendar that guided every minute of her working life. Yesterday's personal column would have been unmarked because writing it down at the start of each year, when she added birthdays, was too painful. Normally she just remembered, the date etched into her memory. The date when their teenage years went from carefree to grief-stricken. The day their mum, Annabel, had died in a single vehicle car accident.

'Earth to Penny . . . Hello?'

'Sorry Angie, I can't believe I missed Mum's dinner, either. Again.'

Penny pushed her hair away from her face, took a deep breath. *This week is an absolute disaster . . .* She struggled to recall the last time she'd set foot on her family's third-generation merino stud. Too long, obviously, if she'd missed the memo about Tim Patterson taking on a farmhand's position.

'Don't leave me hanging. Are you coming home or not? We'd all love to see more of you.'

Penny looked out the darkened window at the skyline of the city she had called home for the last fifteen years. The buildings she shopped in, dined in, worked in, lived in. The life she had so diligently created for herself, that was so far from her country roots.

'C'mon, Pen. You know you want to.'

She could hear the teasing in her sister's voice, her enthusiasm as fresh as the bright sunflowers and dahlias sitting on the bedside table. A mix of emotions ran through Penny's head as she bade Angie goodnight. *Everyone at home sounds happy about it. And Vince is pretty pleased with his miraculous solution. Why can't I muster up the same enthusiasm?*

Four

'Try turning her over again, mate,' called Tim, leaning out the ute's window. His V8 engine purred at the slightest touch of his boot, and he cocked an ear to listen as a second, much softer engine started in the car in front of him.

'You're a legend, Tim,' said Sam Kingsley, stepping out from behind the wheel of the battered station wagon. Tim unclipped the jumper leads from his battery terminals and carefully lowered the hood of his Holden WB. Buffing fingerprints from the metallic paintwork with his sleeve, he unclipped the cables from Sam's jerkily idling engine and looped them back into a neat bundle.

'Thanks for the jump-start. Can I shout you a counter meal? Reckon a pot of pale ale and a steak sanga would go down a treat for lunch.'

'Mate, save your money and buy yourself a new car battery. Or a new car, while you're at it. This is a step down from the Cruiser,' said Tim.

Sam ran a hand through his blond hair and shook his head. 'Don't remind me. Cost-cutting at its finest. Not that you'll see Lara trading in her car or giving up those bloody expensive marathons. You heading to dinner at the farm again tonight? Penny's coming home.'

Tim stared past the rows of tightly packed homes—cookie-cutter houses, as his Nanna Pearl called them—over the power poles and street lights, in the direction of McIntyre Park. He'd only been in the small township of Bridgefield for an hour and already he was itching to get back to the open paddocks and rolling hills that comprised his office.

'Not sure yet. I don't want to intrude. Eddie's always keen, but Stella reckons I spend too much time over there as it is,' Tim said. His sheepdog, Bones, nudged his hand. Tim patted the kelpie's head absent-mindedly. He hadn't seen Penny in more than a decade, but she ambushed his dreams sometimes, working alongside him in the paddocks, just like she had in high school. He shook himself, irritated at her ability to make his traitorous body tingle like a teenager. *Pull yourself together, Patterson, doesn't make a lick of difference to you whether she's a career woman or a milkmaid now. Not your woman. Not your problem.*

Sam smirked at Tim as he leaned against the tailgate. 'All the more reason you should come. Be like old times. Me and Lara, you and Penny. Stella's just jealous. Don't let her tell you what you can and can't do.'

Tim shook his head, guilty for thinking about a girl from his past when he had enough trouble with the woman in his present.

'We'll see. Better head off. Angus wants me to finish the fencing before he gets back from Melbourne this arvo.'

'Slave driver. That's where Lara gets it from. He'll have you under his thumb too, if you're not careful.'

Tim shook his head as he clipped his kelpie's collar onto a chain, securing him to the ute tray. He waved out the car window as he nudged the WB back onto the road.

'You're full of it, mate. Angus's the best bloke I've ever worked for.'

Diana threw up her hands in protest as she stopped for a red light. Though she was a natural at handling a dozen screaming preschoolers and her own tribe of rowdy boys, she was much better suited to the open roads of the Western District. The lights changed and the chorus of tooting that had followed them from the hospital continued. Had she had more energy, Penny might have found Diana's uncharacteristic swearing amusing.

'I don't know how you handle this every day, Penny. It's like I need to stick a sign to the window saying "I'm from the country" so they'll cut me some slack. Bloody hell! That one came out of nowhere,' Diana gasped, flicking her fringe out of her vision.

Penny heard her dad chuckle from the back seat.

'Better you than me, love. And remember, you're the one with the bull bar.'

'You're doing great, Diana. Traffic's always thick around the hospital. We're almost there,' said Penny.

Diana jerked in and out of the traffic, cursing each time she received another toot. Penny breathed a sigh of relief when her street came into view, gesturing to the three-storey apartment complex.

'It's that one across the park, with the decorative green panels.'

Diana nodded grimly, twisting the steering wheel of her four-wheel drive. She parked beside a row of plane trees, their leaves clinging to the last of their greenery before changing colour and floating to the footpath.

I'll miss their autumn display. Penny pushed down a wrench of resentment. Vince's words from earlier that morning scrambled in her head. *It's business, not pleasure. You'd do the same, Pen. I'll have everything packed up and ready by the time your family gets into town.* She knew he was just being practical, but why did it feel like such a betrayal?

Angus poked his head between the two front seats.

'Righto love, you wait here while we collect your stuff. Diana and I will have you loaded up and ready to roll in two shakes of a lamb's tail.'

Diana twisted and reached across to the back seat, pulling a handful of snacks from her voluminous Mary Poppins-style handbag.

'There's an apple, a banana, popcorn, Tiny Teddies and a bag of chips to choose from. Knock yourself out. Let's see if I can avoid getting tooted at in your underground parking lot.' She grinned, shutting the car door gently.

Penny's phone vibrated on her lap as she waited.

She squinted at the bright screen and scrolled down to see a message from Jade.

Hey gorgeous girl, safe travels back to countryside. Love Jade.
PS. Heard Georgie dodged a call from that gossipy reporter re Whitfield Pharma story. Will keep eye on his newspaper column.

Penny groaned. She hadn't even thought about the story being picked up by the press. *Georgie will find a way to put a good spin on it, surely . . . ?* She tapped out a quick reply, cringing as the brightly lit screen made white spots dance in front of her vision. For a person who made a living out of marketing and mopping up clients' messes, the feeling of being on the receiving end was mighty uncomfortable.

Penny watched her sleek black car appear under the roller-door of the communal garage. Diana was hunched over the steering wheel, pulling out an inch at a time. She parked in the street and emerged with a perplexed expression.

'Glad Dad's driving your car home, Pen. Those topsy-turvy blinkers are all over the shop. The boys will be out in a minute with the last suitcases.'

'You're a gem, Diana. And thanks for picking me up from hospital. Vince would have driven me home if his flight weren't booked for this afternoon.'

'Sure he would've,' Diana said, tucking her white shirt back into a denim skirt Penny recognised as one of her older sister's wardrobe staples. 'Speak of the devil,' Diana murmured, nodding over Penny's shoulder.

Vince and Angus emerged from the building, each holding a suitcase.

Penny climbed out of Diana's car. She smoothed down her floral dress and pulled her linen jacket around herself, as a cool breeze followed her father and her lover across the busy road.

The difference between Angus's and Vince's clothes was as clear as the divide between the lives they led, and the two worlds that had shaped Penny so far. She buried her head into Vince's chest, glad he was wearing a jacket so her make-up didn't stain his pinstripe shirt. *You're stronger than this, Penny McIntyre. Where's the go-getter who earned back-to-back Employee of the Year awards? Business is business.*

She straightened up and lifted her chin.

'You'd better smash this secondment, Vince. By the time I get back to Melbourne, I expect you to have the Sydney office on track for their strongest sales period on record, right?'

'That sounds a bit more like the girl I love. We'll both be back in Melbourne before you know it, babe.' He winked and kissed her on the tip of her freckled nose. And with a handshake for Angus and a smile, he slipped into a taxi and was driven away.

Five

Penny stretched in her seat, angling her face away from the sunshine that flooded in through the windscreen as they headed west into the afternoon sun. Her body ached with every pothole they hit, mocking her brave front at the hospital where she had waved away the doctor's concerns about the four-hour car journey ahead. After three and a half hours on western Victoria's crumbling roads, she conceded his point. *He was right. It's like being run over by a truck*, she silently admitted. *Not long now, then I'll curl up into bed and sleep off the road trip.*

She drifted in and out of sleep throughout the drive. Angus's faded work shirt was rolled up to his elbows. One arm rested against the window, the other was draped over the steering wheel. It was a stance more accustomed to the cab of his ute or the old Leyland truck. His conservative 90 kilometres per hour felt especially slow in her sporty European car, which spent more time parked in the garage than on the open roads. She watched his attention dart from the traffic to the paddocks beyond, his lips moving in time to the songs on the radio station he had commandeered.

'Nearly home. Have a good kip?'

Penny nodded half-heartedly, wincing as the small movement rippled through her stiff body. She was grateful she had family who were willing to give up their day to collect her from hospital, pack her city life into the back of two cars, and trek the 400-odd kilometres back before the kangaroos flocked to the dusky roads.

'You'll come good after a decent rest. It'll be okay, love.'

Penny shut her eyes and leaned back against the headrest. She wanted to take comfort from her father's words and wished she could share his matter-of-fact view, but the more she stewed on her enforced leave and Vince's abrupt departure, the more she knew it was far from okay. If she hadn't messed up so badly, she wouldn't need to be ferried back to the farm—the opposite direction to her promotion and her relationship.

'Kids will be happy to see you.'

The thought of her niece and nephews brought a smile to her face.

'I guess that's one benefit of convalescing at home.' Penny saw disappointment flicker across Angus's face. *Way to go, Pen.* She reached out to touch his tanned arm.

'Sorry, Dad, that didn't come out right. I appreciate you helping me out . . .' She trailed off as Angus turned the steering wheel. The car slowed to almost 60 kilometres per hour as a large blue sign proclaiming 'Welcome to Bridgefield—population 200' rolled past, almost in slow motion. Penny looked away.

'Love, we jumped at the chance. You're no inconvenience and anyone who thinks otherwise is a darn fool,' he said quietly.

Penny knew Vince would have a lot of ground to make up before Angus would warm to him. *Hell, he might have a lot of ground to make up before I warm to him again, depending on how these next ten weeks pan out.*

'You'll probably notice a few changes around the place. Tim's come up with some good initiatives. He's a real go-getter, that lad.'

Penny's ears pricked up but she kept her gaze out the window. 'We're working together most days now. Don't know what I'd do without him.'

She waited to hear more about Tim, but her father stayed silent as the sun dipped down to the horizon, its final bow for the day. From the sound of things, 'that lad' was becoming the son Angus never had. And from the sound of his new role at the farm, she would have little chance of avoiding him in the coming weeks.

The noise of barking dogs shook Penny from her sleep. She realised the car was no longer moving. A welcoming party had gathered on the front porch of the farmhouse to watch her return to McIntyre Park. Lara and Sam with their daughter Evie. Diana's husband Pete with their four boys. Angie, whose orange curls were gathered in a messy bun and clashed happily with the red, polka-dotted apron she wore.

'Home, sweet home.'

Her father's voice came from behind Penny as he removed her biggest suitcase from the boot. Penny wiped grit from her eyelashes, ran her tongue across her dry lips and wished she had a hairbrush handy. The children fidgeted impatiently on the front steps, their hands waving furiously to match their eager smiles. She saw their attention diverted beyond her car and the children overflowed down the steps as Diana pulled in close to the house.

'Mummy,' yelled a blond pair of boys in matching flannel shirts, launching themselves at Diana's legs as soon as she emerged.

'Hey, Elliot. Hey, Harry. I should go away more often, I think they've actually missed me,' Diana said, sending a wink in Penny's direction.

The littlest McIntyre—Leo—wasn't far behind them and Penny smiled at the baby commando-crawling across the lawn. He'd barely been rolling, let alone crawling, last time she was home. The two oldest children—Cameron and Evie—looked like they were in clear collusion, whispering between themselves as they rushed towards Penny's vehicle. She unfolded herself from the passenger seat like an accordion, the aching in her hips and knees making her movements jerky after the long drive.

'Welcome back, Aunty Pen,' the pair chorused, sounding like siblings rather than cousins. Their gangly limbs folded around her in a three-person hug, both children almost a head taller than when she'd last seen them.

'Thanks, guys. I can't believe how much you've both grown. You must be eating your parents out of house and home.'

Penny allowed herself to be led towards the house, wrapping one arm around Cameron's shoulders for support. Evie vibrated with excitement as she clasped Penny's other hand, proudly presenting her to the rest of the family.

Angie stepped forward. The youngest of the McIntyre clan, what she lacked in birth order, she made up for with size and personality. She climbed down the stairs, bringing a gust of baking aromas with her, and tugged Penny into an excited hug.

'I'm so happy you're home. I've rustled up the crowd for a family dinner. Hope you're hungry?'

Penny mentally farewelled her plans to slip quietly into bed. Faltering under her little sister's expectant look, she nodded gingerly.

'That sounds lovely. But really, you shouldn't have gone to any trouble,' Penny insisted.

'Nonsense, it's the least I can do. It's been ages since you've been home,' called Angie, her hips swinging as she ascended the steps. 'Come in, come in. Wait till you see what's inside.'

Six

Tim sighed as he carried Stella's suitcase to the car. She stuck out her hand, ripped luggage from his grip and stuffed it into her boot. He tried again to placate her, knowing as well as she did that they could keep going through the motions or they could just call it quits. They hadn't been particularly well suited, right from the start, but he wasn't a quitter.

'C'mon, Stella, it's one dinner. You've got to admit they put on a beautiful spread. And Angus invited us 'specially.'

Stella slammed the boot, then opened it again to tuck a rebellious suitcase handle back in.

'There's not enough room for you, me, Eddie, your Nanna Pearl and the whole McIntyre clan in this relationship, Tim.' Stella kept her hands on her hips as she pressed a dry kiss onto his cheek. 'You enjoy that meal then. And your precious ute. And your crazy family.'

He sucked in a sharp breath at her last jibe—both her words and her long hair flicked him in the face as she walked towards Eddie. Eddie stood with one hand on the roof of Stella's silver sports coupé, puzzling at the seat full of washing baskets, suitcases and a mound of bright fluffy pillows that he had been forever tripping over.

Tim followed close on her heels, resting a hand on Eddie's shoulder.

'Say goodbye to Stella, mate.'

'Stella, Stella,' said Eddie, a mournful look in his almond-shaped eyes.

A stroke of annoyance passed through Tim as he watched Stella hesitate and then press his brother into a quick hug.

Tim hit replay on his CD player, itching to hear Lee Kernaghan singing 'She's My Ute' for a second time as he directed his WB along the back roads of Bridgefield. He'd anticipated tears and an awkward parting as Stella drove off; he just hadn't expected them to come from his little brother, who seemed much more attached to her than he was.

Eddie continued staring out the window, leaning against an armrest they hadn't noticed was battered until Stella had pointed it out last month.

Tim sang and tapped the steering wheel, spinning the tyres as he rounded the dirt track that took him towards McIntyre Park's main entrance. He sneaked another look at Eddie and received a scathing glare in return. Tim blew out a resigned breath. He turned towards the majestic red gum trees that flanked the McIntyre Park Merino Stud sign, confident Eddie would perk up when he arrived at the farmhouse and soaked up the female influence that was so strong in the McIntyre family.

'Chin up, mate. Girlfriends are overrated. We'll save up for our farm much quicker without distractions, you'll see.'

Penny started across the driveway, wondering exactly what Angie had concocted. Knowing her sister, it could be anything from a box full of kittens or a triple-decker pavlova to a pop-up beauty salon inside the lounge room, all prepped with lotions, potions and wax strips to try to perk her up. *Only Angie*, she thought with a smile. Gravel crunched underfoot as she walked towards the weatherboard farmhouse she'd grown up in.

Pete bounded down the verandah steps, past the thick lavender hedge, and wrapped her in a gentle embrace.

'G'day, stranger. Good to see you.' His beard tickled as he kissed her cheek.

'Thanks, Pete. Shame it's not under better circumstances. This was the last thing I was expecting.'

'Chin up, Pen. It's not the worst thing in the world to have to come home, is it? Pretty sure it could be under much worse circumstances.'

'Too right. You could've broken both your wrists and be unable to wipe your own arse. Now *that* would be a predicament,' said her other brother-in-law, Sam, clattering down the steps with a wink. He leaned in, the top of his head bumping her cheekbone awkwardly. She wrinkled her nose at the scent of cigarettes and beer. The charismatic man she remembered from her teenage years, when he and Lara had started dating, seemed to have lost his shine and charm as he'd aged. His hair was thinning and the once football-fit body had turned scrawny.

Sam called out to Angus as he walked towards the vehicles: 'Need a hand?'

'I'm right, thanks, Sam. It's not every day Penny comes home from the city. I'll let you strong lads lug them up the stairs, but at least give me the honour of pulling her suitcases out of the car.'

Penny waited in limbo, unsure if she was ready to head inside the house just yet. The high volume of Diana's boys was already making her head pound and Evie was bouncing a tennis ball against the side of the house. But it was an easier option than the verbal sparring that awaited inside with her second-oldest sister Lara. *Get over yourself. You'll have to deal with Lara sooner or later. Watching your life being pulled from the back of two cars isn't exactly uplifting.*

The sound of a V8 cut through the country air. She pivoted on the gravel, her focus drawn to the dust swirling behind the familiar navy-blue ute. *You've got to be kidding me*, she thought. *None other than Tim Patterson.*

Seven

Penny watched as the Patterson brothers walked towards the house; so different in size and character but both with grey eyes and sandy-blond hair. Tim had a hand around Eddie's shoulders. *Still as protective of his disabled brother as he was in high school.*

'Eddie, do you remember Mac?'

Eddie's cheeks puffed up in a smile that made his eyes almost disappear. His tongue poked out the corner of his mouth as he rushed up to hug her. Penny winced as he squeezed her with childish enthusiasm.

'Hello, hello, hello.'

She couldn't help but soften at Eddie's cheerful welcome. He had grown wider but not much taller since she had last seen him, a sprinkle of stubble spreading across his soft jaw.

'Thanks, Eddie, nice to see you again.'

He clapped his hands together in excitement, bustling to join the men at the back of her car. She watched him go, prolonging the moment before she had to face Tim. A light cotton work shirt stretched across his muscular frame, the sleeves rolled loosely to his elbows. *Still as good-looking as ever*, she noted resignedly, feeling distinctly worse for wear in comparison. Penny turned her gaze to his scuffed steel-capped boots as he cleared his throat.

'Mac.'

No one but Tim had ever called her Mac. His casual familiarity as he stood at her family property, apparently about to join them for a family meal, ruffled her composure. His voice was rougher than she remembered, his face lined from days on the tractor and in the paddocks.

'Tim.' She nodded woodenly. After their break-up in high school, she'd worked hard to keep as much distance between them as possible. Penny lifted her chin, about to join her sisters inside when she saw Eddie carting a small purple suitcase up the stairs, pausing on the top step to shake it like a child with a present under the Christmas tree.

Her hands flew to her cheeks.

Tim caught the look on her face.

'What? You worried he's going to break your suitcase?'

A nerve twitched in Penny's eye. She knew the ornate Venetian glass inside would be shattered. No amount of superglue would fix the figurines, and unless she popped over to the northern hemisphere, she knew she would never replace them. Vince was right. They would have been safer in storage after all.

She felt a wave of exhaustion wash over her and sighed. 'I should have carried that one myself . . . it was fragile.'

Tim called out to Eddie, the edge in his voice evident. 'You're being careful, aren't you, mate?'

Eddie looked up. 'Like a music box.'

He put the suitcase close to his ear and shook it again, fascinated with the tinkling of broken glass. Tim groaned.

'Sorry, Mac. I'll replace it.'

'It's fine. Don't worry about it.'

Penny could still remember the last time she'd said those words, had lied in exactly the same way as if the ruined item was only a cheap, replaceable possession. Her assistant had stumbled while carrying a tray of coffee, just minutes before a crucial marketing presentation. Penny had nailed the pitch in a hastily borrowed outfit, but her coffee-stained pink dress hadn't fared quite so well.

'It's fine, don't worry about it,' Penny had said, as the young assistant had tried to dab espresso from the fluted sleeves, her hands stroking the luxurious silk.

The girl had gasped when she saw the signature red label inside the neckline.

'Oh my God, it's a Valentino. I'm such a klutz.'

Knowing the assistant couldn't possibly afford a replacement on her wage, Penny had glossed over the accident. She hadn't accepted a cent from the apologetic young woman, and she wouldn't be taking Tim up on his offer either. She mentally farewelled the unique glass figurines she'd brought home for safe-keeping.

Penny walked away as quickly as her tired legs allowed. But before she could reach the verandah steps, her foot slipped out sideways on a patch of gravel. Her arms shot out in front of her to break her fall and she landed in a heap.

Every muscle in her body squealed, having just recovered from dropping to the boardroom floor, but she scrambled to her feet with as much dignity as she could muster. Tim and Eddie both rushed over, soon joined by Pete and Sam. Diana thrust baby Leo into Pete's arms and kneeled to examine Penny's knee.

'It's bleeding, Pen. Might be gravel stuck in there too.'

'Bleeding, bleeding, bleeding,' repeated Eddie, the purple suitcase falling to the ground as he covered his mouth with one hand and pointed to her knee.

Penny flapped her hands at the sudden audience.

'It's nothing. It's fine. *I'm* fine,' she said. Tiredness, pain and embarrassment ripped through her.

'Nothing? Just like the little virus you said you had?' Diana's voice was high and Penny realised she wasn't the only one exhausted by the long day of driving. Diana gestured to Tim.

'Carry her upstairs, please. She's not fit for anything but bed.'

Penny balked as Tim walked towards her, but Diana wasn't having any of it.

'Get over yourself. Bed! Now.'

She kept herself as aloof as possible when Tim picked her up. He ducked to avoid the hand-painted 'welcome home' banner and carried her quietly inside.

Penny awoke to a musical conversation between warbling magpies and travelling galahs. The unfamiliar sound was disorientating, so different from the cawing seagulls that lorded over St Kilda.

Must be just on sunrise, she thought, her head groggy with sleep. She blinked at the golden light illuminating the curtain edges, and rolled onto her left side. She gasped as she caught sight of the digital clock.

Is it 9.38 a.m.? Have I slept for that long? Penny sat bolt upright. A pounding in her head confirmed she had gone a long time without any pain relief.

She pushed back the printed Holly Hobbie sheets and eased herself onto the edge of the single mattress. A matching bed on the opposite side of the room, which had once been Angie's, was laid out with a selection of supplies, including a fluffy pink dressing-gown. Diana's other touches were evident in the room too—a vase of roses and a bottle of water.

Good old Diana. She remembered with a shudder how her older sister had ordered her to bed in the same tone she used with her four-year-old twins. A flush spread over Penny's cheeks. Tim had carried her like a kelpie who had rolled in a dead sheep's carcass, only drawing her close to navigate the narrow staircase. He had resumed his rigid stance when they emerged onto the landing, had lowered her to the bed with an air of clinical detachment and then apologised for her broken figurines.

An urge to rush back to the city grabbed her—the same feeling that had washed over her in the final months of high school. The walls had crept in closer and closer, until the day she had packed her suitcase and waved her family goodbye. Penny looked around the room that had seemed so big as a child. The framed photographs on the dressing table were unchanged and the posters remained stubbornly Blu-Tacked to the walls. She tugged at the waistline of her pyjama pants, ignoring the faded stares of Heath Ledger and Matt Damon as she rubbed her sore hip. She shuffled past the trio of matching black suitcases and over a pile of woven baskets, and located her handbag. A box of anti-inflammatories lay on top of the phone chargers, laptop charger and iPad mini. Penny downed three tablets at once and shrugged her arms into the dressing-gown. The clean, familiar scent of her mother's fabric softener enveloped her.

Dogs barked. Gravel crunched. Two car doors slammed and the back door creaked open. Voices floated up from the staircase, followed by the sound of water running, crockery being pulled from cupboards and a radio burbling to life. It felt like she'd just rewound the clock fifteen years.

Eight

Tim reached across the kitchen bench and turned on the radio, filling the room with banjos and crooning.

'A decent kip is just what Penny needs. Even if she won't admit it, she's as crook as a dog. Being home will do her a world of good,' said Angus, nodding at him from across the island bench.

Tim stirred sugar into his coffee, comparing the exhausted Penny from yesterday with the teenager he had once cared about. There was no denying it; Penny was still smoking hot, but her tiny frame had been ravaged by whatever virus she'd contracted. Now she was a pale imitation of the vibrant redhead from high school. He shook away the memory, aware Angus was awaiting a response.

'Won't argue with you, Angus. She looks terrible.'

Angus opened the fridge door and lifted the glass dome off an ornate cake. A caramel macaroon dropped from the cluster of chocolate decorations on top of the masterpiece. It looked like something that should be cut into at a wedding reception, not a weekday smoko.

'You sure Angie's going to be happy about you hacking into that?' Tim asked as Angus reached for the carving knife.

'The moment's passed. It was supposed to be a welcome home cake for Penny, but she was fast asleep before we'd even unloaded all her luggage. No sense letting it go stale. Angie said she'll bake something new for Sunday night's dinner.'

Angus cut a generous slab, then pushed the rich mud cake in Tim's direction. Angie lived half an hour away and she usually called in after work, not in the middle of the day, but Tim couldn't help but glance at the back door as he hesitantly accepted the plate.

'Still don't want to be in your shoes when she discovers you've cut into it.'

'Waste not, want not,' said Angus, lifting the cake to his mouth with a grin.

Tim scooped up his piece; the heady chocolate scent followed by a rich, velvety taste. *Hell, yeah.*

'Annabel passed down her famous cooking skills, didn't she? Don't understand why you're not the size of a house, Angus.'

Angus grinned again, pressing his lips closed to stop the mouthful of cake escaping. The alarm on Tim's watch beeped.

'I'd better head off. Eddie's bus will be cruising past the driveway in a sec. He right to tag along again this arvo?'

Angus nodded, reached for the knife and cut a third slice of cake.

'Course. You don't even have to ask.'

Tim nodded at Angus. Angus had accepted Eddie as part of the bargain and waved away their father's sins with humbling kindness. Not for the first time, Tim wondered how he'd got lucky enough to find a job with Angus McIntyre when no one else in town had wanted anything to do with the Patterson boys.

Penny washed her face and reached for the soft towel, inhaling the same scent of washing powder that infused the dressing-gown, the bedsheets and pillowslips. She sighed at her reflection in the mirror. Angus had brought her lunch and dinner in bed yesterday, but she knew she couldn't hide out in the bedroom for her entire stay. Several familiar voices floated up from the kitchen below. One in particular stood out, prompting her to change out of her pyjamas and into jeans and a soft green knit that set off her complexion.

It's been years since I cared for Tim Patterson's opinion, and I'm certainly not going to let it bother me now. I'm not here to impress anyone.

But a sense of personal pride hounded her as she worked her way through her morning beauty routine. Her toothbrush came away pink and she flossed with more restraint. Next came toner, eye cream over the bags under her eyes that hadn't budged since Christmas, moisturiser and a light application of make-up. She stacked the containers in the top drawer, feeling calmer when each bottle was ordered by height, labels turned to the front, like a beauty store counter.

Downstairs, she found Diana sitting around the table with Tim and Angus, just as she'd suspected. The twins and Eddie glanced up from a game of marbles. Leo cooed at her from his high chair, waving a soggy rusk stick in her direction.

'Hi, Aunty Penny,' chorused the twins.

'Hi, Aunty Penny,' followed Eddie. 'Marbles, marbles, marbles.' Eddie clinked the glass balls together gleefully and they returned to their game. Penny couldn't help but smile, her attention flickering to Tim, who gave no indication of having heard the 'aunty' part of his brother's comment.

Diana pushed her chair back and hugged Penny to her chest, sending a series of shockwaves through Penny's aching joints. She winced, prompting Diana to step away and assess her at arm's length. Looking closely, Penny saw the streaks of grey in her sister's hair, the laughter lines that had merged into wrinkles either side of her kind eyes.

'The country air's already working its magic, I can tell.' Diana moved to the bench and filled the kettle as Penny pulled out a chair.

'G'day, love. Glad you got a decent rest.' Angus nodded from behind his newspaper, sipping tea.

'Tim.'

'Mac.'

Penny accepted tea in a mug that proclaimed 'Cydectin: kills more worms' and a pre-milked bowl of Weet-Bix from Diana. It was a far cry from the breakfast she usually ate and she almost laughed her oldest sister's mother-hen act, as if she considered Penny yet another child to whisk under her wing. But one look at Diana's determined face and Penny knew it wasn't worth arguing.

'You'd better hoe that down, Penny. Chop, chop. I've made you an appointment for Dr Sinclair at 11 a.m.'

Penny spluttered, pieces of soggy Weet-Bix flying across the table.

'What? I've already had a gutful of doctors this last week.'

'But not a *local* doctor. Not one who knows our whole family history inside and out,' answered Diana, her arms folded across her chest.

Penny looked to Angus for support. 'Really?'

He averted his gaze. 'Yep, no use arguing, love. We're only looking out for you,' said Angus, keeping his attention fixed on the newspaper.

Penny plucked at the fine wool knit, suddenly too warm.

'What if I'd still been sleeping at 11 a.m.?'

'Then I would have rescheduled. But I've heard enough about your 5 a.m. gym sessions to know you're unable to sleep past sunrise at the best of times. I factored in a little leeway given your illness and gave you a day's grace, but I knew you'd be up relatively early.'

A snicker of laughter came from the far end of the table and Penny's eyes narrowed at Tim. It was one thing to be railroaded by your big sister, but another thing to have someone else find amusement in it.

'All right, but only because Dr Sinclair might agree this whole ten-week thing is complete overkill.'

Diana climbed back into the driver's seat and dusted her hands on her denim skirt.

'Well, that's the kids settled with Pete. Hopefully they don't tear the place to pieces while we're at the doctor's.'

Penny shook her head, unconvinced. The drive into town had been manic. Trying to appease Leo and entertain the twins with nursery rhymes had required her full attention, and left her wondering how Diana managed to drive with such high-volume back seat shenanigans. *Give me peak hour city traffic any day.*

'Do you leave them at the stock agency often?'

'Nah, only for special occasions. It was too hard when they were little, but now Pete's the manager and the boys are easier to manage, it seems to work okay for short bursts,' said Diana, pulling out of the parking lot.

Penny glanced over her shoulder and watched the twins jumping across sacks of grain and dry dog food. She hoped, for her brother-in-law's sake, that the doctor was running on time today. They skirted around the back of the small town and found a park right beside the Bridgefield bush nursing centre.

Penny hadn't set foot inside for nigh on seventeen years, but the vinyl chairs remained unchanged, the reception area untouched by a paintbrush. The scent of Pine O Cleen disinfectant greeted her like a long-forgotten Christmas tree as she walked through the glass sliding doors.

Penny gave her name to the receptionist, who welcomed her home fondly even though she looked as unfamiliar as the woman discussing toddler toileting routines with Diana. The chatty woman leaned over Diana to introduce herself.

'I've heard all about you, Penny. I feel like I know you already. And aren't you just the spitting image of your sisters.' Her voice was loud enough for all the room to hear, but the sleeping child on her lap barely stirred.

'Diana's just been telling me how she's taken you under her wing. You're so lucky to have a big family like yours to look after you.'

Diana smiled proudly, enjoying the compliment and oblivious to Penny's discomfort at the woman's familiarity.

A sinking feeling settled in Penny's stomach as she looked around the waiting room and wondered how many of the people buried behind newspapers, magazines and mobile phones already knew about her arrival. *Nothing around here stays private for long.*

Nine

A yellowing skeleton smiled back at Penny as she entered the doctor's room. The doctor's hair had faded to a mousy grey, but her smile was as vibrant and welcoming as ever.

'Long time, no see, Penny. I heard you were back in the neighbourhood,' said the physician, directing her wheelchair to the front of the room.

Penny shook her hand, feeling the secure, warm grip of the woman she had admired since childhood, and took a seat next to Diana.

'Dr Sinclair, you're looking well.'

'Thanks. I'm sorry I can't say the same for you though. What's all this about Ross River fever?'

Penny threw a glance at Diana, who raised her hands in mock defence.

'Don't blame me. I didn't say anything.'

The doctor smiled before wheeling herself back behind the desk and reaching for Penny's file.

'It's common knowledge already—don't tell me you've forgotten how fast news travels around here?'

Penny shook her head. *Home, sweet home.*

'Looks like the gossip line has upgraded from dial-up to NBN. I only arrived two days ago.'

Dr Sinclair laughed and referred to her notes.

'Seems we have your records from birth up until 2002, but nothing since then. Who's your current doctor?'

Penny gave her the details for the Acland Street Medical Centre in St Kilda and outlined her illness, skimming over the humiliating collapse quickly and quietly. The longer she spoke, the more the doctor's expression shifted from passive to pitying, and she knew her chance to swing the consultation in her favour was unlikely.

'She's been in hospital too. You might want the details from them,' interjected Diana, brimming with the need to contribute.

Penny shot a severe expression in her direction.

'Lovely, I'll grab those details after an examination. Up you hop.'

Penny slipped off her ballet flats and lay down on the clinic bed. The doctor navigated her wheelchair over and examined her, humming as she scribbled notes on her file. She pulled out an arm cuff.

'Sit up. And sleeve up, too. What made you come see me if you've just got out of hospital? Are you in more pain?'

Diana interjected again. 'I insisted, doctor. With forty-something years of McIntyres under your belt, I knew you were worth a visit.'

'Thanks, Diana. But how about you, Penny? Do you think you need a second opinion?' She looked at Penny.

Diana was suddenly busy with her handbag, a pink glow spreading across her alabaster complexion.

Penny shrugged.

'To tell you the truth, I thought the doctors in Melbourne were making a mountain out of a molehill. Until the hospital

stint . . . the last thing I expected was an enforced ten-week
break.' Her voice trailed off. She met the doctor's gaze and
shrugged again. 'But here I am. Back at home in my thirties,
with round-the-clock care. Barely able to walk to the bathroom
without the effort tuckering me out.'

'At least you're on the right track now, Penny.' Dr Sinclair
returned to her desk and typed as she spoke. 'Did you tell the
Melbourne GP about your mother's history?'

Penny looked up and shook her head. 'I didn't think it was
relevant.'

'I can check the records but this old memory bank is pretty
reliable.' Dr Sinclair tapped her head with her knuckles.
'I remember a note in Annabel's files about a serious fever in
her teenage years—not Ross River fever but an autoimmune
illness, maybe lupus, something like that.'

Penny's brow furrowed. *How come I haven't heard this
until now?* She turned to Diana, suddenly grateful for her
sister's presence.

'But what does that mean for me? Plenty of people get run
down, and I've got the benefit of being young, fit and healthy.'
Penny's voice went up a notch and her hand slipped to her
temples, massaging a tremor by her eye.

'Yes, but we need to keep a closer eye on someone who
has a family history. A viral infection is one thing, but with a
genetic history like yours, it could be a precursor to something
much more serious.'

The doctor placed a hand on Penny's arm. Penny stared
blankly, still processing the news.

'I can see you're shocked. I'll get you to come back to the
clinic after your test results and records are transferred. The
best thing you can do is respect your body. Nourish it with
low-impact strengthening exercises, maybe some mindful

meditation or yoga; whatever it takes to get your mind and body back on the right track.'

Penny felt the doctor squeeze her arm and looked up to see a kind but firm expression on the older woman's face.

'This is a warning, not a death sentence. You need to take your recovery seriously.'

Penny nodded contritely and looked at the slips of colourful paper Dr Sinclair handed her, each advertising a different seniors' exercise class at the nursing centre.

'Forget about the city for a while, switch off your social media, smell the roses, that type of thing. God knows there are plenty growing in your mother's beautiful garden.'

'But you think *this* is going to help? Geriatric exercise classes?' Penny waved the brochures in the air, then flinched at the pain the movement evoked.

'You'd be surprised, Penny. You need to nourish your body, not keep punishing it.'

Penny didn't know whether to laugh or cry at the thought. She knew Vince would be amused when he found out. Her heart sank further as she remembered she still hadn't heard from him. *I'll try him again tonight.*

She tried to move her expression to something agreeable, something that would satisfy both Diana and the doctor, but enthusiasm failed her. Penny was a spin class and boot camp type of girl, someone who had always scoffed at the easy option. Even the Tough Mudder obstacle race had been fun, right up until the mosquito had given her a major virus as the ultimate unexpected souvenir. *Yoga and low-impact aerobics classes will be like watching paint dry.* She looked at Dr Sinclair's serious expression. It seemed like this aspect of her recovery was non-negotiable.

'You're doing aerobics classes with a bunch of senior citizens? What a hoot! I'll have to start calling you Jane Fonda. Please tell me you'll be wearing a pastel leotard and a headband?'

Angie's laughter filled the bedroom and Penny allowed herself another smile. A knack for finding humour in every situation was one of the things she loved most about her little sister. For the past half hour, Angie had entertained Penny with tales about her beauty salon customers. Women Penny had known at high school, and even a few men, were among Angie's customers at the bustling country salon, and she had laughed until her stomach ached at the stories from the waxing table.

'It feels like old times,' said Penny, pulling the blankets up around her chest.

Angie nodded, leaning back against the iron frame of her old bed. 'The only difference is the decade and a half that passed between now and then,' said Angie, helping herself to another slice of mud cake.

That and the utterly different direction our lives have gone since leaving high school, thought Penny. While she had rushed to the city straight after graduation, Angie had taken a local traineeship in the neighbouring town of Eden Creek, waxing, massaging and spray-tanning her way through the local population until she had enough clients to open her own salon.

'Obviously I'd fire any of my girls if they talked about clients after hours, but you looked like you needed a good laugh, Penny. Between your crazy work and my salon, we never get to catch up anymore. We'll try to make up for it in these next few months, okay?'

Penny nodded, pushing aside her untouched plate of cake. The glistening chocolate ganache looked like it held more than her weekly intake of calories, and she wasn't interested in returning to the city with hips like her little sister's.

'Weeks, not months, Angie. You're right though, it's always go, go, go. I would have averaged seventy-five hours a week in the office this month. And all for nothing,' Penny said with a sharp shake of her head.

'Plus all those hours you spend at that fancy gym of yours, and those fun runs. I stand by my decision to avoid exercise at all costs. Never know when an infected mozzie is going to swoop down and bite you on the bum.' Angie laughed, covering her mouth to stop crumbs flying across the bedroom. 'But the good news is, you get to hang out here with us and take exercise classes with the senior citizens. That reminds me, have you caught up with Lara yet?'

Penny rolled her eyes at the mischief dancing across Angie's face. Although Angie and Diana had always tolerated and excused Lara's abrasive manner, there was a tension between the two middle sisters that had not eased with time. If there was an argument to be had at family gatherings, it was almost always between Penny and Lara.

'Not yet, but Dad said she was dropping around this afternoon. Any topics to avoid this month? Is she still on the sugar-free bandwagon?'

Angie groaned and nodded vigorously.

'Holier than thou. She's even worse than you. Don't think I haven't noticed your untouched slice of cake, Pen. But on the subject of conversation killers, best not to ask about Sam.'

Penny thought back to her arrival, several days ago. She hadn't seen anything amiss between Lara and Sam when she arrived at the farmhouse.

'Really? She didn't mention anything on the phone last month. Mind you, she was pretty busy reprimanding me for sending Evie "a ridiculously expensive knit jumper that will be a pain in the arse to wash" instead of making it to her tenth birthday party,' said Penny, putting on a severe voice. Conversations with Lara were usually like that. Penny's attempts at generosity and a genuine interest in her niece were met with suspicion and rebukes. She looked up with a wry grin, expecting to see Angie's amusement. Instead, her sister's face was sombre.

'Give her a break, Pen. Things aren't exactly rosy in her household.'

'Don't tell me they're on the rocks again?'

Angie nodded. 'Yep. I babysat Evie last weekend, when Sam was away and Lara was working a late shift. Poor girl said she missed her dad, but the house was quieter without all the yelling.'

Penny smiled sadly. Even though she often disagreed with Lara, she didn't want her going through another messy break-up and make-up. The last time she and Sam had separated, Lara had sunk into a deep depression. And young Evie had been stuck in the thick of things. *I'll cut Lara a bit more slack instead of rising to her every barb. Muster up a little more patience. Surely it won't be too hard to manage?*

Ten

'So I'm on the train, right, sitting in our usual seat up the front, just swiping through Tinder when a match comes up. And you won't believe who it was, Pen. Are you ready for this?'

Penny adjusted her perch on the bedroom windowsill, nodding into the phone as she listened to another one of Jade's tales from the battleground of singledom. Jade's quest to find Mr Right kept them both amused on their daily commute, over the pounding of the treadmill and the thrumming of the rowing machine. From the sound of traffic in the background and Jade's breathless voice, she knew her friend was late to work. Again.

Penny leaned closer to the window as her friend's voice cut in and out, waiting for the static to clear. The blue-tinted mountain ranges out her window were majestic, but they sure played havoc with the phone reception.

'Let me guess, it was the nudist guy from Richmond. No, no, it was the married guy who forgot to mention his wife.'

'Which one? They all seem to forget about their wives on Tinder. No, it was the seventeen-year-old again, the one that keeps popping up. I think he's stalking me.' Jade laughed down the phone line, her breathing laboured as if she were taking the steps from the train station two at a time.

Penny had a sneaking suspicion Jade was taking advantage of her absence. Their fitness would both be back to square one at this rate.

'What's with all the huffing and puffing? Don't tell me you're already slacking off at the gym?'

'You get a holiday, I get a holiday. It's a win-win situation, Pen. Without you cracking the whip, I'm coasting through the workouts and I bet you're resting a little easier without emails buzzing 24/7? I've got a little project for you though. Keep an eye out for a hunky farm boy while you're down there. We're not all lucky enough to have a Vince waiting in the wings.'

Penny smiled. Jade had orchestrated Penny and Vince's first kiss at the staff Christmas party, ordering the band to play a slow song and shoving them onto the dance floor together, and had been a loyal card-carrying member of team Penny and Vince ever since. She was the only one who knew about the engagement ring, but one of many who agreed the couple were a perfect match. Both were at the peak of their careers in the marketing industry, with a shared charisma and drive, and a confidence that only came from being highly successful in their chosen field. *Jade's right, I'm lucky to have found Vince. Even if he is momentarily ditching me for Sydney.*

A rap rang out from the wooden door. Penny's cheeks burned bright red as she minimised the Facebook search page, dozens of unfamiliar Tim Pattersons flicking off her screen in an instant. She closed the laptop, sat it on her bedside table, and pulled the sheets up over her leggings as the door swung open.

'Knock, knock.' Lara's voice boomed into the room. 'Thought I'd smuggle you in something for lunch. Looks like you haven't eaten in weeks.' Evie followed behind her mother, waving a blue flask and mug in her hands.

'And we've brought you honey and ginger tea,' Evie chimed in, her gentle voice compensating for Lara's brisk tone.

Penny reached for the tray of muffins, a bolt of pain rocketing through her shoulder. She slid back against the cast-iron bedhead with the feeling of uselessness prickling like a clover burr inside her sock.

'Careful, Evie. Don't spill it everywhere,' Lara chided, putting the tray down on the dressing table and turning to her daughter with a frown. The grey nurse's uniform and tight ponytail did little to soften her look.

Penny felt older herself as she noticed the threads of silver creeping into her sister's otherwise russet hair, the lines that gathered around her mouth and eyes, just like Diana's. 'Thanks, they look great. And I haven't tried ginger tea before, so that'll be a treat,' Penny said.

Evie lit up under her praise. Even her sandy ponytail was bouncing, Penny noticed, wishing she could tap into her niece's energy source.

Lara stared out the gabled window, her head turned towards the sheep yards. Angus and Tim had been working there for the last few days, their utes coming and going against the backdrop of dry paddocks and mountain ranges.

'How are you feeling, Aunty Pen?'

'Better than last week. Everything still aches, though, and with everyone's cooking, I'll be as big as a whale by the time I leave,' she said.

Evie grinned back at her, then perched on the side of the bed, her fingers tapping a tune on Penny's laptop cover.

'You could do with a bit of meat on your bones. How long are you staying?' asked Lara, leaning against the window frame, her arms crossed in front of her.

'The apartment is sublet for ten weeks. All going well, I'll be back home as soon as it's free. It's going to be tough. Vince and I have only ever spent three weeks apart.'

Lara's expression twisted in amusement.

'Your Vince sounds like a real catch. Clears out the second you need him and then tries to make a bit of cash from renting out your place.' Lara laughed dryly, studying Penny's face for a reaction.

Penny's temper flared. Lara didn't know the first thing about her and Vince's relationship, had no concept of their standing in the city's corporate and social circles. And from what Angie had explained, it didn't sound like Sam was about to win any Husband of the Year awards. She opened her mouth to reply when Evie interjected, seamlessly deflecting the argument.

'I like your computer, Aunty Pen. Does it have games?' she asked, drawing it onto her lap and flicking up the screen.

Penny reached out as Evie's nimble fingers flew across the trackpad but wasn't quick enough to stop her search for Tim Patterson spreading across the page.

Lara strode across the room before Penny could push the screen shut.

'Why are you searching for Tim on Facebook? He's just over there.' Evie pointed in the direction of the sheep yards, puzzled. She reluctantly conceded the laptop to her mother, who sat it back down on the table and watched Penny with interest.

'Thought you were supposed to tune out of social media? Wasn't that the doc's advice?' Lara said.

She turned to her daughter, poking Evie's shoulder with a stern finger.

'And even if Aunty Penny is face-stalking every man and his dog, it doesn't mean you can help yourself to other people's computers.'

'Sorry, Aunty Pen.' Evie's hangdog expression deepened.

Penny laughed in spite of herself. 'That's okay, Evie. And I hate to say it, but your mum's right. I'm supposed to be having a "sabbatical",' she said, using the air quotation marks she knew irritated Lara. 'It's not easy breaking old habits though.'

She watched her niece's expression morph from despondent to inspired.

'I could change your Facebook password. Then you can't use it anymore,' Evie offered, grabbing at the opportunity for redemption.

'But then how can Aunty Pen snoop around without having to go to the effort of talking to people? You're worse than the gossips at the post office,' said Lara.

Penny passed the computer back to Evie, clenching her jaw. Only twenty minutes into their first catch-up, and Lara's negativity was wearing thin. She tried to rein herself in, remember that Lara was having a tough time at home, but her voice came out louder than anticipated.

'It's called research. And I'll have you know that Vince and I are just dandy. We've got a big holiday coming up in a few months.'

'I'll bet you do. Tough life for some,' said Lara, her nostrils flaring. She had never let Penny forget her suggestion that the whole family should go on an overseas holiday together, not long after moving to the city. The group holiday idea had never gained traction, largely due to Lara's stout refusal, and Penny hadn't raised the subject again.

Penny sank down against her pillow, catching a glimpse of Evie backing towards the door. Her gangly arms hugged her chest and she slipped a lock of hair into her mouth. Penny reached out and rested a hand on Lara's pale arm. Lara flinched.

'I don't want to argue, Lara,' Penny said, searching her sister's face for a trace of softness, and finding only sharp angles and disapproval. 'I didn't even want to come back home, but I had no choice. Least we can do is be civil, and before you know it, we can go our separate ways again.'

Lara gathered up the tray. 'I'll bring food around, seeing Dad hasn't got all day to spend baking—just don't expect me to feel sorry for you. Way I see it, you've brought this on yourself.'

Penny retracted her hand and turned to her niece, forcing a smile for Evie's benefit, as the ten-year-old shrank further into herself.

'It's okay, Evie. Your mum and I were just having a discussion. A difference of opinion, that's all. Thanks for the tea. Come visit me again soon,' she said, beckoning her niece closer. She ruffled the young girl's hair gently.

Evie lifted her chin, pulling the end of her ponytail out of her mouth. Penny watched her glance back and forth between them. Her voice was small when she spoke.

'Are you going to Hawaii again for your holiday? Or Japan? I've put all your pretty postcards in a special box, so I remember where to go when I'm old like you, Aunty Pen.'

A smile tipped Penny's grim expression upside down.

'Just New Zealand this time. I'll send you another postcard, all right?'

Evie leaned in for a goodbye hug. Lara laughed bitterly, shaking her head as she left the room.

'*Just* New Zealand? You'll want a darn good job, Evie. Or a rich fella. Despite what some people think, money doesn't grow on trees around here.'

Penny's chest pounded as she looked out the window, the friction in the room draining away as she heard Lara's feet stomping down the stairs.

Hands still shaking, Penny forced herself out of bed. She reached for the doorhandle, ready to shut the door on Lara's disdain and cocoon herself in the bedroom. But a movement in the hallway made her pause, and she peered out to see Angus's faded shirt at the top of the stairs.

'Dad. I didn't know you were there,' she said softly, wondering how much of their conversation he had heard.

He turned slowly, keeping his hand on the rounded knob at the top of the bannister. Worry lined his face.

'Lara . . . you've got to admit, she's pricklier than an echidna,' said Penny, shaking her head.

'Not nice to see you two bickering like children the second you get home though. She's just trying to help, love. We all are. Especially after Diana filled us in on the doctor's appointment.'

Penny closed her eyes and shook her head silently. *Of course Diana would keep everyone updated.*

'I couldn't bear to lose you too, Pen, not after your mum went so early. And I hate that you feel so ripped off about being at home.'

He *had* heard that bit. Penny searched his face, reading the disappointment and concern in the set of his jaw.

'I'm sorry, Dad. I'll look into the classes Dr Sinclair mentioned. And I'll make more of an effort to enjoy my time here, I promise.'

Eleven

Tim held open the crimson-red door, running his thumb across a paint drip. He tutted.

'Darn paint job is up the creek, Nanna. You should sack the bloke who did this,' he said, as his grandmother stepped up and over her worn doorstep.

Her lilac hair jiggled as if it had a life of its own, the freshly set perm and new lavender tint smelling like the hairdressing salon he had just collected her from. She beamed at him, and he smiled back as he spotted a smear of coral lipstick on her teeth. He lowered the groceries onto the floral hall runner, reached up and tapped his own teeth to signal the familiar problem.

'Lipstick, Nanna,' he said, averting his eyes as she pulled her top dentures out and rubbed them on her skirt, before replacing them.

'Looks like we're both a little sloppy with our workmanship. I couldn't possibly complain about your painting, Tim. Adds character,' she said with a wink.

Warmth filled him as he followed her into the kitchen, where he'd enjoyed a lifetime of hot meals and love from the woman who had all but raised him. He unpacked the groceries into the worn timber cabinets, as Nanna Pearl bustled about making tea. Years of practice made the silent routine seamless and companionable.

Tim's mind wandered to McIntyre Park as he stacked tins, bags and boxes into his grandmother's pantry. Ever since Angus had given him the leading farmhand job, he'd dedicated more brain space to stock rotation and weather than ever before, soaking up Angus's tutelage like a sponge so that when his finances were sorted, he'd have both the money and the knowledge to make his own farm a success. But in the last few weeks, his mind had drifted towards McIntyre Park for an entirely different reason. A five-foot-nine, redheaded reason, to be exact.

'Cuppa's up, darling. Now sit and tell me all about your day. I was so carried away telling you about mine that I didn't even ask you yet. I'm turning into a self-absorbed thing in my old age, aren't I?' she said, carrying over two steaming cups of tea.

Tim shut the pantry door, his low chuckle filling the small room. For a lady who had spent all morning teaching Eddie's disability group how to bowl, then several hours volunteering at the post office and then another hour at the mercy of her relentlessly chatty hairdresser, Nanna Pearl was anything but self-absorbed.

'Well, it wasn't as interesting as your day, that's for sure. More sheep work today, just going through stock. They're looking pretty good for this time of year. Last month's rain helped. I'm heading around to see Sam tonight. Not sure what he's got going on, but he's like a bear with a sore head.'

Nanna Pearl watched him over her teacup.

'That boy has always been a loose cannon. Angus McIntyre is a nice man, more tolerant than most, but Annabel McIntyre would turn in her grave if she knew Lara had ended up marrying Sam Kingsley.'

Tim took another sip of his tea.

'Lara keeps him on a tight leash. And no other bugger stuck up for me when Dad left town.'

Nanna Pearl sighed, placing her cup down.

'Loyalty is one thing, but that Sam has a nose for trouble.'

Tim covered her hands with his own, easily fitting them inside his. Her ruby engagement ring pressed into the underside of his knuckles as he gave her a gentle squeeze.

'Don't worry about it, Nanna. He's all right. Now, tell me more about this yoga class you're starting up.'

His grandmother looked up at him, concern giving way to a mischievous glint.

'We've already had a great response. And you'll never guess who registered today.'

She pulled the teacup to her lips, adding another ring of lipstick to the rim, and grinned at him.

'Mrs Beggs from the general store?',

He watched her eyes dance with amusement. Her coral lips pursed.

'Don't make me spray hot tea across my favourite tablecloth. Mrs Beggs wouldn't fit on a yoga mat, darling. No. We've got a young one signed up. Someone you know quite well.'

She dabbed her lips with a floral napkin and reached into a stack of crosswords and mail, sliding a formal portrait from the pile.

Tim stared down at the gawky teenager in a second-hand suit, unsure where to hold his hands. He instinctively reached up and touched the scar on his chin, now faded. When the photo had been taken, the scar was still fresh—an angry red line of freshly split skin. Standing next to him, in a white debutante dress with all the beauty of a young bride, stood Penny McIntyre. He pushed the photograph back towards Nanna Pearl and gulped another mouthful of tea. Last thing he needed was a lavender-haired Cupid getting the wrong idea.

Twelve

Penny eased her way down the staircase. The coolness of downstairs washed over her like a sea breeze by the time she reached the bottom step.

The unseasonably erratic weather continued, with autumn now turning her bedroom into a hot box. She wiped her forehead with a sweaty hand. The last time she'd been this hot was the feverish days before her collapse, when a sheen of perspiration had made her make-up slide from her face by midday, requiring regular touch-ups in the workplace bathroom. Penny padded across the quiet kitchen, glancing at the clock. *Dad and Tim will be in soon—grab a new jug of water and get back upstairs before they come in.*

She tried her best to stay upstairs when Tim came in for lunch and smoko. It was just too weird. The exception she'd made a few nights ago, when Diana and the boys had invited Tim and Eddie around for dinner, had been an exercise in awkwardness. Both of them looking away automatically when their eyes met, the forced politeness that so strongly contrasted with the harsh words of their teenage parting, the jolt she had felt when their hands touched as he passed her the salad.

So instead of sitting downstairs directly in front of the air conditioner, she stayed upstairs and let the heat add a layer of exhaustion to her still-recovering body. The only consolation was knowing he probably felt as awkward as she did.

Penny filled her empty jug with fresh rainwater, set it in the fridge, and pulled out a chilled replacement. She placed the jug on a small tray, shot a wistful glance at the lounge room, its door closed to keep out the harsh afternoon sunlight, and headed back up the stairs. Three steps up, a noise caught her attention. It sounded like the television had just been switched on in the lounge room. She shook her head. *Don't be ridiculous.* Two steps later, another noise. She strained her hearing and smiled. The sound of cartoons whispered through the warm air. *Diana's boys must have messed with the timer button on their last visit. Maybe the power's been on and off, and it's turned on automatically.*

Penny set the tray on the timber step and walked back down and through the kitchen. The door creaked as she pushed it open. Frigid air rushed out to greet her like a long-lost friend. Elliot and Harry were perched cross-legged in front of the television set, blond curls spilling over their faces, naked except for Spider-Man underpants. Diana was asleep in Angus's recliner chair, patches of sweat marking her thin cotton dress, with Leo splayed across her chest, also asleep. His chubby cheeks were rosy red from teething and his tiny hand was clutched around a teddy bear that Penny had bought him as a newborn.

She crouched down beside the twins.

'Hey guys, I didn't hear you come in. Your air conditioner still broken at home?'

Harry looked up, surprised at the interruption, and put a finger to his lips. 'Shhh, Mummy sleeping.'

Penny nodded, putting her finger to her lips too and glancing at Diana in case his loud response had woken her. She watched her sister stir before returning to a deeper sleep and felt an urge to safeguard Diana's rest.

'Want to come upstairs with Aunty Pen? I'll read you a book,' she whispered, gesturing to the well-stocked shelf in the corner. Harry nodded and returned with a picture book about shearing. He shoved his hand into hers and pulled her towards the door.

'Wait a sec, Harry. You coming too, Elliot?' He was the quieter of the pair and still treated her with aloof apprehension. *That's what you get for visiting so sporadically*, Lara had told her the other day, when Penny had mentioned Elliot's apparent shyness.

Elliot tucked his chin to his chest, but Penny could sense his gaze as she tiptoed to the bookshelf, Harry trailing behind her. She pulled out another book from the same series and brought it to him.

'What about this one? George the Farmer is putting in a wheat crop, just like Grandpa does. Look at his tractor,' she said.

Elliot pulled himself to his feet. A little tug of triumph lifted in her chest as both brothers took her hands and they went upstairs.

⚘

Penny closed the door of her father's office. She walked to the desk, flicked the small fan on and opened the window. Fresh air filtered into the office; the scent of eucalyptus and newly mown grass sent dust motes swirling around the room. It didn't feel like three weeks since she had arrived at the farm, but surely enough, the days had flown past.

Penny sat down in the office chair. The stiff frame creaked and groaned as she pulled it close to the desk, not unlike the way her body had creaked and groaned at the start of her convalescence. She moved aside a pile of paperwork to draw the office phone closer, restacking bank statements and machinery catalogues as she went.

She itched to straighten each book and consolidate the paperwork, so the desk would be clean and tidy like her own. Her mother's laughter rang in her ears as she remembered how they had both taken pains to neaten Angus's office, only to find it back to organised chaos a day later.

'Leave it, Penny. You know Dad can't find anything if it's too neat,' Annabel would say. This room was the only one in the house that she hadn't been given free rein in. As a result, the sparse space felt masculine, from the antique leather chair and antlers mounted on the wall to the dark, heavy timbers and mismatched filing cabinets.

She brushed away the memory, pulling her hands back from the desk, and instead ran her fingers through her hair as she contemplated who to call first. She knew her workmates would be in and out of meetings for the day, but she didn't have the foggiest idea what routines staff at the Sydney office kept. A longing to speak with Vince swept over her, and she dialled his mobile number urgently into the cordless phone.

The scent of Imperial Leather soap hit her as she put the handset to her ear.

'Vince Callas speaking.' His words were peppered with traffic in the background, the beeps and toots of a bustling city.

Her shoulders dropped in relief at the sound of his voice.

'Vince, I'm glad I caught you.'

'Babe, great to hear from you. I tried to call again last night, but it goes straight to MessageBank.'

'Tell me about it, the mobile service is terrible. I'll give you the house number.'

He groaned sympathetically, the familiar sound making her heart sing. She felt the iceberg of isolation melting.

'You still sound pretty raspy, Pen. Feeling better?'

'Getting there. How's Sydney? Have they tried to headhunt you permanently yet?'

'Not yet,' he laughed. 'We helped land another big account today, so we'll be out celebrating again tonight.'

Penny could picture the smile on his handsome face, the same smile that had caught her eye when they'd first met.

'We? I thought you were the only one seconded to the Sydney office?'

A loud noise came from Vince's end; most of his reply was eaten up by the sound of a passing vehicle.

'. . . anyway, I've got to go. Charlotte and I need to make it across town before the meeting starts.' The traffic roared down the phone line at her again, and she only caught the final two words '. . . bye, babe.'

Penny stared at the phone suspiciously, hitting redial. It went to Vince's voicemail. She jerked the phone back into the charger. It sounded like he'd said Charlotte. She usually skimmed through every HR email update so she could keep tabs on the comings and goings of her colleagues and as far as she knew, there were only two women named Charlotte in the whole of Boutique Media. An anxious woman from the Adelaide office, who had self-medicated with vodka at the annual staff awards night a few years ago and slurred her way through an acceptance speech for an award she hadn't actually won. Then there was ice-blond Charlotte, one of Georgie's protégés from the London branch. Her accent was pure boarding-school posh and her short dresses were a regular topic of water-cooler conversation.

Please let him be talking about the Charlotte from the Adelaide office, Penny thought, her mind whirring at the unexpected news.

Thirteen

She pressed the phone keypad and tapped her nails on the desk as it connected.

'Boutique Media. You're speaking with Jade.'

'Jade, I need a favour.'

'Hey stranger, I was just walking past your empty office five minutes ago. I'll move into it if you're not back soon.'

'Trust me, I'm working on it. Just wait until I tell you about my doctor's recovery program, you'll be beside yourself.' Penny sipped from her mug, frowning as the instant coffee met her tastebuds. She still hadn't got a taste for the freeze-dried stuff Angus bought. It wasn't the cheapest or nastiest stuff in the grocery aisle, but it was in a completely different ballpark to her usual daily espresso.

'Pen, I'd love to, but you'd better make it quick. I've got end of the month coming up, and we're already snowed under with the quarterly budget. Can I give you a call tomorrow night?'

Penny looked up at the livestock calendar on the wall, remembering the fever pitch that settled at the end of every month.

'Of course, I clean forgot. Just quickly, did you know anything about Vince going to Sydney with a woman called Charlotte?' She struggled to keep her tone light, but there was no fooling her oldest friend.

'Not that new British one? Charlotte the Harlot? The one that put the "ho" in ho, ho, ho at the Chrissy party?'

Penny winced, remembering the childish nickname she'd suggested over a gingerbread martini. They had giggled at the time, but now it felt ominous. Her worries compounded as she farewelled her friend and promised to recap the following evening. Penny picked up a pen and walked to the wall calendar. She counted seven weeks ahead, flipping from a harvesting photograph to a sunset over green pastures to a shearing shed scene. She made a big, black ring around the box marked 1 June.

'June the first. That's when everything will be back the way it should be,' she said aloud. Her voice sounded shaky, even to her ears, and she picked up the colourful brochures that still lay in the wire wastebasket underneath the desk. *The exercise classes will pass the time until I can go home*, she decided. *If nothing else, they'll be good for a laugh.*

The modest township of Bridgefield spread out in front of the ute as they crested a steep hill. Clusters of houses appeared by the roadside featuring long gravel entryways with established gardens and well-kept farm signs giving way to shorter drive-ways and smaller, messy yards. Neglected weatherboard homes that were once their owners' pride and joy sat desolately on the fringe of town, with dilapidated chicken coops full of weeds and long grass. Sheets of iron clung valiantly to precarious roof trusses. Penny felt a pang of loss for the picturesque settlement she remembered. *Where's the bustling little town, the pride of*

place? The clipped lawns and freshly painted fences she had admired from the school bus window had all but disappeared.

Several new homes proudly fronted the road, declaring their faith in the future of the town, but the faded paint and neglected yards outnumbered the shiny new roofs and hot-mix driveways at least ten to one.

'The town's looking a bit down at heel,' she murmured to Angus, watching a young woman collect her garbage bin in her dressing-gown. 'What happened to the thriving farming community?'

Angus looked around him, seeming surprised, as if the change had been so gradual, he hadn't noticed.

'Well, I guess there's not as much money around these days, love. Young people head straight to the city in search of bright lights and big dreams. Not mentioning any names, of course, but there isn't quite the investment from the next generation.'

Penny noted with relief that the heritage buildings in the main street remained unchanged. The bluestone bricks and red trim of the Shire offices, library and bush nursing centre looked as grand as the day they had opened in 1902. Sandwiched between the town hall and one-person police station was the general store, its striped bullnose verandah a beacon to passers-by and residents in search of a carton of milk or the local paper.

Angus parked directly out front of the store. He reached for his khaki hat and looked at his watch.

'Meet you back here in an hour?'

'Should give me plenty of time,' said Penny. She tucked her yoga mat under her arm and stepped onto the footpath. The smell of stale beer floated down the street as Angus opened the pub's heavy glass doors. He was soon enveloped in the darkness. She continued down the footpath, feeling out of place in her lycra leggings and neon-pink hoody. Taking the steps slowly, she made her way to the bush nursing centre entrance and fidgeted with her shoelaces while waiting for the automatic sliding door to open.

A trio of elderly women greeted her as she stepped inside. She smiled at them, trying to match names to the vaguely familiar faces and read the provocative slogans printed on their shirts, at odds with their white, lilac and silver hair.

'Oh look, Pearl, we've got a young one! Here for yoga are you, sweetie? It's almost about to start,' called the lady with the 'Workout Warrior' singlet.

The names Beryl and Ethel swam to the top of Penny's mind, but the other women came to her rescue as she murmured her thanks.

'Merryl, don't you know who that is? It's the young McIntyre lass. Penelope, isn't it?' The ladies flocked to her, welcoming her home and asking after her father.

'And Eddie told me all about the lambs coming through. Tim said he was pleased with the early autumn lambing trial—is your dad going to try it again next year?'

The short woman with lavender hair looked up expectantly. Penny realised she was speaking with Tim and Eddie's grandmother, Pearl.

Penny searched for an answer, keenly aware their farmhand's grandmother knew more about the merino stud than she did.

'I haven't had a chance to ask, but I'm sure I'll get all the ins and outs during my stay.'

'Give her a minute to settle in, Pearl,' said the tallest woman, shaking her finger. 'She's only just back from the big smoke, probably hasn't even pulled her boots on yet.'

Penny laughed. 'Guilty as charged. But I'm sure it won't be long before I'm touring paddocks and getting the inside scoop on all things merino.'

'Oh, you can't help but enjoy yourself out at that beautiful property. It was so good of your father to show him the ropes; Tim's happier than I've seen him in years. Makes an old duck proud to have a grandson like him.' Pearl hugged her sun-spotted hands to her heart as she spoke, her two friends nodding in unison.

'He's saving for his own farm, you know—such a lovely lad.'

'Always helps me when my Rufus goes wandering. Puts him on the back of the ute, next to Bones, and delivers him back to me,' added Merryl.

The yoga instructor breezed past them, smelling like she'd bathed in a vat of patchouli oil.

Penny bundled her yoga mat back under her arm and followed the trio into a large room. Classical music filled the air as a Mexican wave of yoga mats unfurled across the carpeted floor. Penny spread her feet to hip distance apart as directed, and followed the instruction to invert her body into a downward dog position. Her hair fell down over her face, her thoughts tumbling as blood rushed to her head. But no matter how hard she tried, Penny couldn't forget Pearl's glowing pride in and unwavering loyalty to Tim.

'Gently moving into mountain pose . . .' Penny followed the instructor's lead, straightening up and drawing her arms down by her sides. She turned her head and intercepted the curious gaze of Tim's grandmother. Pearl smiled at her, a flash of coral lipstick parting to reveal perfectly straight teeth. Penny smiled back. She wasn't proud of the abrupt way she'd broken up with Tim, but it was in the past. Tim had obviously rebuilt his life, and she'd been happy to escape the cloud of scandal when she moved to the city. Penny bent into a forward fold, dangling her wrists by her ankles. *It had all worked out for the best, hadn't it?*

Fourteen

'Aunty Pen, watch this,' called Elliot, bobbing up and down in unison with Harry on the trampoline. Penny dutifully looked towards the play equipment, relics from her childhood when occupational health and safety were unheard of, a time when safety nets and soft-fall floor coverings were a ridiculous notion.

Her legs were still aching from the previous day's yoga session. She pulled them up underneath her. It was a pleasant sensation, a definite improvement on the headaches and fever that had plagued her the previous few months.

Diana swept gold and amber oak leaves off the lawn before sitting down, cross-legged, next to Penny and Leo.

'No, look at me, Aunty Penny,' called Evie from the monkey bars, her skirt falling over her giggling face as she flipped backward off the top of the steel-framed structure. She landed on the lawn next to Eddie, who was making daisy chains, and bowed to her audience before running across to join her cousins on the trampoline. Penny had been surprised to see Eddie join their picnic when Angus and Tim headed out mustering, but the children seemed to enjoy his presence as much as he enjoyed theirs. She gathered that the tableau wasn't uncommon.

'This is the good life, Pen,' sighed Diana. She removed her broad-brimmed hat and turned her face up to the late afternoon sun, closing her eyes with a contented smile.

Penny looked around and took in the deep-blue shade of the Grampians to the east, the array of red, yellow and orange trees lining the yard, the deep shadows cast across the green paddocks by the red gum trees, and the happy laughter of her niece and nephews. The air was still and warm, autumn's final nod to summer, and bees lazily buzzed their way across the garden.

Penny closed her eyes and twisted her body into a yoga stretch. 'It might not be the Cinque Terre or fall in Connecticut, but I guess it's not too shabby.'

Diana batted her over the head with the sun hat. 'Not too shabby? Jeez, you're a hard one to please.' Diana laughed, giving her a gentle whack on the shoulders for good measure. 'But at least you're looking better. Must be that "healthy mind, body and soul" caper that Dr Sinclair recommended.'

'Maybe.' Penny caught sight of Diana's raised eyebrow. 'Okay, probably. I'm feeling better,' she conceded, reaching for another lamington. Her strict eating habits had slowly fallen by the wayside, weakening under the temptation of her sisters' baking prowess and the offence they had taken at her constant rejection of their cooking. *It's just a compromise. I'll give up the sweets again as soon as I hit the city limits.*

'These are good. Did you make them?'

'Course I did. Mum's recipe.'

Penny thought about Annabel's recipe book, still sitting in the farmhouse pantry where she had left it years before. Her sisters had copied down their favourite recipes, leaving the treasured original untouched and lonely on the shelf. The more she became reacquainted with the home cooking she had grown up with, the more her mother's faded handwriting had begun beckoning to her each time she opened the cupboard.

'So, what's the latest on Lara and Sam?'

Diana shrugged. Her beaded earrings jangled as she looked in Evie's direction. 'Hard to say. I don't like to jump to conclusions, but from the sounds of things, it's heading south again. Getting details from Lara is like squeezing blood from a stone, and Evie didn't say anything when I picked her up this morning.'

'He was always a bit funny, Sam. Fine on a good day, but other days—' Penny shrugged. 'Though I can't imagine a string of replacements will be knocking on Lara's door. Aside from her dazzling personality, there's not exactly a wealth of eligible bachelors around here, is there? My friend Jade is desperate for me to round her up a wholesome country boy, but they're thin on the ground everywhere, I think.'

Diana shook her head and cast a look at Penny.

'Your Tim is about the only eligible bachelor in the district and I doubt he's looking for another girlfriend. Never liked Stella much, anyway. Walked straight past Mum's roses—in full bloom, mind you—her head bent over her phone the whole dinner. I overheard Mrs Beggs saying she'd gone interstate.'

'He's not *my* Tim. Not since the last millennium. Even then, we were barely together for more than a few months. Six at best.' So Tim was single again. She hadn't been back on social media since Evie had changed her password, though the temptation to hack into the account was stronger than she liked to admit. She turned and looked at Diana squarely.

'How much responsibility is Dad giving Tim, anyway? I spoke to his grandmother at yoga and she seemed to think he's running the place. I didn't realise Dad had virtually adopted him.'

'Why don't you get over your high school tiff and just ask him yourself?'

'Nothing to do with me, I'm staying well out of it.'

Penny turned away and watched Eddie crowning Evie with daisies, his movements careful and precise. He clapped at her delighted reaction, then ambled over, squinting into the sun.

'Cake please, Miss Diana?'

'Sure, Eddie.' Diana handed him a lamington. 'Are you having a nice time with the kids?'

Coconut and sponge spilled from his lips as he nodded effusively. He finished his mouthful with a gulp.

'Yep. Nice time with the kids. Tim got the sheep yet? We're going to have our own farm.' He smiled and lumbered off without waiting for a reply, to join Evie on the swings.

Penny shot her sister a look. 'Before you go all gooey-eyed on me, I've already heard the glowing reports from the older ladies at yoga that Tim's now the town darling.' She adopted a haughty tone, not unlike Charlotte the Harlot's accent. 'Tim Patterson—a pillar of society, a stalwart of integrity. He could almost run for mayor, if only his father hadn't fleeced half the town.'

Diana rolled her eyes. 'Sarcasm doesn't suit you, Pen. Your friends made such a fuss about it all those years ago—are you ever going to get down off your high horse about that whole thing? Pretty sure everyone else has forgotten all about it.'

Penny pulled herself onto her knees and stood up. She dusted the grass from her jeans but couldn't quite brush off the suspicion that she had handled the whole incident badly. She collected the empty mugs and put a lid on the lamington container.

'It's just the facts, Diana. Everyone trusted his father and look how that ended.'

Fifteen

Penny washed the mugs, stacking them on the draining board as the sound of motorbikes filtered in through the kitchen window. She watched Tim enter the backyard, a helmet under his arm. All four children, plus Eddie, ran up to greet him, and he crouched down to their level. Penny set the tea towel aside, ready to head upstairs, when the sound of footsteps creaked across the back porch. She turned to see her dad cradling a tiny lamb in his arms. Its limp form poked out from underneath an old towel.

'This little guy somehow escaped the fox, but he's going to need a bit of TLC to survive the night. I thought you could use the company? Can you slip your Rossi boots on and grab me a few newspapers from the wood shed?'

Penny nodded her head without even realising it, despite the fact she'd traded her workboots for high heels a long time ago. Her answer elicited a small smile from her father and a feeble bleat from the lamb. She returned with the newspapers.

'You never could resist the sick ones, Pen,' he said softly. He shook his head as if to flick away the sentimentality, and his voice was brisk when he spoke again.

'Fetch the laundry basket too, there's a girl, so I can leave him upstairs with you. We'll shift him into a pen if he survives.'

The laundry cupboards were in the same order they had always been. She easily located the basket and a beach towel she had once used for swimming lessons.

'Poor little guy, he looks pretty weak,' said Penny as she returned. She dried off the lamb's damp wool, concerned about its lack of movement.

'I'll rustle up a warm bottle. Don't get too attached. Don't name it. You know the old saying—where there's livestock, there's dead stock,' said Angus, wiping his hands on a faded green shirt before lining the basket with the newspapers and towel.

'Sure, I'll keep an eye on him and throw him on the heap if he doesn't make it,' she said dryly.

Angus turned with a grin, shaking his head as Penny rolled her eyes.

After he left, she turned to look at the tiny creature. It was sleeping and a pink tongue poked out of its mouth. Its chest moved slowly under the towel, the greyish wool tightly curled and long creamy eyelashes fluttering gently. *If you make it through the night, I'll call you Hercules*, she whispered to the exhausted lamb with as much detachment as she could muster.

Tim slung his leg over the quad bike and headed back down the laneway, keen to check one more boundary fence before he called it a night. The tiny crossbred lamb Angus had handed to Penny was an anomaly, the result of a neighbour's dorper ram breaching their fences out of the main joining period. Tim had been the one to discover the mangy-looking intruder in the paddock last October, and he was darned if it was going to happen again and jeopardise their own carefully coordinated breeding program.

He scanned the fence lines, keeping an eye out for loose strands, barbed wire adorned with tell-tale clumps of dorper wool, or any of the neighbour's self-shedding rams among the McIntyre merino flock.

Tim's mind wandered back to the farmhouse as he patrolled the southernmost boundaries, wondering how the orphaned animal would fare in the hands of a country-girl-turned-city-slicker. He had tried to convince Angus to put the lamb out of its misery, but there had been no shaking him from the idea when he'd announced it would be the perfect project to occupy Penny during her convalescence.

Angus is dreaming if he thinks a mongrel lamb will magically rekindle Mac's country roots. Everyone except him can see she's counting down the days until she returns to the city. He hadn't mentioned the calendar squares to Angus, but surely he'd also noticed that she had circled a date a few months in advance, and was consistently marking each day off.

Tim looked out at the hilly horizon as the wind whipped his scruffy hair across his forehead. He breathed in the dry earth, the fresh air that tasted sweeter than any fancy perfume or air freshener. *I'd give anything to have this farm in my family. Mac doesn't even know how good she's got it.*

The lamb stirred at the sound of the house phone, bleating feebly and then loudly as if it were competing against the ringing. Penny looked up from the laundry sink, wiped her hands on a tea towel, and left milk powder lumps floating in the half-made bottle.

'Shush, Hercules, you'll get lunch in a minute.' She cleared her throat, shutting the laundry door as the lamb continued protesting.

'McIntyre Park, this is Penny.'

'Babe, you sound like you're still in the office. Swap Boutique Media for McIntyre Park and I'd swear you were back at your desk. Loved the picture of your baby sheep.'

Penny beamed, delighted to finally catch Vince on the phone. The ongoing game of phone tag between his mobile, his Sydney office number, the farmhouse number and the patchy range on Penny's mobile was getting ridiculous.

'You sound like the twins; they call him a baby sheep too, instead of a lamb. He's going great. I'd forgotten how strong the little blighters could be,' she said, rubbing a bruise on her chin. Hercules had headbutted her in protest yesterday as she was wrestling the empty milk bottle from his foamy mouth. She hadn't noticed it until Evie had pointed it out last night and had been amused by the way her niece had fussed around looking for an icepack instead of focusing on her schoolbooks. Anything to get out of homework, it seemed.

'Can't talk long, babe. We've got a meet and greet with some overseas clients, but great to hear all's good.' His voice trailed off and she heard a muffled laugh.

Penny frowned at the calendar, realising she hadn't marked off the last few days, and picked up a pen as he came back on the line.

'Oh, and keep the cute animal pictures coming through. Don't suppose you're rearing any baby kangaroos or possums? Charlotte's very impressed with your versatility. Love you, babe.'

Penny gripped the phone long after Vince had hung up and chewed on the end of the pen. She didn't like being patronised. A funny taste formed in her mouth, but she wasn't sure if it was the blue ink now leaking out the end of the biro or the way Charlotte's name cropped up so often in their sparse conversations.

⁂

A rap at the door jolted Tim from his laptop screen full of spreadsheets. He ran a hand through his hair, glancing at the clock. Not often they had visitors at 9 p.m. on a Tuesday night. The knocking came again, accompanied by a belated bark from Bones. Tim stood up, pressing save on his budget and finances forecast.

'Coming,' he called softly. His back cricked and crunched as he walked to the door. He switched on the porch light and groaned at the sight before him.

Sam wavered on his front step, rocking back and forth in his worn-out workboots, with a backpack hoisted over his shoulder and a bottle of bourbon in one hand. His face was as rumpled as his clothes, as if he'd just stepped off the bus from an end-of-year footy trip. Tim pulled the door open.

'Lara's bloody well kicked me out. C'n I crash at yours?' he slurred.

Tim looked into the dim evening. Moths flocked to the bright light, undeterred that Sam smelled like he'd been swimming in a football field of spirits. Bones sat at their visitor's feet, his tail thumping against the brick path, looking up at him with faith and loyalty. Tim looked away from his dog and up at Sam, wary of being a halfway house or becoming embroiled in Sam's marital dispute. His gaze flickered to the dusty station wagon still idling in the driveway, windscreen wipers going and the driver's door wide open, despite the rain.

'Jeez, mate, don't suppose I can send you back out in that weather. You've had a skinful by the look of it.'

He stepped to one side. Sam staggered through, thumping his backpack on the ground. It sounded like it held more bottles than clothes.

'Bloody women, not worth the trouble they cause,' he mumbled, launching into a maudlin rendition of their old footy team song.

'I'll change my mind if you don't put a sock in it, Sam. Eddie's asleep,' said Tim, shrugging on a jacket. He jogged out to Sam's car, turned it off and slipped the keys into his pocket. Bones nudged his hand, giving it a lick for good measure. 'It's the least we can do, Bones. And it's only for a night or two.'

Sixteen

Penny laughed as the lamb wobbled on its spindly legs, the little tail wriggling and ears flicking back and forth as it bleated.

It circled the wooden playpen at the far end of the kitchen, impatient for its morning feed. Hercules had grown even stronger after a fortnight of regular feeding, thriving under Penny's care. Angus had shaken his head at the creature spending more than the first nail-biting few nights inside, but after the rocky start, when it looked like it wouldn't survive, he'd softened. Penny liked the animal's company.

'It's more fun looking after you than thinking about my own health,' she told the lamb as she mixed up the formula. The lamb bleated insistently as she walked over to the pen, bottle in hand. She tucked him under her arm, offered him the teat and sat down with the feeding animal on her lap.

Dust swirling along the driveway caught her eye, and she watched two cars approaching the house. Angie's red hatchback pulled right up at the lavender hedge. Bees and butterflies raced for cover as her bumper nudged the grey foliage.

Diana guided her four-wheel drive closer to the house, giving a generous berth to all the surrounding obstacles. Penny smiled

at her sister's foresight as the twins flung open their doors and
bounded out from both sides, hitting the ground running.

She watched both sisters convene in close discussion, their
quick glances towards the house setting Penny's alarm bells
ringing. It reminded her of the conversations she and Jade used
to have when they were two single ladies scoping out wine
bars and discussing their game plan for the night. *If I didn't
know any better, I'd say those two were cooking up trouble.*

'Erk-lees, Erk-lees.'

A tornado of twins rushed in through the back door, their
rubber boots tracking freshly cut grass clippings and mud
across the floorboards.

Two pairs of dirt-covered hands reached up and petted the
lamb before completing the lap of the island bench, narrowly
avoiding their mum.

'Harry! Elliot!' Diana bellowed from the doorway, Leo on
her hip, Angie right behind her. 'Outside, outside, you'll get
Grandpa's floor all dirty,' she said, walking into the kitchen
and shooing her sons out the door like a flock of chickens.

Their yahooing was like an Indian war cry. It had filled the
large room and was most noticeable in its absence.

'And shut the door,' called Diana, but to little effect, as
cold air rushed into the kitchen. She muttered as she closed
the heavy door herself: 'If I had a dollar for every time they
did that . . .'

'I'd be a rich woman,' finished Penny and Angie in unison,
remembering their mother's favourite refrain.

Diana sat Leo down on the floor with a jam drop and looked
wearily at Penny as she pulled out a chair. Penny noticed lines
around her eyes, dark circles that would have challenged any
brand of concealer, had she been wearing it.

'Those two will give me more grey hairs than Cameron or Leo combined. And if *you* keep worrying me to death, then I'll be completely grey before I'm forty,' she said, sneezing into a crumpled handkerchief.

'Are you okay?'

'You don't have a monopoly on illness, you know.'

Angie gestured silently behind Diana's back, scrunching up her face and forming her fingers into bear-like claws. Penny stifled a laugh, turning it into a cough as Diana fixed her with a grumpy glare. She softened after a series of sneezes.

'Sorry, I'm feeling terrible with this cold, and a teething baby doesn't help.'

Penny winced sympathetically. She knew what it was like to be sick and tired of being sick and tired. She walked to the side door and set the lamb down in the backyard with the twins.

'We've come to ask you a little favour,' said Angie, putting the kettle on and pulling mugs from the cupboard.

'Does this involve me forging Dad's signature on absentee notes or ushering heartbroken boys out of the house after you've dumped them? Because that was so nineties.'

'What? No, of course not. I've moved on since high school.' Angie grinned.

'It's for me,' said Diana.

Penny was shocked; Diana never asked for help.

'I promised the school I'd coordinate a craft activity this term, for one lesson a week in partnership with the disability centre. But with Pete's mum on holidays and this damn cold, I can't possibly run the class with these three in tow,' she said, waving her hand outside, where the twins ran circles around the backyard.

Angie placed tea and biscuits on the table.

'I've just been reading Marian Keyes. She's always marvellous and apparently, there's such a thing as baking therapy.'

'That's why Angie and I reckon you'd be the perfect person to take the class, doing baking instead of craft, with the school kids.' Diana looked at Angie, who spread her hands out in a flourish.

'And bake yourself better at the same time!'

Penny's jaw dropped. She shook her head resolutely.

'Me? And a classful of children and special needs people? Baking?' She leaned back in her chair, laughing at her sisters. 'It sounds like pure torture. I'd never sign up for something like that. I haven't baked a thing in the last five years.'

'If it's good enough for Marian Keyes, it's good enough for you,' objected Angie. 'Dr Sinclair thinks it's a great idea. Think of the feel-good vibes you'll get from helping the community.'

Penny ate her jam drop, pretending to consider the proposition. The boys dashed past the window, Hercules following close behind. She laughed at the scene and turned back to the table to see triumph and relief on Angie's and Diana's faces.

'That's great. We knew you'd be a trooper.'

'Thanks, Pen, you're a gem.'

'Woah, I haven't agreed to anything,' said Penny, holding up her hands. 'No, no, no. Sorry. I can't do it. Why don't you sign up for it, Angie?'

'Don't try and weasel your way out of this, Pen. The beauty salon is flat out. I can't possibly stretch myself further, not with my apprentice running off to Queensland like a belated schoolie. And there's no use asking Lara, not with Sam and everything else she's got going on.'

'More drama?' Penny watched her sisters exchange a look and felt more out of the loop than ever.

Diana nodded. 'Lara's turfed him out. Evie's staying at our place while they sort their stuff out. She and Cameron have stayed up chatting well past bedtime the last two nights, but at least the poor thing's got someone to talk to, I guess. And

I'm glad she didn't have to watch her father storm out, kicking doors and waking neighbours. God knows how Lara's feeling about it all. She's clammed up again.'

Angie groaned. 'If you want an update, just ask Mrs Beggs at the post office. She's pretty much an expert on the subject. Now it takes me just as long to collect Dad's newspapers from the general store as it takes to drive from my house back to Bridgefield. She's heard from more than one of Lara's neighbours that she and Sam are as hot-tempered as one another. God knows what other rumours are swirling around.'

The three women sat quietly. Penny tried to put herself in Lara's shoes, but came up with a blank. She and Vince never fought. Although she was pissed off about his minimal contact while she'd been at the farm, she couldn't ever imagine them slamming doors and yelling. She shuddered at the thought. The resentment at falling to the bottom of Vince's priority list didn't sting quite so much these days, now that she was back into the lull of McIntyre Park. In the scheme of things, her predicament was a hiccup compared to the turmoil that must be playing out in Lara's life at the moment. Her mind started to wander to the old Bridgefield scandal that had engulfed the Pattersons, and the subsequent storm she hadn't been brave enough to weather by Tim's side, when Angie broke the silence.

'Come on, Pen. You've got more free time than anyone. What about your healthy mind, body, soul thingy? They'll go together like scones and cream.'

'And God knows I'd do it myself—' Diana sneezed again, a glint of mischief creeping into her expression. 'If you want to babysit these three for me?'

Penny's gaze swung wildly to the window, where she saw Harry smearing Elliot's face with mud. *Or is that sheep poo?* She cringed and searched the kitchen for Leo, who had crawled across to the pantry and was silently but industriously spreading a packet of flour across the floor.

'You'll have another adult helper if you do the cooking classes. And they're all independent kids, least you won't have to change any nappies,' offered Angie.

'Go on, Pen. Never know, you might actually enjoy yourself.'

Penny tipped her head back and stared at the cobwebs gathering on the kitchen ceiling. She sighed as she fixed her sisters with a steely look.

'I'll do this for you, but only as a very special favour for my two favourite sisters. Be warned right now—I'll endure it. There's Buckley's chance I'll enjoy it.'

Seventeen

Pollen blew across the town hall parking lot, wafts from the yellow cypress boughs sending Diana into yet another coughing fit. Penny glanced at her sister, hoping for her sake she looked worse than she felt. She juggled the bag of groceries on her arm, still unsure if she'd be able to convert the basic ingredients into something palatable. If it weren't for Jade's laughter down the phone line, she may well have pulled out.

'Baking classes? You woke me up at 2 a.m. to tell me you're worried about baking classes. That's hilarious, you don't even bake,' Jade had scoffed. 'Closest I've seen are those protein balls that require three glasses of water to swallow. I think you should choose the babysitting.'

Penny hadn't taken offence at her friend's comments; she was kind of right. She'd left the baking behind when she moved out of McIntyre Park. But there was something nostalgic about the suggestion that had kept her from cancelling.

'This is just a one-off,' Penny warned Diana.

'It will be good to get out of the house. And don't forget, you're from a long line of community volunteers. It's about time you gave something back.'

Penny bit her tongue as she thought of their mother's endless bake sale contributions and school canteen duty. Diana had followed in her footsteps, and she knew Angie and Lara had completed various types of community service over the years. Cheerful daisy bushes lined the yellow weatherboard hall. Spider webs hung from the ornate burgundy trim and the tin roof glittered with rust. Diana hunched over, trying to smother another bout of sneezing and coughing. Penny grabbed the baking supplies from her hands and directed her back towards the car.

'Go home and put your feet up before you infect everyone in the town.' It felt good to be ordering her oldest sister around. For once, Diana didn't argue. Penny nudged the groceries and the mixing bowls onto one arm. She pulled against the reluctant hinges of the heavy hall door with all her might. It creaked open and the musty scent of school concerts, Christmas gatherings and multi-generational birthday parties engulfed her.

Noisy chatter and excited footsteps echoed across the hall, and suddenly she was surrounded by a group of children wearing navy aprons over their uniforms. They scooped up the bowls and unthreaded the shopping bags from her arm, then pressed a pink apron into her hand before racing to the kitchen.

She slipped the apron over her head as the students unpacked ingredients for the chocolate cake and jam drops. The feminine design contrasted with her skinny jeans and blouse. She ran her hands over the ruffled hem and floral pocket, a smile pricking at her lips. It would do.

As she entered the small kitchen, Penny noticed a figure crouched in the corner, head down, pulling mixing spoons and baking trays out of the cupboard and handing them to a group of young adults. Penny spotted Eddie at the same time he saw her, and she watched the recognition blossom on his face.

She laughed as he bustled up to her, almost bowling over a young primary school student in the process, only to hesitate when he reached her. He stuck out his hand shyly.

'Penny, Penny, Penny. You cooking with us?'

'Sure am, Eddie. Should be fun.'

She hoped her voice sounded more confident than she felt. It certainly had been a long time between batches of biscuits. But Eddie's bright smile was contagious; her apprehension melted away as she smiled back at him and his group of friends.

'I wasn't expecting to see you here, Mac,' came a voice from behind the crowd.

Eddie and his friends turned to the back of the kitchen. Penny's heart jumped as she saw who was rifling through the cupboards: none other than Tim Patterson. Her smile dropped. Had she known exactly who the other adult helper was, she might have dug in her heels that bit harder.

She looked at the eager faces before her; a range of ages and abilities eagerly awaiting their collaborative cooking session. She looked at Tim's clenched jaw, and realised he hadn't been expecting her either.

As much as she wanted to rip off the pink apron, she knew it wouldn't be fair to bail at this late stage. Penny took a deep breath. *Calm mind, body and soul. What the hell is Tim Patterson doing in the hall kitchen in the middle of the working week? Doesn't he have fences to fix or sheep to drench?* She smoothed out the apron and swallowed a realisation—there might be a lot more to the adult version of this man that she didn't know.

Just as he had in the past five weeks, Tim worked hard to keep his distance. Half an hour into the baking class, he realised it was much easier on a 3,000-acre farm than in the tiny kitchen. The smell of Penny's shampoo followed him around the 1950s room; a fruity aroma sweeter than anything in his and Eddie's bathroom cabinet.

'Sorry . . .'

'No, you go first.'

Tim pulled his hands back as they both reached for the same wooden spoon.

I should have known Diana and Angie were cooking up something when they bribed me with pineapple sponge cake. Extending my volunteer shift at the special school is one thing but helping Penny McIntyre run a baking class—that's a whole 'nother ball game. Almost worth it though, just to see the look on her face when she walked in.

Tim turned, his smile slipping away as he unpacked her reaction. *Was it really that much of a stretch for her to imagine me volunteering and giving back to my community? Everyone else in Bridgefield has moved on—does she really still believe I'm going to follow in my father's footsteps?*

He watched Penny out the corner of his eye as she helped Eddie and his new primary school buddy make biscuits. The apron strings were tied twice around her dainty waist. The ridiculous diet she'd been on in the city might have stripped meat from her bones, but it hadn't robbed her of the ability to wield a spatula.

It was easy to see she was still a natural with the equipment, an inherent talent for cooking running through her veins. Tim watched Eddie fumble with the large bowl, unable to hold it steady at the same time as stirring. Penny reached across and showed him how to hug the bowl into his elbow. There hadn't been much call for baking in their childhood. Baked goods, or more accurately the lack of, had been just another bone of contention between his parents. Tim let the children measure out flour as he fished his phone from his pocket. The room was too quiet; it needed some music. *He* needed some music. He pulled up a Keith Urban album, set it to play, and returned to his team of young bakers. The familiar stream of country music helped ease away the feeling he was completely out of his depth. Three tracks in and they were stirring something that resembled dough.

'Looking good, little guys. Pretty sure they'll be asking us to join the *MasterChef* team soon.' He grinned and looked over at the other group. Even he could see Eddie was sneaking more into his mouth than he spooned onto the tray, but Penny kept passing him the mixture, praising each mound that made it to the tray. Tim turned back to the workbench, mimicking her actions with his group until their tray of biscuits was complete. He walked over to the oven, proud of their efforts until he slid the tray in alongside Penny's straight rows. Their efforts looked distinctly mismatched in comparison.

'Pretty good effort, I reckon. Don't you, guys?'

There was a cheerful chorus of agreement from the older girl beside him and the younger student on his right. He looked up to see Penny's gaze upon him and wondered if she had noticed the defensive edge in his tone.

'I'm sure they'll taste great,' she offered.

'Too right. No need to fancy them up—kids will eat them regardless.'

He wiped his hands on the blue apron and stared back at her grey–green eyes. For the first time since she had returned home, he allowed himself to scrutinise her, to see the woman she had grown into. He clocked the dangly earrings, the ever-present make-up and the carefully pulled-back hairstyle she had chosen for the day. *Beats me why she gets herself dolled up like that every day. She'd be prettier without all that fuss.*

He thought about Stella's make-up, lotions and potions that had once cluttered up his bathroom. *What do I know about women, anyway?* He looked down at his steadily rising biscuits, the misshapen balls merging into the neighbouring rows. *About as much as I know about baking. All the more reason for me to steer clear of all women—high maintenance, low maintenance or otherwise.*

Penny stared back at him boldly, noting the frayed edges of his shirt collar, the hair curling around his ears and the short, scruffy beard that almost covered the thin scar on his jaw. The noise of dishes faded into the background as she searched his face, trying to pick out the differences between the troubled teenager she had turned against when the town had ostracised his family, and the man he was today.

'Image isn't everything.' His voice sounded like a challenge.

She could feel the hostility in his words, had noticed the clunky way he used the sieve and his unfamiliarity with the different ingredients. He obviously wasn't a recreational baker.

'No, but sometimes it's nice putting a bit of effort in,' she said, turning back to her group. Penny kept to her side of the kitchen for the rest of the session, finding herself swept up in the solace of measuring, mixing and guiding the children through the class. *Perhaps it is possible to bake yourself happy,* she marvelled, biting into a moist chocolate cupcake. Her desire to distance herself from Tim disappeared as she inhaled the scent of cocoa that had been her kryptonite for years. She swooned at the decadence of eating a warm, homemade cupcake straight from the cooling rack, mimicked by her star helper, Eddie.

'Mmm-mmm.' Eddie giggled as he peeled back the patty pan wrapper to take another bite. 'Yummy.'

The children murmured their agreement, and Penny smiled as she saw an identical yellow wrapper in Tim's hand as he packed away the blueberry muffins his group had attempted. Their volcano-like muffins were untouched, the sides burned and the insides still gooey. Aware she was taking childish glee in his failure, Penny felt a thrill at her rusty yet superior baking skills.

A cough from the back of the hall heralded Diana's return. Tim strode past her with a container full of biscuits, nodding a quick hello on his way outside.

'Looks like you've made enough for an army,' said Diana. She shuffled over to the bench, a handkerchief scrunched up in her hand.

Eddie came past for the final container of cupcakes and hugged Penny again. His face beamed with pride and joy.

'Seems you've made a firm friend,' Diana said, smiling.

'I guess there's something to be said about baking for pleasure. And Eddie's a lot more easy-going than his brother, that's for sure,' said Penny.

Diana looked like she was about to ask something, but her mouth squeezed shut as Tim returned to the kitchen.

'Baked goods are all packed. Deliver 'em straight back to the school?'

Diana nodded. 'That will be wonderful, Tim. Thanks so much.' He dipped his head in reply before turning and leaving without a glance in Penny's direction.

'See you, Tim. Don't let Eddie eat them all on the way,' she called cheerfully.

Eddie was hot on his heels as Tim paused at the open door.

'I'll get some more practice in before next week.'

'Next week, Penny, thank you,' added Eddie, waving.

Penny frowned.

'There is no next week; this is only a one-off, isn't it?' Her voice came out through gritted teeth as she shot a narrow look at Diana.

'Perhaps I forgot to mention it? You're all signed up for the five weeks,' Diana mumbled, blowing her nose on the handkerchief and sniffling loudly.

Penny's gaze flitted to the back of the hall, where Tim and Eddie were silhouetted against the white sky. She didn't like being forced into things, but she wasn't going to give Tim the satisfaction of knowing she had been unwittingly sucked into one of Diana and Angie's schemes.

She smiled through gritted teeth and nodded, lifting a hand in farewell. There might be some science in this cooking therapy lark, but in the meantime, Diana owed her a serious explanation.

Eighteen

Hercules frolicked around the backyard, donkey-kicking his fluffy legs behind him and wagging his long tail. Penny marvelled at his energy and realised she was feeling relatively spritely herself. She looked at her slender wrists, flexing them back and forth, and spread her fingers out, reaching and contracting them without a hint of pain. Relief filtered through her body. It was the first time in ages she hadn't winced with pain at the mere movement.

The creased pages of Annabel's recipe book fluttered in front of her, and she wound the kitchen window shut. Little puffs of flour rose from the pages as Penny searched for a yellowed slip of paper with her grandmother's precise cursive writing, sidenotes added in Annabel's handwriting. As well as a treasure trove of recipes, the book held a wealth of memories. Just flicking through the pages was like travelling back in time. She traced her finger over the tiny stars and dates next to Annabel's favourites, the mug-rings on the opposite pages where her mum had rested her cup of tea, mid-baking session. Penny smiled as she spotted her own imperfectly formed handwriting underneath Annabel's. 'Best choc cake recipe!!! Penny '96.' And then Angie's scrawl beside a coconut rhubarb cake, highlighting it as a Bridgefield Show award winner a year later.

Penny set the recipe book down gently and fossicked in the pantry for supplies. She had just started folding cream and egg into the dry mixture when Angus walked in.

'You trying to get a jump on Tim for tomorrow's baking class?' Angus placed his Akubra upside down on the kitchen bench, the interior dark with sweat. He flicked the radio on, filling the room with banjo and guitar, and whistled along as he filled the kettle.

Penny laughed and stirred the mixture until it came together into a ball. She pulled it onto the flour-sprinkled benchtop and began working the dough.

'Hardly. It's not a competition, Dad.'

Angus watched his daughter kneading, his expression soft as if remembering the women who had stood before this same window in this very room: generations of McIntyres bringing the same scone recipe to life.

'Whatever it is, it's been good for you. You're moving a lot freer, as if the pain is all but gone. Though I must say, Monday mornings have gone to the dogs without my right-hand man. An hour of volunteering at his brother's school seems to have morphed into a half morning now that he's caught up with this baking class.'

He poured boiling water into two mugs and jiggled both teabags in unison.

'I certainly didn't choose to bake with him.' Penny blew a lock of hair from her forehead, but it fluttered directly back into the same place. With a sigh she relinquished the dough and swiped the hair away with her hand, leaving a trail of flour across her cheek.

Angus laughed. 'Your mother always used to do that. Those short bits of hair would fall into her face time and time again, and her cheeks would end up dusted in flour just like yours.' He smiled at the memory.

Penny's hand went to her face again, feeling for the flour, but she couldn't detect anything except a light layer of make-up.

'There, you've done it again.' He chuckled softly and took a seat across from Penny, resting his weight on the wooden stool. Penny smelled the lanolin on his clothes and saw fibres of wool stuck to his shirt.

'Did Mum always love cooking?'

Angus stood up abruptly and went to rescue the teabags from the mugs by the sink. Leaning back against the counter, Angus lifted a mug to his lips, his gaze distant.

'Baking? Yes. Not so much the everyday humdrum cooking. She made biscuits and cakes with you kids until the cows came home. I'd get back from a day on the tractor and you'd all have cake batter everywhere, hair stuck to your faces with smears of condensed milk, and oats scattered across the kitchen floor.' He smiled at the memory as if watching the scene run across his mind like a film. 'One of you would be licking a wooden spoon, another would be scraping your little fingers round and round the bowl to get the last bits of batter, and the older two would each get a beater to lick.'

The radio changed to a Slim Dusty track and he leaned over to turn it up.

'Barely a week would go by when I didn't get home to this bench piled high with baking, each of you girls urging me to sample a different piece.' Blinking, Angus looked out the window. 'And didn't I love it,' he said quietly.

Penny eased the scone cutter into the creamy mass. Old memories surfaced as she placed each round onto the floured baking tray. She pushed them into the hot oven, dusting off the nostalgia as she shook the flour from her hands.

'So,' she said brightly, hoping to lighten the mood. 'I bet these scones will have Mr Right-Hand Man pleading for a truce.'

'Thought you said it wasn't a competition? I wish you two would build a bridge and get over whatever rift is between you. He's a good man, Penny.' Angus turned the radio down and watched her scrape flour from the benchtop.

'I know you think that, but the apple never falls far from the tree, does it? I might be the only one to remember, but half the town turned against him when Roger's shonky deals came to light. You didn't see all the brawls he got into in the schoolyard, Dad. Then when he split his jaw, right before the deb ball—it was horrible.'

Penny busied herself with the dishes, remembering how genuinely shocked she'd been at the time, and the confusion that had clouded her judgement, unable to separate the Tim she knew so well from his father who'd fleeced the town. *Couldn't Dad see how his own trust in Roger Patterson had been used against him? Was he really willing to take a gamble on Tim, after he lost so much money?*

'The bloke's protective of his younger brother, loyal to a fault, ambitious and hard-working; can't blame him for that. Doesn't mean he's got ulterior motives though, Pen. He's got a dream of owning a farm and I'm mentoring him.'

Penny crouched down and assessed the scones, distracted by the way their side seams split as they rose, almost ready to be prised apart and smothered with butter, jam and cream. She'd done the right thing, putting distance between herself and Tim, but it hurt to hear her father singing Tim's praises, defending him. She picked up the recipe book and traced her mother's name on the inside page. Annabel McIntyre. A kind woman who had lavished baked goods on neighbours and friends. A firm believer in second chances. She slipped the book back into the drawer.

'Maybe I've been a bit hard on him,' she said, reaching for the oven mitts. 'Who knows, I might spare him a smile tomorrow.'

Angus rolled his eyes at her droll tone, amusement tugging at his lips.

Nineteen

'Bugger,' said Tim, thumping his hand on the kitchen bench. 'That was supposed to be baking powder, not baking soda.'

Penny turned away from her group, amused to see Tim's big, callused hands daintily scooping the powder from his mixing bowl. His young charges giggled nervously among themselves. The creases in his brow deepened as he gave up sorting the fine white baking soda from the equally fine white triple-sifted flour and upended the whole bowlful into the garbage bin. His movements were jerky as he reached for a new bag of flour, ripping it open with more force than necessary.

Wonder what's got his goat? Penny had noticed his burned pinwheels and lopsided scones on the baking tray next to her well-risen and neatly rounded offerings, but the sight of Tim losing his cool three times in one lesson was losing its novelty.

'I guess practice makes perfect,' she said, leaving her students to stir their cupcake batter. She looked over his shoulder at the recipe, Pearl's neatly linked script pressed into the page. 'Want to use Mum's recipe instead? It's pretty much bullet-proof and has half as many ingredients as this one.'

'Too late. Already told Nanna Pearl I'm making these.' He checked the baking powder label before passing it to one of Eddie's friends. 'One teaspoon, mate.'

Outside the wind rattled the loose window shutters, and the background conversation turned to the upcoming field days. Tim wiped his hands on his apron, slipping his thumbs through the denim belt loops, and sighed.

'I've cocked this right up, today. Even Bones won't want those burned ones.' His voice was low, his tone curt as he waved a dismissive hand at the trays. Penny thought back to yesterday's conversation with her dad.

'If your kelpie won't, then the chooks will. Or you can feed them to Sam—Lara said he took a dig at her cooking; maybe he should see what properly burned food looks like. Everything okay?'

Tim snorted, his mouth twisting.

'Yeah, you could say that. Not only has Sam hijacked my house and reads my newspaper before me, he's also quick to point out the bulldust about the old man in the *Bridgefield Advertiser*. You know, those crappy columns the newspapers print when there's no real news. "On this day twenty years ago . . . " So, guess what I got to read at brekky this morning? Still makes me wild rereading his charges, the dodgy bastard.'

Penny remembered the way Tim had at first defended his father in the schoolyard when several farmers' sons taunted him about the sheep rustling accusations. She remembered her shame at the time, embarrassment that he, and therefore she, would be forever tainted by association. Her cheeks coloured. She glanced up at Tim briefly, surprised to hear him talk so freely. He must be frustrated. It was the most he'd said in her presence the whole six weeks since she'd been home.

'Do you still stay in touch?'

Tim shook his head, clenching his jaw.

'He doesn't deserve it. He can rot in jail for all I care.'

Penny saw the bitterness in Tim's eyes, a hint of the angry teenager who had fought tooth and nail to keep Eddie out of the foster home system when his father's crimes were confirmed. She wondered what would have happened to their budding relationship had it not been interrupted by his family turmoil and the subsequent fallout. *Should I have tried to help him through it, all those years ago, instead of running away under the weight of peer pressure?* Penny shook off the sudden prickle of guilt. *How many times do I have to tell myself this? Breaking it off was absolutely, definitely the right decision.*

'You can pick your nose, but you can't pick your family,' she said, offering Angus's favourite adage to lighten the heavy conversation. Tim's distracted scowl intensified and she turned back to the restless bakers. Eddie and a primary school student wore mixing bowls as hats, and Tim's group had ditched their bowls altogether to sample the least burned pinwheels.

'Righto bakers, let's get this show on the road. Greta, pull our cupcakes out of the oven, please. Eddie, you can pack up the best-looking scones and pinwheels—they'll be afternoon tea at the nursing home today. No, not those burned ones. Our ones.'

She shot a look at Tim, who was gazing out the window, oblivious to his group using spatulas like drumsticks against the side of the bench. *Does his father's imprisonment haunt him or does he block it out the same way I handled Mum's accident?* She shook her head. *Not your problem, Penny,* she told herself. *Soon you'll be back in the city, far away from small-town dramas.*

The scent of rosemary and garlic filled the kitchen as Tim pulled a roast lamb leg from the oven. He tugged the floral oven mitts from his large hands, switched on the heat under the saucepan of gravy he'd prepared earlier, and stirred it to a simmer. The kitchen was as comfortable as the threadbare flannelette shirt he wore, though he was usually on the opposite end of the bench.

Pearl set down her crossword and ambled over to the stovetop, rugged up in two hand-spun cardigans despite the mild autumn day. Her hair was looking extra purple and even more tightly curled than usual, a sure sign she had spent the morning at the hairdresser's. The flu seemed to have struck half the town, including his ordinarily spritely grandmother, but he knew she would have insisted on her weekly curl and set.

'Smells lovely, dear. You're such an angel, cooking for your old nanna.' She slipped her hand on top of his.

He looked down at her wrinkled hand, dwarfed by his own, and pulled her into a gentle hug.

'You're my number one girl. The roast should be okay, though I can't make any promises about the dessert.'

She squeezed him tightly. 'Nonsense, I bet it will taste fabulous.'

Tim laughed at her optimism, hoping tonight's meal would turn out better than his efforts at the last two baking sessions.

'Your mum would be so proud of you boys,' she whispered, loud enough that only Tim could hear. He glanced into the lounge room; thankfully Eddie was immersed in a *Where's Wally?* book.

'Please don't, Nanna. I know she's your daughter, but she made her feelings pretty clear when she walked out on us all those years ago. You're more of a mum to us than she'll ever be.'

'I know, I know. I just wish I'd looked after you and Eddie better when it all went pear-shaped. I should have packed my suitcase and come home straight away when your father went to jail. It keeps me awake at night, Tim. That and my cranky hip.'

Tim laid his hand on hers. 'I wasn't going to interrupt your big overseas adventure, not in a million years. Old news now, Nanna. Eddie and I managed just fine.' She didn't need details about how hard it had been, the number of people who had stopped and stared at them, the way conversations at the post office had paused mid-sentence when he collected the mail. He'd been too proud, too determined to ask for help, but he was forever grateful for the way she'd smoothed their transition back into the social fabric of the town when she finally returned.

She sighed, her breath coming out like a wheeze.

'You're right. Enough of that maudlin stuff. How are your baking classes? A bit of fun?'

'I'm only doing it for Eddie's sake,' he said, casting a sidelong glance at the sunken sponge cake sitting on the green laminate benchtop. Although Mac hadn't commented on the sponge that had imploded as soon as he opened the oven door, or the jam and coconut slice that had almost slipped out of its greasy tray earlier today, he knew baking wasn't his forte. Nevertheless, Nanna Pearl had oohed and ahhed over the sponge as if it were fit for a queen.

'Young Penny McIntyre would know her way around a kitchen, mark my words. Pretty girl, that one. She's come along in leaps and bounds at yoga. You two have a lot in common, you know, both losing your mothers at a similar age.'

Tim gripped the wooden spoon tightly at his grandmother's comments, keeping his back turned so she couldn't see his eyes lifting to the heavens. She'd shared this nugget of wisdom with him twice already since Penny had returned to Bridgefield, phrasing it slightly differently each time. He nudged the steamer full of beans and corn roughly, not wanting to cut her off again, but keen to halt the heavy-handed hinting.

'Eddie. Set the table, mate. Dinner's almost up.'

Tim reached for the knife and started carving lamb from the bone as Pearl sneezed into her handkerchief.

'Though that boyfriend of hers sounds a bit off. From what I hear, he hasn't even met Angus or visited the farm yet. What type of new-age relationship is that?'

'I wouldn't know, Nanna. None of my business.'

'But she's such a lovely girl. Always takes the time to chat with me after yoga classes. And she's even polite to Olive, though everyone knows Olive's such a terrible gossip. Just like Mrs Beggs and that William Cleary. They were having a good old chinwag about Lara and Sam this morning. Should be a good garage sale, all those lovely things sold up because they couldn't agree on who kept what.'

Tim clenched his jaw as he served up the wholesome but straightforward fare. He'd heard more than he wanted to about the garage sale. In fact, he'd heard more than he wanted to about Sam and Lara's financial affairs and marriage in general. The novelty of waking up each morning to find Sam passed out on his futon couch, half a slab of beer cans littering the lounge room floor, suitcases still stacked in the porch, was starting to wear thin. *There's only so far a friendship can stretch, right?*

Twenty

Rain rushed through the tin downpipe with a roar, cascading over the edges of the gutter each time the pipe reached capacity. Penny sat back in the wicker chair, petting the lamb's soft ears and enjoying the way the curtain of water intermittently drenched the lavender hedge below. Angie's red hatchback splashed through the puddles and pulled up in the driveway.

Angie dashed from the car, shielding her hair with a pile of newspapers. Her jacket was soaked through in seconds as she crossed the gravel and clambered up the steps, grateful for the shelter of the vast verandah. She giggled, shaking like a wet dog. Raindrops flew across the porch and made their mark on Penny.

'Erggh, you're worse than Rusty,' Penny groaned. Angus's black and tan kelpie thumped his tail against the decking at the mention of his name. Penny threw her sister a dirty look before accepting the bundle of mail and soggy newspapers. Nestled among the *Bridgefield Advertiser*, *Stock & Land* and an assortment of window-fronted envelopes for Angus, she found a crisp envelope embossed with the Boutique Media logo.

A shiver of anticipation rippled through her hands as she tore it open. When was the last time she'd looked at the calendar? Surely her ten weeks weren't up yet? She gave a whistle of surprise as she read Georgie's invitation back to work. Hercules skittered away at the sudden noise. Georgie outlined details, dates and schedules that would follow her return to work. Just reading it made Penny a teensy bit tired. Exhilarated too, but realistic that the seventy-five-hour weeks awaiting her would hurt as much as the fitness regime she and Jade had agreed on.

'They've missed me, Angie, desperate to have me back. Apparently, all they need is my medical clearance and I'm good to return in just over a fortnight.'

'It can't be. Already? Sounds like they're not the only one eager to have you back,' Angie said, her voice teasing as she pulled a postcard from the back pocket of her jeans and waved it just out of Penny's reach.

'Don't tell me you've been reading my mail?'

Angie grinned and flipped over the glossy Sydney Opera House photograph. Her voice was loaded with drama as she read aloud: 'Dear Penny, Sydney is great, but it'd be better with you. Sorry about the lack of contact, things are still flat chat. Missing you, babe. Can't wait for our big trip. Love, Vince.' Angie smooched several big air kisses before handing the card to Penny.

'He may as well take out a full-page advertisement in the Briddy newspaper,' laughed Angie. 'Soppy bugger, isn't he? Never calls, but instead pens declarations of undying love. Haven't you told him postcards are prime fodder for the rural rumour mill?'

Penny shook her head with a wry smile, rereading both letters. It was on the tip of her tongue to mention the engagement ring, but she held back. 'I would tell him to pop the postcards in an envelope, but he's not exactly easy to catch on the phone. Fancy a glass of wine, Angie? I feel like celebrating.'

'I've got Zumba class tonight. Have to work off all those biscuits you keep forcing me to sample. I'm so thrilled you've rediscovered baking, Pen. I'll miss your delicacies when you leave.' Angie smiled wistfully. 'And I'll miss you too, Pen.'

Penny looked at her little sister, recalling an overwhelming and teary version of a similar conversation fifteen years earlier. She placed a hand on Angie's arm.

'I love it back in Melbourne, Angie. It's what Mum wanted for me. I'll be able to ace that promotion now I'm back to full strength. Plan a future with Vince. But I promise to visit more often.'

'You'd better. Make sure you enjoy these last few weeks then, hey? As entertaining as it is watching you and Lara try to ignore each other, maybe you should patch things up before you head off? That rumour mill just won't let up. She needs us now more than ever.'

One look at Angie's solemn face and the sarcastic reply fizzled away on Penny's tongue. First Dad and now Angie trying to get her to mend fences. She squeezed Angie's arm. 'I'll do my best.'

❀

A kookaburra perched on the power line, laughing while keeping a close watch on the pair of octogenarians, several seventy-year-olds and one thirty-three-year-old walking laps around the town centre—their new pre-yoga warm-up. The conversation was as light as the walking pace, and Penny was grateful for the way the older women had welcomed her into their group.

'I hear your love letters are steaming up the post office windows, Missy.' Merryl grinned, waving to the sole car driving along Bridgefield's main street.

Penny laughed and her hand reached for the necklace that had arrived in the mail yesterday. Vince had chosen a delicate love heart pendant on a long silver chain. Lara had called in to the farmhouse just as she was unwrapping the gift, and although Penny had tried not to rise to her sister's barb about gifts equating to guilt, it had taken the shine off the gesture.

'I'd hardly call them steamy, Merryl, but it's nice to know he's thinking of me.'

They rounded the corner by the general store.

'Oh, to be young and loved up. Those city boys know how to woo a woman, don't they, Pearl?'

Penny watched Nanna Pearl unzip her fuchsia hoody. Today's T-shirt said: 'CWA—Chicks With Attitude'. The older woman patted her tightly curled hair and tossed a surreptitious glance in Penny's direction.

'I don't know, Merryl. Give me a country bloke any day. There's a lot to be said for integrity and good old-fashioned hard work, don't you think?'

Penny lay facedown on the floor. Her arms were stretched out in front of her, knees tucked under her belly and forehead resting on the yoga mat. Inhaling through her nose, she let the breath inflate her lungs and gently expand her ribcage, enjoying the peaceful moment.

'Moving out of child's pose and onto all fours for a cat and cow,' called their willowy instructor.

Sucking her stomach up to the ceiling, Penny bowed her head. *At least I can tell Dr Sinclair I followed her advice. Yoga twice a week—check. Quiet fiction reading that barely stimulates my brain—check. Gentle walks outdoors—check. Limited social media and zero communication with work—check.*

Age and Herald Sun *subscription swapped for the tiny local newspaper—check. Good food and plenty of rest—check. Baking therapy classes—check. Surely she'll be happy with that update.*

Everyone groaned as the instructor led them into a sustained plank position. Penny felt her muscles shake from the strain, and where she would have once fought vainly to maintain the pose, she gave in to the tremors and lay down on her mat.

'Are you really going to let yourself be out-planked by a seventy-year-old?'

Penny turned to her left, finding herself just centimetres from the neon-green backside of Olive. She hadn't taken to the pre-yoga walks, but she never missed the twice-weekly classes.

'Olive, you're way too strong for a spring chicken like me,' Penny protested.

'Practice makes perfect, Missy; you'll get stronger if you do it every day,' she said.

'I think there's something else I'd rather do every day,' called a voice from the front of the class. The room erupted with laughter, several of the ladies lost concentration and collapsed onto their mats as they guffawed raucously.

'I did not need that image in my head,' replied Penny, scrunching up her nose at the idea of her elderly classmates having a sex life, especially one more active than hers.

'What, don't you think we still do it? Those little blue pills Max got from the doctor are worth their weight in gold,' crowed another lady, delighted to send the class into another wave of laughter before the teacher hushed them all and directed them into warrior pose.

Penny shook her head. She would miss the cheerful and sometimes surprisingly lewd banter in these classes. *I only hope I've got as much spunk when I'm that age*, she thought. *That*

is, if I make it to that age . . . The notion of her precarious
health, and the risks she took in spite of it, prickled at her
conscience like the swarm of mosquitoes at Tough Mudder,
nipping and biting all over. Her mouth was suddenly dry and
she broke her yoga pose to take a sip from her water bottle.

'Use it or lose it, that's what I say, Missy,' called Olive
with a wink.

'Oh shush, Olive. She doesn't need you rubbing her nose
in it,' came Pearl's voice from the opposite side of the room.

Penny felt a wave of gratitude for Tim's grandmother, who
seemed to be the only one willing to pull the class back into
line when the discussions began to dominate the exercise.

But Olive clung to the topic like a pit bull. 'I think she needs
all the advice she can get, Pearl. What, with those pictures
all over Facebook. I could barely believe it when Mrs Beggs
showed me how to search for people on social media. Face-
stalking, she called it,' crowed the old lady.

Several sharp breaths echoed around the room; even the
yoga instructor went silent as everyone turned to Penny.

Penny laughed uncertainly. *What on earth was Olive talking
about? Surely the woman was confused. Vince didn't even have
a Facebook account.* She turned slowly, unsure if she wanted
to know the answer to the question forming on her lips.

'What pictures?'

Olive's warrior pose wavered as she glanced from Penny to
the group, then back to Penny. Her expression was hesitant
now, her false teeth disappearing as she chewed her lip.

'You know, the ones on Facebook? Your boyfriend with
that girl Charlotte? Better hang onto him, not like your sister
and Sam Kingsley.'

Penny dropped down onto her mat, silently taking in the
news as her head adjusted to the abrupt change in position. She

felt a dozen eyes boring into her back as she tried to dismiss
the snippet of gossip. Her arms shook as she pushed herself
up off the mat and resumed warrior position. *Vince wouldn't
dare, would he? Not after last time ...*

Twenty-one

The mobile phone vibrated in irritation. Wrong password. Again. *Darn it.* Penny thumped the yoga mat down on a chair and leaned against the island bench, trying to crack Evie's password. Evie10? Nope. Hercules? Evie2019? AuntyPenny? Nope. Nope. Nope. She blew out a frustrated breath and ran her fingers through her hair. *What type of password would a ten-year-old choose?*

'Penny for your thoughts?'

Angus's quiet voice made her jump, and she looked guiltily at the phone clutched in her hand.

'Dad, I didn't know you were home.'

'Just about to head out, check the stock before morning smoko. Keen for a spin?'

Penny screwed up her nose, her head thundering with different replies. *No, I've got a zillion password combinations to try so I can break into my social media account and see if my boyfriend is messing around on me. Ask me in an hour when I've got enough evidence to prove Olive wrong.*

She looked up, the 'no' falling short as she took in his hopeful expression. *Enjoy your last few weeks.* The golden

rays of afternoon sun danced on the paddocks outside, the
Grampians beyond beckoning her to soak up the final offerings
of country living. A strange feeling squeezed her chest tight,
different from the Ross River fever aches that had taken hold
of her body. *Don't pay Olive any notice. It's probably a storm
in a teacup, anyway.*

'Yeah, I'm just chasing my tail here. I'll get a coat.'

Penny rounded the corner of the paddock, her mind on Vince
instead of the track ahead. She pumped the brakes as the ute
pitched low into a divot. Angus winced as he bumped his head.

'Steady on, Penny. Anyone would think you'd forgotten the
lay of the land.'

'Sorry, Dad. It's been a long time.'

'Too long.'

She pursed her lips, wondering whether she should remind
him that her time at the farm was almost up.

'Seems like only yesterday you were hooning around the
paddocks on the motorbike, making me lists of fences needing
repairs, water troughs with slow leaks, details on which crops
were being hammered by galahs, and your grand plans for
the place.'

She pushed away the nagging worries about Vince and
smiled at the memory, slowing down as they approached a gate.

The rusty ute door creaked open and Angus slid out to
unlatch it. He swung his frame back into the seat.

'So, does your fella Vince like animals? Reckon he'd ever
be interested in this old place?'

Penny pondered the deliberately casual question as she
nosed the vehicle ahead.

'Well, I haven't heard from him much since I've been away,
but he's about as metro as they come,' she said, putting the

brakes on both the ute and the discussion as Angus hopped out to close the gate.

A gust whipped in through the open door and Penny pulled the thick beanie down low over her ears. They were at the southernmost end of the property now and the breeze was steady up on the higher ground. The gum shelterbelts whispered their secrets in the wind, their eucalyptus perfume floating through the air. A kookaburra called in the distance, its laugh answered with an echo from the top of the nearby trees. Livestock murmured in the background.

'Fair enough. But it's a shame, Pen. I always thought you were the most likely to follow in my footsteps. You always had the right attitude towards the animals.' He met her eye, wistful. 'And now look at us. Miss City Girl with her highfalutin' job humouring her old man with a trip down memory lane.'

'It's been great being home these last couple of months, but I'm settled in Melbourne, Dad,' she said, staring straight ahead.

'That's all I want, Pen. As long as you're happy, Vince treats you right, and your work is rewarding, then you're on the right track. I just want you to know you'd always be welcome back home. None of the other girls are even remotely interested in running this place.'

Penny looked away. *Can I honestly say Vince makes me happy? Am I stupid to believe his promises? And why the hell isn't he calling me back?* She pictured the diamond ring again. Just the thought of it calmed the voice of doubt in her mind. *Of course we're happy. What woman wouldn't be happy with a ring like that, an apartment in the city, an award-winning career and our jet-setting lifestyle?*

'I think happiness is pretty subjective, Dad. Look at Lara and Sam. Today's yes could be tomorrow's no, and vice-versa. I need to get back to Vince and my job, let things get back to normal, and then I'll be happy.'

Angus looked out the windscreen, his chin lifting as he stared at the horizon. She followed his line of sight to the rocky outcrop that marked Wildflower Ridge and wondered if he knew Annabel had urged her to choose a career other than farming. She looked from where her mother's ashes were scattered back to her father. *I was always going to upset one of them, no matter which path I chose.*

Angus twisted the radio dial. Penny tapped the accelerator and turned the ute for home.

Twenty-two

Penny checked the street sign and flicked her indicator on for a left-hand turn, steadying the warm banana cake as she navigated into a street full of trampolines and swing-sets. Neat little cottages segued into brick veneers and weatherboard fixer-uppers on the far side of Bridgefield's boundaries. She counted the numbers until she came to 27 Henley Street.

Penny leaned over the steering wheel, assessing the chipped green weatherboards and torn flyscreens in disbelief. A scraggly lawn swallowed up any semblance of a footpath from the gate to the house. She hadn't been to Lara's place in ages—being around her at the farmhouse was more than enough—but surely this dump wasn't hers? *Why would Lara leave the new brick house she and Sam built and move in here? And why did Angie and Diana fail to mention what a shit-heap it was when they helped her move house last week?* She checked the address Diana had given her. This was it. Penny clasped the banana cake in front of her, almost like a shield instead of an intended peace offering. She walked across the yard and hesitantly pushed the doorbell. Pot plants flowered either side of the door, as if apologising for the dingy setting.

She heard footsteps and watched through the glass panels as her sister strode into view. The strong smell of Deep Heat emerged as Lara opened the door, revealing a hallway lined with half-unpacked moving boxes. She wore lycra and held a pair of scissors in one hand and a roll of hot-pink strapping tape in the other.

'Penny, I wasn't expecting you here.'

'I wanted to see Evie. And I baked you a cake to repay all those lunches you made for me when I was unwell. Thanks, by the way, and sorry things haven't been . . .'

She trailed off and shrugged her shoulders, not sure how to even describe their relationship.

Lara studied her chunky sports watch, then looked back at her sister.

'Evie's out, but I'm sure she'll love the cake. Thanks.' Lara smiled stiffly as she reached for the doorhandle.

Penny's hopes of getting the Facebook password sank. She didn't want Lara to know she was disregarding the doctor's suggestion of a social media ban, but Olive's comment at yoga was like a gremlin lurking in the back of her mind.

'I'm just heading out for a run. Wanna join me on the bike?' Lara gestured to a bicycle leaning against the battered garage and kneeled down to lace up her sneakers.

Penny was surprised by the impromptu suggestion; the first time Lara had offered more than a strained smile or barbed comment since she'd been home. *Perhaps the banana-cake olive branch worked?*

For the second time that day, Angie's advice to make peace rang in her ears. Penny shrugged.

'Why not?'

The bicycle cogs jammed, making a metallic grinding noise as Penny eased her way up the gears until she fell into line with Lara. It had been years since she'd ridden anything other than a spin bike, and it seemed Lara's mountain bike had taken personality cues from its owner. The chain had already slipped off twice, the fifth gear was a complete write-off and the jerky brakes needed more than a squirt of WD-40.

They turned left at the end of the street, and within five minutes were surrounded by paddocks and hobby farms. Lara's running shoes thudded along the gravel, broken only by the sounds of the magpies warbling and the hum of grasshoppers along the roadside. It was worlds away from the conversation-fest that characterised Penny and Jade's gym workouts or the steady stream of tooting traffic at their outdoor boot camp sessions. As she cycled, Penny tried to imagine they were two sisters who regularly ran and rode together along quiet country roads. She looked at Lara, inscrutable behind her sunglasses and running hat. *Not likely.*

The familiar landscape steadily grew greener as they neared the lake. The bike tyres rattled across the slatted surface of a narrow wooden bridge, and Penny could see a lacework of algae-strewn rocks beneath the clear, flowing water. The lake was in full view as they left the bridge, emerged from the dense scrub path, and rounded a corner. Vibrant shades of pink, yellow and orange were reflected on the still water, bright enough to rival any high-visibility gym gear.

Penny felt her body adjust to the first decent exercise she had had in months. The recent yoga classes and a few tentative swimming sessions had reinstated a snippet of her former strength, but she knew it would be a long road back to full fitness. Although she handled the brakes more than the pedals as they headed downhill, her shirt was soon as sweaty as Lara's.

'Evie wants you to come to her mid-year concert. At the town hall. June the seventeenth.'

'June?' Penny thought about the big black circle in the calendar. 'I'll be back in Melbourne by then. But I'll make it up to her—you can send her across on the bus and I'll take her to the theatre or something. I think there's a new Disney production out in August.'

Penny tried to gauge her sister's silence with a quick sideways glance, but Lara seemed steadfastly focused on the roadside.

'Listen to yourself. You've got such a stick up your own arse. I forgot how taxing it must be slumming it here in the boondocks.' Lara picked up her speed to surge ahead.

'I love the city, Lara. I know you don't understand, but it's how I like it. I've got a five-year plan and I'm sticking to it. Dr Sinclair is happy with my progress, work can't wait to have me back and the apartment will be free in a few weeks.'

She pedalled her bicycle faster so she could get a better look at Lara's face. Her sister's lips were pressed into a thin line.

'Do you think you're too good for us back here? Let me tell you, Penny, there ain't nothing superior about sitting in a fancy office, wearing some swanky suit and devising ways to screw people out of their money. Angie said you've got it in your head that Mum wanted you to move to the city, but she just wanted you to look at all your options, not build your entire identity on becoming a corporate slave who thinks she's better than all of us.'

'Where the hell has this come from? I thought you wanted some company on your run this afternoon, not a whipping boy.' Penny's legs worked harder to keep up the pace as it escalated along with the tension.

'Nothing compares to your bright lights and endless holidays, does it? Vince probably has an allergy to farms or something ridiculous like that. That's why he's never even bothered to visit.' Lara panted with exertion, sweat making her shirt cling to her back.

Penny's breath came thick and fast, and she felt her heart hammering as her legs continued to pedal. *What a way to mend fences*, she thought furiously. The hurtful comments bounced back and forth in her mind, confusion turning to defensiveness.

Penny swung her bike left to avoid hitting several large rocks scattered across the road. Lara veered to the right and they met back in the middle like a silent stalemate.

'Coming home wasn't an appealing option, but at the time it was the only option. I was perfectly happy in the city and I'll be even happier when I return. I want to get back to my life, back to Vince, back to the city where no one reads my mail before me at the post office or feels entitled to offer advice about my life. No wonder Sam left—I'd be sick of your bad attitude day in, day out, too. Don't take your anger out on me just because your life's gone pear-shaped.'

Penny was unaware that her voice had risen to a yell until she'd finished. The air was suddenly dead silent. Even the birds had ceased their twittering.

Lara stopped abruptly. Penny flushed at the low blow and drew to a halt as her sister doubled over with her hands on her hips, sucking in air.

'If that's how you feel, you're better off in the stinking city with all the other selfish buggers who only care about themselves and their image. You and Vince deserve each other. Go and run back to him and stay far enough away that your shitty attitude doesn't rub off on Evie.' Lara's face was puce as she straightened up, little specks of spit gathering at the corners of her mouth.

'But let's get one thing straight. You don't know the first thing about Sam and me or how hard things have been. You're living in a dream world, Penny.'

Penny eased herself back onto the bike, wheeling it around unsteadily and ignoring the pain from the hard seat. She was still fuming as she rode away, her mind brimming with comebacks that remained unspoken as her tiny remainder of self-restraint finally pulled rank.

Penny wrenched the tap to scorching, letting the hot beads of water melt away the anger. It wasn't only the things Lara had said; it was anger at herself for thinking she could smooth over their rocky relationship with a banana cake and an attempt at civility. *I should have known it would never be so simple with her.* The ride back home had taken twice as long as their descent to the lake and she'd walked more than she'd cycled, pushing the bike up the steepest sections of road, swearing each time the pedals clipped her ankles.

She emerged from the shower, red from the scalding heat, still just as hurt. She towelled off and slipped into a pair of jeans, combed her damp hair and reapplied her make-up before she picked up her phone. Vince's lack of contact was wearing whisper-thin, especially in light of Lara's observations.

Her fingers stabbed at the phone as she composed a new message.

> Exactly what day is our apartment free? Please have it cleaned and ready ASAP. I don't care how much it costs.
> Make it happen, Vince.

She hit 'send' and reached for the painkillers.

Twenty-three

'Don't worry yourself about Lara; you've got bigger fish to fry. I hate to say it, Pen, but Vince and that Charlotte woman were the hot topic at the kindergarten pick-up line,' said Diana, her car aerial decorated with black and white ribbons to match the netball team colours.

Penny's imagination ran wild and she felt lost at sea without access to her social media accounts. *This is getting beyond a joke.*

'At kindy pick-up? I thought Mrs Beggs just cultivated the story to drum up more business?'

'Has he called you back yet, Pen? At least tried to contact you? Maybe you should shelve the Facebook ban and get back online?'

Penny was mute as they travelled the seven kilometres to the local netball courts, the excitement of the children lining the back seats setting her further on edge. Diana parked directly in front of the courts, reached into her cavernous nappy bag and located a tatty iPad case. Scribbles and stick figures decorated the cover and the entire screen was smeared with greasy fingerprints.

Penny glanced at it warily, unsure whether she wanted to touch the murky item, which had evidently been manhandled by her nephews on more than one occasion. As keen as she'd been to get that password from Evie, she was now ambivalent about opening the Pandora's box awaiting her online. As long as she didn't see Charlotte's Facebook page, she could keep telling herself Olive and Mrs Beggs were exaggerating, or that they'd gotten the wrong end of the stick altogether. But if the kindergarten mums had got hold of the whisper too, maybe there was more to it.

'Oh, get over yourself. I promise you won't get gastro.'

Diana ushered Cameron and the twins out of the car, pressed a pink five-dollar note into Cameron's hand and pointed them in the direction of the small tuckshop. A sharp whistle came from the netball court. The junior netballers clustered around the coach for a quick pre-game pep talk before racing into their positions.

'Go get 'em, Evie,' called Diana out the car window, beeping her horn as their niece placed her toes on the goal circle and waved back at them.

The game got off to a flying start. The Bridgefield Magpies converted turnovers into goals, Evie shooting with accuracy to get her team to an early lead.

Penny looked down at the device. Dr Sinclair's voice echoed in her mind, urging her to repeat the calm mind, body and soul mantra. They had talked about the likelihood of getting sucked back into social media and how that would be a backward step in Penny's recovery. And up until then, Penny had felt okay with the break. Empowered even. But the whole Charlotte thing was like a scab begging to be picked. *I'm pretty much recovered now, anyway.* Penny's fingers wavered above the onscreen keyboard. She itched to type in her email address, but something stopped her.

'What's up?'

'I can't do it. I want to know, but I don't want to know. I'm committed to staying away from news and social media, but it's killing me having third-party reports about Vince and Charlotte the Harlot!'

'How about I log into my account and you can watch over my shoulder as we stalk her from there? Then you wouldn't technically be breaking the rules, would you?'

'Thanks, Diana.' Penny racked her brains for Charlotte's surname, tapping her fingers on the car's dashboard.

'You'd better hurry up, so we can find her before the netball break is over. My deal is we have to finish before the second quarter starts.'

Penny groaned, coming up with a blank. She reached for her phone to scroll through her work emails, but it was flat.

'I don't know her surname. And Vince doesn't have a Facebook account anymore, I'm sure of it.'

Diana tapped Vince's name into the iPad's search engine, navigated to his LinkedIn profile and started working her way through his list of contacts. *I should have thought of that*, Penny agonised, peering over her sister's shoulder. *Perhaps I haven't been giving Diana enough credit.* She recognised Vince's photo from an industry awards night the previous year, and a nervous smile crossed her face as she studied his handsome profile. It wasn't long before a familiar blond woman popped up in his contact list. Diana typed the name into Facebook and gasped as Charlotte's profile loaded. One in every three pictures in Charlotte's timeline featured Vince.

'Un-fucking-believable! I cannot believe I'm seeing this.' Penny's heart raced as dozens of photos of the glamorous pair flashed onto the screen.

'Un-fucking-lievable, un-fucking-lievable.' Penny turned to see the cheeky twins chorusing from their car seats and Leo smiling at her with a tomato sauce–smeared face.

'Oops, sorry Diana.' She cringed, before going straight back to the screen. Diana had flicked onto the 'details' section and was scrolling through Charlotte's employment history.

'Go back to the photos. I'm not finished. We already know where Charlotte works,' interjected Penny.

'Give me a minute, Pen, I'm streamlining this for you. And I bet you didn't know she has a Certificate IV in "sensual massage" from the Oxford Natural Therapies Centre?'

Penny gasped. *This is getting worse and worse.*

Diana clicked to the next tab. 'Or that her relationship status is "complicated"?'

Another tab.

'And her last few status updates have been annoyingly cryptic, but attention-seeking rubbish like "the truth will come out soon" and "freedom equals happiness". Looks like we've seen all we need to see here, Pen.' Diana logged out abruptly and shoved her iPad back into the filthy case. She gave Penny a sympathetic smile as the umpire's whistle blew and their niece returned to the court.

'What? That's all you're giving me? That's like offering an alcoholic a drink then cutting them off after one sip,' said Penny, exasperated that her sister would so heartlessly open the wound but not even offer a bandaid.

'Shhh, I promised Lara I'd watch Evie play and she's just about to get another goal. Oi, that's a bit rough!' Diana leaned out the car window and called across the court: 'Steady on, Evie. It's not a contact sport.'

Penny blinked as Diana drew back into her seat and looked in the direction of the netball court. Evie's opponent was being helped off the court, her arm cradled at an awkward angle.

'Did you see that? I'd swear Evie did that on purpose, the little bugger. She'll be on the bench next quarter if she keeps it up.'

Penny stared at her sister.

'How can you concentrate on the netball at a time like this? And what the hell am I going to do about Charlotte? Stunning, skilled in sensual massage, living and working in the same postcode as Vince. I can't lay claim to any of those things right now, let alone compete with her.'

'Un-fucking-lievable,' called Elliot from the back seat again. His brothers laughed.

'You should have seen what your niece just did. The other team's goal defender will be in a cast for weeks by the look of things, and she's standing there like butter wouldn't melt in her mouth. Are you sure this Charlotte girl isn't just living in a fantasy world? Maybe she's schmoozy with all her male colleagues?'

The netball whizzed to and fro in front of the car as Evie's team tussled for dominance. Penny's head moved back and forth, watching her niece shoot goal after goal, but all she could see were Charlotte's timeline pictures running like a slideshow through her mind. *How the hell does Vince plan on explaining this one?*

Twenty-four

Angie spooned another scoop of ice cream into her overflowing bowl.

'So, what are you going to do about it, Penny? Hang and quarter him, or sew raw prawns into his suit pockets so they're ruined by the time he works out where the smell's coming from? I'd suggest the latter—that's what I felt like doing when my last boyfriend nicked off. Might have to join Tinder like your friend, Jade.'

'I don't know,' said Penny, reaching for the ice cream tub. Her brow furrowed even further as she began eating directly from the container.

Angie gestured to the soft brown couch and plonked herself down in her favourite corner. Penny joined her, oblivious to Mr Darcy and Lizzie Bennet romancing their way across the television screen.

'I still can't believe she put all those photos online. As if she was parading *her* boyfriend for all and sundry to comment on, not *my* boyfriend. If I had her phone number, I'd give her a piece of my mind. And if Vince would answer my calls, I'd give him a piece too. Bloody bastard.' Penny rammed another spoonful of ice cream into her mouth, flinching when the metal clipped her teeth. 'He's obviously been sucked in. I bet he doesn't even know Charlotte's got these photos up.'

Angie laughed incredulously. 'If Vince has Facebook, then he knows about it, Penny. She's obviously tagged him in every one of those photos—how else did Olive and Mrs Beggs find them? I thought he'd be the type to update his status and profile picture at least weekly.'

'Maybe his account was hacked, Angie. It happens. He shut it down six months ago after someone posted a heap of penis-enhancing ads on his page. I didn't realise he'd opened a new one.'

Angie took the tub of ice cream away gently and pressed pause on the remote control. Colin Firth froze on the television, a wet white shirt clinging to his chest.

'You really think he's oblivious to the family portrait scenario she's projecting on social media?'

'I don't know. I hope so. I was worried about them working together initially, but I can't believe Vince would make a fool of me like this, or knowingly let Charlotte broadcast her feelings across the internet. Surely he's better than that?'

'Well, let's look at the cold hard facts. Vince has been working away, right?'

'Yes.'

'You haven't had sex for how long?'

'Eternity. Well, before I got sick, really.'

'Okay, and this Charlotte is a divorcee with a specialty in tantric massage who has posted dozens of pictures wrapped around your boyfriend?'

'*Sensual* massage, not tantric massage, Angie. Oh God, this is not looking good, is it?' Penny covered her face with her hands as if it would help the facts realign into a more attractive scenario. *You will not cry*, she ordered, squeezing her eyes shut against the brimming tears. She tried to envisage the engagement ring and the New Zealand plane tickets that were locked up in the storage unit with all their other possessions. She set her jaw and shook her head at Angie's sympathetic gaze.

'He's got to be innocent. Get rid of that look, Angie. We don't know all the facts, and until I've heard it from Vince, I'm going to believe this looks worse than it is.'

'Oh, Penny,' Angie rolled her eyes, 'you are the epitome of glass half full. I wish I could share your optimism, but God help my future boyfriend if I ever caught him in that situation. That type of stuff wouldn't fly with me. No way.'

Penny turned the little radio on her bedside table to the local FM channel, hoping the soft music would help her mind settle. But four or five songs passed without registering as she recomposed the text message again and again.

Call me, Vince.

Too soft. Penny hit delete.

Call me, or else we're over.

Too dramatic. She started typing again.

For God's sake, Vince, I know about Charlotte.

Erghhhhh.

She tried to channel the 'glass half full' attitude Angie had doubtfully commended, searching for the right words to convey her message.

'This is ridiculous.' Penny groaned, thumping the pillow in frustration. She tried to call Vince again, instinctively clutching the phone to her ear as the call failed to connect. *What the hell? Where's the respect? Where's the goddamn loyalty?*

Penny's fingers flew across the screen as she tried one more time.

> I'm coming back to Melbourne early and you'd better be
> there when I get back. CALL ME.

She shuffled to the windowsill, pointed her phone towards the mountain range and hit 'send' before she could change her mind.

🦋

'Penny, Penny, Penny.'

Eddie bounded into the house, his boots squelching on the wooden floorboards as he rushed into the kitchen. Penny glanced up from the tray of biscuits she was scooping onto cooling racks, saw the muddy footsteps behind him and pointed to Eddie's feet.

'Boots.'

Eddie nodded, his happy smile not dampened in the least at her harsh tone. His whistling broke the silence as he placed his boots by the back door.

Eddie returned, embraced her warmly and she tried to soften her rigid stance. The last few nights had consisted of more worrying than sleeping, and her patience was running low.

'Real fast on the motorbike today!'

She looked at his red cheeks, windblown hair and the gleam in his eye, and remembered the test drive Angus had mentioned last night.

'Did you try out the new quad bikes?'

'Yep. Good ones.'

'And what about the snazzy side-by-side ones? The UTVs? Did you like those?'

He tilted his head to the side, wrinkling his nose, and shrugged.

The sound of laughter filtered in through the porch window. She felt a stab of irritation as she watched Tim clap a hand on Angus's shoulder and her father's chin lifted to share another joke that had them both throwing back their heads in amusement. She watched them leaning against the ute tray, their faces as animated as Eddie's. Tim's hair was an almost identical shade to the dry grass in the paddocks behind them, his body fitting the worn denim jeans in a way Vince's never quite could. *How can he be so comfortable around the rest of my family, yet so guarded and wary around me?* She turned back to her biscuits. One bite was enough to know they were her best yet. The thought comforted her, helping take the edge off the tiny shaft of jealousy that had wormed its way into her mind and the residual anger she felt about Vince's alarming lack of contact and what he may or may not be up to in Sydney.

The smell of sugar and melted butter erupted from the porch door as Tim swung it open and stepped inside. His stomach growled at the inviting scent. The farmhouse had a distinctly homely fragrance these days, which seemed to suit the large kitchen.

'Another top-shelf batch of biscuits by the look of it, love. I'll check them for quality control.' Angus grinned, helping himself to two biscuits.

Tim snuck a look at Penny, noting her stiff back and lacklustre welcome. Not that she'd ever fussed over him or gone out of her way to engage him in conversation, but she had seemed a little more relaxed in his company since the day they'd talked about the local paper rehashing his father's crimes. He declined Angus's outstretched hand and reached for the *Stock & Land* instead, ignoring the crunch of biscuits from Angus and Eddie.

'How was the test drive?'

Tim knew without looking up that Penny's question was directed at Angus, not him, and kept his focus on the newsprint.

'Great. We've narrowed it down to two models. They're both in stock at the local dealership, so it's six of one, half a dozen of the other.'

Angus flicked the kettle on and pulled four mugs from the cupboard. He made the tea, leaning over Tim's shoulder for a closer look at a full-page quad bike advertisement.

'Though it looks like they've got them a bit cheaper at the Mildura Field Days. Might be worth the drive, hey, Eddie?'

Eddie nodded enthusiastically, thrilled to be involved in the discussion.

'Did you test the new side by side options?' Penny wiped the spotless kitchen bench a second time.

'Pfft, they're as useless as tits on a bull with all that roll bar nonsense. They're for the buggers who can't ride to save themselves.' Angus laughed, helping himself to another biscuit.

Tim sneaked a glance at Penny and saw the tight set of her jaw. *So that's what she's angry about*, he thought, noticing the way Penny bristled at her father's dismissal.

'I would have thought they're at least worth a test drive, seeing you're in the market for a new one anyway. Did you ask about the government rebates and farm safety promotions?'

'Those incentives aren't worth jack. Quad bikes have served us well for decades—leave those rally cars to the nervous nellies who rely on roll bars and cages.'

Tim watched Penny stalk towards him. Up close she smelled just like a bakery, the sugary scent contrasting with the anger that seemed to radiate from her. She jabbed a finger at his newspaper.

'*The Age* is more my style, but aren't farm accidents at an all-time high?'

Tim spoke softly.

'He's right, Mac. They're just another new marketing scheme, using scare tactics to part farmers with their hard-earned cash.' He looked up from the newspaper, surprised to see Lara jogging up the steps.

'Penny would know all about marketing schemes. Apparently, city suits know more about farming than us backward country folk.'

Penny spun around at Lara's voice, her face darkening as if her sister held an armful of snakes instead of a bag of lemons.

Tim swallowed a sigh, knowing the potential for an argument was increasing by the second.

'I never said that, Lara. Don't you have better things to do than stir up trouble?'

Folding the newspaper shut, Tim clapped Eddie on the shoulder. 'C'mon, man, let's go feed out some hay. Leave these guys to it.'

He nodded a quiet hello to Lara and tipped his half-drunk tea down the sink.

'Quad bikes, quad bikes, quad bikes,' sang Eddie, pointing eagerly to the newspaper. Tim steered him away from the table and handed him his boots.

'I'll meet you back at the shearing shed in an hour, Angus.' But it was as if he hadn't spoken, his boss was wholly focused on his two daughters and the animosity between them.

'Now c'mon, girls, don't be like that,' said Angus.

Tim hastily shoved his feet into his size-12 boots. He tried to hurry Eddie along as the conversation volume moved up a notch.

'You're a nurse, Lara, you should talk some sense into Dad about the old-style quad bikes,' Penny said stiffly.

'Farms aren't any different from any other workplace; the user accepts all liability, that type of thing. If he wants another quad bike, he should get one. You just like spending money, Penny,' said Lara. 'And as someone who's just got out of hospital because of her own pig-headed behaviour, I wouldn't be throwing too many stones about personal safety.'

Tim looked up to see Penny clenching her teeth, angrier than he'd ever seen her. *For someone who seems unflappable, she gets pretty fired up around Lara.* Tim followed Eddie outside, shutting the door on their discussion. After spending years sheltering Eddie from family domestics, he wasn't going to drop the ball now.

Twenty-five

Penny stormed outside as Tim's ute rumbled down the laneway. She heard her dad's footsteps behind her. His hand was warm on her shoulder, his tone appeasing.

'Ah love, don't mind Lara. She's just trying to save me money.'

Penny pushed at the gravel with her toe, the sharp bluestone piercing her skin. She shrugged his hand off irritably.

'I don't know why I bother. I'll keep my opinion to myself in the future.' She shoved her hands into her pockets, frowning.

'Let me take you for a spin on one of the new quads we looked at,' Angus prompted. 'Turn back the clock a few years, get the wind in your hair.'

She shook her head, resolute.

'I think it's a bit too late for that, Dad.'

The house was quiet as Penny kneaded and thumped the scone dough, projecting her frustrations onto the soft blob. She knew their fat content was probably sky-high, but the kneading action was a better outlet for her anger than any of the alternatives running through her mind. Penny refilled her glass of red wine, surprised to see the bottle was almost empty. She took a sip and returned to kneading.

'Steady on, love,' chided Angus. 'What did that dough ever do to you?'

He settled his mug in the sink and folded his arms against his cotton pyjama T-shirt.

'I can't believe we're even related,' she said, slamming the dough against the benchtop. 'I have no problems with Diana, no problems with Angie, no problems with you—except when you shot me down in the quad bike debate—but Lara . . . we might share some genes, but she's in a league of her own.'

'She's had a tough time recently, with Sam and all that. Don't let her get your goat. She's gentle as a kitten; you just need to get past her claws.'

'Talons, more like,' muttered Penny. She could smell the oven was hot enough, felt the dough was ready to roll, but continued to work it emphatically.

'This is baking therapy at its finest. Your Irish author-lady would be proud. What's her name? Marion? And I didn't deliberately ignore your advice, Penny. Tim and I tossed around the UTV pros and cons.'

'Good old Tim, hey? Almost as cheerful as Lara. Tell me, Dad—' Penny pushed up her sleeves, wiped her face on the inside of her forearm, and took a gulp of wine—'is he angling for an inheritance or a way to buy the farm cheaply? Is that why he's here all the time? Yes, Angus. No, Angus. Three bags full, Angus? You may as well tell me now because he sure acts like it.'

She saw Angus's expression change from playful to wary.

'Course he isn't. Damn shame you girls never showed the same interest as him though.'

'I've looked at your books, Dad. I know it's a successful enterprise. I'd hate someone to worm their way into the business and rip you off again. What about those dodgy deals his father was involved in? Sheep rustling, bogus trading. Don't forget about that.'

'Steady on, Penny. Tim is nothing like Roger Patterson and I reckon you know that just as well as I do.' He picked up her glass of wine and poured it down the sink. 'Sometimes you and Lara are more alike than you realise.'

The trilling phone cut through the still air, jolting Penny's wandering mind. She set the lamb down on the grass and jogged into the house.

'McIntyre Park, Penny speaking.'

'Babe, I was just about to hang up. Glad I've finally caught you.' Penny felt anger rising in her chest at Vince's strained tone. *How dare he sound inconvenienced?*

'You're glad you caught me? I've been trying to call you for a week! What the hell has been going on?'

'Nothing, babe, just crazy busy with work. I'm on the phone all day, networking with the Sydney crew and clients most nights. You know how it goes, honey.'

'Networking my arse! I've seen the photos, Vince. Don't lie to me.'

Her voice had dropped from indignant to dangerously low in just a few sentences, and she felt the little nerve in her cheek twitch.

She waited for him to explain, but the line was completely silent. Penny blew out a furious breath.

'You said it would never happen again, Vince.' She looked out the kitchen window, her eye caught by a blue wren teasing the lamb, while her mind replayed the memory of an anonymous brunette slipping out of their apartment one rainy St Kilda evening. *Brunettes, blonds, redheads. He's nothing if not versatile*, she fumed.

'I can explain, Pen. It's not what it looks like.'

'Then leave Sydney right now, so we can fix this.' Penny took a shaky breath, unsure whether to issue the ultimatum weighing on her mind. She thought of the future they had mapped out together, the years she had invested into the relationship, the trust they would need to rebuild to get over this hurdle. The thought of entering the dating scene again made her dizzy. Jade's Tinder tales were only funny because they happened at arm's length. She squared her shoulders and spoke quietly.

'Or send back your apartment keys and get all your things freighted to New South Wales.'

Vince's reaction was immediate, as she had hoped it would be. 'Babe, I fucked up. I've been missing you so much, I just needed some company. If you hadn't got sick, none of this would have happened.'

'Don't you dare turn this on me.'

'Give me one last chance. Please. You know we're the perfect couple. I can't come home right now—I've got a major pitch at the end of next week, and the apartment isn't available until then, anyway.' His confidence was gone and his voice had gained a pleading quality. 'This presentation is my final chance to show the Sydney team what I'm made of. Think of our long-term future, babe. Melbourne's hottest corporate couple, remember? Smashing the corporate ceiling together.'

The wind had picked up outside and rose petals were fluttering past the window. Penny watched them fall softly to the ground, like the pieces of her fractured relationship.

'We could stay in Jade's spare room for the week?'

'True, but . . .' Vince hesitated.

More rose petals floated past. She felt an axis shifting. The compass points keeping their relationship on target had altered, and true north was nowhere to be found. Penny took a shaky breath.

'Penny, you know I love you. It's only another few weeks until I come home. I'll make it up to you then, I promise.'

The ring she'd found buried beneath his socks and cufflinks wedged itself firmly between her sense of self-preservation and her carefully composed five-year plan.

'You can't throw it all away now, babe. We'll get past this, you'll see.'

Penny cradled her head in her hands and tried to believe Vince's words.

Twenty-six

Penny knew she was still a week away from returning to Melbourne, but she ripped open her suitcase anyway. She stalked around the room, throwing loose clothes into her suitcase; anything was better than dwelling on Vince. A text message came through on her phone and she glared at the illuminated device. After barely a handful of texts in the last seven weeks, the messages were suddenly coming in thick and fast. But instead of Vince's name, Jade's appeared on the screen.

> God, Pen, hope you've got some answers by now. Bloody bastard. Will track down voodoo doll for the harlot. Have arranged boxing classes as promised, new term kicks off June. Will Ross River fever come back if you thrash your guts out though? Keep me posted. Find me a cowboy yet? Last night was another fizzer. xxx J

Penny sank down onto the bed, mentally composing a reply that didn't sound like she was sulking. What a crap week. First Lara losing her shit, now Vince humiliating her. She was too mad to cry, and tonight's yoga class was the only thing standing between her and the stash of red wine downstairs. She took a deep breath and typed a reply.

Get your butt ready, Jade, I'm in the mood for boxing. Will check with Dr about virus returning. xx Pen

Penny rolled up her yoga mat and made a beeline for the door. The class had been tougher than usual, but at least her shoulders had lowered a little, instead of hovering at the base of her ear lobes. Arriving a few minutes late had been a smart plan, and if she could just slip out the door before everyone else, she'd avoid the inevitable questions. Olive glanced in her direction, a mixture of pity and apology crossing her lined face, but Penny busied herself stuffing the yoga mat back into its bag. She wasn't ready for a group discussion on the Vince issue. Diana's, Angie's and Jade's interrogations had been bad enough.

The sun had almost finished setting, cutting the sky above Bridgefield into swathes of apricot, gold and grey. The kookaburra that lived above the town hall called out to her as she rushed along the footpath.

She tossed her mat into the back of the ute and fished the keys from the footwell. She wrenched the wheel, preparing to swing the ute around, when a lilac head hurried into her rear-view mirror, lifting an arm in Penny's direction.

'Penny, wait up a sec, will you?' Pearl's purple legging-clad legs moved pretty fast for an old lady, thought Penny, a smile beginning as she noticed how the pants perfectly matched Pearl's hair.

'Tim's taken Eddie to Ballarat for a doctor's appointment, and I don't have the stomach for another ten minutes in Olive's car. Those air fresheners are worse than a funeral bouquet.'

Penny nodded. *So that's why he hasn't been at the farmhouse today.*

'Hop in.' Penny reached over and wrenched open the passenger door.

Pearl shimmied onto the bench seat. 'Beautiful night, isn't it? You'd hardly know winter's on its way.'

'Sure is. Least I'll be back in the city before the frosts really set in,' said Penny, heading through the residential part of town. The small houses slowly spread out and Pearl pointed her towards the blue gum plantations beyond the Bridgefield town limits. Penny waited for the older woman to ask about Vince or use the drive as an excuse to get the inside scoop on the Facebook scandal. But she sat quietly in the seat, a content smile on her face as she watched the last rays of sunshine paint the fresh shoots of grass in the paddocks a rich, Kelly green. An intersection approached. Penny looked at Pearl for direction.

'Left here, love. Then turn right when you get to the mailbox with a set of cow horns. That was Eddie's touch, you see. He gets a kick out of them every time he visits. And Tim's a whiz at rigging that sort of thing up. I thought the blue baling twine gave them a rustic touch, but they kept blowing down in those rotten sou'westerlies. He's mounted them on blocks of wood now—they'll outlive me.'

The sight of two cow horns fixed to the sides of a forty-four-gallon drum came into view. She'd never pictured Tim as the type of man to craft ridiculous postboxes just to make his grandmother and brother smile.

'He's a good man, our Tim,' Pearl said lightly as they drew to a stop in front of her cottage.

Penny thought for a minute before nodding a farewell. For some reason the words remained stuck in her throat.

Twenty-seven

'I've got to get my life back on track, Diana. There's no use sitting around here. Not now that I'm better,' said Penny, scooping Leo onto her lap and tickling his chubby feet. Diana's house had that same warm feeling as their mother's kitchen. Important discussions took place around a sink of dishes or a bowl full of cake batter.

'I could be in Melbourne, finding out where all my major projects stand, liaising with Georgie. Getting these brows waxed back into shape, freshening up the highlights in my hair. Start working off my baking at the gym.'

Leo giggled as Penny waggled her eyebrows. Diana paused, then adjusted the angle of the carving knife and sliced off a slightly smaller piece of cake for Penny.

'I can barely believe you're letting Vince off the hook that easy. And you almost sound excited about working yourself back into an early grave.'

Diana sat the plates on the table alongside a fruit platter. She turned and let out a loud 'Coooo-eee'. A moment later, Cameron, Evie, Harry and Elliot came racing in from the playroom and clamoured around Diana's square dining table.

144

Penny rolled her eyes as she strapped Leo into a highchair. 'Don't you start. I've got enough to worry about without feeling guilty for leaving. We all knew this was temporary.'

'What are you feeling guilty about, Aunty Pen?' The red berry stains around Evie's mouth undermined her serious expression.

'Maybe she's done something bad?' Cameron's hand hovered over the fruit platter, his face twinkling at the possibility of an adult getting into trouble.

'She's feeling guilty because she's running back to the city a little bit early instead of following doctors' orders,' answered Diana, opening the discussion up to the younger members of the room.

'No! Don't go, Aunty Pen!' said Evie.

'We'll miss you again. Stay here with us, just a little longer,' said Cameron. 'Puh-leasssssse.'

'No, no,' offered the twins in unison, unsure what they were protesting against, but keen to join the movement.

Penny turned to Diana, who shrugged innocently and took a bite of cake as she waited for the furore to die down.

'I'm sorry, guys, but I have to go back.'

'Dr Sinclair will get grumpy with you,' warned Cameron, cake crumbs flying from his solemn mouth. 'And we'll miss you. You do even better baking than Mummy, Aunty Lara and Aunty Angie.'

'Wash your mouth out with soap, Cam. My sisters are way better bakers than me. I've done everything else the doctor asked, I'm just leaving a little early. Vince and I . . .' Penny trailed off as she realised her niece was watching her closely. Evie had just dealt with her parents' break-up; no need to introduce more drama, especially seeing they'd never actually met Vince.

'Sometimes, guys, you just have to do what you think is best.' Penny's voice was more confident than she felt. *Am I doing the right thing?* she wondered, looking around at the forlorn faces. She'd loved their company in the last eight weeks. Their faces were anxious, but she was pleased that they didn't let her news spoil their appetites. The zucchini cake she'd baked that morning was disappearing at lightning speed.

'Like when Dad gets mad with Mum and then he's really sorry. Mum said us moving into that weird house is for the best. But . . .' Evie considered the fruit in front of her, prodding at a strawberry with her fingernail. 'But I'm not really sure it's for the best. Our old house was way better. My room was heaps bigger. The carpet in our new house smells like it's been sitting underneath Grandpa's shearing shed.'

Diana shot Penny a look.

Penny smiled gently, stroking her niece's long, blond hair. 'Sometimes adults have to make tricky choices, honey. Even if it doesn't seem like a good idea at the time, it can often be for the best. And yes . . . I'll miss you all too.'

'But Grandpa's house is your home, Aunty Penny. Why can't you keep living there?' Cameron pointed out the window at his interpretation of south.

Although she knew it was the wrong direction to McIntyre Park, Penny followed the small pointed finger, taking in the same view of the mountain ranges that were visible from the farmhouse, the similar tree-studded paddocks, the same rolling green paddocks.

Penny took a sip of her tea, hoping the hot liquid would burn away the tiny part of her that agreed with everything they had said. Forget all about Vince and his wandering eye, banish the seventy-five-hour working week she was rushing back to. Stay here sipping tea and eating cake to the soundtrack of happy children and magpies in the garden. But she dismissed the notion with a soft shake of her head. *I've long since buried that dream, and I'd only be a third wheel for Dad and Tim.*

'It's because of Vince, dummy,' said Evie. 'Don't you know Aunty Penny is going to get married and wear a beautiful princess dress, and then they'll live happily ever after?'

Penny spluttered as a zucchini cake crumb caught in her throat. Diana hid a smile as Evie sipped her glass of milk, a condescending expression settling over her face. She eyed her cousins with a withering look. 'You boys wouldn't understand. I'll be a flower girl, won't I, Aunty Pen?'

The girl had a memory like an elephant. *Why'd I craft such a soppy bedtime story?* In light of this week's turn of events, the fairytale wedding featuring Prince Vince and Princess Penny seemed a heck of a lot closer to fantasy than reality. She closed her eyes. *How could I have been so blind, so confident that the rift in our relationship was repairable?*

'Let's not get ahead of ourselves, Evie. Give Aunty Penny a chance to settle back into things before you go practising your royal curtsey,' said Diana, her hand settling on Penny's shoulder.

'Perhaps you two can be the final pair in the baking class this week, the last one before I leave,' Penny offered, blinking away tears.

Cameron's frown and Evie's pouting lips both softened at the suggestion.

'All right, but only because they sound like lots of fun. We're still not happy that you're leaving,' said Evie.

Penny looked at her empty coffee cup, unfurled herself from the couch and headed into the kitchen for another refill. A spoon rattled against china as Angus snored in his armchair, cradling an empty dessert bowl. She looked out into the night, rain was still beading down the windows and pots full of white flowers danced to the tune of a strong southerly wind. Despite the overnight frost, a freestanding fire kept the farmhouse toasty warm. The ambiance of a wood burner was high on the list of things she would miss.

Penny sighed, running a weary hand through her hair. She remembered her melancholy on the journey from the city to the farm two months ago, convinced the secondment would be like a penitentiary sentence. She thought of the times when she'd been so homesick for her city life and suffocated by the proximity of her family. But as she sat nestled in the couch, drinking yet another cup of coffee to try and unfuddle her puzzled brain, she felt a sense of gratitude. She was grateful for the weeks surrounded by her niece and nephews, the smell of much-needed rain on parched paddocks, the feeling that came from nurturing a sick animal back to health, and the beautiful simplicity of baking herself better.

Penny drained the last drop of coffee, hoping the brew would give her the strength to close the tiny door that niggled and waved the flag for country living. She stood up, collecting the pudding bowl, and reminded herself she would return to Melbourne at the end of the week. Absolutely. Definitely. Certainly.

Twenty-eight

Puddles splashed up over Penny's boots as she ran across the community hall parking lot. She could hear Tim's V8 engine purring down the main street of Bridgefield, the creak of its aged suspension as it negotiated the potholed surface and knew without looking that Eddie and Bones were accompanying him. She fumbled with the hall key, her back to the driving rain, as their car doors slammed. The wind pushed the hall door open for her, and she dripped her way across the wooden floorboards to the kitchen, her arms singing from a load of heavy groceries and cooking equipment.

'Ready for one last class?' she called to the pair as they came through the doorway, their jackets saturated and their hair slicked down against their wet faces.

'Penny, Penny, Penny,' called Eddie. His face lit up like a sunbeam as he ran over to hug her. She smiled back at his cheerful greeting and wondered whether he understood this was their last session together. For a fleeting moment, she envied his simplistic view of life, his full focus on the present.

'Mac.' Tim nodded as he passed her, his voice quiet as he unpacked their supplies.

Tim, on the other hand, thought Penny, *he's probably delighted to see the back of me.*

The hall door reopened and a wave of keen bakers raced across the room. In the flurry of excited footsteps, she felt Tim's presence beside her; an earthy smell of firewood and cut grass. He picked up the wooden spoon she had just set down and rolled the implement between his large hands.

'You okay, Mac? Nanna Pearl told me about Vince,' he said, raising his voice to be heard above the chatter between Eddie and his friends.

Penny turned, surprised at his gentle tone. Her arm inadvertently pressed against his as she met his grey eyes. She searched for a hint of sarcasm or condescension, but found nothing other than concern. She debated how to reply when a familiar voice piped up.

'Are you talking about Aunty Penny's boyfriend, Vince? Dad says he's a knob, but I'm not sure what kind of knob he means . . . a doorknob? Or a knob of butter?' asked Cameron, appearing by their side with a puzzled look on his face.

Tim laughed.

'I'm sure your dad means he's a *snob*, mate. Some of those city blokes are a bit like that,' he said, ruffling the boy's blond hair and sending Penny a wink over the top of Cameron's head.

Penny shook her head with a smile, watching him as he flicked through the recipe book with her nephew. The fifteen years that had passed since they were together felt like two lifetimes ago, but in this hazy light, with a sunshower illuminating the hall kitchen, he looked more like the young man she'd fallen in love with. The way he joked with Cameron reminded her of the way they'd horsed around as teenagers. Friendly teasing, bad jokes. Anything to foil teenage awkwardness until they were comfortable with one another, sure of the other's feelings.

'Righto, Aunty Penny, we're ready. Don't forget to wash your hands, Tim,' said Cameron with a cheeky grin.

Penny smiled. It would feel good to tie up loose ends before she returned to the city. She couldn't change the past, but she could end the final baking session on a good note, with something akin to friendship.

She watched as Tim organised their young charges, tying aprons and overseeing the hand-washing process as she set up the baking equipment. He carefully lifted a shy teenager from his wheelchair to wash his hands at the sink, tickled Evie as she tried to evade the soap pump, and quietly outlined the morning's recipes.

A thought rose to her mind and, as unbidden as it was, she couldn't bring herself to block it out. *I bet Tim isn't the cheating kind.*

One of the children had commandeered the portable radio in the hall kitchen, and Tim found his toes tapping to the tinny pop music. The mood was buoyant in the room, excited voices from happy bakers going about their tasks with smiles on their faces. *Even Mac's happy,* Tim noted, watching her juice lemons with effortless efficiency.

He'd almost got used to sharing the tiny kitchen each Monday and realised with surprise that he might miss her when she headed back to Melbourne. He coughed, trying to dislodge the uncomfortable feeling. *You'll miss this—the group sessions—not her.*

Like a dog with a bone, Nanna Pearl had taken it upon herself to update him on Mac and Vince's relationship dramas during last night's roast. And as much as he tried to tune out, and nod in the right places so it seemed like he was listening, his ears had pricked up when he heard just how rocky their relationship was.

For all of her faults—and there are quite a few—she doesn't deserve to be cheated on, he thought, an unexpected surge of protectiveness bubbling out of nowhere. It was the same feeling that had crept into his thoughts as Sam had ranted about Lara and the McIntyre family, as if he were an innocent bystander in their marriage breakdown. Tim hadn't missed that since Sam had left town. Not one bit.

He looked away, searching for something else to focus on. He landed on Evie as she poured condensed milk into the blender. She had her father's colouring, but thankfully neither of her parent's perpetual pessimism.

'Nice work there, Evie.'

'Thanks, Tim,' she said, her round face turning up to him with unabashed adoration.

He walked around the room to where his group were pressing biscuit bases into fancy hinged tins. *What did Penny call them? Springform tins.*

'Lasagne took longer than I thought. We're almost out of time, Mac. Reckon the blender will hold a double mix?'

'Of course it can. Piece of cake,' said Penny.

She flashed Tim a sudden smile. His body responded as her face transformed from pretty to beautiful. He spun around. Although his hands were already clean, he thrust them under the running water to clear his mind. It was the first time in years he'd seen that smile. He recalled the last time, sitting beside a bonfire with country music blaring from his ute speakers, moments before she had tugged him closer and kissed him with unbridled teenage enthusiasm. *C'mon, Patterson, get a grip. You obviously need to get back into the dating game if one smile has you rehashing old memories.*

Tim threw back a glass of cold water. He watched Penny pour lemon juice into the blender and open the second tin of condensed milk. She set the ingredients aside, wiped her hands on the frilly apron, and watched the students finishing up with the biscuit bases. He followed her line of vision.

'Those smiles say it all,' he said.

Penny beamed again, happiness relaxing her face and making her eyes crinkle at the corners. She was so infuriating at times, self-focused and city-centric, but somehow, she softened during baking classes.

'Don't tell anyone, but I've enjoyed it. Turns out measuring butter and scooping flour are soothing. I'd forgotten how much I love baking,' said Penny.

'Anything would taste better than kale stir-fries and chia seed protein balls. I don't know why you've deprived yourself of decent food for so long.'

She glared at him; a stern expression with a teaspoon of mischief and a shot of straight-up sassiness.

'Says he who couldn't bake a cupcake a month ago. And what's this I hear about you fixing gourmet roasts? Nanna Pearl is sending Olive batty with all the details. You know she's going to land on your doorstep one day, right on 7 p.m. You're a dark horse, Tim Patterson. I'll give you that.'

Tim laughed, glad she couldn't read his mind and discover just how dark his thoughts ran, mainly when she gave him that smile. *Lucky she's leaving in a day or two*, he thought. Something inside him realised being friends with Penny McIntyre was a lot more dangerous than being enemies.

Penny folded her arms across her chest, enjoying the newfound camaraderie between her and Tim. It was an improvement on the strained awkwardness that had marked the previous eight weeks. A screech from the blender and a shriek made them turn in unison.

'Erghhh,' cried Evie. Her hands clamped over her mouth as the blender sprayed its sticky contents everywhere.

With the mixture dripping down her brow, Penny blindly searched on the benchtop for the absent lid. Tim's arms reached around her to flick the machine off at the power point.

The younger children gasped, the older students giggled, and Penny felt her lips twitch as she took in Tim's face. Chunks of cream cheese hung from his stubbled jaw. Beads of condensed milk oozed off the tip of his nose. He pursed his lips, nostrils flaring with amusement as he scanned her face. She smelled the lemon, felt the thick droplets rolling down her cheek and a roar of laughter pealed from her lips.

From the sight of Tim's broad grin, Penny knew she was as much of a spectacle as him. His laughter also echoed around the room, sending the junior chefs into stitches.

Emboldened by the eager audience and feeling suddenly playful, Penny kept her gaze locked on Tim as she reached for the blender.

'You missed a spot, Evie.' She scooped out a handful of the mixture and rubbed it into Tim's hair.

The children went wild as Tim maintained a deadpan expression, lifting an eyebrow and looking back at her quizzically. He leaned in closer, smelling like sweet citrus.

Penny bit her lip with a combination of mischief and anticipation. She felt the heat of his body next to hers and the room faded away as his face took up her entire field of vision. She caught her breath as he ran his finger gently along her cheekbone. She wrenched her eyes away from Tim's to watch his fingertip then travel to his mouth.

'Mmmm, tastes good to me . . . still, reckon it needs more lemon juice though.' His voice was low and husky as he stepped away with a smile, still sucking on his finger.

Hoots of laughter brought a flush to her face. Penny flicked on the tap, allowing the cold water to bring her back to her senses. *What the hell was that? And in a room full of children, to boot.* She recruited helpers and started cleaning up the mess.

'And here I was thinking you didn't like getting your hands dirty,' said Tim. Two shirts dangled from his outstretched arm. 'Lucky I picked up a clean basket of shirts from Nanna Pearl this morning. The green one should fit you.'

Penny smirked.

'Your nanna does your washing?'

Tim shook his head mournfully.

'She kidnaps my laundry basket when I'm at work, holds it to ransom until I agree to let her iron. You don't know how many times I tried hiding the washing before I finally gave in.'

His voice was wistful with a hint of humour—a side of him she had yet to experience.

'But if you don't want it . . . ?'

He dropped the shirt on the bench and walked away. Penny looked down at her sodden and sticky clothing, knowing clean and dry was a much better option. She wiped her hands on the apron.

'I'll be back in a second,' she told the group. 'You guys can finish cleaning up.'

She grabbed the shirt and headed into the depths of the community hall. The brown and orange toilets she remembered from her childhood had since been replaced with a single unisex, wheelchair-friendly restroom. But it wasn't the tiling or the new sink that caught her attention. She stood rooted to the spot at the sight of Tim facing the wall as he pulled the wet T-shirt over his head. His body was toned by farm work rather than weights or gym machines and, try as she might, she couldn't help but stare.

Look away right now, Penny McIntyre. You have absolutely no business ogling another man, especially Tim Bloody Patterson. She took a step backward and tried to reason with her body, turning an unbidden sigh of appreciation into a cough. To distract herself, she lifted the fabric to her nose, curious to know whether it would hold his scent or his grandmother's trademark lavender. Her senses were rewarded with the fresh smell of line-dried cotton and a hint of Tim's woodsy outdoors.

Tim heard Penny cough to announce her arrival. He stayed where he was, changing his shirt slowly, and hoped the straining against his zipper would hurry up and subside.

Have I really gone back to high school days, when hormones trump common sense?

He couldn't remember the last time he'd been turned on in a public setting. He was pretty sure Penny hadn't noticed, but it was embarrassing all the same. He turned around, holding the soiled shirt in front of him, trying not to notice the ripples under her damp shirt that suggested lacy underwear.

'I'll give you some privacy.'

She nodded and took a step into the tiny room. Tim could smell her lemony sweetness again, which pushed him back towards the state of arousal he had just overcome. Two steps closer and they would be chest to chest.

'Thanks.' Her voice came out soft and inviting and before he knew it, he had bridged the gap between them with another step.

Tim felt his pulse quicken as he looked down at the freckles sprinkled across her nose. He watched her eyes darken. Her lips parted. Tim tried to conjure up the reasons why he should walk away, but his brain couldn't think beyond helping her out of that wet shirt and appreciating the body underneath it. He ran a tentative hand over the delicate skin on her arm. It goose-bumped at his touch. Tim studied her, saw the lust that reflected his own, and leaned closer.

'Tim? Tim? Tim?'

Eddie's voice echoed down the corridor. They sprang apart as the footsteps drew closer. Tim drew a ragged breath, adapting to the abrupt change of focus. He looked back at Penny as he strode out of the room, unsure whether her expression was one of relief or disappointment.

Penny cleaned the hall and packed up on autopilot, unable to look Tim in the eye as she shepherded the children back to the school minivan and made her hasty escape. *This is not me,* she admonished herself, looking into the rear-view mirror. Flushed cheeks, cheesecake-speckled hair and dilated pupils reiterated her betrayal. She felt like dying of shame.

How can I possibly be angry at Vince for his infidelity when my hormones are running wild at the sight of a semi-naked torso? Her conscience was scathing, a headache nagging at her temples as the car crunched along the gravel driveway of the farmhouse. *You almost kissed Tim Patterson . . . you stupid, stupid girl.*

She skidded to a halt at the sight on the front doorstep. A plastic-wrapped bouquet of roses sat by the front door. Her jaw dropped as she spotted an aqua box nestled in among the tightly furled blooms. Penny jogged up the steps, horror rather than anticipation propelling her towards the delivery.

She tugged at the white ribbon, her heart pounding. She pulled out a pair of exquisite silver earrings with love heart-shaped pendants that matched the necklace sitting on her bedside table. A sharp breath escaped from her lips, and she tried to pinpoint the emotion.

Relief that it wasn't the ring? Guilt for her behaviour an hour ago? Irritation that Vince thought he could buy her affections? The realisation that up until now his mistakes had always been papered over with excuses and expensive gifts? Disgusted by her internal conflict and how close she had just come to kissing another man, Penny sat down on the wicker chair and hugged Tim's green shirt around herself. She thought about Vince and the future they had planned so perfectly. She contrasted it with a life on the farm with a hard-working country boy by her side. For the first time in a long time, Penny wished she could ask her mother's advice.

Twenty-nine

Angus leaned a broom against the tin wall and flicked off the shearing shed lights, plunging the cavernous space into near darkness. He whistled his way past Penny, the room flooding again with sunlight as he rolled open the large sliding door. Fresh air rushed in, diluting the shed's ingrained smell of lanolin and sheep. They walked together down the rickety steps, Penny holding the bag of mismatched crockery from their pre-shearing clean-up.

'So, you're all set then, Dad. When are the shearers coming?'

'Depends on whether this wet spell holds up. Booked 'em for next month, should be finished sowing the crops by then. I'll go shift that mob in the high paddock closer to home, make sure they're all tickety-boo.'

Penny stood between the ute and the quad bike and eyed her father. The Akubra shaded his face, his sleeves rolled up to his elbows even though it was an icy eight degrees in the pale sunshine.

'It'll be fine,' he said shortly, anticipating her next comment. She asked it, anyway.

'Are you sure you should take the old bike up to that paddock?'

'Are *you* sure you don't want to stay another fortnight, see out your full ten weeks, instead of racing back to the city?'

'Dad, I've got things to sort out. I can't hide away here forever. It's time for me to go.' The thought of seeing Tim again put her on edge. She wanted to fast-forward the afternoon and put a safe, 400-kilometre buffer between herself and temptation. She hadn't mentioned Vince's infidelity, and there was no way she'd be filling her dad in on the extra reason propelling her back to the city. The little voice inside her head, reminding her of what had almost happened in the hall bathroom, was like an impatient bus conductor, frantically screaming 'all aboard'.

Angus shook his head.

'I guess we're both old enough to make up our own minds.' Penny tried one last time.

'The ute would handle it just as well, it's not too wet yet. Rusty could hunt the sheep down from the highest parts.' The dog wagged his black tail, his head cocked to the side, awaiting his command.

Angus climbed onto the seat and started the engine, whistling Rusty up behind him. Penny bit back a reminder about his helmet.

'You take the ute home, there's a girl. I'll see you back there for smoko before you leave.'

He gave Penny a quick wave and set off, dirt flicking up behind the knobbly tyres as he headed towards the far end of the property. She slammed the ute door shut, frustrated that he would take the quad bike across the slippery hills when he could use the ute.

It's a damn good thing I'm leaving today. I have well and truly overstayed my welcome, she thought as she crunched the ute into gear.

Penny yanked the clothes from the wooden hangers and folded them with a speed and technique that would put a professional retail worker to shame. She placed them, one by one, in the suitcases on Angie's old bed. *This whole plan was cursed from the start*, she thought, snapping the lid shut on the first gigantic suitcase and moving to the next. *If I hadn't come all the way out here, I could have kept a closer eye on Vince, worked out a compromise to both stay in Melbourne or both go to Sydney. I should have insisted, listened to my gut instinct to stay. Then again, I should have been able to trust him, dammit.*

Penny stalked to the chest of drawers and pulled out the jeans, shirts and woollen jumpers she'd need for the bitter Melbourne winter. The thought made her pack faster and it was no time before she zipped the third and fourth suitcases shut. She let her mind wander to Boutique Media as she finished packing, the clients who would have missed her, the colleagues who would welcome her back, and the mass of work she could immerse herself in. She pulled the suitcases roughly off the bed. Their bulk took up much of the hallway, so she stacked them on top of each other, leaving a passage just narrow enough to squeeze past.

Arms crossed over her chest, she took one last glance around the dim bedroom. The curtain billowed and a gust of wind raised goosebumps on her bare arms. Almost like the goosebumps that Tim had caused at the hall yesterday. She slammed the cupboard shut, making the photo frames and knick-knacks shudder.

The sky darkened, storm clouds rolling across the hills with the much-anticipated autumn break. The silos were brimming with barley and wheat waiting to be sown, spare tractor parts had been squirrelled into the shed over the previous weeks to ensure they were a step ahead of any possible delays, and the massive machinery had been serviced in readiness for the significant workout. All of which would be done in her wake.

The clouds were now almost a steel-grey and Penny swallowed back a sudden urge to check the weather forecast to see how much rain was expected in the next twenty-four hours. *Get a grip, Penny; it's of no interest to you. Coming home was a mistake, and there's only a few hours until you'll be on the road, closer to where you belong.*

She walked across to the window and closed it. The first raindrops beat against the glass, their trajectory down the pane echoing the disappointment in her stomach. Her phone lit up with a message and Jade's name appeared on the screen.

> Spare bed is all yours. Wine waiting. Ice cream in freezer.
> Takeaway menus ready. Drive safely, Pen xx J.

Penny grabbed her car keys from the bedside table, bumping a silver photo frame. She picked it up, puzzled. It hadn't been there this morning. She touched the sepia portrait gently, smiling sadly at her ten-year-old self, face shadowed by a straw hat obliterating everything except an uneven-toothed grin, the collar of a denim shirt and a small hand clenched in the thumbs up position. She removed the frame backing and reached inside for the print. Penny ran her fingers across her mother's handwriting.

'When I grow up, I want to be a farmer'—*Penny 1996.*

She didn't remember posing for the photo, but she recalled the passion with which she'd declared her innocent career ambitions to anyone who would listen. *Dad must have put it there while I was out.*

'That ship has well and truly sailed,' she murmured to her pre-teen self, tucking the photograph into her handbag. Penny closed the door behind her.

Thirty

Stacking the last mug on the draining rack, Penny scanned the land out the window. Shadows were spearing across the paddocks, the sun drawing closer to the mountains and casting a golden glow over the landscape. *It's just impatience to get going before all those kangaroos come out,* she told herself, trying to magic away the niggling worry about Angus in the high paddock. She sipped from her travel mug of tea, still tongue-tinglingly hot. *He should be back by now.* She thought of the determined look in her father's eye as he'd slung his leg over the bike this afternoon.

She snapped the travel mug lid shut. *Another half hour,* she resolved. *Lara will have a field day if I raise a missing person alarm after only one hour.*

Water trickled over the side of the windscreen wiper reservoir, and Penny pulled the hose away before shutting the car bonnet and reaching for the squeegee. She washed the windscreen with gusto, scrubbing away the layer of dust that had settled during the eight-week hiatus in the hay barn. *He*

probably went the long way around, or perhaps he's going extra slow to avoid running the rams. She looked at her watch.

Relief washed over Penny as she heard a dog barking. She shaded her vision against the setting sun and saw Rusty and the other kelpies bounding up the laneway. The sides of their mouths foamed with lather, tongues hanging out as they panted and dropped down by her side. The quad bike—and Angus—were nowhere to be seen.

The sound of country music pulsated through the shed, and Tim yelled above Adam Brand's latest hit.

'Eddie? Grab me the spanner.'

Tim lay flat on his back, a headlamp illuminating the parts of the engine he was working on. He could hear his brother's footsteps, coarse red dirt grinding like sandpaper on concrete, and called out again.

'Eddie?'

Grease dripped down onto his forehead. Tim groaned, wondering why he'd chosen to do an engine service today, why he'd lied to his boss for the first time and asked for an afternoon off to combat a fabricated headache. *Just another day or two and the awkwardness between Mac and me will be more bearable,* he told himself.

'The spanner, Eddie. Next to the tyre.'

He reached a hand out and felt the weight of the tool pressed into his palm.

'Cheers, mate.'

He tightened his grip on the object, sighing as he realised Eddie had given him his phone, not the spanner. Tim drew the phone to his side. *It's probably afternoon tea time anyway.* He struggled to adjust to the bright screen and squinted at the display. Three missed calls from McIntyre Park. His pulse kicked up a notch as he improvised with a pair of pliers to tighten the bolts. *Mac? Or Angus needing a hand?*

Tim shuffled out from under the vehicle, wiping his greasy hands on a stained workshop rag. Immersed in organising his toolbox, Eddie threw Tim a disgruntled look when the music dipped in volume. Tim brushed the dirt from the side of his face and pressed the phone to his ear.

A smile danced on his lips as he heard Mac's voice on the recording, but his expression quickly changed as her anxiety came through.

'Tim? Dad's not home. Hoping he's with you in another paddock or something . . . Call me back.'

He grabbed his jacket from the workbench and released the jack that had raised the ute to a workable height. Eddie clambered into the passenger seat as Tim listened to the remaining two messages. Mac's voice became more strained as she told him she was about to start searching. Tim gunned the V8 engine and shot down the driveway, the workshop lights still blazing and music playing to an absent audience.

Gospel singing cut through the tense air in the ute cab, but neither Penny, Lara nor Eddie paid any attention to the local radio station. Penny craned her neck around, her chin almost on Eddie's shoulder as she scanned sections of long grass and thick shelterbelts for a glimpse of the red and black quad bike.

'Look, look, look,' shouted Eddie, pointing out the window. Lara slammed on the brakes and they rocketed forward in their seats, following the line of his outstretched arm to Tim on the ag bike.

'Tim, Tim, Tim.'

Lara let out a frustrated growl and slammed the ute into gear again.

'We're looking for Dad—Angus—not Tim, Eddie.'

Penny felt a protective surge towards the young man sitting beside her, oblivious to the situation but happy to be included. 'Don't take it out on him, Lara. He doesn't understand.' She received a smile from Eddie but felt her sister twisting away irritably, muttering under her breath.

Penny braced herself against the dashboard as they hurtled down the bumpy track, coming within spitting distance of a surprised kangaroo.

'Can you slow down?'

'We don't have time to fart-arse around, Penny. If Dad's had an accident, he'll need every extra second we can give him.'

The craggy cliff face loomed into view, casting the last shadows of the day across the northernmost boundary of McIntyre Park. Penny's hand went to her mouth as Tim dropped the motorbike he was riding, engine still running and wheels still spinning. He hurdled a barbed-wire fence that stood between him and a boulder in the rocky paddock. Her gasp pierced the air as she realised the stone was actually one of four black wheels pointing to the sky.

'Oh shit.' Lara stomped on the accelerator and pulled the ute up as close to the fence as possible.

Fear wrapped itself around Penny like a cloak. Her fingers fumbled with the doorhandle, and she stumbled across Eddie to exit the vehicle before it had stopped rolling. Lara and Penny raced through the long grass, side by side. Penny's jeans tore on the barbed wire as she skimmed the top of the fence, and blood trickled down her leg as she ran towards her father's crumpled body. A radius of flattened grass was smeared with dark-red blood around one side of the bike, his escape attempt apparent. The mass of machinery had pinned his leg, a short, jagged bone protruding where the handlebars held it hostage. Tim crouched over his pale face.

'Angus, are you okay? Angus? Angus? C'mon, mate.'

Lara nudged him out of the way, feeling for a pulse. Penny held her breath against a silent scream. She doubled over, hot bile burning her throat, and added to the collection of McIntyre bodily fluids on the ground.

'He's alive. Call an ambulance,' screamed Lara, casting a withering look at Penny's heaving body.

Penny clamped a hand over her mouth and hurried back to the fence. The four-wheel drive heading towards them jerked to a stop. Pete and Diana launched out of their car and hit the ground running. Penny called to them as they raced past.

'Lara's onto it. We'll call for help.'

Angie stepped out of Diana's car too, her face pale. Her reluctance to take another step closer to the chaotic scene in the paddock was obvious; a fear of blood and gore that dated back to their mother's accident.

'Dad's lost a lot of blood. Take Eddie back to the house and call the ambos,' Penny panted. Eddie, who was still sitting in the ute, watched wide-eyed and fearful as she wiped the vomit from her mouth. For once, she was grateful for Lara's presence. They would need every scrap of her medical knowledge to keep their father alive until the paramedics arrived.

Thirty-one

Penny sipped from the disposable cup, cringing. The catering coffee was barely drinkable, unable to mask the taste of chlorinated town water that matched the bleach-scented hospital waiting room. Instead of the swarms of staff, interns, patients and visitors she'd dealt with in the city, the Horsham hospital was quiet with a buzz of country efficiency. She tossed the half-empty cup into the bin as the emergency room doors opened. A nurse looked up from her clipboard, calling to the child cradling an arm in the corner. Penny rushed past the child and his mother to speak with the nurse.

'Excuse me, is there any update on my dad—Angus McIntyre? The ambulance brought him in an hour ago . . . from Bridgefield?'

The nurse shook her head as she held the door open for the new patients.

'Like I said last time, they're still doing their best to stabilise him. We'll give you an update as soon as we can.'

Penny slumped back into her seat. The quiet room was providing way too many opportunities to reflect on Angus's injuries and yet-to-be-announced prognosis. She hesitated then reached for a magazine. Normally she avoided communal hospital literature, but tonight the need for momentary escapism trumped the potential germs. Diana shuffled closer along the row of chairs and leaned her head on Penny's shoulder.

'I hate waiting like this. It's almost harder than waiting for the paramedics to arrive. At least they only took forty minutes.'

'I'm just glad they got to him before all his veins collapsed— the ambos said they wouldn't have got the IV in an hour later,' said Angie, hugging her arms around her oversized jacket. She reached into the pocket and pulled out one of Angus's handkerchiefs.

'Stop harassing the nurses, Penny. They'll tell you when they know something. And Dad might not have needed any pain relief an hour later,' said Lara quietly. 'By then, he might have been dead.'

'You would've laughed if I'd raised the alarm an hour earlier, Lara. Don't even try and pretend otherwise. You could have put us both in hospital hooning around the farm the way you did. Eddie, too.'

'That's rich coming from someone who caused this whole accident.'

'What? I told him *not* to take the quad bike. I told anyone who'd listen how damn dangerous those vehicles are. Nobody. Wanted. A Bar. Of. It.' Penny forced the words out through a clenched jaw, pressing her lips together.

'Give it a break, you two,' said Angie, resting a hand on each of her sisters' arms.

Lara flinched at the touch and jerked her arm away, as if she'd been zapped with an electric prodder.

'Telling Dad not to do something is like a red flag to a bull—I thought everyone knew that.'

'It's nobody's fault, Lara,' Diana warned.

Penny saw Tim look up from his tatty car magazine, his
attention darting between the four sisters. Eddie's attention
pricked up too. Judging by the dark circles under his eyes,
Penny figured he was as tired as she felt. Pete remained quiet,
glued to the muted television in the corner, lips moving to the
teletext.

'Bet she was too busy packing her bags and updating her
Facebook status even to notice he was missing. Hashtag:
leaving today. Hashtag: bring on the city. Hashtag: city slickers
anonymous.'

Penny stood up abruptly, the chair scraping beneath her as
she stood over Lara. She felt her fists bunching at her sides,
fingernails biting into her palms as they trembled with fury.

Tim couldn't help but overhear the conversation and felt guilty
that he'd been working on his ute while Angus was lying in the
paddock, drifting in and out of consciousness. The paramedics
had been the epitome of calm as they'd forced fluids into
his system with an IV and got his blood pressure up to one
hundred. He hadn't been much use at the scene, apart from
helping Pete lift the quad bike from Angus's battered body,
and there wasn't a great deal to do inside the waiting room,
apart from wait. But he wasn't going to sit there and let Lara
heap blame on Mac. That just wasn't right.

'Chill out, Lara. It's useless throwing blame around now.'

Tim dropped the car magazine onto the seat beside him
and walked towards the McIntyre sisters. Penny's freckles
were even more prominent against her pale skin, interspersed
with flakes of black mascara. Her eyelashes were clumped
together as she looked up at him, the pain in her eyes raw. He
wanted to wrap his arms around her, shield her vulnerability

and take her pain as his own. He shoved his hands into his
dusty pockets instead.

'I should've been there helping him today. But we can't
change what's happened, so how about everyone calms down?'

He nodded his head at the security guard who was walking
towards them. Penny resumed her seat between Angie and
Diana, while Lara sat back in the chair, crossing her arms
tightly across her chest. The burly guard returned to his post
at the front counter, his gaze remaining on the quartet of
sisters. Tim stole a quick look at Penny as he returned to his
chair and his heart constricted as she gave him a sad smile.
Eddie's drooping chin lowered and a snore slipped from his
open mouth. *I should've run him back to Nanna Pearl's house
instead of dragging him up to Horsham.* But shock and a
frenzied need to keep the ambulance in his sights had robbed
him of logic, and darned if he was going to ask Nanna Pearl
to drive in the dark to collect Eddie or miss an update because
he was back at a motel room with his brother. He picked up
the car magazine and forced himself to be patient.

Penny stared at the double doors every time a nurse entered or
exited. Tim had finally decided to leave at midnight after the
initial update, but she knew his few hours in a crappy motel
bed wouldn't be much better than her fitful sleep in the plastic
waiting room chair. The doctor had been circumspect, saying
they'd know more after the operation.

Activity in the waiting room had slowed around 3 a.m.
but started picking up as soon as first light crept in through
the windows. Tensions and volume levels had run even higher
in the half hour since Pete had returned, their four boys and
Evie bouncing with energy and questions.

When's Grandpa coming out? Can I have a chocolate? What does this button do? Can I have another squirt of the hand gel? Penny reached into her handbag, fished out a packet of chewing gum and dispersed it among the children.

'Good thinking, Pen. Should buy us a minute of peace, at least,' said Angie. She leaned in closer, talking from the side of her mouth. 'See that nurse near the admissions desk? She comes in for the full monty every month. Hairy as a yeti, she is. Takes twice as long to wax her . . .'

'Angie!' Penny poked her sister in the arm, her head swivelling to catch a glimpse of the tall woman wheeling a patient across the waiting room. 'She might hear you. And what about client confidentiality?' She turned in her plastic chair, noting a hint of mischief in Angie's red-rimmed eyes. As much as Penny appreciated the mood-lightener, she could sense the slight hysteria behind Angie's inappropriate aside.

'I'm only telling you and you're not likely to blab to anyone, are you, Pen? This waiting is sending me batty.'

Penny stretched, her body begging for some respite. She stood up and strolled across the room before Angie breached any further confidences.

'For heaven's sake, Harry, leave the vending machine alone,' called Diana, frowning as the boys started jabbing at the buttons again. 'You'll break it and then there'll be trouble.' The edge in her voice sharpened as the twins protested.

Penny reached down and scooped Leo from Diana's arms, trying not to cringe as her little nephew rubbed a tube of half-eaten yoghurt onto her rumpled shirt.

'C'mon, Leo. Let's go see what the big kids are up to.'

Diana shot her a grateful look before stalking off towards the beleaguered vending machine. Penny sat down with Leo next to Cameron and Evie. The older pair were huddled over an iPad, four hands working the touchscreen in unison.

'What are you guys up to?'

'Dad just sent me a message on Facebook, so we're writing him one back,' said Evie.

Penny's eyebrows rose. From what Angie had told her last week, Lara had severed all ties with Sam after a final blazing row on Tim's doorstep.

'Cool. Where's Mum now?'

Evie looked up from the screen, waving a hand towards the nurse's station. 'Somewhere in there, Aunty Pen.'

Penny jiggled Leo on her knee as she scanned the area. Uniformed staff bustled busily behind the glass doors, but Lara was nowhere to be seen.

It was another half hour before Lara swept through the 'staff only' door and back into the waiting room, her jaw set in a hard line. Penny sat on the edge of her seat. She drew Leo closer, holding him like a shield against the news—bad news by the look of it. Different scenarios ran through her head. *Did he make it through the operation okay? Does he have to be airlifted to the city?* Leo cried out against the sudden constriction and Penny forced herself to relax.

'He's out of the operation, should be in recovery shortly. The orthopaedic surgeon is on his way. Apparently, the injuries are worse than they thought.'

Penny chewed her lip, biting back a dozen questions. If it were Angie or Diana with the medical career, she wouldn't hesitate to push for more information, but Lara . . . not Lara.

The double doors swung open once again, ejecting a middle-aged African surgeon into the waiting room. Penny stood at the same time as Angie and Diana and walked towards the doctor with a mixture of dread and anticipation. His kind tone was heavily accented.

'I have good news and bad news. Angus is a strong man. He's awake now. His pelvic fracture is stable—thankfully no damage to internal organs. We used a plate and pins to secure the pelvis during surgery, similar to the pins used in his ankle. The compound fracture of his fibula is quite complex, and there's severe swelling where the bone penetrated the tissue. We pulled a large amount of dirt and grass out of the wound, probably where he tried to drag himself out from under the bike, but we've cleaned and stitched it as best we could. He'll have a significant scar there.'

Penny felt faint thinking of the dark-red mass around her father's left ankle, the technical details reaffirming the agony he must have been in as he waited for them to arrive. And that was the good news ... she held her breath, steeling herself for the rest. The doctor looked each of them in the eye, his expression serious. Penny shifted Leo to her other hip, unable to keep still.

'The shoulder is more difficult. We knew it had fractured from the X-ray, but the MRI confirmed a severe brachial plexus injury, meaning the nerves supplying the arm have been damaged high up in the armpit. He can have further surgery at a later stage, such as nerve grafts or nerve transfers, to try to restore function to his right arm, and there's a small chance this might improve. We'll know more in a few weeks.'

Penny tasted blood as she chewed on her lip, trying to match the mental image of her active, quietly capable father with the broken man lying in the paddock.

'He won't be returning to farming, then,' said Lara, shooting a look in Penny's direction. 'Not with a useless arm.'

Penny bristled as she met her sister's gaze. *Why does she have to insinuate it was my fault?* She felt Leo squirm in her arms and swallowed the defensive remark and instead murmured quietly into the child's soft hair as the doctor shook his head.

'No. Angus will be in hospital for several weeks, then months of therapy just to get motion back in his hip and ankle. If he was an accountant, perhaps he could learn to type with his left hand. But at his age, with those injuries . . .' The doctor paused, his expression sympathetic. 'Manual labour is highly unlikely.'

Thirty-two

The swish of the double doors made them all look up. An elderly nurse padded towards them.

'It's been a long night for you lot, hasn't it? Those chairs don't lend themselves to comfort. Your dad's just settled into room five. Third door on your left, down that corridor. Make sure you get outside after you've seen him though—you look like you could all do with some fresh air. Catch a bit of shut-eye after your long night?'

Penny nodded at the nurse. They'd been camped out in the hospital for almost fourteen hours, but it had felt as long as a wet week. She was pretty sure she wasn't the only one of her sisters craving a hot shower, a soft bed and a strong drink, but those luxuries paled into insignificance next to seeing their father.

'He won't be much company for the next day or two, but at least he's stable now,' said Lara, leading the way down the corridor. Penny stuffed a soggy sausage roll into the bin as she followed.

'Do you think he'll be angry about his arm?' asked Angie as they turned into the surgical recovery ward.

Penny shrugged. 'He won't be thrilled. But it's better than a coffin.'

A gasp escaped her lips as she walked into room five. The large window illuminated the abrasions and livid purple bruises along the side of Angus's face. His skin was otherwise pale, his eyes closed. She watched his deep and even breaths underneath the crisp white bedsheet. The monitors connected to his wires and drips beeped, adding to the noise thumping inside Penny's head. She walked to his side and smoothed a wayward tuft of hair that stuck out at an odd angle.

'You gave us a bloody scare, you old hoon,' she said, fighting to keep the wobble out of her voice. Her lips grazed his rough cheek. His eyelids fluttered, and she watched him struggle to form silent words. She felt Angie behind her, reaching across to hold his bandaged hand.

On the opposite side of the bed, Lara pulled a chair to his knee and Diana sat in the chair by his shoulder.

'It's okay, Dad. Just rest,' whispered Diana, placing a hand on his chest.

Penny bit back tears at his frailness, the way his eyelashes stopped flickering at Diana's instructions. Before long, his chest fell back into a steady rhythm of sleep. She looked at the bandaged arm that proclaimed no more drenching, no more hauling bags of wool across the shearing shed and no more hoisting injured sheep onto the back of the ute.

'Knock, knock.'

Penny turned to see Tim in the doorway. He held a machinery magazine and the *Stock & Land* in one hand, a bunch of grapes in the other.

'How is he? How did the surgery go?'

Tim's eyes looked even darker than usual, with a smudge of purple underneath them. He looked from Angus back to

Penny. She wiped her cheeks, sifting through the technical jargon for a succinct wrap-up.

'Well, it's not looking good for his shoulder. The nerves are all torn.'

'Doc said his brachial plexus is stuffed. Possibly paralysed in his right arm. The pelvis and ankle will heal in time, but the arm probably won't,' said Lara.

'Right.'

Penny glared at Lara, irritated by her terse interruption. Eddie's frightened voice rang through the silence.

'Angus, Angus, Angus.' Eddie hovered behind his older brother, alarmed as he scanned the room. His grip on Tim's arm drew red welts to the surface, and he jumped as a nurse came up behind him.

'Ahhhh!' he yelled, looking frantically around the room for an escape route.

'Shhh, mate, it's okay. It's okay,' soothed Tim.

Although his voice was quiet, Penny could hear the emotion tinging his words, and she realised the extent of Angus's injuries had also thrown him for a six. She stepped away from the bed and relieved him of his load.

'Thanks, Mac. Those are from us. The grapes were Nanna Pearl's idea. Apparently, every patient needs grapes. I'll get this guy home. The machines are freaking him out, but I'll call you tonight. You'll be at the farmhouse?'

Penny paused, her tired brain struggling to work out what time of day it was. For all the hours she'd killed in the waiting room, she hadn't even thought of cobbling together a plan beyond seeing Angus. If the sky hadn't been light outside the window, she could have sworn it was almost dusk.

'You want me to give you a lift back to the farmhouse? Or you're probably catching a ride with Diana?'

Penny considered the two options. The idea of spending an hour and a half in Diana's car with four stir-crazy children, a teary Diana and a frazzled brother-in-law was unappealing, but she wasn't sure she could handle the trip squashed between Tim and Eddie on the bench seat of his WB ute, straddling the gear stick.

'I'll work something out. You get Eddie home.'

'I'll detour to the farmhouse, drop you off,' said Angie.

Penny nodded, relieved that someone was capable of pulling a coherent plan together. Tim turned to head out when a nurse walked in.

The nurse clucked her disapproval. 'Family only for the next few days, thank you very much. Mr McIntyre doesn't need any excitement or hoo-ha.'

Tim and Eddie took their leave and let the nurse bustle around checking monitors and adjusting the drip.

'It's okay, Brenda, we were all just heading out,' said Lara, walking the nurse out of the crowded room and waiting at the door.

'We'd better get home too. Pete's got someone holding the fort at the stock agency, but he'll be tearing his hair out with the kids,' said Diana.

'C'mon, Pen, lets follow them out. At least if I fall asleep at the wheel, Diana and Pete can tow us the rest of the way home,' said Angie, managing a smile between yawns.

Penny looked down at her father. She wanted to stay longer, but it made more sense to get back to the farmhouse, snatch some sleep and a shower, and return to Horsham in her own car. That way she could come and go as she pleased. Angus's eyes remained closed. *Just a couple of hours, then I'll be back.*

It wasn't until Penny noticed Diana weaving across the wide hospital corridor, typing into her phone, that she realised she still hadn't called Vince. She tugged her mobile out and was pulling up his name in her contacts list when Lara broke the silence.

'That's it, then. Better sell the farm,' she said, jamming her hands in her pockets. She said it in the same indifferent tone she'd announced her separation from Sam. Matter of fact, no outward display of emotion, as if she were telling Evie to do her homework.

It's a miracle my niece knows how to smile and laugh with that type of example, thought Penny.

'Is that a joke? It's not even funny. It's a bit bloody early for these types of discussions, isn't it?' Penny looked down the corridor towards Angus's open door, hoping he hadn't heard Lara's comment.

'What—you think he's going to work the farm with one arm and all those injuries? You're dreaming.'

'Maybe we can share-farm it, or agist the land,' said Diana uncertainly.

'We could hire someone to work it full-time until we figure out what to do. Perhaps Tim?' Angie's voice was just as hesitant, as if discussing the farm's future gave their father's injuries a finality.

Penny shook her head. Both suggestions were better than Lara's, but still, neither sat comfortably with her. They walked a little further before Penny broke the silence.

'We don't need to rush into anything just yet. A share-farm arrangement or agistment would involve a lot of set-up, and Dad said he's on the cusp of shearing and lambing. And Tim's just about to sow the crops. You can't lump that on someone at the last minute and hope it goes well. Dad's put a lot of work into this season. It was shaping up to be one of his best,' said Penny, indignant on Angus's behalf and surprised at how much she'd absorbed in the last two months.

She looked at her sisters' faces; each had a different expression—unsure, upset and indifferent.

'We are absolutely not selling the farm,' said Penny. Her voice was firm. Determined.

Lara kept walking, arms crossed over her chest. Penny matched Lara's pace, staring across the corridor at her with an unwavering gaze.

'Well, let's ask Dad about that tomorrow then, shall we?' Lara's voice held a challenge.

Penny nodded, lifting her chin and increasing her pace a little. 'Yes, let's.'

'Ah-hem.'

Lara was the first to break eye contact and look over Penny's shoulder at the sound of another voice. Penny twisted and saw the tall nurse Angie had pointed out earlier, walking behind them.

'Sorry Francine, just a little family walk and talk going on here,' said Angie.

Penny couldn't tell whether her sister's awkward smile reflected the tension crackling through the corridor or her guilt for sharing this woman's intimate waxing details.

The nurse nodded as she kept pace with them.

'Sounds like you're arguing over sheep stations,' she said, looking between Lara and Penny, clearly unaware just how accurate her comment was.

Penny looked across at Lara warily, giving a slight shake of her head. *Not today, Lara. Not here, not right now.* She hoped the silent stalemate could keep until later, and judging by the minute nod of Lara's head, she seemed to agree. The farm sale wasn't raised again as they walked towards the car park. The silence between them felt heavy, and Penny pulled her jacket closer against the chill. A sense of foreboding prickled at her skin as the four sisters splintered in different directions.

Thirty-three

Angie picked up speed as the houses turned into industrial businesses and tractor dealerships. The road then opened up and an expanse of prime cropping land whipped past the windows. Penny tried Vince's number again, cursing when it went to voicemail a second time. She knew the mobile phone coverage would wax and wane as they skirted around the Grampians and resigned herself to leaving a message.

'Vince, I've got some bad news. Dad's been in an accident. He's in hospital. Anyway, I'll call you later, after I've had some sleep. Love you.'

She set the phone down and avoided Angie's sceptical gaze. She stared at the paddocks, wondering whether they'd been sown with wheat, barley, chickpeas, lentils or canola.

'I can understand Vince is a busy man, but you cut him an awful lot of slack, Pen. He must be bloody good in bed.'

Penny continued staring out the window. It was no use trying to convince Angie or explain the engagement ring. Unless she saw Vince in action, at the helm of a boardroom in his suit and tie exuding charisma and power with clients lapping up his every suggestion, she wouldn't understand. And their sex life . . . it had been so long since she'd lain beside Vince that she barely felt qualified to comment. The month before she was hospitalised had been a write-off. No quantity of cold and flu tablets had been able to mask her internal aches enough to focus on the passionate form of pain relief Vince suggested.

Rusty danced on the end of his chain, watching Penny's every move as they pulled up at the farmhouse. She waved Angie goodbye and strode over to the dogs, dust swirling down the driveway and sandblasting her skin with each gust. The other three kelpies were busy gnawing on fresh bones, but Rusty sat to attention, his ears pricked.

'Who fed you guys?' She stroked Rusty's black and tan head, wondering which of the neighbours had taken care of the animals in their absence. His tail thumped against her leg as if to remind her the bush telegraph could be a blessing, not just a curse.

She gave Rusty one last pat and turned back towards the farmhouse.

A small bouquet sitting on the back step was another surprise. The harsh wind had blown most of the delicate petals from the peonies and a film of red, Western District dust covered the green stems. She didn't have to read the card to know the flowers were from Vince, and made a mental note to ask the local florist to put deliveries inside the back door next time. She picked up the flowers and leaned on the unlocked doorhandle with her elbow, pushing it open with her shoulder.

The two surviving peonies were recovering in a vase of fresh water when Penny heard a vehicle pull into their driveway.

'Yoo-hoo. Anybody home?'

Penny turned around to see a short, stocky figure silhouetted in the doorway. He moved into the house, his clothes still as ripped and paint-spattered as ever and his familiar smile as generous as always. A distant neighbour and father of one of her high school friends, he had barely aged in the last two decades.

'Mr Harvey?'

'Good to see you home, Penny. Sorry to hear about your dad. Bess sent me round with lasagne and fruit cake, though I bet you'll have half of Bridgefield baking for you this week.'

Gratitude welled inside her. As desperate as she was for a shower and change of clothes, she wasn't going to turn away casseroles and cakes that she wouldn't have time to cook.

'There's something to be said about small communities. No matter what happens, nobody goes hungry.'

'Fat chance of that with Bess around. Not a moment too soon though—can't have you fading away to nothing. Give me a call as soon as you need a hand checking your dad's paddocks. I threw the dogs some tucker earlier, too. Figured you had enough on your mind.'

'Thanks, Mr Harvey. I hadn't even thought that far ahead, to tell you the truth.'

He brushed off her comments with a shake of his head, looking down at his dusty boots.

'Angus was a big help to us when I had my knees done, an' Lord knows your mum baked enough cakes and meals for the community during her lifetime. Too short it was. Too short.'

Penny looked away, her heart too heavy and her head too tired to stroll down that part of memory lane right now.

'But your father, he's a tough bugger. I'm sure he'll be back in the paddocks in two shakes of a lamb's tail.'

Penny wished she could be as optimistic.

'I sure hope you're right, Mr Harvey. Thanks again.'

'Don't mention it. I'll swing past the house tomorrow to check your sheep, let you know if there's anything amiss.'

Penny watched his ute drive down their driveway and felt another wave of appreciation for the community spirit around her.

'Hey babe, I was just thinking about you. Terrible news about your dad. Is he going to be okay?' Vince's warm voice was like a cup of hot chocolate.

Although the farmhouse fire was stoked up and the oven was on, Penny still couldn't shake the chill from her quick trek to the wood pile and back. She let his comfortable conversation wash over her, the mundane work news and updates from their social circles like a balm to her tired, worried brain. Penny stretched out in the recliner that smelled like Angus. It was undoubtedly the comfiest seat in the suite and she could see why her father gravitated towards it every night.

'He was pretty dopey when I saw him last. His pain medication is pretty strong. But he came through the operation okay. And he had a few minutes of being awake this morning,' said Penny. She was about to start explaining the extent of his injuries when Vince's voice cut over the top of hers.

'Did you get my flowers, babe? I know how much you love those pretty ones, although they were supposed to be a 'perk-you-up', not a 'get-well-Angus' bunch. And I've got the apartment all sorted.'

'The flowers were pretty. Thanks.'

Penny glanced at the two naked stalks in the vase, their shrivelled petals having dropped to the table in defeat just hours after she had brought them inside yesterday. *Was it really only yesterday? It feels like an eternity.* She leaned her head back against the soft chair.

'When are you coming home, Pen? You could collect me from the airport Friday, save me getting a taxi?'

Penny was silent. Friday seemed a long way off. She looked out the window at another trail of dust coming down the driveway. Even over the barking dogs, she recognised the hum of the V8 engine.

'Babe? You there?' He blew out a sharp breath. 'I've been like a monk here in Sydney, I promise. Nothing for you to worry about . . . Babe?'

She dragged herself out of the armchair and walked with the phone to her ear.

'Sorry Vince, I've got to go. I don't have the brainpower to think about this now—can we talk about it later?'

'What do you mean? I've said sorry. I've done everything else you asked. What more can I do?'

The frustration in his voice was drowned out by a knock on the door. She walked across the kitchen.

'It's not about you, Vince. My dad's in hospital. I'll be staying here a little longer to sort things out. Can you do me a favour, please? Actually, make that two. Cancel my appointment with Georgie's doctor. I'll text you the number.' The knock on the door came again, louder this time. Penny's voice lowered. 'And stay the hell away from Charlotte.'

Tim usually walked straight inside when Angus was home, but he felt funny about waltzing into the farmhouse when he knew Penny was the only one home. He tapped on the door a second time and lifted the esky containing Nanna Pearl's borrowed Tupperware containers, a bottle of wine and a six-pack of beer.

Her eyes were underscored with dark circles when she answered the door, flitting from his face to the phone in her hand. He got the uncomfortable feeling he was interrupting something and suddenly wished he'd waited until tomorrow to drop the food and drinks around.

'Food delivery. I wanted to find out how Angus is doing and figured we could commiserate over a drink, but . . .' His voice trailed off as Penny closed her eyes and rubbed her temples. *What are you even doing here, Patterson? The last thing she wants is you intruding.*

'But that's obviously a crappy idea, so I'll just leave you to it.' He clunked the esky onto the deck and spun on his heel, regretting his ill-conceived attempt to clear the air between them.

'Wait.' Her voice sounded as weary as she looked. 'Dad's the same as yesterday, stable but groggy. Thanks for helping, Tim. And thanks for the meals on wheels. I've got one of Bess Harvey's casseroles ready for dinner, but those meals won't go to waste. Is it your famous lamb roast?'

Tim nodded as he shoved his hands in his pockets. *Don't say it, Patterson. Just walk away now.* But his mouth was quicker than his brain and he plunged ahead, searching her face.

'About the other day at cooking class . . .'

Penny's gaze dropped to the phone in her hand again. He saw her cheeks flush.

'I don't know what I was thinking, Tim. I'm so embarrassed. I'm not like that, no matter how terminal my relationship is. Please, can we forget it even happened?'

Tim pressed his lips together, squeezing his vulnerability into a sharp line of pain. *Great work, Patterson. Kicking goals here.* He nodded slowly, making a zipping gesture across his compressed lips.

'Yep, too easy. Glad we're on the same page,' he lied.

He turned away, unable to handle the relief flooding into her features, and berated himself for misreading the situation.

'I'll catch you tomorrow, Mac.'

'Night, Tim.'

Thirty-four

'And with wool prices currently on the rise, we can expect to see better stability in the markets . . .' Penny stopped mid-sentence, folded up the newspaper and placed it on Angus's bedside table. She stroked his pale forehead, careful not to bump the wound near his eyebrow. Perhaps he was trying to send her a sign in his sleep, trying to communicate that he was sick of her regular reading sessions, tired of listening to wool prices and market reports that were utterly irrelevant to him in his current state of health.

She looked back at the newspaper's colourful front page. The lead article highlighted two more fatalities on Victorian farms. She hadn't had the heart to read that piece out loud, nor the editorial or letters to the editor about the same subject. It would have sounded way too much like 'I told you so', even though her audience was not in any position to contradict her or complain.

'You're one of the lucky ones, Dad,' said Penny, surveying the bandages, splints and casts decorating his body. She fossicked in her handbag for an apple, dislodging her notepad. She bent down to collect the slip of paper that fluttered to the floor, which was a scribbled version of the Melbourne-to-Sydney flight schedule. Three days ago, it had seemed like a sound solution—fly up to Sydney and confront Vince face-to-face—but now . . . the idea had fallen by the wayside, just like rescheduling the work medical, eating regular meals and bothering with her daily blow-dry and make-up routine. She clasped Angus's hand and longed yet again for her mother's advice to help straighten up her jumbled list of priorities.

'You can't even step away from that thing for one second, can you?'

Lara's hostile voice rang out across the room. Penny looked up from her phone to see her sister standing in the doorway, trackpants and a hooded top replacing the nurse's uniform she'd been wearing earlier.

Penny saved the draft email she was composing and checked the time. Over an hour had passed as she replied to work emails on her phone, the novelty of decent reception keeping her glued to the chair by her father's bedside. Penny had planned to be halfway back to the farm by the time Lara finished work. She squared her shoulders, unwilling to reward her sister with the reaction she so obviously wanted.

'And how was your day, Lara? Mine was fine, thanks for asking,' said Penny, mimicking the saccharine tone Diana used with the children when she was at her wits' end.

'Your priorities are up the creek. We were almost orphans a few days ago and you're sitting there on Facebook or whatever, checking to see if your idiot boyfriend has posted any new photos of himself and his new girlfriend.'

Lara snatched the chart from the back of the bed frame and flicked through Angus's medical notes.

'Or let me guess: you were messaging your boss, telling her you'll be a day late returning to work due to a highly inconvenient farm accident? Selling the farm is the best idea, obviously.'

Penny leaned over and kissed her father's cool cheek. She collected her bag and phone, leaving the newspaper on Angus's bedside table.

'Give me a break, Lara. He's been in hospital for less than a week—doesn't mean we need to whack a "for sale" sign on the front gate.' Penny pushed past Lara to get to the door and was halfway down the hall before Lara called out to her.

'Hey, Penny. The quicker we sell the farm, the quicker you can get back to your beloved city, right?'

Penny kept walking, not wanting Lara to see the doubt in her eye.

☙

Penny looked up from the newspaper. After a week of reading aloud to Angus, she'd almost reached her saturation point for articles about wool prices, crop advice and new machinery releases. She folded the paper and placed it next to another fresh bag of grapes on his bedside table. The simple act of reading the articles aloud to her father always made him smile and if he noticed her skipping the ones about farm accidents, he didn't mention it.

Diana swept into the hospital room, her hair unruly and a large, jammy smear on her wrinkled white T-shirt.

'I've only got a minute. The twins need collecting from a birthday party in ten minutes. Just wanted to see how Dad is today? Did they say any more about the nerve damage after those tests?' Her words were rapid-fire, miles away from her usual calm demeanour.

'The EMG tests weren't so good. No response to the nerve conduction survey or the needling. Maybe surgery down the track, but for now, they're more interested in managing the pain and starting rehab.'

Diana ran a hand through her hair, adding to the dishevelled look. Penny noticed a tremor in her hand and brimming tears.

'Are you okay? Sit down, tell me what's wrong.' Penny was worried. Diana never fell apart. Even in the darkest days following Annabel's death, Diana had remained the rudder of the family.

Diana slumped down in the seat—no customary straight back, no steely reserve as the tears rolled down her cheeks. She threw her hands up in the air, a low cry coming from her haphazardly lipsticked mouth.

'It's everything. Dad is never sick, never injured. He'd hate being fussed over like this, hate the farm being ripped out from under him like Lara is suggesting. She called me about it again yesterday. There's no changing her mind. Leo's still teething, Harry hasn't been sleeping through either, and Pete and I keep fighting about McIntyre Park.' Diana's sobs amplified in the room, but Angus remained asleep.

Penny wrapped her arms around her eldest sister, puzzled by the floodgates, but understanding the sense of flailing around and waiting for the dust to settle before they could work out the best path forward. Lara's words had weighed heavily on her mind overnight, her stomach curdling with distaste each time she thought about them.

'Have you had any other ideas?'

Penny shook her head, feeling just as helpless. 'Nope, I just know Lara's still stuck on the idea of selling. She's got a real bee in her bonnet about it. Thinks it's a win-win for everyone.'

Diana drew a shaky breath and wiped her eyes with an ironed handkerchief. 'I could have strangled Pete last night, seriously. I thought our nest egg was still sitting in the bank, perfect for investing into a farm-share arrangement, but unbeknownst to me, Pete's locked it into a five-year term deposit. Reckons it's generating interest for the kids' school fees. Frugal bastard.' Diana spat out the words, more irate than Penny had ever seen her.

Penny looked at her watch, sending an apologetic look to her sister. 'What time did you say the birthday party finished, Diana? It's half past now.'

'Oh, shoot.' Diana scrambled to her feet, smoothing down her skirt with damp hands. 'Don't mind me. I'll be better after a glass of wine and a good night's sleep. But before I forget, here's Dad's mail and another soppy postcard from Vince. Looks like he's back in Melbourne, desperately awaiting your return.' Diana thrust the bundle of envelopes into Penny's hands.

Penny ripped open an envelope addressed to her, the pathology clinic logo matching the letterhead inside. She smiled and leaned out the doorway.

'My bloods have come back perfect, Diana. Ross River fever is all cleared up.'

Diana's retreating figure turned but didn't pause as she sped down the corridor.

'Good,' she called back. 'We're going to need every ounce of strength possible to get through these next few months.'

Penny paused at the door as her sister's words echoed down the corridor. *Months? Who said anything about months?*

Thirty-five

Tim stepped into the farmhouse laundry. Angus's coat still hung on its usual peg, but the shoe rack looked empty without his large boots. He wondered if they'd been cut off him in the ambulance. *Should get him a new pair as a 'welcome home' present*, thought Tim. The door slammed behind him, bringing with it a gust of wind that swept through the house and into the kitchen, ruffling the curtains and blowing hair across Penny's face. He almost grinned at the sight. Her hands were covered in egg whites and breadcrumbs, almost as if she'd been tarred and feathered, and she tried unsuccessfully to push her fringe out of the way with her forearm.

'Here, let me help with that,' he said, striding across the kitchen.

She stood quietly as he reached across the island bench and lifted a lock of hair from her face.

'Sorry Mac, wind caught the door before I could stop it. Windy enough to blow a dog off the chain.' He stepped away, pulling the wringing wet shirt from his shoulders and slicking his own hair away from his forehead.

194

Penny washed her hands and threw a tea towel over her schnitzel production line.

'No worries. You look like you could do with warming up. There's soup on the wood-fire if you're keen for an early lunch?'

Tim nodded and headed back to the laundry to wash up. He didn't need soup to warm up—being so close to her again was the equivalent of eating a bowl of chilli. He called out over the running water.

'Might grab a takeaway mug, ta? Bit of baking therapy underway?'

He strolled back into the kitchen. Penny stood there, a puzzled look on her face as she assessed the mixing bowls and measuring cups spread across the counter. Annabel's recipe book was propped open to the desserts section and she grabbed one of the yo-yo biscuits piled up on a wire cooling rack.

'I was only going to make soup and schnitzels but you're right, it seems to have morphed into a full-blown baking session. I've invited everyone to dinner tonight. I think we could all do with a nice meal. You and Eddie are welcome to join us.' She turned to retrieve the pot of soup from the top of the fire.

Tim watched her with a smile, his thoughts scattering in all directions. Mac cooking for him in just the apron, no clothes between her skin and the thin floral fabric. Mac the same age as Nanna Pearl, her need to nurture continuing until soft tissue rounded her angular hips and padded out her slim build. He pictured himself standing by her side, after fifty or so years of companionship. A memory jumped out at him, snatching his fanciful notions away: a vision of Penny in a blue-and-white school uniform, shiny shoes and braided hair; the smile that had been reserved just for him morphing into a frown a few months into their relationship, the corners of her mouth turned down with distaste as her friends, and then finally Penny too, whispered about him in the schoolyard. He remembered her sickly pallor, her fragile body as he'd carried her upstairs on her return to McIntyre Park. Then the citrus-scented woman who had invaded his thoughts ever since that cooking disaster in the community hall. *Which is the real deal?* He shook his head, trying to clear the many faces of Penny McIntyre from his mind.

Penny was unnerved by Tim's silence. She felt like shoving the soup ladle in her mouth. *First, I've ignored the farm accounts and put off a phone call to Georgie in favour of slaving over a hot stove. Second, I've come up with the ridiculous idea of an impromptu family dinner including Lara—the last person I feel like being civil to—and third, I've invited Eddie and Tim, a man who could rival Colin Firth in a wet T-shirt competition. Maybe Diana isn't the only one losing the plot around here.*

Tim cleared his throat.

'We wouldn't want to impose.'

'Well, the invitation's there. I know we haven't always been on the best of terms, but I'm thankful for your help, Tim.' She turned to face him again, proffering a mug of steaming soup, and he bit back a smile at the trail of biscuit crumbs down her chest.

'And I know Dad would be grateful too.'

The corner of Tim's mouth turned up, followed by a flash of conflict that raced across his features so quickly Penny thought she'd imagined it.

'Thanks, we'll come. Routine will probably do Eddie some good. He was freaked out by the whole accident and hospital thing.'

He opened his mouth to say more, but the shrill ring of the telephone stopped him.

'Might be the hospital,' said Penny, reaching for the phone. She hoped it wasn't Georgie. It would take another few batches of biscuits before she worked out how to handle that call.

Vince's enthusiastic greeting boomed into the kitchen and Tim waved a silent goodbye, retreating from the house with the mug in hand. Penny listened to Vince's animated account of the presentation he had just finished, but her focus was on the navy Holden heading down the driveway, Bones the kelpie bracing against the wind in the back. The maple trees whipped from side to side as he passed them, the very last red and yellow leaves floating from the branches and flying into the paddocks.

She forced herself back to the phone call, her boyfriend's voice bringing her back to the topic at hand.

'. . . apartment's all shipshape like you wanted. Everything's out of storage and back in its place. The only thing missing is you, babe, and then it will all be back to normal.' She heard the eagerness in his voice, his contrite effort to please her.

Penny thought of Angus lying paralysed in hospital, Lara's flippant idea of selling the farm, Angie's and Diana's uncharacteristic behaviour in the last few days and her flickers of unwanted attraction to Tim, of all people. How could things possibly go back to normal now?

Thirty-six

Penny wandered away from the saleyard canteen, freeing the bacon and egg roll from its wrapper. She took a generous bite of the warm, salty concoction, determined to ignore the number of calories and hoped it wouldn't smudge her lipstick. Rolls for Eddie and Tim were tucked under her left arm; they would have to share the last bottle of orange juice. She headed back towards the market where all the action was—a chorus of auctioneers, keen bidders and noisy livestock, dozens of small groups lingering to discuss their purchases, others bustling ahead to inspect upcoming pens of sheep.

'Hup a bid, hup a bid. Who's gonna give me a bid?' the auctioneer called from his walkway high above the pens of sheep, at least six feet above the crowd. His hands waved as furiously as his rapid-fire voice, taking bids higher as the auction got underway.

Penny had always enjoyed the markets as a child, relishing the opportunity to weave in and out of the crowd with other farm kids, occasionally stopping to eavesdrop on adult conversations or beg her parents for some spending money. Tim had been right: the markets were a good idea in a week that had been fraught with tension. He had changed her mind about cancelling their pre-arranged load, explaining their market ewes were in perfect sale condition. She was glad she'd accompanied them to the sale. *At least I'll have something positive to report back to Dad this afternoon*, she thought, scanning the crowd.

Tim's yellow-and-navy-striped rugby jumper made it easy to spot him at the back of the bidders, where he was gesturing with his hands as he spoke to another man. Eddie stood beside him, enjoying the spectacle of the frenzied auctioneer trying to get the best money for a mob of motley-looking ewes. Their sale pen had fetched twice as much as this lot.

Penny approached Tim and Eddie, only recognising their east-boundary neighbour, William Cleary, when it was too late to walk away.

'Ah, here she is. Penelope, you must have felt your ears burning.'

'William, nice to see you again,' she said, nodding to the rake-thin older man as she handed out the rolls. She had never warmed to William or his family, even though Angus seemed to get along with him just fine. And Tim too, from the look of things. Her mother's comments about their gossipy neighbour had stayed with her long after Annabel had passed away, and she knew that any snippets of news spread faster than a bushfire when William Cleary was within earshot.

'Sad business with Angus. Lucky it didn't finish him off altogether.'

Penny gaped at the comment. Distracted by the bidding action, William didn't even notice the impact of his words. She shot Tim a glance. He had stopped mid-mouthful, egg yolk running down his chin, a pained look on his face.

'Anyway, I was just saying to Timmy here that I'll lend a hand whenever you need. Or get the old girl to bake you a

cake or two. Give her something to do with all her spare time.'
His dry laugh turned into a splutter.

Penny walked away before her temper got the better of her.
She felt sorry for his wife, who probably had as much spare
time as the next overworked and under-recognised farming
woman. *There's no way we'll be accepting any help from him*,
she thought, stalking towards the bidding arena.

'Penny McIntyre, you haven't changed a whisker,' said a
familiar voice. Penny turned and recognised the face beneath
the chubby jowls and tent-like shirt of the woman next to her.

'Rachel Harvey? I haven't seen you in what, fifteen years?
Are these all yours?'

Penny gestured to the tribe of children huddled around her
school pal's legs, each decked out in peaked hats, polo shirts
and a rainbow of rugby jumpers.

'Yeah, but I'm happy to loan them out if you need a new
form of contraception. Dad said he called round last week.
I'm sorry about Angus. Is he on the mend?'

Penny was pleased to see her high school friend's humour
was still the same, albeit buried under the weight of mother-
hood. She watched Rachel ruffle her children's hair fondly,
the tender gesture overriding her words.

'Dad's pretty banged up, won't be much use on the farm
when he gets out of the hospital.'

'So, are you going to have a crack at running it?'

'Not likely. I'm heading back to Melbourne as soon as we
get Dad sorted.'

'Rushing back to the rat race, eh? Your mum pegged you
as a high-flyer from the start, didn't she? You always did
have the gift of the gab, I suppose. Well, for what it's worth,
I reckon you can take the girl outta the country, but you can't

take the country outta the girl. I can just picture you back on the land.'

Penny shook her head and steered the conversation in a different direction.

'Are you still with . . .' Penny paused, trying to remember the name of the farmer her friend had married straight out of high school. The name slipped into her mind as a short man wearing a baseball cap sauntered towards them. 'Andrew?'

'Yep, same old, same old,' Rachel said, turning as her husband's hand snaked around her waist. 'Not much has changed around here, has it, Andy? You remember Penny?'

He lifted one of the little girls onto his shoulders, the resemblance between father and daughter unmistakable.

'G'day, Penny, you're a blast from the past. The father-in-law mentioned you were home. I hear you've hooked up with Tim Patterson too? Better late than never.'

Penny spluttered her orange juice. 'He's working for my father, but that's about it.' Penny looked behind her at Tim, who was still cornered by William. As if he felt her gaze, Tim looked up, a small smile lightening the pained expression on his face. She shook her head. *Tim's a big boy; if he can't extricate himself from a conversation with someone who calls him Timmy, then he deserves the ear bashing.*

Rachel elbowed her husband in the ribs. 'You've been hanging around that post office too long,' she scolded. 'Don't mind Andy, he gets the local gossip all mixed up. She's got a city boyfriend—remember the postcard story? Though that might be off now, given the whole Facebook saga.'

Penny grimaced, wondering if there was anything about her life that wasn't public news.

'Well, I'd heard Tim had something going with one of the McIntyre girls. Sorry, Penny, I must have got the wrong end of the stick,' he said, tickling his daughter's toes.

'Nope, not me. Anyway, I'd better check our next mob. They'll be under the hammer any minute now. Nice to see you both,' Penny said, wondering whether the town's rumour mill had somehow got wind of their near-kiss in the hall. *Not that I care*, she reminded herself, edging her way into the bidding circle.

Penny caught sight of the photographer just as he lowered his gigantic lens. She dropped her hand from Tim's arm, wondering whether the camera had been trained on her when the auctioneer called out the final bid, or if the photographer had been busy capturing the shocked reaction from the rest of the crowd as their final pen of McIntyre Park ewes topped the sale. She stepped away and slipped into the fold as congratulations floated around her. What had made her fling her arms around the six-foot sandy-haired man standing beside her? And what would everyone in Bridgefield think if the newspaper printed the photo of her and Tim in next week's *Stock & Land*?

'Bloody great price, Timmy. Angus will be proud.' William Cleary clapped Tim on the shoulder like a proud father. 'Might smuggle a few through the boundary fence, cheaper than buying 'em.'

She watched people who had lost money to Roger Patterson crowding around Tim. She wondered how long it had taken them to get over the sting of Roger's betrayal, how long until they had spoken the Patterson name without bitterness. She turned and walked out of the bidding arena. Life had been a lot easier when she still thought Tim Patterson was tarred with the same brush as his father.

Thirty-seven

'I think Lara's avoiding me,' said Penny, scooping a prawn into her mouth. Another counter meal seemed decadent while Angus continued to lie in the hospital, sleeping more than he was awake, but Penny had eaten all the casseroles she could handle for one week and the hospital cafeteria left a lot to be desired. It hadn't taken Angie and Diana much convincing to meet her at the hotel for lunch, though the open invitation to all three sisters was met with radio silence from Lara's end, just like Penny's invitation to the family dinner at the farmhouse earlier in the week.

'She could just be busy—you know the way they change up night shifts with on-call stuff and then throw in a few early shifts?' said Angie, fork dangling next to her mouth thoughtfully. Her ability to see the best in everyone was humbling, and Penny sighed resignedly.

'Well, she still manages to run for an hour or so every day; I don't think anything gets in the way of that. She's going to campaign hard for the farm sale, whether we like it or not,' said Penny, shifting the salad around on her plate.

'I think Dad's accident just flustered her. I'm sure she's not serious—she loves the farm as much as we all do, doesn't she?'

Diana leaned forward, quickly scanning the hotel playroom where the twins were burning off energy, before responding.

'Well, I hate to say it, but I agree with Penny about the sale. Pete said the succession planning team at his stock agency deals with family farming conflicts all the time, and it usually boils down to money. She might be angling for an early inheritance?'

'Get out of here.' Angie shook her head doubtfully as Penny nodded.

'Think about it,' said Diana, warming to her subject. 'You've got good money coming through with your beauty salon, Angie. Penny's investments have set her up financially, and Pete and I have a solid income and savings plan. So solid, he's tucked our nest egg away, out of reach,' she said, an edge to her voice. 'There's only one of us without that type of financial security.'

'What's the deal with Sam? Won't he pay child support?'

'Pfft, he was even worse with money than Lara. The best thing he did was crawl under a rock somewhere, never to be seen again,' said Diana.

'She'll never find another guy who's willing to put up with all her hostility. She should have begged him to stay,' said Penny.

Diana shook her head, unconvinced.

'You were in the city when it all went belly-up the first time. You didn't see how she was. And when I asked her about the recent split, she told me she never wanted to see him again.'

Angie shrugged. 'Well, that didn't last long. Mrs Beggs at the shop said he was back in Bridgefield this morning. Filling up at the servo.'

Diana's response was immediate, her eyes growing wide.

'Really? Does Lara know?'

'I forgot to ask. Things have been crazy this week. I haven't seen Lara since the weekend. She isn't answering my calls either.'

Diana swore under her breath, pulling her phone out of her pocket and dialling as she strode across the hotel dining room.

'What was that all about?' said Penny.

Angie shrugged again. 'Your guess is as good as mine, but Diana's not happy.'

'Bugger. Don't look now, but William Cleary is walking our way. Saw him at the saleyard earlier this week—I'd forgotten how much he can talk.'

'He's more of a gossip than Mrs Beggs. Is he drunk?' Angie spoke under her breath.

Penny watched the way he slopped the beer over the edge of his glass as he staggered towards them, took in his flushed cheeks.

'Maybe.'

'If it isn't the McIntyre girlies, out to lunch. Fancy seein' you twice in a week . . . P'nelopeee. And little Angela.'Cept you're not so little anymore, are you?' He laughed, spraying beery breath across the table.

Penny pushed the remains of her prawn salad away, her appetite disappearing.

'We'd love to stay and chat, William, but hospital visiting hours have just started,' said Penny. She gathered her handbag from under the table. Angie tossed a napkin over her plate and followed Penny's lead, equally keen to get moving before he launched into a long-winded story.

'Don't get your knickers in a knot, girlie. Say g'day to old Angus from me. Tell him he's done a good deed selling the farm to Timmy. Needs a good break, that boy.'

Penny grabbed William's arm as he lurched directly into their table, and spun him around with a little more force than necessary.

'What are you talking about?'

Other diners turned in their seats as William stumbled again, slopping more beer down his chest.

'I heard all about it at the post office. Apparently, Timmy got a good deal. Should help your old man outta a rough spot, with his being a cripple now . . .'

Penny shook her head in disbelief, gobsmacked. *He must be joking . . . ? Tim wouldn't have . . . couldn't have . . . surely he hasn't been to visit Angus overnight and cooked up a deal without us knowing?*

Penny felt sick to her stomach, suddenly dizzy with the need to get to the hospital.

Thirty-eight

Penny stalked down the corridor, her stride agitated and her glare furious as she went straight past the nurse's station.

'And where do you think you're going with a face like thunder? Not planning on disturbing Mr McIntyre, I hope?'

Penny swore under her breath as she stopped and turned towards the no-nonsense nurse, Brenda.

'He's had enough on his plate with your cranky sister storming in here earlier.'

'Lara was here?'

'Yes, but I sent her packing as soon as I overheard the tone of their conversation. She may have worked here once upon a time, but it doesn't mean she can upset my patients like this. I won't stand for it. My stockings nearly fell down when I heard the alarm going off on his monitors.'

Penny summoned up all of her professional poise to talk the stern nurse into allowing a two-minute visit, but her plan was thwarted before she'd even taken a step towards the room, by the twins screaming their way up the hospital corridor. A harried Diana and Angie arrived at the nurse's station in time to hear Brenda's final words on the subject.

'No, no, no, no, no. I've had just about enough of this circus. We'll call you if Mr McIntyre needs anything more today. Otherwise, you can clear off until you've all calmed down.'

Beep, beep, beep. The Mercedes' over-speed alert chimed at her and Penny looked down at the speedo, easing back from a silky 130 kilometres per hour.

The northernmost tip of the Grampians stretched before her as she whipped down the country highway, white posts and dead kangaroos blipping past as she drove towards Bridgefield. Diana and Angie were just visible in her rear-view mirror.

Penny thumped the steering wheel with her fist as she recalled the dejected look on their faces at the hospital an hour ago, the frustration that had driven her fingernails into the palms of her clenched hands.

All three of them had tried to call Lara but to no avail. Likewise, Tim's mobile was either switched off or out of range. She felt like throwing her phone to the ground and crushing it with her pointy-toed boot. Penny knew precisely where she planned on shoving that very same boot if William's slurred words held an ounce of truth.

There was nothing to do but head for home.

Penny swiped at the radio dial, hoping music would calm her bubbling fury. She toggled through the stations, one eye on the road, one on the digital display, until she stumbled across a heavy rock program. AC/DC was a stretch even for her eclectic music taste, but somehow the thumping drums and screaming electric guitars seemed like perfect company for her mutinous thoughts.

A silver ute loomed on the horizon. With a spotlight on the roof, mud flaps that almost reached the ground and enough rust spots to be considered terminal, the vehicle was a slow-moving billboard for farm machinery and local Bachelor and Spinster balls.

Penny rolled her eyes as the stickers for the Colac Titpullers B&S, the Eel Skinners and Duck Pluckers B&S and the Poochera Pissants Ball loomed into view. Her foot jabbed the accelerator as she thought of Tim. *Backstabbing bastard, just when I thought I could trust him.*

She eyed the driver as she flew past the car. Instead of the teenage boy she had expected, she was face-to-face with a man about her own age. One arm rested on the windowsill and lazily gripped the wheel, the other around the shoulder of a small child. The little girl waved joyfully, pigtails bouncing as she jiggled in her booster seat.

Penny's anger abated briefly and she waved grimly before pulling back into the left lane, memories of perching proudly in the front seat of her father's ute—the one that now sat lifeless in a machinery shed—overshadowing her anger. As a child, she hadn't seen the rust or the dents, only the pure joy of talking about sheep and wool as they ran errands in town. No hurry. No fuss. Just father and daughter time in a dusty old ute, a relic from Angus's past he couldn't fathom parting with.

A beeping noise drew Penny back to the present, and she looked in her rear-view mirror to see Diana's four-wheel drive indicating to turn off the highway. The old silver ute was just a dot in the distance when Penny braked and cursed. *Have I honestly been away so long that I've just missed the turn-off for home?*

☙

Penny slammed her car door and had covered several metres before Diana had even rolled to a stop beside her. Car doors slammed behind her, but Penny marched towards the pen of sheep and the three figures silhouetted against the tin shed.

Brown grass crunched under her boots, dust swirling with every jerky step. Penny's grip on her emotions was as tenuous as the lacklustre start to winter.

I'll throttle her. And him, she thought, as Tim's, Eddie's and Lara's laughter carried over the sound of barking dogs and jostling sheep. It was beyond belief. Lara barely smiled these days and she'd only heard Tim's deep laugh twice since she'd been home. Once with her father and then in the hall kitchen, just minutes before her lips were millimetres from his.

Penny slowed fractionally as she heard panting behind her. 'Wait, Pen. Calm down before you bust an artery. Diana's putting the kettle on.'

Angie's shorter legs struggled to keep up the pace and she jogged a few steps as the smell of sheep wafted towards them. Penny spotted Eddie and Lara at the far end of the yards. The sheep yard gate screeched as Bones and Rusty pushed a mob through the race. Tim released the sheep he was drenching, lifting his drench gun in greeting as they arrived.

Penny shoved her hands into her jeans pockets, face steely as she turned to Angie.

'We'll need more than a cup of tea to smooth this over.'

Thirty-nine

Raised voices danced off the corrugated iron. Spooked sheep skittered in the holding pens, bunching up against corners, the smaller ones scrambling to save themselves from being crushed. A wind whipped up out of nowhere, coating them all with dust.

'You've got a bloody nerve, Tim Patterson. And you too, Lara. You should be ashamed of yourself, upsetting a sick man who can barely tell what day of the week it is. There are laws against this. You can't convince him to sell the farm when he's not in his right mind.'

Tim set the drenching gun down, his large hands swiping at the dust that had settled on his face.

'It's not like that, Mac.' His voice was quiet and steady, but the quick glance he gave Lara was all the confirmation Penny needed.

'Have you been in cahoots with Lara all along, intending to be the first bidder if and when the property came up for sale? Don't you have a scrap of dignity? Either of you?'

Penny's voice shook with anger and she squinted against a gust of dirty wind, the fine particles of topsoil finding their way into her mouth. She spat viciously and ran her tongue along her gritty teeth.

Lara glared at her. 'Dad's not going to run it himself anymore, is he? I'm just being practical,' she said, swinging her legs over the railing to stand beside Tim.

Eddie followed, his movements less fluid, and he straddled the top rail unsteadily. Penny's anger faltered a little as she watched Tim assist him, gently coaxing his brother all the way over.

'What's with all the secret squirrel stuff though, Lara? Penny and I should be part of these discussions. Diana too.' Angie's chest had stopped heaving, her measured tone contrasting her sisters' harsh words.

Lara looked from Penny to Angie, and then over to Eddie. She shrugged.

'Penny shot the topic down. No use banging my head against a brick wall there. Figured I'd ask Tim and then go direct to Dad,' said Lara.

Even though Angie had asked the question, Lara directed her answer at Penny, as if she knew the flippant tone would further incense her.

'Settle down, Mac. You're going off half-cocked,' said Tim.

Penny felt the blood pulsing through her temples, a thin red haze settling in front of her vision.

'We're talking about a farm, not some petty debate about rissoles versus sausages for dinner,' said Penny. She stabbed a finger in Tim's direction. 'A *family* farm. And I think this should be a *family*-only discussion. Without any tyre kickers around.'

There was a groan from Angie. A smirk from Lara. Penny wasn't sure whether it was another gust of wind or her words that caused Tim's expression to harden, but she felt the civility between them evaporate with a jolt.

Tim put an arm around Eddie, shaking his head as he guided his brother towards the ute. Confusion crossed Eddie's face.

'Penny, Penny, Penny?' He turned and headed in her direction, distressed.

Tim reached for Eddie's arm and steered him the opposite way. His voice was tight as he spoke, and Penny saw his self-control wavering each time he unclenched his jaw.

'Not now, Eddie. It's time for us to go home.'

Penny squeezed her fingers into a fist, wishing she could retract her last sentence. She wiped the sweat from her forehead, leaving a line of dirt in its place, and looked to Angie for backup.

'Angie? Come on. Am I the only one who cares about the heritage of this place? Or Mum's memorial rock up there on Wildflower Ridge? What are we going to do if we sell? Roll the great big boulder down the mountain and pop it in the front yard of some tiny townhouse?'

'I think we all need to calm down, Penny,' said Angie.

Penny threw her hands in the air. 'Seriously?'

Lara laughed dryly, thriving on the conflict. She leaned forward, close enough that Penny could smell the mixture of sweat and lanolin on her skin.

'You haven't even been up to Wildflower Ridge in years. If you're so nostalgic, Penny, why don't you have a crack at running the bloody place? Put your money where your mouth is? Now *that* would be hilarious.'

Penny clenched her jaw indignantly and took a step back, her boot striking an empty drench drum beside her. The thump set off another round of barking from the dogs and added to her already rapid heart rate. Her ego stung as Lara continued to laugh, and anger took hold of her once again.

'I'd manage just fine, but I've got better things to do. Laugh all you want, Lara. At least I'm not trying to sell Dad's farm out from under him.'

She turned and yelled at Tim and Eddie's retreating figures, the words flying from her lips before she could stop them.

'You can stick your offer up your bum, Tim. Unless Dad says otherwise, McIntyre Park is not for sale.'

Tim didn't acknowledge Penny's parting shot, unwilling to expose the hurt and anger written across his face. It was no secret he'd been working hard and ploughing his savings into a farm deposit. And it was only a matter of time before his and Lara's casual conversation was pumped into the Bridgefield gossip mill and churned out as a full-blown, signed, sealed and delivered sale offer. But Penny's reaction had cut to the core.

Never, not bloody once, did I consider swindling Angus.

His fingers tightened on the steering wheel as he swung himself into the ute. Without waiting for the click of Eddie's seatbelt, he twisted the key in the ignition and let the red dirt fly behind him.

'Penny, Penny, Penny . . .'

Eddie's voice came out as a whimper.

Tim eased off the accelerator. 'Don't worry about her, mate. We should've learned from the past and given her a wide berth from the get-go.'

The implicit comparison Penny had made between him and his duplicitous father brought bile to his throat. *I'm nothing like him*, he told himself, swallowing the acrid taste. Tim felt like punching something, the way he had fought through the pain all those years ago. His fists unclenched a little as he looked at Eddie, who was still mumbling out the window. They both hated fighting and if history was any judge, it certainly didn't impress women either. Teenage Mac had taken one look at his grazed knuckles and detention slip and fled in the opposite direction, no second chance. He swore under his breath.

You might not be a fraud, a fighter or a thief, but you're just as much of a fool as him if you thought McIntyre Park would ever be yours, Patterson. You should have fobbed Lara off the second she asked if you wanted to put in an offer.

Tim shook his head, mentally cataloguing the spirits cabinet. It would take more than beer to deliver sleep tonight.

Forty

Penny shoved the general store's glass door. The doorbell trilled
and the smell of warm pies and newspaper ink immediately
engulfed her. She stormed past shelves of overpriced toilet paper
and bags of flour. She wasn't here for shopping, she was here
to deliver a piece of her mind.

Penny rang the bell next to the cash register twice, craning
her neck to look into the staffroom at the back of the store.
Mrs Beggs, the long-standing postmistress and general store
operator, jumped out of her chair, looking Penny up and down
as she approached the counter. Penny opened the conversation,
but the postmistress overrode her words.

'Mrs Beggs, I—'

'By goodness, Penny, you're all grown up. No wonder those
postcards keep coming, with a figure like that.' Mrs Beggs
whistled as she reached across the lolly jars on the counter and
squeezed Penny's shoulder. Her warm touch and even warmer
reception caught Penny off guard, her scathing serve about
circulating gossip and reading other people's mail frozen on
her tongue as Mrs Beggs chattered away.

'How's Angus doing? I've been thinking of you poor girls. First your mum dying so young, now your dad so terribly injured. And with that big farm to run too, mmmm. Terrible, terrible,' said Mrs Beggs. She hummed as she bustled around behind the counter, pulling a wad of envelopes from a pigeonhole and scooping up a thick stack of newspapers, a handwritten 'McIntyre' printed on the top of each page.

Penny shook her head. The cloud of anger that had delivered her direct from the sheep yards to the post office was just waiting to erupt.

'Mrs Beggs, I need a word. You can't—'

'Ah, lovie, you don't have to say anything. I know you've been through a lot recently. What, with your illness and all your boyfriend troubles.'

'That's what I'm here to talk about. I don't appreci—' Penny was interrupted once again, this time by the jingling doorbell.

The shopkeeper looked over Penny's shoulder at the next customer. The rest of Penny's sentence faltered as she turned to a man standing behind her, trickles of blood covering his chin.

'Bandaids, Mrs Beggs? Where do you keep the damn things? I'm all out, and this scratch is bleeding like a stuck pig,' came the gruff voice from beneath a bloodied handkerchief.

Penny backed away from the bleeding man. *Looks like more than a scratch to me.* Penny's stomach weakened as the image of blood-smeared grass and Angus's gory ankle beamed into her mind. Her gut clenched and she felt like throwing up the remains of Bess Harvey's zucchini soup.

'Over on the back shelf, John. Behind the birthday cards. I'd love to chat more, Penny, but I can't stand here gabbing all day.'

Mrs Beggs pushed the bundle of mail and papers towards Penny, then reached under the counter and retrieved a wicker picnic basket.

Penny tried to calm her heaving stomach and steer the conversation back to its original direction.

'Mrs Beggs, please.'

But the woman soldiered on, talking over the top of Penny as if she hadn't heard her speak.

'Lookey here, I almost forgot. This basket is for you.'

Penny hesitated, unsure if she should accept a gift from someone who had caused her so much trouble, however well intentioned.

'Go on, take it. The ladies and I had a bake-up on the weekend 'specially for you and Angus.' Mrs Beggs pushed the basket towards her. A carton of eggs and a bag of biscuits sat on the top of a towering pile of plastic containers, fresh lemons and individually wrapped trays of cake.

'We're planning another bake-up next weekend too—that is, if you like what you see there. And Gilbert, my hubby, will come to help with the farm work each evening after he closes the servo.'

Penny looked at the older woman, her body rounded from years of readily available pastries and an undeniable talent for cooking. Mrs Beggs scanned Penny's tired face, her tongue still for the first time, as if she knew Penny's unspoken anger was impotent in the face of such generosity.

'Go on, there's a girl.' She reached over and gave Penny's arm another squeeze.

Penny swallowed a sigh as she accepted the heavy basket.

'Thank you, Mrs Beggs. That's very . . . generous. Please pass on my thanks to your friends. And Mr Beggs too.'

Mrs Beggs nodded, then shuffled between Penny and a shelf of second-hand books, calling to her customer as she weaved through her store.

'Hold on, John. Bandaids are over this way. It'll be easier if I just get them.'

ॐ

'Arghhh. Town water,' said Angus, grimacing as he swallowed a mouthful. He set the cup down onto the wheelie table, next to a messy half-finished crossword and a notepad full of illegible bullet points.

'If I don't choke to death on these horse tablets, then this sad excuse for water will surely finish me off. The dogs wouldn't even drink this fluoridated, chlorinated muck. Bring us a jug of rainwater when you're in next, eh, love?'

The return of his humour was as welcome as the steady rain that had fallen over the last week. Penny studied her father's face, his eyes glinting against the fading yellow and light-purple bruises, the jagged wound along his cheek that would be another daily reminder of his accident. *Not that he'll need reminding.* She looked at the plaster casts on the left side of his body, the firm sling around his right shoulder. *Just getting around and learning to rely on his left hand will be enough of a challenge.*

'You look like you're sizing me up for a coffin, Pen. Where's your smile, love?'

His left hand rested on hers, warm and steady. Weeks in the hospital had softened his hands; the customary calluses had all but disappeared. His muscles and presence seemed to have shrunk as well, and the outline under the sheets looked like a shell of the strong man who had roared off on the quad bike three weeks ago. *And here he is comforting me,* thought Penny. She forced a wan smile, unsurprised when it turned into a yawn. She'd had no trouble falling to sleep as rain pounded on the tin farmhouse roof, but it was the 2 a.m. wake-ups and worry-fests that were taking their toll.

'No coffin required, thank God. Though by the look of that list you've got right there, I might need to order one in

my size. A girl could die from exhaustion doing all those jobs
in a day. That's if I could read your left-handed writing.'

Angus picked up his notepad.

'The physio reckons it'll get neater. And these are the jobs
for the next month, not the week. Just give it to Tim, he'll
know what to do.'

Penny gritted her teeth at Tim's name and wondered why
Angus wasn't furious at his and Lara's plan for the farm. She
opened her mouth to ask him how he felt about the proposed
sale when loud footsteps echoed along the corridor.

Penny looked up to see Lara leaning against the doorframe.
She greeted Angus with a smile that didn't make its way to
Penny. Instead, Penny received a look that was as tight as the
bun that held her sister's hair hostage, a hint of challenge still
lingering in her red-rimmed eyes. Penny stayed in her seat,
determined not to be rushed out the door again as her sister
walked in.

'Are you okay, Lara? You look like death warmed up.' Angus
reached out and Penny watched her flinch at his gentle touch.

'I'm fine. It's nothing.'

Lara leaned in to kiss his cheek. As she straightened up,
Penny saw a purple shadow on her white skin, more vivid
than those on their father's body. Curiosity trumped anger as
she watched Lara discreetly tug her shirt down. *How can she
afford that fancy cupping therapy when she can barely afford
to rent a decent house? Would have thought she'd turn her
nose up at natural therapies.*

'How's it going in here, Dad? Sick of these four walls yet?'

Lara stood by the side of the bed, blocking Penny's view.
Her athletic body was toned under the thin layer of lycra
and Penny wondered whether she ran just so her body was
exhausted enough to sleep. *If my conscience was as guilty as
hers, I wouldn't sleep a wink.*

'I've wooed all the nurses with my rugged country charm, scoffed as much hospital food as one man can stomach and reread all the newspapers cover to cover. So yes, I guess you could say I've almost outstayed my welcome.'

'Hate to break it to you, Dad, but I think you'll be in for a few more months yet,' said Penny, leaning around Lara to meet Angus's eye.

Lara turned with a scowl.

'Give him some credit, Penny. Dad doesn't need negativity.'

'That's rich coming from you, Lara.'

'Righto, righto, girls. Give it a rest.'

Angus tapped his pen on the table. 'We all know you can't flog a dead horse.'

Penny stood up, wary of the defeat in Angus's voice and sick of Lara blocking her view.

'I've got loads of time to think in here. Maybe Lara's right. I've got Buckley's chance of running the farm anymore. It isn't much good to me if none of you girls are interested in farming.'

Lara lit up. 'I knew you'd see reason, Dad.'

Penny shook her head slowly, disbelief weighing on her shoulders.

'I never thought I'd hear you say that. You love McIntyre Park.' She watched him turn his head away to look out the window, but she knew his mind was 150 kilometres south.

'Let's explore all the options before you make that call. Please, Dad.'

Penny slipped past the nurse's station. She turned the handle of his door, finding Angus asleep. Late afternoon sunshine glowed through the large window, forming a golden square on his pillow that matched his yellow bruises. A posy of pink roses from Diana's driveway sat in a fresh vase next to a box of chocolates. Penny tossed a bag of wrinkly red grapes into the wastebasket. She knew who had delivered them and was pleased she hadn't been visiting at the same time.

She watched her father's peaceful breathing. His earlier comments had surprised her. *Yes, he's pretty injured and yes, it's true none of us have pursued a career in farming. But to even consider Lara's stupid suggestion? Outrageous.*

'Penny. You came back,' said Angus, his voice low and sleep-addled. 'Angie just left.'

'I'm only dropping you in some food. I'll let you get back to sleep.' He closed his eyes, a smile on his mouth. She walked towards the door, but his sleepy voice continued the conversation.

'You're a good daughter, Penny, always were. Used to think you'd run the farm. My little country girl, grown up to be a city woman. If anyone could do it, you could.'

Penny spun around, her heart hammering in her chest. His eyes were still closed, the only sound in the room the ticking of the cheap clock he'd asked her to buy. She watched his chest rise and fall as he slipped back into sleep, the smile still lingering on his lips. Penny's little twitch suddenly sprang to life again, flickering under the skin by her temples. Was there a grain of truth in his semi-lucid ramblings? *As a farmer's daughter, I make a pretty good marketing executive, but that's about the extent of it.* She'd closed the door on that life long ago . . . hadn't she?

Forty-one

Penny packed away the mop bucket and powered up her laptop, the smell of Pine O Cleen lingering on the freshly washed floors and polished benchtops. It had taken longer than she expected to whip the farmhouse back into a tidy state, stopping to study little mementos as she swept, mopped and dusted each room. Annabel's sewing basket was overflowing with half-finished projects that had been rifled through but not returned to the cupboard. Last year's Christmas cards sported six months of dust on the mantelpiece. Dog-eared farming brochures seemed to have multiplied in her father's absence.

But the real rabbit's hole had been the old photo album lying open on a coffee table in the master bedroom. Penny had lost an hour leafing through the pages, a smile tugging at her lips as she saw more photographs of her young self in overalls, in murky swimming pools, on horseback and in school concerts. Annabel's striking figure jumped off the page as she hugged her children, smiled for the camera and hammed it up with Angus. There were candid family photos, passport photos, school photos and a ghastly formal family portrait that had thankfully never reached the lounge room wall.

A batch of new emails jostled for her attention as soon as the laptop had fired up.

Georgie's email address was well represented. Penny opened the latest message, feeling guilty for neglecting her work emails in the wake of Angus's accident.

Dear Penny,

I hope your father is recovering. Assuming you received the bouquet of flowers from Boutique Media . . . ? I need to discuss your return from leave. Charlotte Harris has kindly offered to step into your role if you're no longer interested. Her work is receiving high praise from clients and colleagues alike. Can you please call me?

Georgie

Penny frowned as she reread the email. She'd extended her leave after the accident, but not once did she tell Georgie she was uninterested in the promotion. She rushed to the telephone, punching in the number she knew off by heart.

'Boutique Media. Anna speaking.'

'Anna, it's Penny. Is Georgie at her desk, please?'

'Hey, Penny. I haven't heard from you in ages. How are things with you?'

The young woman's voice sounded perkier and more confident than Penny remembered, and she felt pleased for her assistant. Anna seemed to have come a long way since the Valentino dress and coffee catastrophe.

'Excellent thanks, Anna. Dad's recovering from his operations and I'm strong as an ox.'

'All . . . right . . .' Anna's voice faltered, then lowered. 'To tell you the truth, I'd heard otherwise. I thought you'd be back by now, but Charlotte said you were going downhill again.'

Penny spluttered, sending a jet of tea across the dining table.

'Charlotte Harris? Downhill? That's ridiculous. My dad was in an accident, that's why I've been away longer. I've barely even spoken to Charlotte since she began with Boutique Media.'

Penny strode to the sink for a cloth, hearing the hesitation in her PA's reply.

'Given the client complaints, she thought you needed more time to recover, get back on the ball.'

Penny sat down at the dining table, tossing the dishcloth at the puddle of tea she had slopped across the worn surface.

'What complaints? Is this *Candid Camera* or something?' She had managed to push Charlotte to the back of her mind for the last few weeks, but hearing the woman's name made her angry again.

'Put me on with Georgie. I've got to sort this out.' Penny fumed, trying to make sense of the conversation.

'Penny, darling. I've tried to call several times. The home phone rings out and your mobile is always switched off.' Georgie tutted down the phone line and Penny scrambled to adopt a professional tone.

'Georgie, I feel like there's been a miscommunication. I haven't received any flowers from Boutique Media, I'm not going downhill as some people seem to think and I know nothing about this alleged complaint.' Her words came out fast and firm. 'Please fill me in.'

Penny's temper surged as Georgie outlined her understanding of the situation and the incorrect details of her health and priorities, as reported by Charlotte.

'The client complaint was only verbal, mind you, and you can't shoot the messenger. Charlotte has been invaluable in your absence, Penny. You would get along well if you made an effort, darling.'

Penny glared at the phone.

'Vince knows her well enough for the both of us, Georgie. We certainly won't be sharing an office when I get back. I can't believe she'd stoop this low.'

'Let's not allow a little indiscretion to get in the way of what's good for Boutique Media. You were very focused on that promotion and still have an excellent shot at it. Do you still want to apply?'

It was Penny's turn to hesitate. Hercules's woolly head bobbed past the kitchen window as he careened around the backyard. She stood up and shut the photo album on the far end of the table, carefully constructing a reply in her head before speaking.

'I most certainly do, Georgie. I don't plan on giving up my city life or everything I've ever worked for. I'm trying to find a way of keeping things here afloat too, if you'll allow me to make a few special requests?'

Undeterred by Georgie's hesitant response, Penny took a deep breath and began to outline her plan.

Dry food rattled into the dog bowls. Penny gave each of the kelpies a pat as she chained them up for the evening. Afternoon rain had filled their water bowls to the brim and she tucked the food bowls under their kennel verandahs to stop them getting waterlogged.

Penny dodged puddles as she passed the machinery shed and skirted around the house yard to the chook house. She swapped two scoops of grain and a bucket of kitchen scraps for several fresh eggs. Light rain danced on the strong wind, masking the sound of the car until it had pulled up into the driveway. Penny squinted against the rain and wind, her shirt folded up like a pouch to hold the eggs. Between the wisps of hair blowing over her face, she could just make out the shiny boots, cream moleskins and white shirt of their visitor.

'Can I help you?'

She walked towards him, abandoning the direct route to the porch that offered respite from the weather. Penny wasn't in the habit of inviting strangers into the house, especially ones who looked like they were trying to replicate an R.M. Williams catalogue. The man raised a clipboard over his head to protect his neatly parted hair and stuck out a hand. Penny stared at it.

'Sorry, I haven't got a free hand. I'm Penny McIntyre. Who are you after?'

'G'day. Joe from Western District Property Valuations. I'm doing an assessment and valuation of McIntyre Park.'

'You're kidding me? You heard Dad was in an accident, did you? Thought you'd better get in early? You can nick off, you vulture.' The eggs clinked as she took a step towards him, wanting to slap the tape measure from his belt loop.

He inched back towards the squeaky-clean car, his hand fumbling with the keys as he eyed her warily.

'It's okay, Pen, he's got an appointment,' said Angie, stepping out from the passenger's side. Penny gawked at her younger sister.

'Angie?'

'Lara organised the valuation, but she was called into work. She asked me to come instead.'

Penny clutched the eggs to her body, trying to fathom how Lara had sucked Angie into doing her dirty work.

'She can't just bulldoze Dad into selling. We haven't explored the options yet. I wouldn't put it past Lara to pull a stunt like this, but I can't believe you'd go along with it, Angie.'

Angie swiped the rain from her face, avoiding Penny's eye.

'Just let him do his job without a scene. Then we'll all know where we stand.'

'Where we stand? I'll tell you where we stand, Angie. On fourth-generation McIntyre land. This soil is practically running through our veins, whether we like it or not. I don't know where Lara's bank account is sitting, or yours for that matter, but obviously those dollar signs are clouding everyone's judgement.'

Forty-two

Penny sipped at the wine, aware the likelihood of Angie joining her was declining as rapidly as the level of sauvignon blanc in her glass. An hour had passed since she had texted her sister a peace offering.

No use waiting any longer, or I'll be finishing that bottle of wine for dinner. Penny took hold of the borrowed Tupperware dish and loaded it into the microwave.

Whether Mrs Beggs' 'apricot royale' casserole contained chicken or pork was a mystery, but the smell made her mouth water in anticipation. Penny looked dolefully at the two places she had set and spooned a portion onto just one plate as the back door slammed. Relief washed over her. *Thank God. For a minute I thought she'd actually sided with Lara.*

'Better late than never—I thought you'd gone to the dark side, Angie,' Penny said, her frown clearing to a smile as she pulled the empty plate towards her.

Tim shook the rain off as best he could, but he continued to drip across the laundry floor as he padded inside the farmhouse. His stomach growled as he inhaled the smell. It was like walking into Nanna Pearl's kitchen when she dished up her famous hotpot. Penny stood with her back to the laundry, dishing up food. Plastic freezer containers filled the sink instead of saucepans and chopping boards. He smiled at the pile of gravy-soaked green capsicum on a side plate. Whoever had cooked those meals mustn't have known about her dietary preferences. He pulled himself up and dropped the smile. *You don't know much about her either these days, Patterson.*

'Sorry to interrupt, Mac. I'm just after Pete's phone number, I need him to give me a hand.'

Tim watched Penny turn. It wasn't hard to read her expression. He glanced across and saw the table set for two. Whoever she was expecting, it certainly wasn't him. Water beaded down his saturated shirt, but it felt colder inside the farmhouse than out in the pouring rain. He'd avoided her all week, limiting farm updates to text messages and bringing his lunch box to work, but he couldn't skip this visit. A flat phone battery, a bogged ute and a busy schedule had made sure of that.

'You? I'm still not happy with you, Tim. Especially when you're dripping all over my clean floor,' she said, pointing a finger at the puddle of water pooling beneath him. He shoved his hands into his back pockets, mopping the damp spot with his odd socks.

'I figured. Are you going to let me explain, or just trust the rumour mill?'

He watched her pinch the bridge of her nose and saw the fight go out of her features.

'Don't bother. It's a moot point, seeing the farm isn't even for sale. Let's just leave it. What do you need help with?'

Tim's eyebrow flickered. Her reaction was a lot more restrained than her earlier take on the topic. He watched her stick her chin out a little higher, a measure of steel underlining her quiet words.

'Ute's bogged in the paddock behind the shearing shed. Pete'll have to yank me out with the tractor.'

'You don't need Pete. I'll grab a jacket.'

Tim wrapped his large hand around his chin.

'You driven a tractor anytime recently?' He studied her face. 'How about you steer the ute, and I'll hop on the tractor?'

Penny drew herself up taller as she walked towards him, her nose reaching the top of his shoulders. She tilted her head to look directly at him.

'Just like riding a bike.'

The tone of her voice brooked no further discussion. Tim watched in surprise as she skirted around his puddle towards the coat rack, and pulled on Angus's Driza-Bone. She tucked her hair up into a beanie and tugged on a pair of elastic-sided workboots, the first time since high school that he'd seen her wearing anything other than fancy labels or perfectly pressed seams. Although he was still angry with her, he felt another tug of attraction as he watched her slip back into her old skin. He pulled his damp boots on and held the door open for her.

'Some things you only need to be taught once, then you've got it for life,' she said, ducking under his arm and looking a hell of a lot like the determined teenager he once knew.

Penny pulled into the parking spot close to the top of the ridge and tugged at the ute's handbrake. She looked up at the rocks towering above her. From a distance, the mountain range appeared blue, but up close it unfolded as a patchwork of chocolate, ochre, slate and toffee, peppered with little outcrops of vivid green and bravely balancing boulders.

She left the keys in the ignition and headed for a faded white post marking the trail to Wildflower Ridge. Weeds and creeping greens had claimed the narrow gravel track as their own. Penny found her way through the grasses guided by memory. The crisp June air burned in her throat as she trekked the steady incline.

Little birds fled and drop-tail lizards scampered out of her way, unused to company on this side of the mountain. Overgrown branches pushed at her body, trying to keep the mountainside for themselves. Penny slipped defiantly between them, turning her back to the cliff face as she looked out over McIntyre Park. The clouds had disappeared, leaving sapphire expanses and streaks of strong yellow sunshine. The distant rumble of neighbouring farms' tractors floated across the paddocks; they looked as tiny as the little cast-iron toys Leo, Elliot and Harry played with. Satisfaction buzzed inside her as she recalled the way she had handled the tractor last night. Her hands had known exactly which levers to pull as soon as she'd sat down in the cab, gaining reluctant approval from Tim. It hadn't taken them long to remove the ute from its boggy confines.

Penny reached the end of the barely-there path, resting her hand on a final white post that pointed directly upwards. A damp patch rubbed underneath her backpack as she pulled herself up onto the first rock. Dirt and sand slipped between her fingers, coating her jeans with fine dust as she scrambled towards her goal. Several sandstone boulders later, she reached the top of Wildflower Ridge. The freesia stalks were up but not yet blooming, and wildflowers were still another few months from their annual display. Even without the showy blossoms, the view was captivating.

Penny ran her hand over the smooth surface of her mother's memorial rock, tracing the simple lettering on the plaque: *Annabel McIntyre 1955–2002.*

She spread her jacket across the ground, its purple fabric standing out against the dewy grass. The rock warmed her back as she leaned against it. Birds called around her and eagles soared past on warm air currents.

If she closed her eyes, Penny could almost go back to the first time she had visited the outcrop as a child. Banished from school with chickenpox, she had been out exploring the walking tracks with her mum. Penny remembered being enamoured with the little goat track that led to the wildflowers, the great rock and the spectacular vista. The way she had stuffed wildflowers into Annabel's ponytail, her mother giggling as she added more to her buttonhole. Little had she known they would scatter Annabel's ashes there seven years later, after a car accident stole her from their lives. A familiar weight of guilt settled on Penny's shoulders as she remembered the argument they'd had just before the accident, the hurtful words thrown between them. Annabel's insistence she at least consider a university degree, and Penny's determination to start an on-farm apprenticeship. *Would you still be here today, Mum, if we hadn't argued?* Tears had clouded her mother's vision as she'd backed her car out the driveway.

Penny had tried to assuage her guilt the best way she knew how, by honouring her mother's last wishes. And as much as it had hurt to shelve her own dreams and aspirations, she'd gained a strong sense of satisfaction from channelling her grief into high distinctions and top honours at university, then an award-winning career.

'I miss you, Mum,' said Penny, her words floating to the edge of the bluff and flicking away into the wind. 'I'm sorry I haven't visited, but I'm back now. I know it's not what you wanted, but I think it's time to set a few things straight.'

Forty-three

Penny shuffled uncomfortably, her bum tender from too many hours in the stiff plastic chair. Usually she was up beside Angus, but today she was relegated to the foot of the bed. Pete gave Diana a kiss and squeezed his way out of the narrow room. He hoisted Leo onto his shoulders and gave them all a mock salute.

'Right, I'll take these munchkins to the playground for an hour.'

'Thanks, Pete. Make sure they wear their jackets. Cameron, help keep an eye on your brothers. You too, Evie.'

The cousins scattered down the corridor, arguing over the first ride on the flying fox.

The hospital room was quiet in their wake, each of the McIntyre daughters waiting for their father to start the discussion that had already driven a wedge between them.

'Righto, girls, I'm all ears. What are we gonna do about this farm?'

Angie toyed with her handbag clasp as if she were expecting a rabbit to jump out at any minute. Lara leaned in for the first word, just as Penny opened her mouth.

'Let's sell.'

'Don't sell.'

Angus fixed Lara with a wistful gaze, then Penny.

'It would have to be you two on opposite sides of the coin. What about you, Angie? Diana?'

Diana stepped in, her voice measured.

'I thought we could offer to buy part of the farm and share-farm the rest, but Pete's got our nest egg invested elsewhere. I think he's more interested in managing the stock agency than managing a farm,' she said, her lips pursed with disappointment.

'Don't worry yourself, love. We all know Pete's a great bloke and a top stocky. But he's never been much of a farmer. Plus, you've got your hands full with all those kids. Angie?'

Angie looked up from her lap, unwrapping a chocolate bar. Penny noticed the absence of enthusiasm that usually oozed from Angie's every pore.

'I don't know. It would be terrible to see a random share-farmer run it into the ground. Then again, it's too big an asset to leave in limbo. I can see sense in selling.'

Angie's ambivalence hit Penny like a punch in the stomach. She gaped at her little sister, not sure she knew the woman she was sitting next to. *How has Lara poisoned her so quickly? Where's her backbone, where's her fight?*

Lara stepped in, her voice animated. 'There's nothing to gain by leasing it, Dad, considering your injuries. It wouldn't be the same living in the farmhouse while someone else worked your land, bred from your sheep. If you sold, you'd have a fresh start. I think Tim can get a deposit together and I certainly wouldn't say no to an early inheritance. If not for me, do it for Evie.'

Penny reeled around at Lara.

'That's a low blow, Lara. Sam's tight-arse tendencies have really rubbed off on you, haven't they? Keep the children out of this; they love it as much as we do. Well, as much as some of us do.'

Lara bristled. Penny looked out the window, ashamed at her jibe.

'It's a win-win for everyone, Penny. Dad can buy a smaller, low-maintenance house, go on a cruise every year for the rest of his life, get an automatic ute to better suit his arm. And if he decided to give us an early inheritance, which would be a very generous and helpful option, we'd all benefit,' said Lara.

Penny met Angus's eye, his resigned expression softening as she shook her head resolutely. Vince could wait. Work would manage. Her apartment would still be there in six or twelve months, however long it took Angus to get back on his feet.

She took a deep breath.

'No. McIntyre Park doesn't need to be sold, not if I can help it. I'll run the farm until we find a better solution.'

Penny ignored the snort of laughter from Lara's side of the room. A flicker of hope flashed across Angus's face as he held her gaze.

'What about the city? Your fancy job won't keep while you mop up after my mess. And from what Angie's told me, that boyfriend of yours is already a liability. You sure you want to leave him unchaperoned for any longer?'

Penny glared at Angie again, the knife of betrayal wrenching deeper in her stomach.

'Let me worry about Vince. Georgie has agreed to a trial job-share arrangement, so I can work from home and still apply for the promotion. I'll make it work, trust me. Have I failed at any of the goals I've set for myself yet?' The thrill of her announcement gained momentum and an unintended edge of cockiness wiped the smirk from Lara's face.

She held her breath as Angus digested her decision.

'Okay,' he said, rubbing a hand along his jaw. 'That could work. I'll give you a shot at managing the farm on two conditions. One, you have to make sure the on-farm ram sale goes smoothly in September—it's our bread and butter and we're renowned for running a top-notch event. And two, you have to keep Tim on as leading farmhand.'

Penny's elation faltered at the second clause. Years of event management, marketing launches and client functions meant the ram sale was a no-brainer, but the idea of working day in, day out with Tim was unthinkable.

'Can't we hire someone else? One of the Guthrie boys from down the road? Tim isn't exactly my cup of tea.'

'Be practical, Penny. Tim knows the place almost as well as me, and he's a hard worker. He won't let us down.'

Penny looked around the room at each of her sisters. Diana nodded her support, Angie looked out the window as she devoured another chocolate bar and Lara watched in amusement.

'She's delusional, Dad. Look how quickly she ran away to the city after school. She's pulling your leg.'

Penny stood up, indignant.

'If I say I'm going to do something, Lara, I do it. Last thing I want to see is McIntyre Park sold. Not to any Tim, Dick or Harry. I'm running this farm, even if it means working alongside Tim Bloody Patterson.'

Forty-four

Penny skipped up the farmhouse steps and shook the rain off her jacket as she walked along the verandah. Butterflies inside her stomach nipped and tickled at the same time, excitement intertwined with fear.

A vase of crimson gerberas waited on the doorstep, bright in the overcast afternoon. Their presence threw a new set of butterflies into the mix, ambivalent ones that ducked and weaved, asking if she was doing the right thing. She opened the card.

Hey babe, hurry home soon. I've got something waiting for you. xx V

The colourful petals waved like little red flags, reminding her she still had to break the news to Vince. And for a tiny moment, an image of Charlotte opening the white-ribboned ring box whipped into her brain. She took a deep breath, hoping her decision to stay on the farm wouldn't compromise all of her other dreams, and went inside to call Vince. His voicemail clicked in. She hung up.

🍇

The wind rushed past Penny's bare arms as she thundered down the driveway, exhilarated by the speed. It was just what she needed to blow out the cobwebs and chase away the fog from another restless sleep.

'It's got more go than the old quad,' she yelled to the salesman, as she rolled to a halt and switched off the UTV ignition. 'The rollover protection looks sturdy and we could fit a sick sheep on the back, or at least the kelpies and a few square bales of hay,' she continued, climbing off and circling the vehicle for another look.

A hard top and three seats were sandwiched between a short bonnet and small tray; the whole thing perched on four chunky wheels and an exposed suspension. *It looks like something the Special Forces would use on covert operations through the jungle.* Penny smiled at the thought as she removed her helmet, deliberately ignoring the fact that her jauntiest mission on the vehicle was likely to be collecting fly-blown sheep and spraying out insecticide.

Brian unclipped his seatbelt, his neatly pressed shirt and jeans now covered with mud spatters from Penny testing out the traction through a shallow, boggy drain. His bushy moustache burst free of its confines as he removed his helmet and wiped the muck off his helmet visor.

'Probably not a good day to wear my white shirt, was it?' He laughed, looking down at his splotched clothes. 'Not to worry, it was worth it to see the views from your top paddocks, Penny. Those panoramas are priceless,' he said, wiping the dirt off his arms.

'Yep, they're hard to beat, Brian. Though you should see them from the top of the ridge—even more spectacular. The Ranger ate those rocky creek beds for breakfast, didn't even falter on the steep inclines.'

'You'd be making a good choice. A Polaris UTV is an investment in your farm's safety. At least you'll get a government
rebate. They're throwing millions at this quad bike scheme,
and a Ranger side-by-side should earn you about a thousand
dollars back.'

She did the sums in her head as Brian rode the vehicle up
the ramps onto his trailer. The final bill would be close to
$20,000, and she was still wary about spending so much of
her father's money without his express approval.

*Should I head to the hospital, ask Dad's opinion, or just
go ahead and wear the consequences? He did give me the
chequebook*, she told herself, *and safety should be a priority.*

'It handles well, better than I expected. I think you've almost
sold me on it, Brian,' she said begrudgingly, trying to get her
conscience over the line.

'I'm sure Angus would love the opportunity to check the
sheep with you. He couldn't do that comfortably on a four-
wheeler, but he could with the type of legroom you have here.
We could have one to you by the end of this week, or if you
wanted this display model, we could knock a grand off it,
plus the promotional discount. I can have it cleaned up, fully
serviced and back here by 10 a.m. tomorrow.'

She rocked back on the heels of her boots, weighing up
the risk. *Who's running this farm? Me. Who's making the
decisions? Me. Who's going to wear the blame if this financial
year sends us bust? Me. Well then, make a call*, she told herself.

'I guess it is tax deductible, right? And I'd be silly to miss
out on your only sale of the year.' She reached out her hand
to seal the deal.

Brian's smile widened as he pumped her hand and clapped
her on the shoulder. 'Absolutely, Penny. I knew you were a
smart woman.'

𝖃

Tim and Eddie unloaded the final boxes of drench from the back of the ute and closed the machinery shed door. Squinting in the low sunlight, Tim did a double take as he watched Penny walk over, her frame swamped by Angus's Driza-Bone. Rusty bounded over to greet her and she was soon surrounded by all the working dogs. She ruffled their heads as they sniffed at her mud-spattered jeans.

Eddie leaned in for a hug as if it had been months since he'd last seen her, instead of a week.

'Penny, Penny, Penny. More cakes, Penny?'

'Farm work to do today, mate. Meet your new manager—ta-da.'

Mac, managing the farm? You've got to be kidding me. Tim ran a hand through his hair incredulously, watching her pirouette in a pair of elastic-sided boots.

'What? Since when?' Tim couldn't hide the surprise in his voice. Kylie Minogue running for prime minister would have been less of a shock than this news. He wished Angus had at least called to give him the heads-up.

'Since last night. Don't look so worried. I'm a fast learner. It should all come flooding back quickly.'

'But . . .' Tim's brain whirred on overdrive as he tried to comprehend the new working dynamics, the minefields that lay in wait.

'For how long? A week, a month?' *Until the bright lights beckon, or Vince crooks his little finger?* A surge of frustration pulsed through his body. The thought of someone playing farmer on a property he would have loved to buy was a tough pill to swallow. His jaw clenched as he shoved his hands into his pockets.

'Until we can sort out a better arrangement that doesn't involve selling McIntyre Park. I want to make this work, Tim.

And Dad says you're a non-negotiable. Can you teach me the ropes?' Penny stuck out her hand.

He looked at her flushed face, her sparkling eyes, the speckles of mud that blended in with her freckles. *So she already tried to negotiate me out of the arrangement? Bloody hell.* Working at McIntyre Park was a far cry from owning it, but not many local landowners offered above-average wages, treated their farmhands with the respect and gratitude that Angus offered, or extended the same courtesy to Eddie. Tim reached out a hand, ignoring the sparks that came from her touch, and nodded silently. *At least I'll be here to pick up the pieces when she comes to her senses and runs back to the city.*

He turned and walked over to the machinery shed, following the urge to fix something or pull something apart.

'Oh, and keep your eye out for Brian tomorrow—he's collecting the old quad bike and dropping off a replacement.'

Tim stopped abruptly, remembering the ute he'd passed on the way from town.

'Don't tell me you've been talked into one of those UTVs?'

Penny dusted her hands on the front of her jeans, nodding.

'My first executive decision. You can't put a price on safety. I manage multi-million-dollar marketing campaigns for a living, surely I can make a reasonable decision about a farm vehicle we urgently need.'

Tim pressed his lips together. *Less than twenty-four hours in the manager's chair and she's already making rash decisions. Maybe job hunting wouldn't be such a bad idea after all.*

The phone display illuminated the dark bedroom as it rang loudly through the dark house, still set to the volume Angus preferred so he could hear it when he was out in the yard.

Penny rolled over to answer it, rubbing grains of sleep out of her eyes.

'McIntyre Park, Penny speaking.'

A soft laugh came from the other end.

'Vince, do you know what time it is?'

'You weren't sleeping, were you, babe? Sorry.'

She pulled the blanket up higher on her chest, wishing she'd put another log of red gum on the fire before bed. They were only a few weeks into winter, but the cold snap that had failed to bring rain and instead left a layer of ice on the stock trough indicated they were in for a chilly winter.

'Between trips to the Horsham hospital and working through Dad's to-do list, I'm in bed early these days.'

'To-do list? The apple hasn't fallen far from the tree, I can tell. Surely your old man doesn't expect you to do all his dirty work? What about that lackey who answers the phone like he owns the joint? He slacking off already?'

She yawned again. 'Tim? He's about as far from a slacker as you can get. It's long days for everyone at the moment.'

'Lucky you're coming home soon—you'll be back into your usual routine in no time, Pen, nursing a leisurely scotch instead of being tucked up in bed at 10 p.m.'

Penny rolled onto her side, wondering what else he'd forgotten. He was the only one who liked an evening scotch; she always stuck to wine. His slip made it easier to say the next few sentences.

'I'm going to stay a little longer, Vince. Manage the farm for a bit.' She'd hoped to be a bit more awake for this particular discussion, but she was alert enough to hear the incredulous laugh down the phone line. All of a sudden, she hoped he would choke on the scotch, spraying it across the pristine white sofa he'd insisted on.

'What's funny about that, Vince?'

'Farm manager . . . Baby, you're the fastest-rising corporate star in Melbourne. Before you got sick, your wage was higher than mine, and that's saying something. You were made for suits and heels, not . . . not CWA meetings and sheep shit.'

Penny pushed herself up into a sitting position, trying to keep her voice even. She knew he wasn't going to throw her a celebration party for her new position, like the cocktail extravaganza he'd suggested when she nailed the last Boutique Media promotion, but she didn't expect downright derision.

'What are we in, the 1950s? It's only temporary, while Dad works out what he's going to do. You can come visit on weekends, and I'll head up to the city a few times. It'll be fine.'

She heard him take a sip of scotch as he considered her news.

'Well, I won't say I'm thrilled, but it sounds like you've made your mind up . . .'

She nodded into the dark, knowing ten-year-old Penny would be pretty damn proud of thirty-three-year-old Penny at this very moment.

Forty-five

Penny jumped as her mobile phone trilled in her pocket, the synthetic music jarring with the calling sheep and twittering birds. The shearing shed buzz was just audible over the sound of the animals. *Angie?* It felt like an age since Angie had last returned her calls or visited the farmhouse. *Maybe she was finally coming to her senses?*

She tried not to feel disappointed when Jade's name appeared on the screen.

'Hey stranger, where have you been the last two weeks? I've been trying to track you down, see how the boss-girl is faring. Why are you shouting?'

'Sorry, I forgot the reception is almost decent now they've boosted the phone tower. I've only just started getting service anywhere other than my bedroom windowsill. It's a luxury.'

Penny cradled the phone between her shoulder and her ear as she latched the gate behind her. The freshly shorn sheep bounded around friskily, happy to be rid of the weight of their wool. She clapped her hands, urging the stragglers at the back to join the mob.

'Sorry I missed your calls, I meant to get back to you. We're in the thick of shearing now, and I pretty much fall into bed at the end of the day. How are things?'

'Nothing new. Nose to the grindstone, smashing it at the gym so I can still party on the weekends. It's not the same without you though. That boxing class is torture. I can barely believe you suggested it and then dumped me.'

'I'm sure you're still fit as a fiddle. My fitness, on the other hand . . . you wouldn't be impressed. Manoeuvring wool bales and squatting down to pick up dags off the floor is the extent of my workouts this week. But at least my biceps are impressive.'

Penny shielded her face against the glaring sun, watching the dogs funnel the mob through the narrow gateway up ahead. She could hear traffic in the background from Jade's end.

'Sounds like you're getting into the swing of things there, Pen. I probably wouldn't recognise you without your make-up and heels. Don't tell me you wear braids and a checkered shirt too?'

Penny looked down at her work shirt, grinning at the criss-crossing pink and navy lines.

'Can't confirm or deny that accusation, but you'll be pleased to know my hair is blow-dried as usual, not a braid in sight and my make-up is intact as always. No need to drop my standards just because I'm outside the city limits. In fact, some of those roustabouts in the shed could do with a little foundation and blusher.' Penny laughed, the lightness of the conversation filling the void from Angie's absence. She entertained Jade with stories from the woolshed as she finished walking the sheep to their paddock. '. . . but at least the shearers are all wearing shoes this week, and the wool's coming off nicely.'

'I have no idea what you're talking about, but you sound happy.'

Penny laughed again, leaning against a fence post.

'Yep, it just gets under your skin somehow and then *bam* . . . the next thing you know, you're ordering a felt hat to match your new flannel shirt. It's the least I could do for Dad. It would rip his heart out to sell right now.'

'Good for you, Pen. How's Vince? I saw him out on the town last weekend. Is everything okay there?'

Clouds skirted past the sun, plunging the paddock in shade. Penny kicked at the ground, using her boot to dislodge a leafy weed.

'He's a bit sulky at the moment. Thinks I've lost my marbles staying here longer than absolutely necessary. He'll come round,' Penny said, the false cheer hollow even to her ears. *He'll have to.* 'Look, I'd better go, Jade. I'll be back in Melbourne soon for a client meeting. We'll catch up then.'

'Righto, cowgirl. Which reminds me, you can call off the search for a cowboy to bring home with you. I've found a winner this time. A new guy just moved here from Tassie. I think I found him the second he reached the mainland, can't wait to introduce you soon.'

Jade's excitement added an extra bounce to Penny's step as she headed back to the shed. Diana had been right about the lack of eligible bachelors in the district. No matter how many nice things the old ladies in town had to say about Tim Patterson, she wasn't blind to his sneaky ways. *I was right all along, and there's no way I'd be setting him up with Jade. Not if he was the last bloke on Earth . . . Because you still have feelings for him*, a little voice whispered as she shut the gates and called the dogs back in her direction, ready to shift the next mob of sheep. She shook her head. It had nothing to do with emotions and everything to do with trust.

※

The bottle of red wine was empty by the time Penny and Diana retired to the lounge room. The kitchen was spotless, the floors swept, the boys bathed and listening to Pete's bedtime stories.

Penny slumped onto the couch. Her back was sore from another day in the shearing shed, but the offer of dinner at Diana and Pete's was too good to pass up.

'So, fill me in on Vince,' said Diana, perching on the edge of the couch. 'He stopped moping yet?'

Penny leaned back against the puffy cushions.

'Nope, he's still campaigning for a weekend away. Which would be great if we weren't in the middle of shearing. At least that's still tracking well. I don't know what all the fuss is about.'

'Tim could probably handle things by himself for a few days. Sounds like everything's on schedule.'

'I told Dad I'd run the farm. I can't just slip away for a dirty weekend at one of the busiest times of the year. Vince has to suck it up.'

Pete popped his head around the lounge room door, a new bottle of wine in his hands.

'Fancy another, ladies? Diana, the boys are after a goodnight kiss.'

Diana pulled herself off the couch. Penny shook her head, getting up to leave.

'No thanks, Pete. I've got to get home—another big day of shearing tomorrow.'

Pete settled down in the armchair opposite Penny, flicking on the television behind her. Football commentary filled the room as he topped up Diana's glass and poured one for himself.

'Yeah, guess you'll need it finished before the storm hits next week.'

Penny hesitated, one eyebrow raised. 'Storm? My weather app doesn't say anything about a storm. I know there was meant to be a front Monday, but apparently, they've down-graded it to patchy rainfall. Only a 5 per cent chance of rain for the whole week.'

'Not according to the Bureau of Meteorology.' Pete pulled a phone from his top pocket. 'Now they're tipping plenty of rain Monday, Tuesday and Wednesday. You might get your dirty weekend after all,' he said with a wink.

'It can't rain, I've already got the week planned. The shearers are due somewhere else the following week and I don't want shearing to run into lambing. The window between the two is close enough already.'

'Listen to you, Penny Mac. We'll make a farm girl out of you yet.' Pete laughed, affecting a deep voice. 'Obey thy weather gods. Delete all weather apps. Monitor thy official BOM site, and ye shall be rewarded.'

She shushed him as she scrambled to access the Bureau of Meteorology site, cursing her reliance on the weather app that had sufficed for the last decade.

Penny pushed the wethers into the sheep yards, slamming the gate shut behind them with a few choice words. The mob had split and doubled back several times as she rounded them up, making the dogs work twice as hard and the task twice as long. Her frustration levels had risen every time the lead sheep rolled his eyes at the open gateway, splintering the group when he baulked. Had he not already been castrated, Penny would have happily volunteered to stretch a little green ring around his testicles until they withered and fell off. She was surprised Angus hadn't already sent the troublesome ringleader off to market.

'You ladies were like angels compared to those idiots,' said Penny, as she walked passed the heavily pregnant ewes she had penned up earlier that morning. Dark clouds cast shadows over the farmhouse, turning the pale weatherboards a charcoal-grey in the distance. She was clinging to the chance of forecast winds blowing off any early rain, disregarding Tim's suggestion of rescheduling the shearers for later in the week

I don't care if Tim likes it or not—these ewes will be lambing on the boards if they're not shorn soon.

The lead shearer pulled the radio's power cord out of the wall, plunging the shed into silence. He bustled the appliance under his muscular arm, shaking his head. His team packed up their handpieces quietly, their singlets and jeans as clean as they had been upon arrival.

Penny headed to the door, her small body silhouetted against the cloudy sky. She pointed to the clock above the tally board. 'It's only 8 a.m. How about we give it another hour and then see if the wool's dry enough? Please?'

A young wool classer snickered, earning him a clip around the ear from his boss.

'Pull your head in, boy. Her old man's banged up in hospital, and it's not her fault she can't tell a damp sheep from a dry one.'

Penny cringed at his pitying tone.

He turned to her, twisting his faded terry-towelling hat in his hands. 'Sorry Miss, we've all shorn two sheep each and had a vote. They're too wet.'

'How about tomorrow? Surely they'll be good to go tomorrow?'

'Let's say Wednesday. Won't waste my time trekking over when they're still likely to be wet. Can't afford to have a crew of sick contractors.'

Penny stepped aside to let them walk past. She watched them load into a collection of utes and four-wheel drives, the laughter between two young lads drifting up to the shed.

'She's blind as a welder's dog if she can't see the moisture in that wool,' said one, his cocky grin faltering as he caught her glaring at him.

Penny turned and stormed back into the shed, avoiding Tim's gaze. Embarrassed by her own impatience and misguided optimism, she yanked plastic containers from the fridge and shoved the biscuits and sausage rolls into the freezer. The scones she had got up at 5 a.m. to make would be rock-hard by the time the shearers returned. Penny tossed them into the bin.

'Chooks would be happy with those. And you could save a few for smoko,' said Tim, walking into the tearoom.

'I'm not in the mood for "I told you so", Tim.'

Normally, she would have set them aside as animal fodder instead of landfill, but a stubborn streak reigned and she continued to pitch the fluffy golden mounds into the bin.

Tim watched her take her anger out on the baked goods, recalling the way she'd overruled his decision to cancel this morning's shearing. He could handle hard yakka, shrug off poor weather and manage bad-tempered animals or Eddie's meltdowns. But damned if he knew how to deal with Penny McIntyre in a flap. He could see she was trying, and her work ethic was better than he'd expected, but he didn't understand her impatience to keep things to such a rigid schedule. It reminded him of Stella and her relentless quest for perfection.

'Farms don't run like clockwork, Mac. Calling shearers when the sheep are blatantly wet just makes us look bad.'

She spun around, and he was surprised to see the fire in her eyes.

'I thought you'd be happy to see me stuff up. Aren't you still desperate for the first option on the farm?'

Her words burned like a branding iron. *Am I that transparent?* A nibble of guilt lodged in his body as he realised his shot at owning McIntyre Park hinged entirely on her failure.

Am I really that type of guy? Tim closed his eyes, torn between his dreams and the man he wanted to be.

'Too right, I'd love to buy this place for Eddie and me. But regardless of what you might think, Mac, taking advantage of anyone or setting someone up for failure is not my style.'

He kept his words soft but felt the hardness clench around his heart, daring her to challenge his integrity. 'I'll keep this farm running as best I can in your dad's absence, but we need to work as a team. Okay?'

He watched doubt flicker across her face, vulnerability quickly replaced by determination.

She jutted her chin forward, meeting his eye. 'Okay.'

Tim turned and whistled to the dogs as he took the shearing shed steps two at a time. If he didn't know any better, he'd swear Penny McIntyre had just entrusted him with her confidence. *Am I really prepared to set aside my dreams to meet Mac's expectations?*

Forty-six

'How are things in the rehab ward, Dad? Your room's a bit bigger at least,' said Penny, leaning down to kiss Angus on the cheek. She refreshed the fruit bowl, topped up his jug with rainwater and unloaded new magazines onto his bedside table.

'Don't fuss, love. I can reach them just fine. It's a bit quieter than the acute ward too. Taking a bit to get used to this contraption, though.' Angus jerked his thumb towards the wheelchair. 'I much prefer hobbling around like a cripple with the single crutch instead of going in circles in that thing. The moon boot weighs a ton, but at least I'm mobile. Well, semi-mobile.'

He caught her staring and reached up self-consciously to touch the jagged scar on his cheek, tufts of stubble surrounding the raised red welt.

'It's not easy shaving left-handed either, but I'm having a crack. Don't want to scare off all the new nurses at this end of the building.'

He winked, earning a laugh from Penny.

'Lara said there were a few hold-ups at the farm. Got all those sheep shorn yet?'

Penny shook her head, her futile attempts to stick to the schedule still a sore point. It didn't surprise her that Lara was keeping him abreast of the delays.

'Hopefully, the rain stops soon. The sheep are still too wet to shear. But it's all going well otherwise. The community support was excellent those first few weeks, and I haven't managed to run the place into the ground yet.'

'Good to hear, love. I was a bit worried you might have bitten off more than you can chew after that Ross River fever jazz. How's your body? You're not pushing yourself too hard?'

Penny shook her head. 'All good, Dad, you'd never even know I was sick. Dr Sinclair said relapses can occur, but generally you build up an immunity to the virus. I paid the high price upfront, now it should all be smooth sailing.'

'I'm glad, love. Those few months were tough going, but if nothing else, it delivered you home.'

'Me too, Dad.'

She looked away as tears glistened on his lashes.

He coughed loudly and made a fuss of searching for his notepad in a drawer.

'Here, I've got another list—just as a back-up, mind you.' His handwriting was distinctly neater than before, and he smiled when she said so.

'It's the McIntyre determination. We've got it in spades, Penny. But you'll want to be onto those sheep the second they're dry. If it gets too close to lambing, you'll be flat out like a lizard drinking. I never liked shearing after they've got lambs at foot either—a higher chance of the littlies being separated from their mums. That's a headache you don't need.'

'I'm doing my best, Dad,' she said, trying not to gulp as she read his full-page list.

Ducks flapped and flew away from the dam as Penny drove through the boggy paddock, picking her path carefully. It might be too wet to shear, but she was still determined to shave a few jobs off Angus's lengthy list, plus some of her own. The ute rolled to a stop when she found what she was looking for.

With quick, quiet movements, she pulled the rifle from the passenger footwell and loaded shells into the magazine.

Bracing against the open window frame, she eyed up the lame ram in her sights, one back leg dragging uselessly as he walked, and released the safety catch. It had been a long time since she'd had to euthanise an animal, but she didn't want Tim to think she was cherry-picking the cushy jobs. She'd need his help to load and bury the sickly sheep afterwards, but this was a job she could tackle herself.

Where there's livestock, there's dead stock, whispered Angus's voice in her mind. She took a steadying breath, focusing on putting the animal out of its misery instead of her own empathy, and gently pressed the trigger. The ram staggered and fell to the ground. Penny reinstated the safety catch, relieved it was a clean shot and a fast death. She set the gun down and whistled for the dogs.

Penny's phone buzzed and the dogs jumped onto the back of the ute as she located it under a box of ammunition.

'Boutique Media' flashed on the caller ID.

'Hello, Penny speaking.'

'Penny, it's Anna. I'm after your report for Georgie. The background report on the Leonard Group branding?' Keyboard keys clicked at Anna's end.

'Sorry, Anna, I haven't finished it yet. It's not due until next week though, isn't it?'

'Didn't you get the memo? The client wants everything ready for a spring launch. I'm pretty sure Charlotte put everyone in the email loop after last week's meeting.'

Penny gritted her teeth. It was news to her.

'Is she around? I'd love to chat with her.' Penny tapped her fingernails as music played in her ear.

'Boutique Media, you're speaking with Charlotte.'

Penny's irritation increased as the English accent purred down the phone. She could picture Charlotte sitting in her office, undoubtedly rearranging it in her absence.

'Penny, here. In future, I'd appreciate better updates about timeline changes, thanks. I'll get the report nailed this afternoon, but I don't like being set up.'

A false laugh tinkled down the phone line.

'Sorry darling, my mistake. I'll get the tech boys onto this mystery email. Maybe it's been diverted to junk mail, given your limited contact with Boutique Media these days.'

Penny pinched the bridge of her nose, praying for patience to deal with the colleague who seemed hell-bent on stabbing her in the back. She slammed the ute door and looked up to the skies, hoping the light drizzle would cool her temper.

'I'll visit the office as soon as shearing's finished. Spend some quality time with my boyfriend, Vince. That type of thing.'

Charlotte laughed again. 'You really are a little country bumpkin, aren't you, Penny? I hope all those little lambies don't give you too much trouble. Ta-ta.'

Penny swore at the phone.

I'll get the shearing finished on time and make the damn client meeting—just you wait and see, Charlotte.

Forty-seven

'What do you think, Rusty? Will Georgie be happy with that report?' Penny hit 'send' on the email before leaning down and scratching the kelpie's ears. Won over by his melancholic brown eyes, Penny had started letting him inside on occasion. It seemed like the kelpie appreciated company as much as she did, both of them overlooking the McIntyre rule about animals indoors. Showing the same intelligence that made him a top working dog, he sat by her side obediently as she tackled her marketing to-do list, then moved onto the draft media releases and press alerts promised to Anna, before handling the farm accounts.

Angus's desk was now as neat and orderly as her city office, and she had found it easy to get an overview of his recording system. She eased through the main ledger and logged onto the farm's bank account. The moon and stars twinkled at her through the window by the time she'd paid all the invoices for chemicals, fencing wire, shearers, diesel and insurance. Another job ticked off Dad's list and three major jobs crossed off my Boutique list.

Penny switched off the computer and stretched her arms to the ceiling. She fought an impulse to rest in the comfy office chair and tiredness washed over her as she loosened her sweat-stained shirt from her waistband. *Definitely shower time.* Her eyelids drooped further, the effort of getting upstairs beyond her.

Just one minute, she bargained with herself, easing back into the chair and closing her eyes.

Penny jolted awake with a snort to something wet licking her hand. She gingerly opened her eyes, the digital clock burning the numbers 11.24 p.m. into her retinas. Rusty's tail thumped on the floorboards.

'Ergghh.' Penny groaned as she peeled herself out of the chair and walked the dog to the back door. Windburn she hadn't noticed made her face feel stiff and hot.

'C'mon, Rusty, out you go. It's bedtime.'

Penny looked up from the laptop screen as Angie's reflection loomed into view. She swivelled the chair around to face the doorway, surprised but pleased to see her younger sister.

'Hey, Angie. Long time, no see.'

Angie looked away, her expression aloof.

'Dad asked me to collect the farm insurance documents. He's got to get them all signed to start the WorkCover stuff,' said Angie.

Penny frowned, wishing she could erase the strain between them. It was hard to believe they'd been so close a month ago, just like old times. 'I could have taken it in. But while you're here, check this out.'

Penny leaned back, proud of her hard work revising the McIntyre Park Merino Stud logo, brochures, flyers and advertisements for the on-farm ram sale.

'What do you think? Pretty snazzy, aren't they?' Penny's enthusiasm flagged as she took in Angie's restrained nod.

'Not bad. They're a big improvement on the black-and-white ads Dad usually puts in shop windows around Bridgefield.'

'Exactly. All part of my plan to bring more buyers to the sale,' said Penny, pointing out the distribution list that incorporated websites, print media, farming magazines and rural newsletters.

'Won't that be pricey, though? Are you likely to turn enough profit to cover extra expenses?'

Penny nodded. 'You've got to spend money to make money, Angie. You should know that with your beauty business. I got a cheap rate through my work contacts, and it beats sitting around dwelling on this wet weather.'

'I guess so. Reckon you'll get the shearing finished next week?'

'Hopefully. If this rain clears up like it's supposed to, we should have a good run. We're already cutting it a bit too fine. Hey, have you seen Lara recently? Mrs Beggs seems to think Sam's back in town for good. Don't tell me they're trying to make a go of things again?'

Angie averted her gaze again, looking at the pale square of paint on the kitchen wall; the bare spot beside Diana and Pete's wedding portrait that once held a framed photo of Lara and Sam at the altar.

'I don't know,' shrugged Angie. 'She said she was calling into the farmhouse later. Maybe you should ask her yourself?'

'What's all this about glossy brochures and national advertising? Sounds like a waste of time and money to me. You should be looking for ways to economise, not spend,' said Lara. Her face was as downcast as the waterlogged roses alongside the house, but with none of the sweet aroma or soft, pretty petals.

'Great to see you too, Lara. Yes, I'm very well, thanks for asking. You?' Penny shook her head as Lara barged through the house, heading straight to the office. She shrugged at her niece, who was still wrestling with her gumboots on the porch.

'Hi, Aunty Pen. You look pretty today,' said Evie, beaming at her.

Penny leaned in to hug the girl, wondering if she would always feel the need to compensate for Lara's austere manner, and was surprised when Evie kept her arms wrapped around her neck longer than normal. She wondered whether it had anything to do with Sam's return to town.

'Thanks, honey. You must have been eating your veggies these last few weeks. You're almost taller than me,' she said, tucking her new winter-weight shirt into her jeans.

She slung an arm around Evie's shoulder, bracing herself for Lara's criticisms as they walked to the office. Lara stood staring at the printed proofs sitting on Angus's desk.

'Why are you even stuffing around with this, Penny? Sure, it looks flash, but the best customers are always repeat customers. Everyone knows that.'

Penny rolled her eyes, her voice calm for Evie's benefit although she was seething.

'This isn't my first shooting match, Lara. I do this for a living. You stick to nursing and running, and I'll use my marketing background to advance the ram sale, okay?'

Lara moved away from the desk, scowling.

'Go ahead and waste your time then, see if I care. Just don't clean out Dad's bank account trying to make yourself look good. Tim's savings deposit is sorted. He's just waiting for the green light from Dad.'

Penny swallowed hard. Tim had given her his word that he wasn't trying to buy the farm out from under Angus; surely he wasn't stringing them both along?

⸙

Penny dried her hands on a tea towel and sat at the bench to continue revising the final Leonard Group media release.

The scones in the oven had barely started to rise, and she was only halfway through the document when the home phone rang. Penny checked the timer on her way to the phone—still another six minutes until they needed to come out of the oven.

'McIntyre Park, Penny speaking.'

'Babe, it's me. I know you can't make the weekend away, but how about a quick overnighter for the cocktail festival on the Yarra tomorrow? Boutique Media has sponsored another marquee for the night, all the best clients will be there just waiting to be schmoozed. You know you want to,' he said, his voice playful, like when they'd first met.

'Hey, Vince. Cocktails sound divine. It was a blast last year.'

'But . . . I can hear an excuse coming up.'

She sighed. Sometimes Vince knew her too well.

'But I've got my hands full. Shearing is ramping up again tomorrow and I really can't leave. Not while it's in full swing and, by golly, I hope it stays in full swing for at least another six days.'

'You know it'd do you good to show your face at a work function, considering you're working remotely and things aren't going exactly smoothly.'

'Things are fine. Who said it was anything other than smooth?'

The oven timer beeped madly and she grabbed an oven mitt with her free hand, shrugging the phone between her jaw and her shoulder.

'It's not so much what I've heard, it's just the vibe around the office. I try and stick up for you, of course, but you've got to give something back, babe. Mingle with our peeps. Show the team you value your job.'

Penny swore as her wrist touched the wire rack. She dropped the hot tray onto a trivet and ran her puckering skin under cold water.

'What? No, Vince, I'm not swearing at you. I just burned myself. I *am* pulling my weight with daily updates, background research, input into the advertising campaign—but I can't make the cocktail event. I've got to go, love you.'

She hung up the phone, her enthusiasm for baking vanishing along with the sound of Vince's protests. She threw the oven mitt across the bench and slumped down into her chair. Rusty's tail wagged against the table leg, his head cocked quizzically to the side.

'I'd make it if I could,' she told the dog. Penny skimmed over the press release one more time, then the media alert, and hit 'send' to her entire media address book.

I'm not going to be pressured into anything, she told herself. *Vince can say all he wants about his peeps and his schmoozing, but my most important priority at this very minute is getting shearing underway. Then I'll have time to show my face in the office.*

The laneway linking the paddocks to the shearing shed was smooth and fresh, each piece of gravel washed clean by the downpour earlier in the week. The kookaburras called in the red gum trees as Penny strode back to the shed, admiring the butterflies as they fluttered past in search of flowers. Three successful days of shearing combined with an exceptional outlook for the rest of the week was exactly what the doctor had ordered.

She called the dogs, interrupting their attempt to flush rabbits from the long grass, and tucked cold fingers into her sleeves. She flexed her arms against the crisp air, the evidence of her newly toned biceps lifting her mood as she turned towards the farmhouse.

The sight of three cars in the main driveway wiped the goofy look from her face. She pushed her body to a jog, trying to work out why Angie, Lara and Diana had all converged unannounced on the farmhouse. *Is Dad okay? Has there been another accident? Are the children injured?* Sweat soaked Penny's dirty work shirt as she ran up the laneway.

Puffing, she reached the shearing shed. The buzzing and whirring of the equipment continued, despite the gathering at the house. *It can't be an emergency if they're still shearing.*

Penny forced herself to slow down and catch her breath as she walked the remainder of the way home. Smoke curled out of the chimney. As she got closer, Penny spotted a familiar outline in the corner of the lounge room. Her father's favourite spot in the house. *Surely not . . . he couldn't be home already.*

Forty-eight

'Surprise!' Five little voices crowed in unison as Penny came through the back door.

Slipping off her boots, she hugged her niece and nephews, swung Leo onto her hip and rounded the corner into the lounge room. A riot of pain coursed through her body as her knee smashed into the frame of the sofa. She winced, clutching her knee. Shock and confusion about the rearranged furniture made her blurt out the central question on her mind.

'What are you doing here? I thought you had a few weeks left in rehab?'

Her father's face fell and the vibe in the room was as awkward as the furniture configuration.

Penny tried to think of something to say that would smooth over her abrupt comment, but nothing came to her lips. She was grateful when Cameron broke the silence.

'Grandpa's home, Aunty Penny. Isn't that great?'

'And look at his funky wheelchair, it's so much fun,' said Evie, running to the side of Angus's recliner for a demonstration.

Penny reined herself in, lowering Leo to the floor, and walked across to kiss Angus. It was nice to see him. She smiled down at his face, noticing how he looked a lot more like his old self now that he was home where he belonged, away from the artificial lights and clinical setting.

'It's great to see you back. Welcome home, Dad.'

'Thanks, love. I'm looking forward to sleeping in my own bed.'

The wheelchair nudged her leg in the same spot she had collided with the sofa, and she cringed as a cheeky grin appeared on Evie's face.

'I'm going to practise for murderball. Watch out, Aunty Pen.'

'Careful guys, it's not a toy. And don't bang into Grandpa or Aunty Penny's leg!' Diana threw Penny an apologetic look and raised an empty cup.

'Tea?'

'I'd love a cuppa,' said Penny, 'but I've got four stands running and shearers that'll be begging for afternoon smoko any minute now.' She walked over to Diana and lowered her voice to an urgent whisper. 'He's looking better already. Don't get me wrong—I'm thrilled to see him home—but when on Earth was this decided?'

'Lara announced it this morning. Said she was collecting him with Angie.'

Penny glanced at Angie standing by the wood-fire, again deep in conversation with Lara. She swallowed hard and glanced at her watch, aware she was cutting it fine. She'd already learned the hard way about standing between a hungry shearer and his tucker.

'I offered to have him at my place, but between Cameron's sleepwalking, Harry's night terrors and Leo's teething he'd never get a full night's sleep.'

'I just can't believe she'd yank him out of the rehab ward. Last time I visited, he could barely shower or dress,' said Penny.

Penny stalked across the room. The wood-fire crackled and glowed, but there was no time to stand and warm her hands.

'Lara, Angie, could you help me get some more firewood?' She looked pointedly at the near-empty wood box beside the roaring fire.

The three sisters headed outside. The woodpile was dwindling, another reason why she'd been letting the fire go out overnight, and only restarting it when she came in for the evening. Penny started collecting an armful of wood, keeping her voice light.

'You two look pretty pleased with your big surprise. Wasn't Dad supposed to stay in the hospital for at least another week or two?'

'He was sick of it, Pen. You should have seen him yesterday, he practically begged me to smuggle him out,' said Angie, studying the fiddleback on a large piece of red gum, the grain crimped like a clip of merino wool.

At least she has the decency to look a little guilty, thought Penny.

'That's funny, because the nurse told me he needed another fortnight of rehab.'

'Angie's just being nice. He wanted to be back here to keep a closer eye on the farm. Make sure you don't do anything rash,' said Lara, flicking a huntsman spider off the piece of firewood in her hand. It hit the ground running, moving fast to find a shadowy space.

Penny jumped out of the spider's frenzied path, forcing a dry laugh.

'He probably wants to make sure you're not putting up the "for sale" signs, Lara. He's going to need a lot of care. I hope you plan on offering full nursing services?'

'I'll come around now and then, but weren't you the one Dad just nursed back to health? Surely it's your turn to repay the favour?'

'Repay the favour? You're kidding me, Lara. I'm up to my eyeballs already and I don't have time to argue,' Penny shot back. Angie and Diana roping her into baking therapy classes was one thing, but full-time caring duties on top of farm work and job-sharing with Charlotte was a whole different ball game. *Why don't I just introduce Lara to Charlotte and they can come up with a watertight plan to send me completely batty?* Penny squeezed her eyes shut, trying to calm her mind, relax her shoulders and unclench her jaw, then looked back at the farmhouse windows. Pleasure at seeing her father finally home was mixed with the frustration that Lara was setting her up for a fall.

'I'll look after Dad because that's what families do, but I won't forget this, Lara. Karma will bite you in the bum one day.'

Tim pulled the shearing shed door open, squinting into the bright sunshine. Goosebumps prickled his skin as he scanned the laneway. *It shouldn't have taken her this long to return the sheep to their paddock.* He'd counted out the runs himself, filled in the tally books and set Penny's trays of slice and fruit salad onto the battered tearoom table, where the shearers had started devouring them at a rapid rate. But it wasn't like her to dilly-dally. A pang of concern lodged itself in his chest and he shook away far-fetched reasons to explain her tardiness. *Don't be ridiculous, Patterson. Fat chance of two serious accidents in two months at the same farm. And she was on foot anyway, numb-nut.* He took the steps two at a time and an unexpected sense of relief washed over him at the sight of Penny jogging across from the farmhouse. He looked beyond her, to the trio of cars parked in the driveway.

Sweat sucked Penny's work shirt to her body, showcasing a figure that had been haunting his restless dreams and attracting covert glances from the team of shearers. He felt his irritation rising as he realised just how much their interest irked him, as if they wanted to discover whether she was as sweet as the chocolate slice and cakes she baked.

Tim shoved his shoulders back, burying the unwanted twinge of possessiveness, and walked towards her. One look at her tightly knitted brow and the thunder in her eyes, and he knew the driveway traffic jam wasn't just a pleasant social visit. Though from what he'd seen recently, the McIntyre sisters didn't seem to do pleasant social anymore.

'What's up, Mac? Smoko's almost over. Thought I was going to have to send out the search party.'

'Dad's home.'

Tim whistled low. He hadn't expected to see Angus at the farm for another month or so. Admittedly, it would make crosschecking farm arrangements a little easier, but Penny didn't look like she saw it that way.

'He'd be pleased about that,' he said cautiously.

Penny blew out an exasperated breath, rolling her eyes to the blue sky.

'He might be, but I'm not. I'm not a nurse and I've got enough on my plate without this. I don't know the first thing about rehab or physio. He'd better be able to wash himself. There are some things a daughter shouldn't have to see.'

Tim turned back to the shed, hiding the grin that threatened to expose just how sexy he found her anger. The fiery scowl and wrinkled-up nose were easier to appreciate when they weren't directed at him.

'I'm sure the others will pitch in. Best boss I've ever worked for. At least you know he'll be a good patient.'

'He'd better be.'

The UTV engine idled as Eddie swung the gate open. Penny drove through, collecting him after the gate was firmly latched. Eddie loved the new side-by-side bike and he rushed to help shift mobs of sheep, check water troughs and return the freshly shorn animals to the far paddocks. The expression on his face when he climbed aboard was priceless, and she saw how he yearned for the open air, relished being useful and treated each day on the farm as a new adventure.

Tim was waiting for them as she pulled up outside the shearing shed, Bones lying by his side.

'Got a minute, Mac? Might need to review our final week of shearing. New alert just came in from the BOM website,' he said, leaning an arm against the UTV's roof.

Penny groaned. Eddie mimicked her reaction.

'Just my luck, when we're so close to finishing. And with lambing starting next week. What are they tipping?'

Tim pulled his phone from his back pocket, angling the cracked screen away from the sun. Like his scuffed boots, grease-stained shirts and ripped jeans, the phone had been put through its paces. And if the duct tape holding the back cover together was any indication, he expected it to last a lot longer. She reached into her pocket for her own phone and opened the bureau's website from her 'favourites' list.

'There's a massive front with hail, thunder and lightning expected mid-next-week. Looking like two or three inches on the worst day, with howling westerlies. Not pretty.'

'Do you think we can get the shearing finished by then?'

'We'll have a red-hot crack. Otherwise, we can push through this weekend, then pen up the last few mobs in the shed while the worst is coming down, and we'll be able to work through next weekend.'

Penny leaned her forehead against the steering wheel. Georgie was counting on her to lead the client meeting that weekend, and she knew it was a prime opportunity to assert some control over the project. Pulling out was the last thing she wanted to do.

She looked up at the sky, the fluffy white clouds against a brilliant blue offering no hint of the looming forecast. *Please hold off another week*, she begged silently.

Forty-nine

'Welcome home, Dad,' said Diana, placing a rogue raspberry back on top of the black forest cake. Angus looked up from his seat at the head of the table and raised his glass of orange juice.

They toasted his homecoming. The children giggled as they clinked glasses of juice, pleased to be included in the celebrations.

'I'm chockers, but I'll still have a shot at that cake. Stunning, love. You've outdone yourself.'

Diana flushed with pride.

'Better late than never, Dad. Hopefully, it tastes all right,' said Lara, passing the knife down the table, oblivious to the dirty look from Diana.

Angie cut and served the cake, hesitating as she reached Penny's side.

'Hey, Pen. How's things?'

Penny weighed up the pros and cons of being light and breezy, or answering honestly. She looked at her sister's freshly painted nails and pushed her ragged fingernails into her lap. Angie's sudden support of Lara defied logic. She rebuffed her younger sister's first attempt at reconnection.

'Rushed off my feet with shearing. Working my guts out at night trying to keep on top of marketing,' said Penny. She jerked her head in Angus's direction and lowered her voice. 'And my patient over there is an added challenge I could've done without. But apart from that, just peachy.'

Angie looked at Angus, her tone defensive. 'He seems pretty good to me.'

They both looked up as Diana's husband leaned in between the two of them, little pieces of cake clinging to his beard.

'What's all the whispering, you two?'

'Nothing, Pete. You might want to keep an eye on the boys though. Elliot looks like he's had too much sugar.'

They turned their attention to the end of the table. Evie and Cameron were perched on the dining room floor, rolling a soft ball back and forth underneath the table, as the twins scurried between adults' legs and table legs trying to intercept it.

Pete laughed. 'They're just playing. Time for another slice of cake, methinks.' He drifted across to the dessert platter, leaving the sisters to their conversation.

'You try helping him get dressed, Angie, or reminding him to do his physio exercises. You haven't seen him in a mood yet. I'll send him around to your place, then you'll see.'

At that moment, just as Angie rolled her eyes, Angus let out a shriek.

'Arghh, little bugger nearly ran into my ankle! Friggin' hell. Watch where you're going, mate.'

There was a gasp from Diana as she pushed out her chair and rushed to Angus's side. Pete scooped Elliot up and took the sobbing child into the lounge room.

Angie's mouth dropped open at the outburst.

'I've never heard him speak like that. Except when the ram charged him last summer,' she said.

'Exactly. Dad's losing his temper more and more. If he's that angry with the kids, imagine how grumpy he is with me. It's not fun.'

'Give him a break, Penny. The poor guy, he said they've cut his pain medication. It must be hard adjusting to his new normal, seeing you working in the paddocks, doing all the things he loved.'

'I hope that's all it is, Angie. Something tells me there's more to it than that.'

⁂

Penny signalled to the truck driver with her hands, calling out to swing further left as his flat-top tray inched closer to the loading ramp. It was the first load since shearing began, and she got inordinate satisfaction from seeing the heavy bales lined up on the small truck.

'Woah up. That'll do it,' Penny yelled, raising both palms to him.

Penny waited for the truck driver to tie down the bales, looking to the horizon. The sky remained blue, the clouds non-threatening. Hopefully, next week's storm was an exaggeration. She took her phone out of her pocket to check the weather once again.

The bureau website flashed away to an incoming call. Penny smiled as Vince's name appeared and stepped down from the ramp to take the call.

'Vince, how are you going? You should see all these wool bales. It's a pretty impressive load.'

'Hey, babe. That's why I'm calling. I'd love to. How's this weekend sound?'

She laughed, walking away from the action above her. 'That's keen. How good are you on the end of a broom? The shearing shed roustabout is off with gastro—she threw up all over the tearoom this morning, so I could use an extra set of hands.'

'You make it sound so sexy.' He laughed dryly. 'I'll give it a shot, as long as you promise to wear your tightest jeans. I've missed that hot body of yours. We can get cosy in your old bedroom. Maybe take a detour out in the fields, a little lust in the dust?'

She could hear the smile in his voice and felt her body respond with a sizzle. It *had* been a long time. Vince wasn't the only one missing their physical contact, and she was on the verge of agreeing when Tim's whistle cut through the air. She turned to see him hunting another mob into the shed. The movement brought her back to her senses. As a complete rookie, Vince would be more hindrance than help in the shearing shed. Her single bed creaked each time she rolled over. It was never going to be an ideal setting. And with Angus's mood swings, he wasn't likely to be the most accommodating host while she was busy working.

'You know what, maybe it's not a good idea, Vince. I've got another huge weekend of shearing, trying to get them finished off before the big storm next week. But all going well, I'll be back in Melbourne Saturday for a client meeting. Then we can make up for lost time.'

'Penny, my angel. You're killing me. You say that now, but I bet you'll cancel, like last time.'

Tim whistled again as he moved directly underneath the loading ramp, shielding his face against the glare. He waved as she spotted him below, pointing to his watch. She covered the phone with her hand as she nodded at Tim.

'Only twenty minutes till lunchtime, Mac. Want me to flick the oven on?'

'Thanks, Tim.'

She watched Tim head back inside and returned the phone to her ear. Vince was still protesting.

'Babe? Who's that?'

'No one just . . . just our farmhand. I've gotta go, Vince. Next weekend, I promise.'

'Penny, c'mon. I miss you.'

'Me too. But honestly, Vince, it won't work this weekend. I'll be in the shed all day and fall into bed, completely knackered, at 8 p.m. That is if I've got all the catering done beforehand.' She started walking up the steps, her mind now focused on the task of preparing lunch for four shearers, two shedhands, a wool classer and a wool presser, plus Angus, Tim and herself.

Vince sighed, his playful pleading turning to frustration. 'I can see why Georgie is getting nervous about your commitment, Penny. I'm wondering the same thing myself. I'll talk to you later when you've got a spare minute.'

Penny paused mid-step and the phone went silent. She stomped up the steps and shoved open the tearoom door. *How dare he question* my *commitment? And what the hell has Georgie been saying?* She squared her shoulders and tried to convince herself that living this double life was worth all the drama.

Fifty

Penny opened the oven door, the rush of heat making her necklace sizzle against her neck. Instead of the golden-brown mounds of pastry she'd been expecting, the sausage rolls were flaccid on top, oozing out the sides and burned underneath. *What a bloody mess.*

'For Pete's sake,' she muttered tipping them into the bin.

It was her fifth late-night baking session of the week, and feeding the team of hungry shearers had become a chore. She now wished she had offered the shearing team a lunch allowance, instead of supplying it herself as her mother had always done.

'It's enough to put you off cooking altogether,' she said to Rusty, whose indoor visits were more frequent than her father approved of.

'Dogs are supposed to live outside. You'll ruin them as good workers if you let them inside and treat them like pets,' he had growled yesterday, when Rusty came in to clear up crumbs under the table.

The bee in his bonnet about the dog was one of several divisions that had opened up after his much-anticipated return

276

home, including complaints about her cooking, snappy remarks about the new UTV and unsolicited criticism of her farm-management skills.

She turned down the oven temperature with a sharp flick of her wrist and began setting up another slab of puff pastry on the bench. As she mixed minced lamb with crushed garlic and fresh rosemary, she puzzled over her father's behaviour.

How can he be so cranky when I'm only trying to help? If anyone can sympathise, it's me, she thought, rolling the pastry over the meat filling and setting it on the baking tray. *I know what it's like to feel useless, when you can't do a darn thing to fast-track recovery. Why won't he take my advice and help himself?*

She shook her head while forking an air vent into the top of each sausage roll, and slipped the new batch into the oven. Her laptop pinged, the bright screen lighting up the dining table.

The email from Georgie made the burned sausage rolls pale into insignificance. She scrolled through urgently.

> Did you reread that press alert before you hit send yesterday? Three of the Melbourne journos have called to clarify. These blunders are becoming way too regular for my liking, Penny. Call me.

Penny's pulse quickened and despite the late hour, she reached for the phone.

The clinking of glass against porcelain floated through the laundry window. Penny stripped off her jacket, beanie and boots and discovered Diana bustling around the kitchen.

'A cleaning fairy, direct from the heavens. You're an angel, Diana.' Penny's voice was groggy, and she felt grit underfoot as she headed straight to the kettle. She heaped two teaspoons of coffee into a semi-clean mug and added milk and sugar before remembering her manners.

'Want one?'

'No, I'm good. I knew things were busy, Penny, but I've never seen the kitchen in this state.'

Penny looked around. Newspapers competed for bench space among media releases and marketing reports. Crumb-covered plates sat between an open jar of vegemite and the toaster. Empty Tupperware and casserole containers lay abandoned and homeless at the far end of the bench, awaiting their mystery owners. She nodded, pouring the boiling water. The mug warmed her cold hands as she took a sip.

'I was up until 2 a.m. last night trying to fix a work stuff-up, then the alarm smashed me at 5 a.m. The kitchen is in a pretty good state, considering. Don't look in the bathroom,' she said, resting her head against the wall cabinets, hoping she had at least kicked her underwear to the bottom of the heap on the tiled floor.

'You know I don't like to interfere,' said Diana, setting the dishcloth down.

Penny quirked an eyebrow.

'Really, I don't. But as your big sister, I have to tell you when things are spiralling. And this is definitely spiralling down.' Diana surveyed the room, her lips pursed.

'I was going to tidy this afternoon.'

'Didn't you learn anything from the Ross River fever thing? I know you're trying to do it all, but you don't want to risk a relapse.'

'I'm going okay. It's just a rough patch with shearing and a cantankerous patient. It's not like you can talk, Diana. You're stretched as thin as Glad Wrap with all the kids' stuff, school council, weekend sports and dance rehearsals. And you still manage to get home-cooked meals on the table every night.'

Diana gripped Penny's forearm and squeezed it lightly.

'Don't make an example of me. Half the time I'm a prime example of how *not* to do things. But I do all of it for love. You reap what you sow with kids, so I've got a vested interest in my madness.

'Can you honestly say the money you earn at Boutique Media, and the hours doing your hair and make-up—despite being ridiculously strapped for time—are worth the effort? How many hours have you spent worrying about Vince this week? Would the shearers even care if you gave them a thirty-dollar meal allowance instead of providing food?'

'At least I'm having a go, Diana. I'm trying my best.' Penny shook Diana's hand off and clunked the mug down on the bench, smoothing her hair defensively.

'But are you working for the love of it? Or for the money? Or the image? I hope it's all worth it, Pen.'

Penny blew out a furious breath as Diana's words cut close to the bone. Her voice was loud as she replied, any concern about interrupting Angus's afternoon nap evaporating in anger.

'I thought families were supposed to support each other? I've got Lara and Angie in cahoots, Dad's lost the plot, I still don't know if I trust Tim, and now you're on my back. What do you expect me to do? Magic up a clone who can keep my career running smoothly while I try to keep the farm afloat? All these things I'm juggling are important to me. I can't drop the ball now.'

Diana closed her eyes. Her lips moved as if she were counting silently.

Despite her irritation, Penny could see the startling likeness between Diana and their mother. A pang of sadness rolled over her and she took a deep breath.

'I'm sorry for yelling.'

'Penny, I'm worried about you. You've got to prioritise or lighten your load somehow. Otherwise, you'll be heading straight back to the hospital at this rate. I'll come back and help later if you're ready to accept it.'

Diana gave Penny a wistful look as she left the kitchen. Penny worked on autopilot, stacking the remaining dirty dishes in the sink.

'For God's sake, can you keep the racket down? Some of us are trying to sleep,' said Angus. He leaned heavily on the walking stick as he turned towards his bedroom.

Penny swiped at the tears that rolled down her face and fell into the sink, wishing she could go to sleep herself and wake up in a week's time.

Fifty-one

'I've liaised with all the journalists and they've promised to delete the old press release and media alert. None of them had taken it through to the print stage yet, thank God. I can't believe I approved a marketing campaign that featured the wrong spokesperson,' said Penny, holding her head in her hands. Her voice was low and she hoped the doors between the kitchen and the bedrooms would provide enough of a sound barrier. The last thing she needed was Angus hobbling into the kitchen to berate her during a work call, or for him to overhear her epic stuff-up.

'It's lucky Janet saw the funny side of your little slip-up. She quite liked being quoted as the head of Tyrrewong Logistics, even though she's never worked in that field,' said Georgie with a sniff. 'Unfortunately, the actual Tyrrewong CEO didn't find it quite so amusing. He's been on the phone again this morning, demanding better service for his hard-earned investment.'

'I read through the media releases and press alerts, honestly, Georgie. I even tweaked a few of the PR team's sentences. I don't know how a glaring error like that could have gone unnoticed by so many sets of eyes.' Penny felt her eyes burning with mascara and sat up straighter to stop herself rubbing them. She fished a wrinkled sheet of paper from the pile in front of her, tracing her fingers over the place where she had inadvertently referred to Janet—the head of their former client, Whitfield Pharmaceuticals—as the spokesperson of a completely unrelated company. Her face was almost as red as the pen highlighting her glaring error.

'The rest of the campaign will be seamless, I promise, Georgie.'

'It's not good enough, Penny. You've been impossible to get hold of. You haven't been into the city once since you began working remotely. Not once. And Charlotte said she's had to rework your reports and presentations so that they are up to par.'

Of course Charlotte would lump me in it. She's taking every opportunity to dig the knife in. Penny looked around the kitchen, the surfaces now shining as a result of channelling her anger into something productive. And anything that wasn't already spotless would be sparkling clean directly after the phone call.

'I'll fix it, Georgie. We'll be finished shearing this week, so that's a huge weight off my shoulders. Let me meet with the Tyrrewong CEO when I come to town next Saturday, smooth it all over.'

Georgie cleared her throat; the pause was longer than Penny would have liked.

'I think you need to choose. Your duel focus is coming at a very high price.'

Penny slapped the light switch, hoping the bright light would help banish her mood. *I've worked my guts out for Boutique Media, only to be dropped like a hot coal at the first sign of*

weakness. Where's the bloody loyalty? Have they forgotten my twelve years of devoted and unblemished service?

She snatched at the dishcloth on the bench and polished the surface to a sheen. *A high price? Don't talk to me about a high price.* A rumble of thunder broke through her cleaning frenzy, and she looked at the window as dark clouds thrust the farmhouse into darkness.

Penny threw down the cloth and rushed to the back door, scrolling through the forecast on her phone as she went. Steely clouds reproached her through the laundry window, despite the distinct absence of rainfall on the weather loop. *Forecast or not, those clouds aren't lying,* she conceded, shoving her boots on.

Another bolt of lightning flashed, followed by a roll of thunder as Penny hurried outside. Black-bellied clouds clustered from the farmhouse to the far mountains, each one darker than the next. She ran for the shearing shed, the storm masking the sound of Tim's ute until it was alongside her.

'Jump in, Mac. Let's get the rest of the sheep in the shed.'

Penny ran to the passenger side and had barely sat down before the ute surged forward.

Tim swore as he flicked the windscreen wipers on to clear the speckles of rain, the drops getting heavier as they gained on the shearing shed. Sheep shifted restlessly in the yards, huddling against one another for shelter.

He watched Penny wrench the ute door open before he'd come to a complete stop, just as the skies opened. Tim pulled the handbrake on and rain pounded at his bare arms, drenching his shirt within seconds of getting out of the car. He knew they'd missed their opportunity and Mac's desperate attempts to get the sheep undercover wouldn't make much difference now they were already wet.

'We're too late, Mac. Leave it.' He kicked the wet earth, frustrated he had trusted the forecast instead of keeping a closer eye on the sky. *Rookie mistake, Patterson, and one that'll push us into lambing.* He'd overheard enough of Penny's conversation with Vince to know she had city commitments the following weekend and berated himself for not penning up more sheep before the storm hit.

Penny ignored him and opened the gate on the side of the shearing shed. Hair was plastered across her determined face as she skirted back around the mob to try to push the confused sheep up the ramp and into the shelter. But the pregnant ewes jammed in the race, swirling like a turbulent ocean. He climbed the rails, gaining on Penny as she let out a frustrated cry.

'Get in, you buggers. C'mon.' She clapped her hands. The wet slapping noise was drowned out by another flash of lightning and burst of thunder. 'C'mon. Get up.'

The smell of wet wool surrounded her, the staccato of water hitting the tin underlining the futility of her efforts.

'They're too wet already.' He yelled to be heard above the rain.

She glared at him as if listening for a hint of mocking or triumph. Tim reached out an arm as her face fell, her mask of control gushing away like the water overflowing the gutters. She jerked away, kicking the nearest fence post in anger. Her expression seesawed between helplessness and frustration, tiredness and pain.

He let his hand fall to his side. *Mac doesn't need you, Patterson, she doesn't want your pity or sympathy.*

He walked away as she slammed the gate shut. A sudden wail of pain replaced her swearing. Tim turned and ran to her, his protective instincts growing as she cradled her hand against her body.

'You okay?'

Penny lifted her hand, looking away as she offered it for his inspection. Tim gently unfurled her clenched fist

'Your fingernail's going black already. But at least there's no blood and no bones sticking out.' He felt the heat of her quivering body, despite their wet clothes, and drew her into an awkward hug. Her cupped hand rested gingerly against his waist and he huddled his body around hers to shelter her from the rain.

Penny allowed Tim to embrace her, screwing up her face against his firm chest.

'You're like a bull at a gate. What are we going to do with you, Mac?'

The familiar stirrings of desire washed away the pain as Tim mumbled sympathetically into her hair. She smelled the washing detergent in his sodden clothes. Her brain danced into dangerous territory, inappropriate answers to his question bursting into her mind as his chin brushed against her forehead. She angled her head a fraction, until she could feel his warm breath on her skin.

'Are you sure this is what you want?'

Penny closed her eyes, breathing in his scent, thinking about the relationship she'd allowed to keep limping along in her absence, the way her body responded to Tim's proximity. Was this what she wanted? Scruffy Tim Patterson, with his odd socks, more family baggage than a cruise ship and an embrace that made her feel secure and protected. The rain continued to pour down. Her body screamed 'yes.' Her mind cried 'hell no'.

'I mean, farming's worlds away from your city life. It's crazy running yourself into the ground for something you don't want.'

Penny stiffened, realising he had meant the farm, not him. She used her right hand to lever herself away from him, as angry at her own traitorous body as his words.

'Thanks for the vote of confidence, Tim. I thought you were being sympathetic and then you shoot me down?'

'Mac . . . I'm just trying to help.'

She blew out a loud breath, pushed past him and swung open the ute door.

Angus's voice crackled over the UHF radio.

'On channel, Tim? On channel?'

'Dad, it's me.'

'Tell me you got all those sheep in before the downpour? You won't be able to scratch yourself if shearing runs into lambing.'

She flopped into the seat, her body and mind limp.

'Nope. We're just going to have to suck it up.' Penny shoved the UHF handset back into the holder.

Can this week get any worse?

Fifty-two

Magpies called from tree to tree, and the smell of fresh earth lingered as Penny walked to the shearing shed. The red and orange sunrise cast a rosy pink glow over the corrugated iron, and raw bluestone gravel crunched underfoot, naked without its usual red-dirt coating.

Dry ground either side of the path showed no evidence of last night's sudden downpour. Penny knew the wool would be too wet to shear or press, but a stubborn sense of determination propelled her towards the yards. She climbed in and whistled to Rusty. The kelpie jumped to do her bidding, nudging a handful of ewes into the race. Penny leaned over the metal fences to inspect the wool on the first sheep. The soggy brown wool parted to reveal fine, creamy crimped fibres. Damp fibres.

She moved to the second sheep, her black thumbnail contrasting with the wool, and then the third. They were all damp. Penny released the ewes from the race, their swollen teats jiggling as they walked back to their mob.

'Mac.'

Penny shielded her eyes from the sun's first rays to see Tim at the top of the shearing shed ramp.

'If we put them back into the paddock and the wind picks up, we might still finish by Friday,' she said. Her voice was hopeful, trumping the anger and embarrassment from last night. She scanned his face, trying to pre-empt his reply, but his expression was guarded, as it had been when he'd dropped her back to the farmhouse. As if he'd known she had mistaken his question about what she wanted.

'Worth a shot, but the weather doesn't give two hoots about your deadlines, Mac. That's what I meant. Your colour-coded priority lists and rigid timeframes don't mean much in farming. All the uncertainty would drive you crazy, I reckon.'

Penny flicked her head, trying not to flinch as her stiff muscles caught and pulled.

'Pfft, usually I thrive under pressure. It's just all this juggling. You have no idea how many balls I've got up in the air.' She closed her eyes, wrapping her arms around herself as a shield against the uncertainty clouding her mind.

'Try me,' said Tim, his voice patient.

Penny laughed dryly as the stream of questions jostled for pole position. *Will we finish shearing in time for lambing? If not, how will we manage the increased workload? Can we ace the on-farm sale? Will I still make this client meeting and snatch my promotion back from Charlotte's claws? Is there anything left of my relationship with Vince? Will Angie, Diana, Lara and I ever heal the rift between us? Will Dad snap out of his awful funk? Will we sell the farm? And why am I the only one that cares? Can I really see myself running it?* She pinched the bridge of her nose.

'No wonder you're losing sleep.'

Penny's eyes flew open and she clamped her hands over her mouth.

'Tell me I didn't just say that out loud?'

Tim shrugged. 'I don't think the sheep will tell anyone. I'm pretty good at keeping things to myself.'

Penny groaned, her cheeks flushing as pink as the sunrise-tinted tin. *What on Earth made me vent like that? To Tim, of all people?* She busied herself with unlatching the gate, mentally cursing Jade and Angie for their absence when she so desperately needed a sounding board. She threw an apologetic grimace over her shoulder.

'Sorry about that. I'd better take this lot back to the paddock.'

One small consolation soothed Penny's embarrassment as she whistled to the dogs. At least she had stopped before she got to the confusion in her mind about Tim Patterson, and the way he had crept into her mind as she tossed and turned last night.

✿

'You've missed a call from Charlotte. She seems like a lovely lady. Very friendly,' said Angus, folding up his newspaper. He placed it down on the pile of magazines and crossword books resting on the wheelchair and grabbed his walking stick.

Penny laughed dryly.

'She can be friendly all right—too friendly. As long as you've got a Y chromosome,' she said, suppressing an offer of assistance that was likely to be peevishly rebutted or rudely ignored, depending on his current mood.

Angus drew himself into a standing position. She winced as his face clouded with pain, wishing she could offer him some comfort or at least convince him to continue the stretching exercises recommended by the hospital physiotherapist. But if the last week was any indication, offering her two cents was as useless as flogging a dead horse.

Penny set about making morning tea as Angus hobbled across the lounge room, pausing at the arm of the sofa before continuing into the kitchen.

'And Vince called too. I don't know what you see in him, Penny. He sure doesn't float my boat. What's this about a trip to Melbourne next weekend? Did you forget about my appointment with the quack in Horsham? If it's too much trouble, I'll ask someone else,' he snapped.

Penny placed a cup of tea in front of him, adding a slice of his favourite chocolate cake.

'Steady on, Dad. I've asked Diana to take you to Horsham. With my luck, we'll still be shearing then, anyway.'

Angus rolled his eyes, looking more like his grandsons after a scolding than his sixty-four-year-old self.

She searched his face for a hint of the kind, gentle-natured man she knew so well, and sighed. *Hopefully, Dr Sinclair has some suggestions because this grumpy, self-pitying act is starting to wear thin.* This morning he tipped his cup of tea into the pot plant because it wasn't strong enough and screamed at Rusty for being underfoot. The old Angus never raised his voice, especially to the working dogs, and would have commiserated over another shearing delay or at least asked about it when she'd arrived home last night, drenched and shaking. Penny gulped the last of her tea and reached for the phone. It was high time to make an appointment at the bush nursing centre.

'Dad, the dial tone is still going. Didn't you hang it up properly?'

Angus paused mid-bite, the cake crumbs around his mouth giving him a wolfish look.

'Yep, I left it off the hook. Saves me dealing with idiots like Vince. And that reminds me, can you cook something better than brown rice and bean sprouts tonight? Nothing wrong with a good square meal of meat and three veg.'

Penny's face fell. *Ungrateful old bugger*, she thought, punching the number into the phone.

Blustery conditions made for heavy going, but one look at Cameron—belted into the passenger seat with enough layers to rival the Michelin Man—and Penny knew her decision to buy the side-by-side was worthwhile. A wide grin was evident behind the visor of his full-face helmet, his head swivelling from one side of the paddock to the other as they checked the stock.

'I reckon a ride on this Ranger will cheer Grandpa up.'

'Maybe, Cameron. We just need to give him more time and space to recover,' said Penny, calling against the wind. The chat with Dr Sinclair had helped ease her mind and she felt better knowing she had a few tools in her arsenal to handle Angus's mood swings. 'He'll get better soon. I'll make sure of it.'

The dogs ran alongside the UTV, eager to stretch their legs after a quiet few days. The freshly shorn sheep grazed in the sparse paddocks, awaiting the hint of new growth still weeks away from providing enough sustenance for them.

Cameron opened the gate, reclipping his seatbelt as soon as he clambered back in. The paddock of pregnant ewes was one of the last mobs awaiting the shearers' blades. They huddled against a shelterbelt on the far boundary, the low scrub protecting them from south-easterly wind gusts. Penny watched Rusty sprinting across the grass, his focus on a stand of majestic red gum trees. Cameron followed her gaze.

'I think Rusty's found something, Aunty Pen.'

'You're onto it, mate. Let's check it out.'

She turned the UTV towards the superannuated trunks, a tingle running down her spine as she saw Rusty standing beside a prostrate ewe. Penny cut the engine, removed her helmet and motioned for Cameron to go slowly as they approached on foot. The ewe kicked her back legs, trying to get away. Her rounded belly shuddered, and Penny saw a small water bag and hooves protruding from under her tail.

'It's okay, girl,' Penny murmured, crouching down for a closer look. 'I think our first lamb is on its way, Cam, whether we're ready for it or not. It's been twenty-ish years since I've pulled a lamb, but we'll have to give it a shot.'

The wind swirled around them as they waited for the ewe's next contraction. Warm liquid flowed over Penny's hands as she positioned them around the tiny hooves, ready to pull. After a moment, the sheep forgot about their presence and began pushing.

As the soggy wool heaved and the sheep snorted heavily, Penny eased the lamb closer towards her.

'Cool, I can see the nose. And there's the rest of the head.' Cameron's delight lit up his freckled face.

'Come back in a fortnight, mate, and you can help me deliver a few more,' said Penny, as the rest of the lamb slithered out. 'What a big bugger he is. No wonder she had trouble.'

Penny wiped her hands on the grass, stepping away to let the mother claim her offspring. Cameron slipped his hand into hers as they walked back to the UTV.

'How cool was that, Aunty Pen? I reckon farming's the best job ever.'

Penny smiled, looking back at the newborn they'd helped welcome into the world.

'It's pretty hard to beat.'

Frogs croaked and burbled away in the dams, their calls echoing across the property. The moon was voluptuously full, casting a luminescence over the yard and paddocks beyond. The promise of a bright day ahead lingered on the still horizon. Penny sipped her tea as she watched for shooting stars, searching for a sign she was about to make the right decision.

Instead of the twinkling skyscrapers and traffic streams she had once admired from her apartment windows, she soaked up the hazy Milky Way, its natural beauty undiminished by streetlights or headlamps.

She tugged Annabel's old woollen beanie lower over her chilly ears and wrapped Angus's jacket closely to her body. She thought back to previous occasions she'd searched for answers in the night sky. The time after her fight with her mum, when Annabel had pushed the university brochure into her hands. *What would life be like if Mum had encouraged me to stay on the farm, instead of dismissing the idea?*

Penny took another sip from her mug, gagged at the tepid tea and set it down on the deck. Rusty nosed her hand, angling for attention, and Penny stroked his glossy coat as she fast-forwarded to a few weeks after her mother's accident. Evenings when she'd sat in the wicker chair again, tears rolling down her face for the mother she had lost, the rift between them that had never been resolved. And then, just a few short weeks after that, she'd curled her feet underneath her on a moonless night, pledging to that very same blanket of stars that she would do what it took to make Annabel proud.

Penny felt a familiar twinge of regret as clouds rolled over the moon, casting the paddocks into darkness. She weighed up the dream she had shelved so many years ago in favour of the career and lifestyle she had devoted her adult life to, to honour her mum's aspirations. *Did Mum really believe the cash bonuses, the overseas trips, the lurks and perks of*

*a city life would make me happy? What was it about farm
life that she'd been so set against? And why didn't she have
the same dreams for the other girls?* Lara's words from the
bike ride rushed back to her. Or was it true that Annabel had
urged them all to look at their various career options and
she'd misunderstood? She sighed, feeling like she was going
around in circles.

'What do you think, Rusty?'

The dog's tail thumped against the boards, and a smile
spread across Penny's face as she observed the stars twinkling
brightly in the moon's absence. Even in darkness, there was
light. A shooting star streaked across the sky, a flash of bril-
liance before the moon broke free from its cloud.

Perhaps there really is no place like home, she thought,
stroking the dog's velvety ears. She shuffled the options around
in her mind until the right combination settled into place, and
sighed. *I know what I want to do—what I need to do—but
am I brave enough to take the next step?*

Fifty-three

Nerves urged Penny to walk faster across the driveway. She fumbled with the back doorhandle, almost dropping the armful of brochures.

'I'm home, Dad,' she called out through the laundry, as she tugged her arms from the jacket. A grunt of acknowledgement filtered from the lounge room and Penny tucked Dr Sinclair's bundle of information into the laundry cupboard. She would share it with Angus after a cup of tea and a piece of his favourite cake. *More chance of a warm reception*, she thought. But first, it was time to make the second call she'd been mentally rehearsing all morning.

She pulled the phone from its charger, took the stairs to her bedroom two at a time, and sat in the window seat as the call was connected.

'Boutique Media, Charlotte speaking.'

'Charlotte, it's Penny.'

'About time. I wouldn't normally take calls in the middle of lunch, but I've been picking up way too much slack for you and it's got to stop. Seriously, you're crazy if you think I'm going to keep bending over backward for you.'

Penny shrugged off a catty thought about Charlotte's willingness to bend any which way for Vince and straightened her shoulders. *When they go low, we go high.*

'I need to talk to you about the client meeting next weekend if you can spare a second?'

'You're lucky my lunch date isn't here yet. Let me guess. Are you too busy wrestling snakes and dodging kangaroos to finish the presentation? I suppose you need me to do all the work for you again?'

'You know as well as I do, Charlotte, that I've done my fair share on this project. But as it turns out, I won't make the meeting.'

'What? You can't renege on this now, Penny. I've got three other projects on deadline. Georgie is going to have kittens.'

'I've just spoken to Georgie,' said Penny. Her gaze wandered out the window to Tim loading hay bales onto the tractor forks. She ignored Charlotte's impatient huff, leaving the silence to linger for a beat longer.

'I've got bigger fish to fry out here. You want my job so much, it's yours.'

A gasp came down the phone line.

'You're leaving marketing for farming? You've got to be kidding me.'

Penny watched the dogs running behind the tractor as it motored down the laneway. The corner of her lips twitched at Charlotte's reaction.

'I don't expect you to understand, but yes, I've resigned.' Penny felt a weight lifting as she said those two words for the second time that day. Even Charlotte's laughter, like sandpaper on stainless steel, wasn't enough to extinguish the thrill.

Penny rose from her seat, her finger hovering over the 'end call' button. But as Charlotte's laughter subsided, a familiar voice whispering in the background caught her attention.

'You ready, babe?'

Penny froze. It wasn't just any voice. It was Vince's voice.

The breath caught in her throat, her mind jumping from one justification to another. *Working lunch? Maybe it's someone else?*

She strained to hear over the background noise, cupping her ear. There it was again. The man she had thought she would marry. Penny felt a hollowness in the pit of her stomach for the wasted emotion and brainpower she had poured into salvaging their relationship, her vision for their future that was pockmarked with more holes than a slice of Swiss cheese. Vince's phone had been switched off all morning and he still hadn't responded to her urgent message to call her back. Now she knew why.

Penny cleared her throat, calling loudly into the phone.

'Charlotte? You still there?'

The muffled sound and background voices went silent.

'Oops, I thought I'd hung up.'

'I just wanted a final word about Vince. You can have him too. I wouldn't touch him with a ten-foot barge pole.'

Penny's hand trembled as she hung up the phone. She wasn't sure if she'd done the right thing, but damn, it felt good.

Lightning flashed across the pre-dawn sky, illuminating the farmhouse at the end of the driveway as Tim turned the ute towards McIntyre Park. As if in reply, the kitchen lights flickered on, and his heart beat faster when he saw Penny opening the curtains, her silhouette graceful as she strolled around the kitchen. Tim blew out a breath, wishing away the buzz of attraction he felt whenever he thought about her. He'd managed to avoid her the last few days much to Eddie's disgust, who began each day with her name on his lips. Eddie had an excursion this morning. He would be sitting down to an early breakfast with Nanna Pearl right now, fuelling up before he joined a busload of other special needs people to see a theatre show in Hamilton.

It's gonna be hard on him if she heads back to Melbourne, thought Tim, brushing his feelings aside. *When, not if, Patterson.* He didn't dwell on his thoughts about losing her to the city a second time and instead cast his mind to the day ahead as he neared the house. The rain would at least give him an opportunity to tidy up the shed.

Tim twisted in his seat, assessing the tin building that housed the machinery. Another bolt of lightning struck to the west. The intense flash of light dulled, but he could still see a strange yellow glow coming from the shed window. Tim squinted, then slammed on the brakes. *What the hell?* The gravel squelched beneath his tyres and he hit the ground running.

'Mac! Mac!' He vaulted onto the deck, and ripped the back door open. 'Quick, Mac. The shed's on fire!'

Fifty-four

Penny recoiled at the smell of burned plastic and squinted against the onslaught of acrid smoke as Tim flung open the shed door. A coughing fit made her bend double, but she forced herself to straighten up. McIntyre Park was her family farm, she wasn't going to let someone else do all the dirty work. She tugged the neck of her jumper over her mouth and nose before following Tim inside.

Flames climbed up the vertical blinds and licked at the workbench, devouring a stack of old newspapers. The black benchtop had blistered and buckled, but otherwise, the damage was minimal. She breathed a sigh of relief and yelled above the noise.

'You take the extinguisher, I'll get a blanket.'

She grabbed an empty grain sack from the shelf and flung it against the wall. Her back pressed against Tim's as they worked on opposite ends of the fire. Tim blitzed the flaming bench with retardant as Penny worked her way upwards. The smell of singed arm hair floated into the putrid air. Eventually, the flickering flames vanished.

Penny panted, her arms aching as she threw down the sack. She strode outside and ripped the jumper from her face, too busy drawing mouthfuls of fresh air to appreciate the kaleidoscope of pink, silver and orange stretched across the sky, or to notice that the storm had cleared. She doubled over, trying to breathe more easily, when Tim's feet appeared in her vision. She felt his warm hand on her shoulder.

'Nice work, Mac—we got there just in time.'

He cleared his throat roughly as he shuffled through the charred bench clutter. Clinking porcelain rang out. 'Missing a few mugs? There's still a few more on the bench, all cracked and blackened. I'm no firefighter, but I'd say the fire started at Angus's old radio. Looks like he's been spending a bit of time out here.'

Penny spat out a layer of foul-tasting grunge before turning back to Tim, wiping a sooty hand across her mouth.

'Lucky you spotted it before it reached the jerry cans and the chemicals.'

'Or the machinery. Kinda tricky to finish the winter crops with a scorched tractor.'

An air of cohesiveness swirled around them as they walked towards the house together. Penny tried to slow her movements in contrast to the adrenaline pulsing through her body. Tim's impeccable timing had just saved them thousands of dollars.

'I've had that radio for donkey's years. It's still as good as the day I bought it,' said Angus, rubbing sleep from his eyes.

Penny pushed a mug of coffee in front of him and wiped her hands on a fresh pair of jeans.

'Not anymore, Dad. But it could have been a lot worse. Imagine if we'd seen it an hour later, or if it was the middle of summer. The farmhouse, the shearing shed and who knows what else would have gone up in smoke—all in the blink of an eye.'

'She's right, Angus.'

Penny turned to see Tim behind her and felt grateful for his support. In her father's khaki shirt and slightly short jeans, he looked like a mini Angus. His tone was calm and measured compared to Angus's defensive voice.

'Well, what's a fella supposed to do now? I've got no little hidey-hole anymore. These four walls are driving me insane, and I'll go mad if I have to do another month of those stupid stretches.' Angus thumped his wrist on the table like a petulant child.

Penny pushed past Tim and emerged from the laundry a moment later with the armful of brochures. She placed them on the table and took a seat next to Angus.

'I've spoken to Dr Sinclair. She gave me some pamphlets about the National Centre for Farmer Health. They've got loads of resources . . . counselling, support groups.'

She looked up at her father. His lips were pressed firmly together, his gaze unseeing out the window.

'I know you've had a rough few months, but let me make you an appointment, see what they have to offer. There are groups for people who've been through farm accidents, Dad, both online and in person. Let me help you fix this.'

She waited for his answer, but he remained silent. She could smell his shaving cream, sense the loneliness and despair underscoring his hostility, and yearned for her mother's ability to talk him out of a bad mood.

Tim nodded at her before taking his cup to the sink. He slipped into the hallway. She turned back to Angus. His good hand played with the edge of a leaflet, worrying the corner with his thumbnail. Penny watched his shoulders shudder silently. He pressed a wrinkled handkerchief to his face.

'I've already lost one parent, I can't sit back and lose another,' she whispered.

Angus's voice was gravelly, raw emotion stilting his speech. 'I'm a miserable old bastard. I don't know . . . it's hard to . . . tried to drag myself out of this hole.' He reached for the coffee with shaking hands, droplets splattering onto his faded shirt. Clearing his throat, he set the mug down with a clatter.

'It broke my heart when your mum died and you rushed away to the city, like I'd buried two of the most important women in my world. And what do I do when you come back and try running the farm? I'm jumping down your throat and finding fault because I wish it were *me* out there in the paddock. *Me* working the dogs. *Me* managing the shearing. Too busy feeling sorry for myself.'

Penny reached for his hand and covered it with her own. She silently wiped away her tears as she watched her proud father fumbling with memories and regrets.

He squeezed her hand. She pressed it back.

'Even if everything had burned to the ground this morning, we'd still have each other. It's not too late to get things back on track, Dad.'

Angus blew his nose, his eyes red as they met hers.

'Okay, I'll talk to the doc. But I want you to be straight with me. I might be a useless cripple, but I'd have to be blind as a welder's dog to miss the rift between you and Lara. And now Angie too? You'll need a ten-ton dozer to smooth that over.'

Penny looked out the window at the machinery shed, the damage that could have been so much worse. Would she look back at her fractured family unit one day and feel that it too had disappeared in the blink of an eye? She needed to fix this fissure before it festered into an impassable canyon. Penny pushed up from the table and reached for her phone.

Fifty-five

Chairs scraped against the wooden floorboards, and plastic plates were handed around as the aroma of cheese and tomato filled the kitchen. Penny lifted a piece of pizza from the box and groaned as grease dripped from the limp slice.

'Plenty of room for improvement at the takeaway place,' she said, looking around the table with a forced smile.

Lara stiffened at the comment and opened her mouth to reply when Evie piped up.

'It's the best pizza ever, Aunty Pen. Everybody loves Pino's,' she said, her braids swinging from side to side.

'Sometimes, if we're lucky, we get to order pizza on the last day of school,' added Cameron.

'Pizza, pizza, pizza,' said Eddie, demolishing his piece and reaching for seconds.

They sat around the dining table like actors in a play. Penny watched Lara murmuring to Angie, Angus talking with Tim at the far end of the table, and the children spread out between Pete and Diana. Diana rescued a loaf of garlic bread from Harry's laden plate and doled out slices to the rest of the table. Elliot took advantage of her diverted attention to flick

303

pieces of mushroom at Leo, while Cameron and Evie sat shoulder-to-shoulder beside Eddie.

This lunch is the weakest excuse for a family meal this table has ever seen. Where's the happiness? Where's the hum of carefree conversation? Almost as absent as Annabel.

Penny dismissed the thought and sampled a second slice, hoping the Hawaiian was better than the supreme. No such luck. She pushed the plate aside and tried for another smile.

'The Italians wouldn't call this pizza, Evie. One day, when you're older, you can travel to Rome. Their pizza is so tasty, you'll never eat this stuff again.'

'Here we go again, Little Miss Jetsetter sharing pearls of wisdom, with just a touch of superiority. How novel.'

Penny saw Lara's eyes narrow as she spoke. Always watching, always ready with a negative comment.

'We're here to try and work things out, Lara.' She held her palms up in front of her. She wasn't going to let this fail before it had even started. Penny's gaze flickered to Tim. Their fledgling teenage relationship was a prime example of something she'd let wither and die without the skills or experience to save it—damned if she was going to keep repeating the same mistake.

'On that lovely note, I'll kick this family meeting off to a start. We all need to get things off our chest so we can move forward. We did this exercise at our last team building day; I think it'll be good. Everyone says something positive, something constructive and something they'd like to improve.'

Penny scanned the room and moved on before Lara could offer any further snide remarks.

'I'll go first. I'm pleased everyone made an effort to come for lunch today. Offering to run the farm hasn't been a light decision, nor has it been easy. I know things have been strained these last few months, but I've officially quit my job in Melbourne so I can concentrate on the farm and get our family back together. I'm open to suggestions, but I want to make this work. For all of us.' Penny felt everyone's attention on her, from Diana's proud smile to Angie's surprised silence.

Angus raised his glass of water.

'Hear, hear. I'll drink to that. I've got an apology to make too, for being such a miserable bugger. I'm happy to have all my girls around this table, and Tim and Pete and the kids. Your mother always said blood was thicker than water and it's time we remembered that.'

The smile on his face is like blue skies after a week of rain, thought Penny. His whole presence had lightened after she'd shared her decision.

Lara pushed her sleeves up and leaned on the table.

'Don't be sucked in, Dad. She can't spend fifteen years ignoring us, then suddenly show an interest in the farm the second it's convenient. From what I've seen, Penny hasn't exactly excelled herself in farm management, and she's downright mad for throwing away her career for a six-month stint playing Farmer Joe. Selling is still the better option.'

Penny chewed on her bottom lip but remained silent, steeling herself for more. Diana waved her hand, inadvertently sending a piece of garlic bread flying into the middle of the table. Everyone was quiet as her voice boomed out.

'How about you pull your head in, Lara, and stop being so contrary? You should be supporting Penny, not tearing her down at every opportunity.' Diana turned in her chair as she jabbed a finger at Angie.

'And you, Angie . . . why aren't you thrilled Penny wants to stay? I thought you'd be delighted, but you've gone off into some parallel universe with Lara. What's happened to everyone?'

Angie dropped her slice of sweaty pizza onto her plate, rubbed her nose and burst into tears. Penny felt caught in an emotional storm. Angus's backflip, Diana rushing to her defence but unwittingly sabotaging the harmony she was trying to achieve, and now Angie breaking down at the dinner table. Lara, for all her faults and attitude, was the only one still true to form. *I need to steer this discussion back to safer waters before it gets way out of hand.*

'Diana, I appreciate your support, but can you keep it to one positive, one constructive and one way forward?'

'This is a load of crap, Penny. Your city psychology won't work here.'

Before Lara could open her mouth again, Evie burst into loud, unrestrained sobs. Penny braced herself against the urge to rush around and comfort her niece. *Lara just couldn't help herself, could she?*

Evie looked up, fear and weariness written across her freckled face as she tried to regain her composure. She took a deep breath, her face reddening as she yelled at the room. 'I'm sick of all this arguing. Everyone is always fighting.' She burst into a fresh wave of tears as all eyes turned to her.

Another cry came, this time from Eddie, who rocked back and forth in the chair, a grimace on his face as he held his hands over his ears, traces of greasy pizza stuck to his boyish jaw.

Tim ran a hand over the top of his brother's blond head as Eddie let out an anguished moan. He knew he had just minutes before Eddie would be in full-blown meltdown mode, and Tim felt a stab of irritation that he'd put him in this situation. Protecting his brother should have trumped his selfish interest in the McIntyre family dispute, especially when he'd known their discussion had the potential to get heated. He looked up at Penny, who was pulling her chair out from the table. *When was she going to tell me she quit her city job?* Anger bubbled up inside him as he realised what that meant for his role at McIntyre Park. *You should've stayed away, let them sort it out themselves.*

Tim stood, gritting his teeth as Eddie's moaning picked up a notch and drowned out Evie's shuddering sobs and Angie's sniffles. He felt the weight of everyone's attention turning towards them, ambivalence tugged at his heart. *I don't belong here.* It was time to put some distance between himself and the McIntyre family, something he should have done weeks, probably months, ago.

'It's all right, mate, let's get you home.' Tim tried to ease Eddie out of the chair, his shoulders stiff and unyielding under the soft flannelette shirt.

Penny crouched down by Eddie's side, her soft words somehow unknotting the compact shape he had curled himself into. Eddie stood slowly, still clutching his ears and keeping his eyes squeezed tightly shut.

'Will he be okay? It hasn't quite gone to plan,' said Penny, rubbing the back of her neck. Her expression was flat and Tim felt a twinge of sympathy for her thwarted family reunion.

'I should have kept him home.' *I should have stayed home too.*

He steered Eddie away from the table. Penny flinched as he swept past her, her movement hurting him more than she could know. Tim paused at the doorway.

'We're off, everyone. And just for the record, my positive is helping you guys get your stuff sorted by leaving the farm. My negative is getting close to achieving my dream and then watching it slip away, and my constructive is a recommendation that you find a new farmhand. I can't do this anymore.'

Angus struggled with his crutches, trying to get to his feet. 'Steady on, Tim. Don't leave like this. Let's sit down and discuss it civilly.'

Tim shook his head as he forced boots onto his brother's feet. 'Don't get up, mate. I shoulda stayed out of this whole debate. It's been a bloody roller coaster. For me, for Eddie, for everyone. Sorry, Angus.'

He watched Penny close her eyes briefly, felt her following them outside, but he didn't trust himself to say anything more. His thoughts skittered between his promise to help her and his commitment to himself to one day own the land beneath their feet. He was no better than bloody Vince. His movements were jerky, filled with self-loathing as he bundled Eddie into the ute.

'I'm sorry, Tim. I didn't expect it to turn into a circus.'

'It's my fault. I shouldn't have even entertained Lara's suggestion to buy the farm, or made promises I can't keep. To Angus. To you. To myself.' Tim studied his dusty boots, the heels worn down, the leather scarred and scuffed from years of hard work. Hard work that had got him no closer to his dreams.

'So that's it? You're walking away?'

'I've overstayed my welcome here, Mac. I'll arrange you a fresh set of hands for Monday morning, but apart from that, I'm done.' He climbed into the ute before he could change his mind.

Penny's stomach twisted as she watched Tim slide into the ute. The thought of him walking away from the farm both terrified and thrilled her. She lifted her hand as his engine roared to life, and his tailgate disappeared down the driveway. *Why the ambivalence? Haven't you just spent months cursing Tim Patterson and his presence at McIntyre Park? At least there's no buyer waiting in the wings now.* But her victory felt hollow as she walked back inside.

Voices rang out from the kitchen as Penny slipped her boots into the shoe rack. A packet of lamingtons was keeping the younger children occupied, but she saw that the discussion had continued in her absence and her oldest niece and nephew had more pressing matters on their minds.

'But why do you even want Grandpa to sell the farm, Mum? That's such a stupid idea,' Evie yelled, screwing up her mouth.

'She's right, Aunty Lara. Everybody else wants the farm to stay like it is. Aunty Penny is trying her best,' said Cameron.

'And we get to come and visit while Grandpa still owns it. Please tell him to keep it, Mum. Please, please, please.'

Evie turned to Angus and Penny could see the mix of emotions swirling as the young girl fought back tears.

'We've got a bit to sort out, Missy. Leave your mother be.'

'But Grandpa—'

Lara's voice cut across the whining tone.

'Evie Kingsley, dammit. Listen to me. I. Said. Drop. It.'

Penny looked at the tense faces around the table, the tired and strained conversations far from what she'd set out to achieve. As if providing an exclamation point for Penny's realisation, Evie shoved the table and its weight wobbled under the force of her anger.

The glasses in the middle of the table jiggled, their empty rims ringing out over Evie's irritated growl. The colour rose in her pale cheeks and in her anger, Penny noticed she was a dead ringer for Lara, whose cheeks and neck were also flushed. Lara spoke again, her tone louder as her patience stretched to its limit.

'It's an adult subject, so stay out of it, Evie. You kids need to leave us to sort this out.'

Diana winced as Evie blew out a quick breath and darted across the room on her toes as if she were intercepting a ball on the netball court. She grabbed hold of Lara's forearm and dug her fingernails into her mother's skin. Lara wrenched her arm away, clamping a hand over the bright red welt.

'I hate you, you mean old cow. I wish I could live with Dad.'

The colour dropped from Lara's face in an instant. Penny held her breath at the tense scene, unable to drag her gaze away from her trembling niece, her enraged sister or the welt that was forming on Lara's arm.

'Get in the car. Now.' Lara hissed the words through gritted teeth, her glare red-hot as she issued the order.

'No.'

Penny tried to think of a way to defuse the tension in the room, but before she could come up with a solution, Lara's hand snaked out and slapped her daughter across the face.

The stinging sound of flesh on flesh shot across the room. A red mark appeared instantly on Evie's flushed cheek before her face crumpled in disbelief. Penny gasped. Angie's hand flew to her mouth. Pete scowled, reaching for Cameron's hand and dragging him to his side. Angus's walking stick clattered to the floor, breaking the silence. Cameron startled like a gazelle, pulled against his father's hand. He leapt to Evie's side and clutched her hand.

'C'mon, Evie, let's get out of here.'

The two children fled the room, shock written across Evie's face as she followed her cousin.

'What the bloody hell was that? You didn't have to hit her,' yelled Angus, his face turning puce as he leaned towards Lara. 'Your mother and I never once raised a hand to you. She'd be turning in her grave right now, Lara.'

Shame flooded Lara's already flushed features as she pressed a hand against her pursed lips. Her knuckles turned white in her fist and she squeezed her eyes tight, blocking the horrified stares from around the table.

Fifty-six

A pot of tea, thought Penny absently, as she tried to digest the scene. She rose from her chair slowly, soothing her shaken nerves and went about the ritual of making tea. Annabel's teapot was right at the back of the cupboard; the box of tea leaves hidden behind hard packets of long-forgotten jelly crystals and rusty tins of spaghetti. She glanced back and forth between the boiling kettle and the dining table. The children had devoured the lacklustre dessert. Angus flicked through the local paper angrily, turning the pages at a pace too rapid for reading, not even noticing the pieces of coconut the twins were flicking across the table. Diana and Pete conferred in the corner, their conflict palpable. Angie's head was tucked in close to Lara's. Even though they were all shocked by what they'd just seen, Penny knew Angie would be trying to reassure Lara.

Lara raised her head from her hands and looked up as Penny placed the teapot on the table. Her eyes were as red as the fingernail marks in her arm. Her expression was far from conciliatory.

'Don't look at me like that, Penny. None of you know what it's like to raise a child single-handedly. You wouldn't have a clue how hard it is when the buck stops with you. Every. Single. Day.'

'I didn't say a word. I think we could all do with a cup of tea though.'

Penny set mugs in front of everyone and walked around pouring tea, before resuming her seat next to Angus. The hot beverage stung her lips and she took another sip, the physical sensation easier to deal with than the emotion.

'Happen often, does it, Lara? Hitting your only child?' Diana's words were gravely quiet. Pete's hand settled on her arm, but she shook it off without a backward glance. He stood up, smoothing his beard with a nervous hand.

'I'll take the kids to the lounge room, leave you guys to it. Keep it calm, Diana.'

Lara waited until the twins and Leo were out of the room before responding. 'Have you ever seen Evie with bruises or a black eye, Diana? Everyone loses their temper occasionally. I bet you've resorted to a wooden spoon.'

'Don't start throwing stones. This is not about me.'

'It's never about you though, is it? Such a bloody martyr, working your guts out for beatification while us heathens blunder around as best we can.'

Diana snorted, although no trace of amusement showed on her face.

Angus looked up from his newspaper. 'Stop it, you two. You should be ashamed of yourselves, bickering like children. If I had two good arms, I'd bang your heads together.'

Angie unfolded her arm from around Lara's shoulder and pulled away. Penny had seen that set of her jaw before, the only sharp edge on her rounded face, when she'd insisted on the baking therapy classes. It was the first sliver of division between Angie and Lara since they'd teamed up about the farm sale.

'It's time to tell them, Lara.'

Lara pushed her chair back in anger.

Angie flinched at the sudden movement but continued nodding. 'It's gone too far now. You're pushing shit uphill.'

Lara shook her head, the nerve in her jaw working overtime as she stared at Angie. 'Don't you dare.'

Penny looked at Angus and Diana, but both were as puzzled as she was.

'Tell us what?'

Fifty-seven

Tim pulled into Nanna Pearl's driveway, one arm on the steering wheel, the other rubbing Eddie's shoulder.

He felt like driving until the ute ran out of petrol, as far away from Bridgefield as his fuel tank would take him, but he needed to think about Eddie. Put his brother's welfare before his own turbulent emotions, ignore the combination of shame, pride and lust attacking his conscience. Their bachelor pad held no appeal in contrast to the farmhouse, which was undoubtedly a family home even when the relationships within it were in a state of flux. Nanna Pearl's was the next best thing and he had instinctively pointed the ute in her direction.

He helped Eddie out of the car, walked him across the covered carport and sat him on the church pew beside her back door.

'Take your boots off, mate. We're at Nanna's now.'

Eddie's moaning had stopped, but his groans brought Nanna Pearl to the door as Tim eased the boots off.

'Oh, you poor little mite. What's wrong, precious?' The knitting in her hand fell to the church pew, forgotten as she wrapped her arms around her grandson.

'Shush now, it's okay,' she soothed. Eventually, Eddie's distress calmed under the same familiar crooning that had soothed them both through their mother's abandonment and their father's incarceration. Her gaze shifted to Tim. He blanched under her scrutiny.

'Bad day at work, mate?'

'You could say that. Had a fire in the machinery shed this morning—it's all right, we sorted it,' Tim added, assuaging his grandmother's alarm, 'and Mac's hell-bent on getting her family back on track, so she threw together a family lunch. If I were smarter, I would've steered well clear, but with Eddie's bus dropping him off at their driveway right on midday, it seemed a good option.' He blew out a frustrated breath, raking a hand through his already messed-up hair.

'From the look on both your faces, I'm guessing it didn't go to plan?'

'Nope. It was going to be a shitstorm right from the start. Lara's been on the warpath for weeks, Mac's focused on rigid timeframes, Evie's like a little wildcat, and Angus is more like his usual self, but his mood can still chop and change like the weather. I should have known better, but . . .' He looked into his grandmother's face. The thick lines in her soft skin were as much a part of her as the lavender scent and the purple hair.

'Sounds like you knew it was going to be tough, but it was worth the pain to support someone you care about.'

He searched her face, wondering just how much she knew. From the look of understanding and the gentle squeeze from her hand, maybe he hadn't hidden his feelings as well as he thought. *Care about? Like, love, hate?* It was hard to know exactly what his feelings were towards Penny, which didn't make it any easier.

'Penny's a lovely girl, Tim, and she has a good heart. They all do, they've just been sidetracked along the way. They'll pull through. And when they sort themselves out, you'll know where you stand with that farm.'

Tim looked up sharply. Of course, she would have heard all about the farm offer, the way his ambition had driven a deeper wedge between the McIntyre sisters. She knew better than anyone that his heart was set on a property of his own, for himself and Eddie.

'A little birdie mentioned it at yoga. You know how these things work. You'll have all this when I die, lovie.'

Tim looked around him, the small yard filled with flowers and garden statues, surrounded by paddocks that had been carved off years ago to repay his father's debts. He loved her little cottage, but without the acreage, it fell well short of his farming dreams.

Tim mustered up a smile and squeezed her hand back gently. 'I'd rather have you any day, Nanna.'

∽

Penny wrapped her hands around the mug and took a sip of her tea, hoping if she made the first step, then everyone else would follow. But the rest of her family ignored their tea as they waited for Lara to fill them in.

Angie tried reasoning with her again. 'They'll understand, Lara. They're family. Hiding it all has made things worse, not better. Almost pushed us to the brink. And all for nothing.'

Angie looked at Penny as if issuing a silent apology for abandoning her, before returning her focus to Lara. Penny perched on the edge of her seat, straining to understand what they were talking about. Her impatience got the better of her and the words tumbled from her mouth uncensored.

'What haven't you told us? What else have you done, Lara?'

Penny felt the force of Lara's glare like a laser beam.

'Come on, girl, spit it out,' said Angus, his voice deflecting Lara's attention.

Lara froze like a rabbit trapped in the headlights, squirming in her seat. With a curse, she jumped to her feet and ran from the room.

Fifty-eight

The light rain had lifted in the minute or two it took Penny to shove her boots on.

Lara was sitting in the driver's seat of her battered car, engine running, wipers scraping aimlessly against the now dry windscreen. Rusty weaved between Penny's legs, his tail thumping as she strode down the steps.

'Lara. Let's put it all behind us and go back inside. You can't drive anywhere like that, you'll plough straight into a tree, the state you're in.'

Lara lifted her head from the steering wheel, tears falling down her cheeks.

'I can't bloody well go back in there. Dad will disown me when he hears the mess I'm in.' She spat out the words bitterly.

Penny tried to imagine a scenario that would make Angus McIntyre disown any of his family, but failed.

She reached in through the window and flicked off the windscreen wipers, then pulled the key from the ignition.

'Come on. Whatever it is, we'll deal with it together.' Penny opened the car door and covered Lara's cold hand. She pressed it softly and coaxed her out of the car. For the first time in a long time, Penny felt like she was the older sister and wrapped her arms around Lara's stiff form. Lara didn't embrace her, but nor did she push her away. *At least that's something.* Another thought niggled at the back of her mind. She peered into the back seat. It was empty.

'Evie's not in there, I already checked,' said Lara.

'She's probably forgotten about it already,' Penny lied, wanting to ease Lara's burden. 'She'll be curled up in front of the telly, feeling bad about giving her mum a hard time.'

They pulled off their boots, feeling all eyes on them as they re-entered the kitchen. Questions lingered in the air as thick as the smell of stale takeaway. Penny flicked the kettle on again and tossed the spent pizza boxes into the garbage bin. She brewed a fresh pot of tea and emptied and then refilled the untouched mugs on the table.

Lara pushed her mug around in circles, twisting it clockwise then anti-clockwise. Penny had worried she would bottle up after her first false start, but once she started talking, she didn't stop. No one dared interrupt. Nerves threaded themselves around her words.

'Sam came to the house the other month. Then he turned up at the school gate occasionally, just flexing his power, taunting me. Evie was ecstatic. There was no easy way to tell her that this man with boxes of Lego and bags of chips could break bones without a backward glance.'

Her hand left the mug and curled out in front of her, as if studying a long-forgotten injury. She gently furled it into a fist and took a shaky breath before continuing.

'At the time I was so frantic about Dad's accident, unsure if he'd pull through or not, that I didn't realise why Sam had come back. It wasn't until I fronted him with a cricket bat and told him to get out of town or I'd file a restraining order.

Then he waved his trump card in my face and told me to push for the farm sale.

'This is . . . this is really hard to talk about. It's . . . Sam and I. Sam . . .' She blew out an anguished breath, her fingers tracing over the raised welts on her upper arm.

'Sam likes to hurt me . . . it started small. But I couldn't make it stop. And if I refused, he threatened to tell Evie how disgusting I was. Apparently, one night he was filming us secretly. And that's why I wanted to sell the farm. So I could buy that video off him, before he uploaded it online and shared it with everyone I knew. Starting with you, Dad. And then he was going to use it as leverage to get full custody of Evie.'

Lara's voice petered out to a whisper in the last sentence, and she sipped her tea. Her sight remained anchored to the table. Penny's sympathy grew as she listened, any irritation vanishing in the wake of Lara's revelation.

She racked her brain, trying to think of any occasions Sam's behaviour had indicated any of this, or a time she had noticed bruises, or fear, on her strong albeit prickly sister. She came up with a blank. *It's because you weren't there*, a voice inside her accused. Then she remembered the mark on Lara's back at the hospital. The way Evie had behaved on the netball court, at the table. Penny washed away the feeling with a mouthful of cold tea but confusion grew in its wake. *That doesn't make sense. If he was hurting Lara, why wouldn't the footage give* her *leverage?*

'It'd never hold up in court, Lara. The video sounds like it exposes Sam for the scumbag he is,' said Penny.

Lara shook her head. 'I can't bear to think of anybody seeing that video. I just can't risk it, Pen. But that's not the worst of it. If blackmail and domestic abuse weren't enough,

Sam added in a clincher. He said if I told anyone or contacted the police, he'd take our daughter.'

❧

Angus threw back a shot of whisky and pushed his glass towards Diana.

'That bastard. I can't believe I trusted Sam, welcomed him into our home, clapped him on the shoulder and drank beer with him when Evie was born. You should have said something, love. We would have chased him off with a shotgun, not a cricket bat. I'll have another dram, thanks, Diana.'

'How could I, Dad? I had no evidence, nothing to take to the police. Just a few threats and memories of the bruises and cracked ribs.'

'We would have helped, Lara. We're your family, that's what we're supposed to do.' Diana poured Angus and then herself a glass of whisky and cringed as the fiery liquid burned her throat.

Penny looked at Angie, incredulous to see Diana drinking straight spirits.

'He's got me over a barrel and there's not a damn thing I can do about it. Except get him the money and be rid of him.'

Penny saw guilt seeping through Lara's resignation.

'But how did you know about it too, Angie? You and Lara have been thick as thieves these last few weeks. I should have known something was up,' said Angus.

'I bumbled my way into it when I saw Sam at the supermarket last month. He told me he might move back to town. I pressed Lara until she caved and suddenly the farm sale seemed a pretty viable compromise for Evie and Lara's dignity.'

Penny leaned forward, the hurt from Angie's well-intentioned abandonment softening amid the magnitude of Sam's threats.

'When he says, "take Evie", does he mean he'll fight for custody? Or does he mean take, as in "abscond"?'

A shiver went down Penny's back as she watched her sister's gaze dart around the room, suddenly jumpy.

'Custody . . . I'm sure he meant custody.'

The ringing telephone cut through the silence, making Lara jump in her seat. Diana answered it, then turned to Penny with a question on her face. She covered the receiver.

'It's Vince.'

'Vince?' Penny shook her head, flicking her hand dismissively at his intrusion.

'Sorry Vince, she's not available. What? You're in Bridgefield? Right now?' Diana gave Penny a confused look and shrugged as she held out the phone.

Penny swore under her breath as she walked to the phone. She gave Vince directions in a clipped tone, then sat back down at the table and surveyed her sisters. Their shoulders were slumped, their expressions grim. Even Angus seemed lost in thought.

'So, where do we go from here? Convince the police to throw Sam in jail?' Penny said.

Angie looked up, her eyes tired and sad, lacking their usual sparkle. 'I don't think verbal threats are enough to lock someone up, Pen.'

Lara pushed back her chair. 'I'm heading home—maybe Evie's decided to walk the seven kilometres. I sure as hell can't stick around to witness that idiot Vince sweet-talk his way back into your life.'

Penny snorted. 'I'm not going to let him, but I can't just send him back to the city, another four hours of driving, without even saying hello, can I?'

'Says who? If Sam's taught me anything, it's that bad behaviour doesn't deserve a second chance. Or a third. You're worth ten of those bastards.'

'So are you, love. You all are,' said Angus, resting his hand on top of Lara's.

Penny surveyed the kitchen. Her family was united in despair. It wasn't the way she'd wanted to forge ahead, but at least it was a start. She stacked the dishes on the bench, looking out at the paddocks as her mind jumped from one drama to another. Were they going to clear all this up? And how was she going to manage the farm without Tim's photographic memory of each flock, each paddock and the jobs that needed doing? As much as she hated to admit it, his work was second to none. *I'm going to miss him in more ways than one.*

Fifty-nine

Diana and Lara bustled up their families in the lounge room, ready to leave, as Penny and Angie cleared the table.

'Elliot, put that down. It's time to go.'

'Cameron?'

'Pete, can you grab the nappy bag? Evie? Cameron . . . ?'

'Switch it off, Harry. Pete, where's Cameron?'

Pete walked into the kitchen, nappy bag and robot toy clutched in one arm, Leo in the other. Harry and Elliot trailed behind him, but Cameron was nowhere to be seen.

'How am I supposed to know where he is? I took one for the team and watched the bloody *Lion King* for the millionth time. I thought he was with Evie.' Pete frowned at Diana.

'Evie . . . Cameron . . .'

Lara strode into the kitchen, her brow furrowed, chewing her lip as she scanned the room.

'They haven't been back here, have they? Cam? Evie?'

Penny shook her head, her pulse racing as Diana and Lara both called for their children, anxiety marking their unanswered calls.

The brass knocker rapped against the wooden door and Penny sprinted to open it, hoping Cameron and Evie had just been playing a trick. Her heart sank when she saw it was Vince.

Apart from a few creases at the elbows and hips of his navy suit and the coating of dust on his black loafers, Vince looked as perfectly poised as ever. Penny inhaled the aftershave she'd bought him last Christmas, but it didn't give her any joy. She ran a shaky hand through her half-arsed ponytail and stepped away as he leaned in to kiss her cheek.

'What the hell are you doing here, Vince? I don't have time for your games anymore.' She looked beyond him to where Pete and Diana were canvassing the yard. Angie and Lara had split up to search the house from top to bottom. Angus sat, tense and frustrated by his uselessness, in the recliner as the children watched another Disney classic.

'I miss you, babe. I know I screwed things up big time, but I want to make it up to you.'

'It's too late. Even if I wanted to, I can't trust you again.'

'Don't say that, we can come back from here. Penny and Vince, the dream team. I know I hurt you, babe, but it will never happen again. I swear on my mother's grave.'

Penny sucked in a quick breath. *How could I have fallen for this guy?* She opened her mouth to point out that Mrs Callas was still alive and well, which was more than could be said for her own mother, but his finger pressed against her lips, demanding silence.

'No, no. Don't say anything more. I've got something you're going to like.' He slipped his hand into his breast pocket and pulled out a ring box.

Penny closed her eyes, shaking her head as he dropped to one knee. *Was it really just months ago that I so desperately wanted this proposal, craved the question he's about to ask?* Here in the weak afternoon sun, when her family was tearing the place upside down searching for missing children, his proposal felt like a cheap afterthought.

'Get up, Vince. Don't even bother. Haven't you noticed a hint of chaos since you arrived? Have you even asked me how I am, or how my father is? Or introduced yourself to my family?' Her angry voice matched her flashing eyes.

Vince looked around him, surveying the surroundings he'd overlooked in his rush to propose.

'What's everyone doing? I passed someone along the road earlier, but they didn't even wave. I thought you said waving was mandatory around here.'

Penny jumped on the snippet of information.

'Near our driveway? What type of car? Blond hair? Any children with him?'

'Steady on. I'm about to propose and you're more worried about a blond man who may or may not have been driving past? Have you replaced me that quickly?'

Penny pushed past him and ran towards Diana. Vince followed, keeping a wide berth of Rusty, who stayed glued to Penny's leg.

'What's going on, Penny?'

'My niece and nephew are missing, and I've just found out my sister's ex-husband threatened to snatch their daughter.' She called out towards the machinery shed.

'Diana! Pete! Vince just saw someone suspicious driving past.'

They jogged over. Vince shifted in his loafers as he received the undivided attention of two frantic parents.

'Well, if you categorise not waving or smiling as suspicious, then . . . yes, I guess he was. Average guy, some crappy old station wagon. I didn't notice his hair colour or any children. I was too busy swerving off the side of that single-lane road.'

Pete's shoulders dropped.

'Could have been anyone. Thanks, anyway.'

'Have you called Tim yet, Penny?'

'Not yet. I'll try Nanna Pearl's house now, Diana. You guys heading to the shearing shed? Make sure you look underneath too, they could be below the catching pens.'

Vince piped up, his face animated.

'Is this Tim the farm lackey you were talking about, Pen? The one with the dodgy father in jail? I'd be hunting him down if my kids were missing. The apple never falls far from the tree.'

Pete spun around and grabbed a handful of Vince's crisp, white shirt. 'You've got no right to waltz in here wearing your wanky suit and stirring up trouble. Tim's a bloody good bloke.'

Penny's eyes widened. Diana's husband was ordinarily placid and mild-mannered. She'd never seen this side of him. She grabbed Vince's arm and pulled him out of Pete's grasp. She watched his jaw clench at the dirty mark on his $200 shirt. He shook off her hand as they turned towards the house.

'Since you're here, Vince, you can make yourself useful. Come inside while I call Tim, then I'll give you a job. We need to find those kids before someone else does.'

Sixty

Angus dragged his damaged leg into the footwell of the side-by-side and allowed Penny to buckle up his helmet. He winced as she strapped the seatbelt into place, accidentally brushing against his hip.

'Sorry, Dad. Hold on tight.'

She pushed the UTV forward. The smell of damp earth and fresh grass whipped past them as they headed down the laneway. A tight smile crept across Angus's face.

'Not a bad way to travel, is it?'

Angus nodded, scanning the paddock. 'Better than sitting in front of the cartoons while everyone else searches. Good thinking delegating that job to Vince. Young Evie knows this place better than Cameron. You'll need an extra set of peepers to scout out their hiding spot.'

She slowed to open a gate, scanning the dam ahead for any sign of bright clothing or— Her heart dropped into her stomach as she thought of the worst-case scenario.

'You don't think they'd go into the dams, do you?' Penny pushed the accelerator down, urging the UTV towards the water. She held her breath until she reached the embankment

and exhaled with relief when a solitary duck flew away, rippling
the otherwise clear surface.

'They're not toddlers. I'm more worried about that bastard,
Sam. If I'd known about him and Lara, I'd have taken a shotgun
around to his place and sorted him out myself. I might not
be able to hold a gun right now, but heaven help him if he's
snatched those two.'

❧

'Cameron? Evie?' Penny's voice was already hoarse from yelling,
but she searched the machinery shed a final time.

'This isn't funny anymore. Come out now, please.'

A mouse ran across the back of the shed and a crow cawed,
heckling her efforts as she did a final sweep of the area, climbing
into the machinery cabs to ensure the children weren't hiding
inside. She jumped down from the steps, holding her breath
to walk past the shrivelled lump of blackened electrical cable
that had caused this morning's fire. A fast-moving front sent
rain pelting down her back as she pulled the sliding door shut
behind her.

*Where are they? Hiding or taken? And to think I was
standing here this morning, breathing a sigh of relief and
counting my blessings after the fire.*

She pulled her jacket closer, accepting the cold as penance
for her misdirected priorities. She thought of the children's
winter jackets still lying on the laundry bench, which would
have warded off hypothermia.

The rain she had repeatedly cursed for delaying the shearing
slammed hard against her failings. *I've been so short-sighted.
The holidays and expensive clothes I used to covet. The
replaceable material things like houses, sheds, apartments
and jobs. All that time I wasted worrying about Vince and
Charlotte. Even a family rift seems trivial in comparison to*

this. Penny swiped at her tears as regret washed over her. *How could I have accepted Lara's surly veneer without noticing something was terribly wrong? Was I that self-absorbed and hell-bent on proving myself that I missed her cry for help?* The sound of rain on corrugated iron interspersed with the echoes of 'Cameron! Evie!' pulled her out of her wallowing.

There would be no replacing these two precious children if they fell into a dam, or worse, slipped into Sam's hands. The thought made her stomach curdle. She looked at her watch as the sun dipped closer to the horizon. Almost 4 p.m. They could be anywhere by now. It was time to revise their plan of action.

'I've checked the closest paddocks, the machinery shed twice and the old cubby house in the shelterbelt. Still no word from Tim either, it keeps going straight to MessageBank,' said Penny.

Angus piped up. 'He must be out of range. Try him again. He's the type of guy you need around in an emergency, not like whatshisname in there.'

Penny didn't bother defending Vince. His complete lack of assistance, apart from a suggestion they call the police, was underwhelming. *Dad's right, I can't believe I wanted to marry that man*, she thought, throwing a dark look in the direction of the lounge room.

She punched Tim's number into the phone for a fourth time and pulled it to her ear as the others continued their updates. Pete wrapped his arms around Diana, pulling her tight against him as she blew her nose.

'We've done inside, outside and underneath the shearing shed, inside all the farm vehicles and cars. Nothing.'

'They aren't in the house, Pete. We've accounted for every cupboard and Lara did a clean sweep of every room after me. If they're hiding, they've got a good place,' said Angie.

Lara let out a strained sigh, looking at the old clock beside the calendar then glancing outside where the last rays of sun had turned the paddocks a rich, golden-yellow.

'I can't imagine Sam would take them. There'll be big trouble if they're hiding. I'll . . . I'll . . .' Lara squeezed her lips shut, blinking back tears. 'I know my hot temper got us into this mess, but if Evie's hiding, I'll need every ounce of self-control not to shake her.'

'Thought you would've learned your lesson by now, Lara.' Diana's voice was high-pitched, desperation making her wild. She pressed her face into Pete's broad chest with a sob.

Penny leapt in, sensing the knife edge both her sisters balanced on.

'Don't start that again—we'll find them.'

But her words were too late. Diana's comment was like diesel on an inferno.

'Don't you think I feel bad enough already, Diana? Anything else you'd like to add?' Lara yelled, her eyes blazing. 'Maybe you could just write a stat dec stating I'm an unfit mother and Sam would do a better job raising Evie? Or perhaps you could help Sam upload his porno to YouTube, save him taxing his tiny brain? Would you be happy then? Would you?'

Lara's yelling brought Vince to the doorway. Penny watched his mouth fall open as he caught the last sentence. She could see judgement tainting his expression, the way he pulled himself up a little taller and took a step away from the tableau, distancing himself. In that instant, Penny knew her feelings for him had well and truly shrivelled up. *These people are my family, as crazy as it may seem to an outsider, and I won't be jumping ship, no matter how rapidly it's sinking.*

'Settle down, love, we're all worried,' said Angus, his voice weary.

Lara caught sight of Vince in the doorway and shook her head at his expensive suit, the way he had failed to observe the unspoken shoes-off policy and his complete uselessness in the crisis. Penny started towards him, hoping to usher him out before he said something stupid. Lara growled at him from across the room.

'What the hell are you staring at?'

Within seconds, Lara had scooped up a glass from the table and flung it towards him. Vince ducked as it shattered against the wall, showering the plaster with shards of glass and coating him with a spray of whisky.

Sixty-one

Tim's boots clattered on the steps and he yanked the back door open. He searched Penny's face for answers, sweat beading on his forehead after the panicked drive over.

'Have you found them, Mac?'

Penny shook her head, anguish at their lack of progress written in her tight-knit brow and pained expression.

He swore softly, assessing the anxious faces in the kitchen. Although Vince wasn't at the table, Tim knew he was in there somewhere, the only likely owner of the Monaro in the driveway. Any other day, Tim would have stopped to admire the classic car, but the safety of Cameron and Evie trumped everything else—even his own irritation at the buffoon's unexpected arrival.

'I got here as quick as I could. Eddie's with Nanna Pearl. She said Sam called in to her cottage last night, borrowed a few litres of fuel to limp his crappy old wagon to the petrol station. Damn lucky he didn't turn up at my place, the bastard. I had no idea he'd be capable of anything like this,' said Tim. Slipping off his boots, he followed her inside, noticing a strong smell of whisky overlaying the takeaway pizza aroma. An open bottle and several glasses sat on the table, forgotten in the panic.

Angus pushed himself up with his walking stick, reaching out unsteadily to shake Tim's hand.

'Thanks for coming, mate. That's the first lead we've had all afternoon. It must have been Sam driving down our road earlier. Bloody mongrel. Wait till I get my hands on him . . .'

Pete and Lara flew to their feet, pressing Tim for information he didn't have until Diana raised a hand and spoke over everybody.

'Wait a minute. You should stay here, Dad. Just in case we're barking up the wrong tree with Sam, and the kids are hiding. No use all of us scouring the Bridgefield countryside. I'll stay with you. Angie, you'll stay too?'

'I'll man the phone.'

Angie nodded at Diana, and Penny rushed to the door, stumbling a little. Tim's hand shot out to steady her and a little zap of electricity ran between them. Their eyes met. She'd felt it too. He looked away, begging his frantic mind to focus. *You're done here, Patterson, not to mention her boyfriend's visiting and the kids are missing. For God's sake.*

'You won't be keeping me home. I'll drive,' said Pete, shoving his phone into his pocket.

Tim pulled his boots on as Penny grabbed a jacket from the coat rack, trying not to watch the way her body wriggled as she shrugged her arms into the mud-spattered Driza-Bone. She dragged a beanie over her ponytail and called orders into the kitchen.

'Angie, get on the phone to Mrs Beggs at the general store. If anyone knows anything, it'll be her. If you don't have any luck, give Olive from yoga a call. Between the two of them, they'll find out Sam's new address in a jiffy. Call my mobile and let us know.'

Tim nodded at Angus and flashed a tight smile at the stricken sisters left in the kitchen. He felt the weight of their expectation, a lump in his stomach forming at the thought of returning to the farmhouse without the two missing children. *What if we can't deliver?*

❧

Penny pulled the seatbelt across her waist and frisked her top pocket. She groaned and leaned forward, speaking over Pete's shoulder.

'Stop! My phone's still on charge upstairs. I'll be back in a second.'

She jumped out of the four-wheel drive, sprinted through the kitchen and took the stairs two at a time.

Pulling the phone from its charger, she knocked a pile of paperwork to the ground. As she skirted around the mess, she spotted Evie's handwriting. She picked up the card, running a finger over the neat lettering.

Get well soon, Aunty Pen. You're my favourite aunty. I love having you home and I can't wait to visit you in the city when you're better too. Love from your favourite niece, Evie.

Penny hugged it to her chest before setting it next to the framed photo of Annabel and herself.

She knew her mother would have lain down in front of a bus to save her children. *Cameron and Evie might not be my children, but I'll do whatever it takes to find them.* She ran down the stairs, two at a time again. *Hopefully, we're not too late.*

❧

Penny sat wedged between Leo's backward-facing seat, a bag of toys and Tim's leg. She could feel his body heat through

the denim and wondered if he would notice her temperature
skyrocketing in such close confines. She flicked the back-seat
air vent open as her mobile buzzed and read Angie's message
out loud.

'Head towards the old homestead on Kent Road. Sam's
charmed Mrs Simmons into a three-month lease with a view
to buy.'

Pete pumped the brakes, fishtailing on the slick road, and
swung the car towards the west. His headlights flashed across
paddocks of red gums and lambs, windscreen wipers trying
valiantly to keep up with the heavy rain.

The glare of red and blue lights illuminated the sky ahead
of them. Pete swore as he flicked on his indicator, pulled off
the road and waited impatiently.

'We don't have time for this.'

'Not a word about Sam or the kids until we've had a chance
to speak to him ourselves. Last thing I need is everyone knowing
about that video,' said Lara, her face desolate.

Penny nodded, her stomach twisting as a policeman
approached the car. *I wonder if Pete feels equally torn about
lying to the local constabulary*, she thought, pleased to be in
the back seat.

'Hey, Matt. How can I help?'

'G'day, Pete. Didn't realise it was you. Hey, Lara. What are
you up to this evening? No Diana or kids tonight?'

Penny squinted as he shone a torch in the back seat, instinctively moving closer to Tim. He greeted them both by name,
even though she didn't recognise him and she fought the urge
to beg for his assistance.

'They've got a school thing. We're just out for a drive,' Pete
lied. 'But we'd better keep going, mate, unless there's anything
I can help you with?'

The policeman pulled a breath-testing machine from his belt and fitted a fresh tube.

'Just blow into here, Pete, and I'll leave you to it. Gotta be seen doing the right thing in the community—friends and strangers alike.'

Pete complied with the request, his composure impressive.

'Clean as a whistle. Be careful on the road, mate. There's some fruit loops out there.'

'Too true. Night, Matt.'

Pete kept an eye in the rear-view mirror as he pulled back onto the road. He drove carefully as the police car turned and followed them along the highway.

Lara exhaled with relief as Matt sped up and overtook them. Penny prayed they wouldn't regret the decision to tackle Sam on their own.

Paddocks of sheep gave way to rows and rows of blue gums. Pete flicked off the headlamps, eased the car into a short, straight driveway and aimed for the brightly lit homestead. He paused beside a utility shed. Penny felt her legs quiver as Tim unbuckled his seatbelt.

'I'll head up to the house as soon as I've scoped out the sheds. Be careful. I've seen enough of Sam on a footy field to know he'll come out swinging if we push him too far.'

Lara made a dismissive sound. 'Don't I know it.'

The smell of eucalyptus flowed into the car as Tim slipped into the darkness. Pete continued towards the house and pulled up beside a silver wagon. Penny opened her door apprehensively. A dog barked in the distance. Lara and Pete's boots echoed on the driveway as they followed a line of bushes and shrubs to the front door. Penny scanned the floodlit yard, blinking rapidly to keep the rain out of her eyes. She jogged past clipped hedges and well-tended flowerbeds, keen to keep up with the others. A creepy feeling prickled the back of her neck as she contemplated what they would find inside.

Sixty-two

Ornate leadlight panels flanked the front door, and Penny saw a shadow cross the hallway inside. Lara rapped again on the door.

Finally, Sam's face appeared behind the wavy, tinted glass. Lara stepped up, so she was almost nose-to-nose with him when he pulled the door open. 'Where are the children?'

A smile spread across Sam's face as he shook his freshly shaved head. He ignored Lara's question.

'Family reunion, eh? If you'd given me notice, I would have baked scones.'

His laugh made the hair on Penny's neck prickle even more, and she glared at him as she entered the house. She tried not to flinch as he locked the door behind them and searched for her niece and nephew as they filed down the antique-filled hallway.

They stopped in the kitchen.

'Where are they, Sam? We're not leaving until you tell us,' said Pete, crossing his arms.

Sam raised his eyebrows, gesturing to the empty dining room.

'Fetched a great price on the black market. Little blue eyes. Innocent faces.'

Penny's jaw dropped. Lara raced towards her ex-husband. Pete grabbed Lara's arm and pulled her back to his side.

'My bad. I shouldn't joke about these things. Still a feisty one, aren't you, Lara? I thought I'd broken those habits.'

Sam pulled a mobile phone from his jeans pocket and dangled it between his fingers.

'How's the farm sale going? Remember what I said would happen if you told anyone about our little arrangement?' Sam lifted an eyebrow as he typed into his phone.

'It's not an arrangement, Sam, it's blackmail. I was getting you the money. You shouldn't have forced my hand by dragging Evie and Cameron into this mess.'

Sam turned the phone screen around, and even from a distance, Penny recognised an email layout. His finger hovered over the 'send' icon.

'Well, you won't mind if I send this to your precious father then, will you?'

Lara clawed against Pete's grip.

'NO! Don't send it.'

Sam pressed the screen. A 'swoosh' sounded as he turned to Pete.

'And what about you, Petey-boy? Would you like to see her all trussed up like a Christmas turkey too? Bet your Diana wouldn't know a whip from a ball gag.'

Pete's hands curled into fists. A scream pierced the air before Lara hurled herself at Sam. Penny took off and ran through the kitchen, her shoes slipping on the tiles as she scoured the bedrooms.

'You can look all you like, Penny, but you won't find them in there,' called Sam as he batted away Lara's advances.

Penny scanned every room she passed, but there was no sign of the children. She stared out the dark windows as she backtracked towards the kitchen, knowing Tim was relying on them to distract Sam while he searched the sheds and gardens. She took strength from his presence somewhere beyond the glass and whispered the mantra that had helped her through months of illness: *Calm mind, body and soul. Hold it together, Pen. Everyone's counting on you.* She took a deep breath and re-entered the kitchen.

Tim pulled the torch from his pocket and flashed it around the dark hay shed. He swiped absently at the cobwebs, ignored the mice running across his boots as he swung the beam left and right. No sign of Cameron or Evie in here either, the third outbuilding he'd checked. He called out, hoping against logic that they were hiding at the very top of the towering square bales, the small shaft of space where cobwebs hung from the steel purlins like Nanna Pearl's lace curtains. His hope faded with each shed he found empty. His boots squelched as he jogged towards the main house. The yard was neat as a pin, no overgrown garden to contend with. He switched off the torch so as not to alert Sam to his presence.

Tim's guts had knotted and clenched as soon as he'd received Mac's message, trying to reconcile his childhood friend with the man who had somehow morphed into an abusive husband, right before his eyes. He spat on the damp grass, feeling guilty for letting something so big fly under his radar. *You were his friend, you should have known something was going on.* His breath came faster now, and the scorching in his lungs felt a puny price to pay for the shame of his obliviousness. *Can't focus on that now, need to concentrate.* His desire to find the children chafed against a burning need to protect Lara and

Penny, and beating himself up about misguided loyalty wasn't going to help either of those objectives.

A light came on in another room as he drew closer to the house. He hoped they'd had better luck inside than he'd had outside. *Pete will have him covered*, he reassured himself, knowing the stock agent stood at least a foot taller than Sam. He'd seen Diana's husband handling cattle; he'd be able to give as good as he got. Tim resisted the urge to check on them through the windows; instead he skirted around the squares of bright light projected through the glass. Picking up his pace, he ran through the trees' shadows until he reached the carport.

The verandah lights flickered on automatically. He flattened himself against the brick building, trying to stay out of their glare as he inched open a rusty latch on the side entry. Tim winced as the metal bar scraped against the catch. He threw a look back towards the house, hoping the rain would cover the sound. The garage smelled like oil and mummified mice, with a strange overlay of fresh bleach that made his pulse race. *Someone's been cleaning in here.* Tim shut the door behind him and switched on his torch. His heart leaped at the sight in front of him.

Sixty-three

Penny watched Pete and Lara wheel around as she walked into the kitchen. She shook her head sharply at their sad faces, her gaze then darting to Sam.

'Nice of you to join us again, Penny. Find anything you like back there?'

Penny ignored his smug smile as she pulled her phone from her pocket and showed him a screenshot of her bank balance.

'How about a compromise, Sam? I'll transfer everything in my bank account right now if you destroy that video and release the children. It's all yours. No strings attached.'

Lara let out a rush of breath.

'Penny, you don't have to do that.'

'Shut up, Lara. It's my money and I'll do what I want with it. It'll be worth every cent if it gets him out of our lives. And I'll fast-track the farm sale the second I get home tonight. You have my word.'

Sam smirked.

'Your savings are small fry compared to what I'm fishing for. A quarter of a mill won't even scratch the surface compared to the proceeds of McIntyre Park Merino Stud. I think it's the least I deserve for putting up with a basket-case wife and having my child poisoned against me.' His voice dripped with venom as he glared at Lara.

Lara yelled, charging at Sam a second time. Her eyes were wild with anger as she raked her fingernails down his face. He grunted, swinging a clenched fist. Lara dropped to the floor, blood streaming from her mouth. Penny cried out, horrified, as her sister crawled away. Sam aimed a kick at her torso, the tip of his boot connecting with a sickening crunch. Lara collapsed back onto the floor. Penny's own instinct for self-preservation battled with the urge to drop to Lara's side and protect her from further harm. *Calm mind, body and soul.* It took all of her self-control to inch away from her sister and creep closer to the kitchen bench.

'Stupid bitch. Look what she made me do,' said Sam, flexing his fingers indignantly.

Pete's voice came out in a snarl.

'You wife-beating, child-snatching arsehole. Get away from her.'

Sam's face transformed into a confident mask, his breathing heavier as he winked at Pete.

'Lucky she likes it rough.'

Penny fumbled behind her back. She clasped a drawer handle and pulled it open as Pete's self-control reached its limit. He shook with fury as he approached Sam, flailing punches left, right and centre. Penny fished in the drawer until her fingers clasped the first weapon she could find.

'Where are the kids, you fucking sicko?'

Pete continued to rush at Sam, grunting with each blow. Penny tossed a glance over her shoulder, seeing the implement she'd grabbed was a meat mallet. She held it behind her back, trying to work out how and when to intervene as Sam used speed against Pete's bulk. Pete reeled from a series of sharp jabs to his face, one eye instantly swelling closed. His heavy punches began lagging as Sam danced around him.

Penny felt sweat dripping down her back. The room's temperature rose in a sweaty, blood-scented fug. The men panted as they squared off against one another. Fear gripped Penny as Sam ducked a sluggish blow to deliver a lightning strike to Pete's windpipe.

Pete fell to the floor. Sam's face lit up in triumph as he swiped a bloody hand across his brow. His excitement was palpable, perverted even, as if he were getting a kick out of the whole thing. Penny looked at the door, wishing Tim would choose that moment to burst into the room. The door didn't budge, and she realised she was now acutely vulnerable, stuck in a room with a man who apparently enjoyed inflicting pain.

A nasty smile crossed Sam's blood-smeared face. His voice came out in sharp gasps, evidence that Pete had landed a few good punches before he'd hit the deck.

'You were always stronger than your sister, weren't you, Penny? The prettiest one with the best head on her shoulders, good at running away with her tail between her legs.' His eyes travelled lazily along her body, scrutinising her breasts as he spoke. Penny shuddered as he came closer. 'You should do that now before things get really messy. Unless, of course, you take after your sister. You like that type of thing too, do you?'

Lara pushed herself up into a sitting position. Pete lay where he had landed, his eyes still closed. Blood trickled down the side of his face.

Penny felt her phone vibrate in her pocket but didn't dare relinquish her grip on the mallet. She shook her head, knowing she was the only one who could get herself out of this situation.

'You've got it wrong, Sam. Lara's the strong one. But when you mess with one McIntyre, you mess with us all.' Penny windmilled her arm as if she were sending a cricket ball down the pitch. The meat mallet crashed down on Sam's left shoulder with a sickening thud. She lunged at him, head down as her knee connected with his groin, then thrust her head upward, feeling a jolt of lightning arcing across her skull as it connected with his jaw. The impact slammed them into the tiles. The wind whooshed from her chest. She curled up on the cold floor.

Penny closed her eyes against the pain. Her body and her mind fought for dominance, and she used the last of her strength to suck in air and scramble away from Sam's body. His eyes were closed and she noticed a raised spotted pattern on his forehead. Dazed, it took her a few seconds to understand what the marks were. She looked across at Lara, who kneeled beside her ex-husband, her hands wrapped tightly around the mallet.

Lara's voice sounded far away and Penny smiled faintly at her words.

'Nice move, sis. I think this bastard needs a lot more tenderising though.' She flicked the mallet down onto his forehead again. The dull thud instantly caused another square of dots to appear on his skin.

'Steady on, Lara. We don't want to kill him.'

Lara giggled.

'Says who? Only thing stopping me is a jail sentence. Help me tie him up before he regains consciousness. Check his room for ropes or duct tape. There's bound to be some in his bedside drawers.'

Sixty-four

Tim ran through the hallway, terrified by the silence that had greeted him as he'd flung open the back door.

'Everybody okay in here?'

'Nothing an ambulance won't fix. But still no kids. How about you?' Penny's voice was hopeful as she called out to him.

'No kids either.' Tim approached the doorway, his eyes wide as he surveyed the kitchen. He blew out a sharp breath of relief at the sight of Sam tied up like a wild boar. Lying on his front, his hands and feet were fastened together behind his back. Pete waved feebly from his position propped up against the wall, a bag of peas pressed against his head. Lara tried for a blood-spattered smile but only managed to wince. Her hand cradled her ribs.

'Jesus, Mac, I leave you alone for five minutes and it turns nasty. What have you been teaching her, Lara?'

He saw Penny cringe at his choice of words, and shame suffusing Lara's blotched face. *Get your foot out of your mouth, Patterson.* He walked across the room to inspect the binds keeping Sam immobile. Penny had used lashings of duct tape around his ankles and wrists and had linked the limbs with baling twine.

She flashed him a grin, looking almost giddy with relief. 'If you can't tie knots, tie lots, right?'

He nodded, impressed with her handiwork. Sam rocked back and forth, testing his binds. A rush of anger surged through Tim's tense body when he saw spit flying in Penny's direction.

Tim bent down close to Sam. He felt like smacking him in the face to shut him up, but there had already been enough violence for one night.

'Bloody bitches. They're crazy. Help a brother out, would you, Tim?'

Tim shook his head, pulling the socks from Sam's feet. He grimaced at their damp warmth and pushed them into Sam's mouth.

'No brother of mine would ever disrespect a woman like that, Sam. I can't believe I trusted you, called you a mate for all those years. I'm going to give you a little break while we all catch our breath, and then you're going to tell us where Cameron and Evie are.'

Penny leaned over, her floral scent calming him as she secured Sam's socks with a strip of duct tape.

Penny ripped open every cupboard in the lounge room until she was sure she'd checked all the nooks and crannies. She returned to the kitchen as Tim swept through the bedrooms and bathrooms a second time.

Frisking Sam's body with distaste, she pulled a mobile phone and an iPod from his pockets. She handed the phone to Lara, crouched down and embraced her gingerly.

'I wish you'd told us, Lara. It would have explained a lot.'

She watched the hardness ebb away from Lara's face, regret replacing the hostility she customarily reserved for Penny.

Lara hung her head. 'How could I? I made a pact with myself when I left. I didn't want his actions to rule the rest of my life or feed the rumour mill. So apart from the counsellor at the women's helpline, no one else knew. And I managed pretty well until you came home, flaunting your high heels, your high-income lifestyle that I desperately wanted. The opportunities and freedom that were never an option for me. And then I finally manage to leave this bastard—' Lara laughed dryly—'for all of a month or two, before he wormed his way back into my life. He would have got custody of Evie if the authorities had seen that bloody video. It was his fantasy not mine, but I'm the one caught on camera.'

Penny worked hard to keep her face neutral, knowing sympathy was the last thing her sister wanted. Her heart ached to think of the pain Lara had endured, the emotions she'd cloaked in bitterness. She was sceptical such a video would have helped Sam, but it was obvious Lara thought so.

Lara busied herself with unlocking Sam's phone. She typed in two passwords, hitting the jackpot on her second attempt.

'Not smart enough to change your password though, are you, Sam?'

Penny averted her eyes as Lara scrolled through his photos and videos.

'Quite a collection here. You haven't wasted any time trawling the Western District for other suckers to film, have you?'

'I'll archive the email on Dad's computer. Then you can choose whether to destroy that version or keep it as evidence,' Penny suggested.

'Don't delete them all—we'll need something to give the police,' said Pete. 'Kidnapping, creating and distributing non-consensual pornography, extortion, blackmail, domestic violence . . . they'll be interested to see that. Give us a look at the iPod. Can't imagine it's his.'

Penny passed Pete the device and he flipped it around in his hands.

'Looks like Cameron's.' He pressed a switch on the side, taking a sharp breath as the screen lit up. 'Justin Bieber, Taylor Swift—definitely Cameron's. Where did you get this? Where's my boy?' Pete took the mallet from Lara and stood over Sam's prostrate body. Blood from his broken nose dripped onto Sam's face. Pete's eyes darkened as he grappled with his self-control. His voice came out in a tight snarl.

'Unlike you, I don't get any joy from hurting people, so I'm going to give you one last chance to explain.' He ripped the tape from Sam's face, watching him gag as he spat the socks from his mouth.

'I don't have him, I swear. I don't even know where Evie is. She buggered off just before you got here. I wasn't going to hurt them. You've got to believe me.'

Pete shoved the socks back into his mouth and put a new strip of tape over it.

'I wouldn't believe you as far as I could throw you. We're calling the cops.'

Penny ended the call to the police station, but before she could put the phone back into her pocket, it began vibrating again. 'Home' was written across the screen. She put it on speakerphone, so Pete and Lara could hear.

'Any sign of the kids?'

'We've got Cam,' cried Diana, her voice breaking. 'The neighbours dropped him home a minute ago. He knocked on the Clearys' front door, wet as a shag and inconsolable. But physically he's fine.'

Penny felt a rush of relief and watched Pete's swollen hands come to his bruised and bloodied face, tears streaming down his cheeks. She took a shuddering breath, her lip trembling as she clocked Lara's frozen expression.

'Evie?'

'No. But Cameron said she went with Sam. They both did, but he dropped Cam off a kilometre down the road, told him to wait in the Clearys' hay shed until I picked him up. He waited and waited, then made his way to the Clearys' cottage. Vince left too, something about an event he needed to prepare for tomorrow. What's happening at your end? Everyone okay?'

Penny let Vince's departure wash past without a second thought; nothing he did surprised her anymore.

'All accounted for, but no Evie. Sam reckons she went missing just before we arrived, but he's such a lying bastard, it's hard to know what's what. We'll keep looking.' Penny felt like kicking Sam for emphasis but restrained herself. She ended the call and moved to Lara's side. Lara's mute distress was worse than her sarcastic remarks and whisky-throwing rage. Penny ground her teeth and scowled at Sam.

'We'll find her, Lara. If it's the last thing we do.'

Tim walked back into the lounge room, pausing as he listened to the tail end of Penny and Diana's conversation.

'Penny, Lara, Pete. You'd better come see what I found in the garage.'

Sixty-five

Tim used his torch to guide them down a hedged pathway to the garage. He slid open the latch and fumbled for the light switch.

Penny squinted against the sudden burst of artificial light, opening her eyes slowly to inspect the workshop. She jumped, her breath catching in her throat as a cat brushed up against her legs, pressing its body against her.

'Damn cat, nearly gave me a heart attack. Scoot, puss.' Tools hung from the wall, an extensive collection of ropes lay in one corner and buckets of paint lined the workbenches. They stepped around an antique tractor in the middle of the room and followed Tim up a narrow ladder.

He passed the torch to Penny and climbed onto the mezzanine level. Penny moved up the last few steps. She gasped at the scene before her, crawling in next to Tim. Her head almost touched the ceiling as she kneeled beside him.

Lara got to the top of the ladder, grimacing with pain. She assessed the room silently. A freshly made bed took up the majority of the floor space, cartoon characters smiling up from the quilt cover. A hanging rack of pink clothes stood on one side, and a bookshelf full of books and Barbies on the other.

'Looks like he was preparing for a visitor,' she said softly.

Tim pressed his lips together.

'More than just an overnighter.'

Pete's voice floated up from the bottom of the ladder.

'Don't leave me hanging. What is it?'

'Sam's made up a bedroom for Evie.' Penny heard Lara's voice falter, but then the familiar McIntyre determination shone through in her next sentence. 'She's got to be here somewhere. I'm going to keep looking.'

☙

The garage door creaked closed and Pete's and Lara's voices rang out as they extended their search outside.

'What if we don't find her, Tim? I thought finding her in a dam would be unbearable, but . . . Maybe it's time to call the police?'

Penny leaned her head on Tim's shoulder, letting go of the tears she'd held back for Lara's sake. His arms reached around her, and she sobbed to the faint soundtrack of a badly wounded and desperate mother calling her daughter's name.

Tim stroked her hair and held her until the tears ran dry. She wiped her face with his shirt. His chest was warm underneath the thin, wet fabric. She looked up into his eyes.

'I'm sorry about the farm too, Tim. I never meant to sabotage your dreams. Can you please come back and help me? No more drama. No more aggro.' She was tempted to tell him what she did want more of, starting with a T and ending with an M, but stopped herself. *Now is sure as hell not the right place for this type of discussion. He doesn't feel that way, anyway. His behaviour confirms it time and time again.* She recalled the exceptions to the rule—the shirtless moment in the hall bathroom and the time she'd jammed her finger in the gate. The way his body had betrayed him, speaking a timeless language more powerfully than the words that continually pushed her away.

Tim's grey eyes flashed, his gaze suddenly as chilly as his rain-sodden clothes.

'I don't know if I can, Mac. It's been . . . a rough ride. Let's talk about it later, after we find Evie.'

He pulled away and crawled past her. She saw the sadness in his face as he turned to step down the ladder. Penny hugged her feelings to her chest, glad she'd held them back. It had already been one of the most emotionally taxing nights of her life, without heaping rejection on top of it all.

Rickety rungs creaked and flexed as Penny followed him down the ladder. She moved cautiously, only relaxing when she felt Tim's strong arms either side of her, steadying the ladder. She hesitated, breathing in his nearness as she waited for him to step aside. But he didn't.

'Penny?'

She turned slowly, her first name sounding unfamiliar coming from his lips. Her pulse raced at his proximity. If she let go of the rails and turned fully, she knew she'd be eye-to-eye with him. And then, if she just leaned in, her lips would brush up against his. A flutter of hope swelled in her belly, and she gripped the sides of the ladder tighter, guarding herself against hurt.

'Yeah?'

His breath came out in a rush, as if he'd been holding it. He let go of the ladder and stepped away, staring at the floor.

'It feels wrong to think about anything other than Evie right now. You know what I mean?'

Penny blinked away guilty disappointment, reality crashing into its place. She shrugged, stepping down onto the dusty concrete.

'Sure. Let's give Lara and Pete a hand. We can't rely on the walking wounded to cover much ground.' She forced lightness into her voice to disguise the foolishness she felt.

Tim held the door open for her. She ducked under his arm and kept her chin tucked to her chest as she walked out into the relentless rain.

A strong wind whistled through the whippet-thin blue gum trunks along the boundary, teaming up with the rain to skew the noises around her. Penny couldn't hear Pete or Lara anymore, but she picked up Tim's voice to her right, and a series of short, sharp barks ahead.

She felt movement at her legs again and almost tripped as the clingy cat wound its way through them and stopped directly in her path. It was the first feline she had seen that didn't mind being wet, and she trained her phone torch on the tabby as it bounded away. She took a step towards it, halting as her brain mocked her movements.

Great idea, Penny. Following a cat? And a dim-witted one at that. Next, you'll be showing it a missing person poster and expecting an answer. She looked back towards Tim, his light beaming across the far end of the utility shed. She shook her head and continued calling as she headed in the cat's direction.

'Evie. Evie.'

She watched the cat walk behind a stand of trees. The barking she had heard earlier became frantic and she picked up her pace. The hems of her jeans were soaking wet, but the cold and wind dropped into insignificance as she rounded the corner and spotted a series of raised dog kennels.

'Evie?'

Her heart sang as she heard a familiar voice reply through the rain and wind.

'Aunty Penny? Aunty Penny!'

Penny rubbed her eyes and craned her neck to make sure she wasn't imagining the small body climbing out of the sheltered box, but there she was, wet and shivering, her own flesh and blood. The dog in the adjoining cage licked Evie's face as she crawled along the wire enclosure and unlatched the door.

Penny hugged her niece to her chest, squeezing her tight as relief flowed through her body.

Sixty-six

Tim tapped the roof of the police car as Matt pulled away, lights flashing. It was done. Sam Kingsley was officially being escorted off the property. He hoped the courts would go hard on him. *That scumbag deserves the full force of the law,* he thought grimly, watching the tail-lights disappear into the night.

Tim ran a hand over his unshaven jaw, stifling a yawn as he walked towards the ambulance. The rain had subsided, but wet denim chafed against his legs. Flagging adrenaline amplified the cold that was seeping into his bones. He had waved away the paramedics' blankets, directing them towards the real casualties, but the call of dry clothes and a hot shower beckoned now that Evie was safe and Sam was in police custody. Tim leaned on the ambulance door, his gaze fixed on Evie's small hand linked with her mother's, clinging to one another as they were prepped for transport.

'A few X-rays and we'll know whether those ribs are fractured.' The paramedic was the same man who had attended the quad bike accident, his movements calm and measured as he checked the stretcher's anchor points.

Tim smiled wearily.

'Hey Missy, you riding in the ambulance too? Bet your mum's pleased to have you looking out for her again.'

Evie rewarded him with a brave smile, the woollen blanket slipping around her shoulders to reveal many more layers, each working to combat the rapidly dropping temperature and ward off hypothermia.

'I'll take good care of Mum. Can you meet us at Grandpa's farmhouse afterwards? Please, Tim?'

Tim nodded, swayed by the girl's resilience. *At least I'll have an hour or so to shape tonight's drama into a child-friendly recap.*

Lara's voice came from the stretcher. The pain medication made her softer, reminding him of Penny.

'Thanks, Tim. For everything.'

He waved away her gratitude as the paramedic closed the doors. *If a ten-year-old can still smile and stay strong after something like that, then you've got no excuses, Patterson. Find her.*

He walked along the homestead driveway, scanning the floodlit yard for just one person. He ignored the eager *Bridgefield Advertiser* journalist, stepped around the unmarked police car that had delivered a pair of detectives from Horsham, and walked behind Pete's car to the driver's side. A phone screen illuminated Penny's face. Her body sagged against the door as she spoke. Tim watched her rub her eyes and guessed she was every bit as tired as she looked. He wanted to whisk her back to the farmhouse and carry her upstairs to her old cast-iron bed, like he'd done when she'd first arrived back at the farm. The desire to make her warm, safe and comfortable immediately surpassed his own needs.

He lifted a hand to tap on the window, but paused. *Manners, Patterson. Let the girl finish her conversation before you barge in like a caveman.*

He took a step backward, trying to sort his thoughts out as he waited, when the volume suddenly increased in the car, heated words spilling out into the frigid night.

'Our relationship was over six months ago, let's stop pretending otherwise. Keep driving back to the city, Vince. This is where I belong.'

Tim's heart surged, his mouth rising into a goofy smile as one of the hurdles between them crumbled. Penny hung up the phone.

He knocked on the window, a sheepish apology on his lips as he saw her jump at the noise.

'You scared the hell out of me,' she said, opening the door and landing an indignant punch on his shoulder.

'Takes more than that to scare you, Penny McIntyre. You were brave today, really brave, and I reckon Lara knows that too.'

Her expression softened, searching his face.

'Just doing what a good sister should, even if it was long overdue. All's well that ends well, I guess.'

Tim watched her turn the heater up a notch, as she shivered at the influx of cold air from the open door. *A smart man would close the door and jump in the passenger side,* he told himself, but somehow his feet wouldn't budge. He wanted an answer to the question that was rolling around in his head. Pete had filled in the blanks about the fight that had taken place in the house while Tim was scouting the outside of the property. Before he went any further, he wanted—needed—to know.

'I heard you offered to pay Sam off and push for the farm sale.'

Penny crossed her arms over her chest and nodded. Her tired eyes were crinkled at the corners, her make-up washed away by the rain and tendrils of strawberry-blond hair stuck out at all angles from her head.

'I learned a lot of things today, things I wouldn't have believed if you'd told me them yesterday. But one thing I know for sure. Family and relationships are worth more than money, pride or image. I would have transferred my savings in a heartbeat and sacrificed everything to salvage my family.' Her voice was bright and sharp, her words marked with certainty.

He reached a hand to her porcelain cheek, the warmth of her skin gently thawing the remains of his resolve.

'My life's been turned upside down since you arrived back at McIntyre Park. I was kidding myself thinking I could stay away from you, Mac. You make me want to be a better man, and I'm hoping you'll give me a second chance.'

He felt hope uncoil in his heart, but remained rigidly upright, waiting for confirmation they were on the same page. She leaned in and nodded, her fingers reaching up and caressing his stubbled jaw as his heart did a barn dance in his chest. *This is how it's supposed to be,* he thought, closing his eyes and bending down to kiss her.

'Ah-hem.'

Tim wheeled around to find an older policewoman with a notepad.

'Sorry to interrupt. I just need a final word with Miss McIntyre. You've given your statement, Mr Patterson, so you're welcome to leave now.'

Disappointment washed over him. Now that he'd finally told her how he felt, he wanted to shout it from the top of the mountains. He sighed as Penny turned back towards the homestead, where the police had set up a makeshift office. A cheeky smile over her shoulder made his heart do the quick-step and he settled into the passenger seat, awaiting her return.

Sixty-seven

The wood-fire popped and crackled, casting a golden hue across the lounge room. Penny curled her knitted slippers under her and tucked her hands around the mug of Milo, stifling another yawn. Her pyjamas were soft and warm, but her fatigue abated just a little more each time she looked over at Tim—there was too much promise in his face and love within the room to consider sleep just yet.

'And tell 'em, Aunty Penny. Tell 'em what you said about the puppies.' Evie was animated despite the ordeal, and she was clinging to the promise Penny had made in the relief of discovery.

Penny glanced at Lara, whose head was resting on Evie's shoulder, one arm clutched gently across her bandaged ribs. She saw a twinkle in her sister's eye. Lara spoke for them both, smiling at the audience who had already heard this tale tonight. Penny knew it was a happy ending to a story that could have gone so badly wrong, and would listen to this rendition on an infinite loop if it made her brave young niece smile.

'She said you could have one. I would've agreed to all six of them if I'd been the one who found you huddled in the dog kennels, being guarded by a bunch of kelpie pups. So I guess we're lucky Aunty Pen discovered you.'

Angus leaned forward, passing Evie another of Penny's chocolate biscuits.

'Always knew you were a smart girl, Evie. Heading for the hills at the whiff of danger proves it,' he said.

'I just didn't feel good at that house, even though Dad said I could train the pups with him, and he showed me my new bedroom. It was like the trees were whispering secrets. That's why I ran off and hid. Do you think he'll want a dog in jail?'

Lara's face hardened, and Penny imagined the minefield she and Diana would have to navigate as they filtered the events of the night for their children. Angus reached over and ruffled Evie's golden hair.

'Don't you worry about that. What's important is you and Cameron being safe and sound, and all of us being here together.'

He's right, thought Penny. She surveyed her family, all crammed into the lounge room they had grown up in. She felt contentment and relief in equal quantities, wrapped together with a bow of romantic anticipation.

'We could all have a pup!' Evie looked around the room, a hopeful expression that would sell ice to an Eskimo.

Angus groaned.

'It's not coming inside like that slob over there.' His tone was light as he jerked a thumb at Rusty, who lay sleeping on the hearth.

'We'll have one too, won't we, Daddy?' Cameron's sleepy eyes pleaded with Pete, who smiled indulgently.

Angie nodded enthusiastically. 'My landlord in Eden Creek said no pets, but I'll have a red-hot crack at convincing him.'

Penny watched Tim rise from the couch with a short nod in Evie's direction.

'Bones is getting old and he could do with the company too. Wait till I tell Eddie,' he said.

Penny was glad Eddie had missed all the drama; his sunny world had already been disrupted enough with all their recent arguments, accidents and surprises. She watched Tim move towards the door and slipped her feet out from underneath her.

'If Vince hadn't gone back to the city in such a hurry, we could have sent him home with one too. Though he didn't seem much of an animal person,' said Cameron.

Tim turned to Penny. She felt her cheeks flush as he scanned her face. She kept her gaze fixed on him as she answered.

'Nope, I made a big mistake there. It turns out he's not an animal person, Cam.'

The corners of Tim's mouth twitched as he lifted a hand to farewell the room, his distraction visible. Angus coughed delicately. Penny could feel multiple pairs of eyes on them, but there was only one gaze that mattered to her at that very moment.

'I'm more interested in a man who loves animals as much as me, who works with his hands and knows his way around a paddock or two. Can you think of anyone who fits the bill?'

Evie giggled, a bubbly sound that mimicked the tingle in Penny's belly.

She watched a delicious smile crease Tim's face.

'I might know a guy . . .' He inclined his head towards the back door. 'If you walk me to the ute, I'll give you his number.'

Penny set her Milo down on the coffee table and sidestepped her family members to cross the lounge room floor. Pausing at the back door, she caught a glimpse of her freshly scrubbed face and flannelette pyjamas in the laundry mirror. She automatically reached to pull out her hair tie, when Tim touched her hand.

'Leave it. I'm more interested in the real Penny Mac. The one who loves animals as much as me, who works with her hands and knows her way around a paddock or two. And I have no trouble thinking of someone who fits the bill.'

He reached down and cupped her face in his hands, closing his eyes as he lowered his face towards hers. Penny felt a shift inside her as his gentle lips pressed to hers, a sense that everything was exactly how it was supposed to be. She snaked her hands around his waist, relishing the gentle movement of his mouth against hers. Pleasure swept through her body as she parted her lips, lifted her chin up higher and kissed him with all of her might.

Tim threaded his hands through Penny's silky hair and drew her closer. He felt her lips curving into a smile as their noses bumped together, and she breathed his name. He felt the tip of her tongue run across his bottom lip and remembered the reason he hadn't been able to get Penny McIntyre out of his mind.

Sixty-eight

Penny awoke to a crowing rooster. She stretched like a cat, her body gliding across the crisp cotton sheets as she reached for Tim's side of the bed.

Although he wasn't there, the linen was still warm and she knew he must have slipped out quietly before his alarm woke them both. Breathing in the smell of his deodorant and shampoo, she lazily rolled back onto her side of the bed and fumbled for her phone. The rooster continued crowing, and she questioned the need for any other alarm: his morning routine was like clockwork. But she couldn't be angry with the early bird, not with such a big day ahead of them. The bright screen dazzled her as she checked the time.

It was a little after 5 a.m., early enough for some stretching before sale-day preparations began.

After stepping into her leggings and T-shirt, she sleepily started her yoga routine, her brain waking up as she went through the now-familiar downward-facing dog, cat and cow stretches, and warrior poses. Fresh breath flowed into her body, bringing with it anticipation and nerves about the sale.

Calm mind, body and soul, she told herself, focusing on her
breathing each time a worry broke into her bubble of serenity.

Yoga done, she breezed through to the shower, washed
her hair and pulled it back into a comfortable ponytail. She
grabbed her sunscreen from beside Tim's toothbrush, and
smoothed it over her freckled cheekbones and down onto
her décolletage, where the sun seemed to sneak in and cast a
permanent shadow on her fair skin. Her green twill shirt set
off her complexion, and she smiled at the white embroidery on
her pocket. 'Penny McIntyre—McIntyre Park Merino Stud.'
The simple label gave her more satisfaction than any lanyard,
business card or nametag from her past.

Magpies warbled outside the kitchen window, trumping the
rooster for volume as daylight peeked in. The fabric curtains
slid easily on their new tracks—one of last week's farmhouse
beautification projects—and Penny pushed the windows ajar.
She found a handpicked rosebud on the benchtop next to a
note from Tim.

> *Best luck today, Mac. You'll smash it. I'm running into town
> for a quick pre-sale errand, see you there soon. xx T*

She lifted the dew-glistened rose to her nose, inhaling the
sunshine and sweetness, and silently gave thanks for whatever
powers had helped everything align so beautifully. *It's going to
be a good day,* she decided as she sipped her morning coffee.
A perfect day.

Tim waved to a local farmer and pointed him to the rows
of utes and four-wheel drives already filling the makeshift
parking lot alongside the shearing shed. There wasn't usually
much call for parking supervisors at ram sales, but a high level
of enquiries from the advertising campaign had indicated this

would be their biggest sale yet. Penny's marketing skills made him prouder than he could have imagined, and he'd been keen to offer his services as chief parking director. Tim looked at the plethora of South Australian number plates, buyers who had come across the border to inspect the McIntyre Park breeding lines. *They won't be disappointed*, he thought, feeling another surge of pride as he scanned the record crowd. Penny walked into view, her fitted green shirt freshly ironed and dark denim jeans tucked into her boots. She'd spent half an hour polishing them last night, working her worries into the rich brown leather, which was already dull with dust. He smiled and raised a hand as she paced past the sheep pens, knowing she wouldn't rest easy until the final hammer fell.

A quick glance at his watch confirmed another half an hour until the auctioneer would start. He called Eddie over to him. Like Tim and all the McIntyre clan, Eddie wore a green twill shirt and a big smile. He held up a bag of embroidered green caps he'd been charged with handing out to the prospective buyers. It was half empty already. Tim gave him two thumbs up, impressed with his brother's fast work.

'Great job there, mate. You'll have a hat on everyone in the crowd by the day's end. Do me a quick favour, would you? Grab me some tucker from the CWA stall?'

Eddie set off in the direction of the catering tent, where Nanna Pearl, Olive and Mrs Beggs held court. Penny's baking was hard to beat, but Tim still had a soft spot for Nanna Pearl's chocolate cake. He tapped his chest pocket, checking to make sure the keys to his surprise were still there. Tim wondered how long it would take Penny to realise the shiny red ute parked next to his Holden WB didn't belong to a buyer or a stock agent. She'd spoken about replacing her Mercedes with something a little more farm-friendly, and he was pretty sure he'd made a good choice. A smile curled his lips, anticipating her reaction. *Today is going to be a perfect day.*

≫

Lanolin and shoe polish scented the warm air. Penny jiggled with nervous energy. Her heart raced as fast as the windmill in the paddock as she waited for the auctioneer to start the proceedings.

'Good weather for it,' panted Angie, her face flushed from the short walk. The sisters looked remarkably similar in their green shirts. Lara had turned her collar up smartly; Angie and Diana had tucked their shirts into their jeans.

Penny fiddled with the silk scarf she'd tied into a knot at her throat. It was supposed to shade the triangle of red skin that had got sunburned in yesterday's spring sunshine, but it was more annoying than helpful. She untied it and stuffed it into her back pocket, then pulled it out and wrapped it around her wrist like a bracelet. If it all went pear-shaped, she could use it to mop up any stray tears. *Think positive, Penny, you've got this.*

'Amazing weather. Reckon you've nailed it, Pen.' Lara flashed a smile in her direction, before scanning the crowd for the children. Penny watched her lips move as she counted five little blond heads among the crowd, then relaxed.

'This is it,' whispered Penny, as the auctioneer lifted his arm for silence. She felt three pairs of hands squeezing her shoulder, her back and her arm as the auction got underway.

≫

The morning of the sale passed in a blur. Each ram topped the previous price, and the mood was buoyant over the lunch break. Penny felt an arm slip around her waist and Tim's lips pressed down on the top of her head. She looked up at his smiling face but couldn't bring herself to relax.

'It's looking good, Mac. Told you we'd smash it.'

'Don't count your chickens before they hatch, Tim. Still got plenty of rams to sell this arvo.'

'Suit yourself. I'm going to raid the tucker tent. Pretty sure it won't top your baking, but I'll give it a go,' he said, heading to where the CWA ladies were conducting a roaring trade.

Food was the last thing on Penny's mind, but she turned and waved at them, stifling a giggle at Nanna Pearl's outfit. She recognised the smart jacket and pleated tweed skirt as one of the many woollen, silk-lined suits she had donated to the local op-shop, along with her collection of high heels, handbags and the remains of her corporate wardrobe. The outfit looked wonderfully jaunty teamed with Nanna Pearl's lilac hair and pearl earrings. The distraction settled her nerves a little as the auctioneer signalled the end of lunch.

A familiar voice came from just behind her.

'Penny!'

Penny whirled around to see Jade step out from the crowd. Her friend squealed and rushed forward for a hug. Penny breathed in Jade's perfume as she embraced her friend. It was delightful to see Jade's cheeky grin after so many months, and wonderful that her two worlds were coming together at last.

'Here's the lady of the moment. And don't you look great in green. Have I missed much? The drive took longer than I thought, especially those winding roads near the Grampians.'

The auctioneer called the crowd to order. The bidding started high and Penny was torn between catching up with her friend and seeing how the rest of the sale went.

Jade reached into her handbag and plonked a familiar green bucket hat with white embroidery over her pixie haircut.

'I love these freebies. Better see what else I can score from your young niece and nephews. They tell me they've got McIntyre Park notepads, magnets and pens as well. Catch up in a bit.'

Penny smiled as Jade walked away; her new hat clashed wildly with her leopard-print shirtdress and brown high heels. As much as she longed to thread her arm through Jade's and give her a proper farm tour, it would have to wait until the auctioneer pounded his hammer for the final time, and all the guests were gone. Penny looked back at the circle of bidders and jumped when a warm hand slipped into hers.

Tim beamed at her, offering first dibs on the range of delicacies he had procured from the CWA stall. She shook her head, her attention going straight back to the auctioneer.

'Still not hungry. But do you hear that, Tim? The ram prices are sky-high,' she said, turning back to him briefly before spotting the red-nosed man approaching them.

'Hello, Penelope, g'day, Timmy. I mean Tim.'

William Cleary extended his hand, pumping Penny's up and down with a surprisingly gentle grip.

'I just wanted to say no hard feelings, eh? Looks like you've excelled yourself here today. I'm now the proud owner of ram number seventy-eight. Will be good to try a few crossbreeds,' he bumbled, his gaze meeting Penny's and then darting away.

Penny's face spread into a smile. 'No hard feelings, neighbour. And thanks for bringing Cameron home.'

They both looked up as the auctioneer moved onto the next pen and started the bidding off again.

'They're selling like hotcakes today, ladies and gentlemen. Now, who's going to make the first bid on ram number ninety-one?'

Penny sank down into the borrowed plastic chair, oblivious to her feet sweltering in her boots and the dust stuck to her hot brow. *I've done it*, she thought incredulously. *We've done it.*

Her face broke into a broad smile as she looked at the empty pens that had been full of rams only eight hours earlier, as healthy and impressive as the figures at the bottom of the auctioneer's tally.

Animated conversation swirled around her as her family worked, stacking up chairs and collecting leftover programs and auction numbers, but she was too overwhelmed to absorb anything other than their triumphant success. They had sold all the rams and broken a McIntyre Park record. Angus eased himself into the seat beside her.

'Nicely done, Penny. I'm proud of you.'

She held back tears as Angus reached over and hugged her, his walking stick wedged between the two of them.

'You've set the bar high. Reckon you'll be able to beat that next year?'

'I'll give it my best shot.'

Exhausted yet exhilarated, Penny tucked the tally into her top pocket and rested her hand on his knee. Tim walked past, carrying a bulging garbage bag in each hand.

'How's my top-selling farm girl going?'

Penny jumped up and kissed his cheek. He dropped the bags into the dirt, a puff of dust clouding up from underneath them, and picked her up by the waist.

'If we weren't heading out for dinner directly after this, I'd show you just how impressed I am, Mac. But I guess I'll have to wait till later,' he murmured into her ear, his voice low and throaty.

'It's a date,' she whispered back, unable to wipe the smile off her face.

Epilogue

Sunlight filtered across the valley in streaks of gold and primrose, painting the paddocks below a vibrant green. Canola crops added to the vitality of the fields, their bright-yellow petals providing a sharp contrast to the pastures dotted with white mobs of sheep, and a riot of purple and pink flowers moved in the soft breeze. *I'm no expert, but those are the prettiest wildflowers I've ever seen*, marvelled Penny, admiring their delicate petals and green strappy leaves.

Penny stretched her arms above her head, settling into her cross-legged seat on the picnic rug. She had arrived early at Wildflower Ridge, setting off before everybody else so she could have a few minutes to herself before the whole family arrived. She couldn't pinpoint a moment when they had all been at Annabel's memorial site since the day Angus had secured the plaque to the big sandstone boulder, but it felt like the right thing to do.

'Just you and me, Mum,' she said, resting her hand on the rock. She could smell the spring air rustling through the grass, almost like her mother's fresh, clean scent, and smiled. She knew Annabel was out there, watching over them in some way, and that she would be pleased with the family unit that had emerged stronger than ever.

Her heart filled as she heard the sound of engines floating across the valley. Cameron and Evie would be here soon on horseback, followed by Lara and Angus in the UTV. Angie was helping install the extra seats in the back of Diana and Pete's four-wheel drive when she had left, and Tim had promised to join them with Eddie.

Placing a kiss on her fingertips, she pressed them to the rock again and then turned to start unpacking the picnic.

'Happy birthday, Mum.'

Acknowledgements

Thank you, readers, for picking up this book and taking a chance on a debut author. As a country girl with a heart full of stories, a head full of words and a lifelong dream of becoming an author, I am bursting with delight at the opportunity to share this book with you. I hope you enjoyed meeting the McIntyre family in Wildflower Ridge, and I look forward to properly introducing the rest of the McIntyre girls in the very near future.

To my first readers—my beautiful mum, sister Zoe and Nanna Linnell; beta-readers—Lindy, Amber, Kayleen, Jayne and Karen; tutors at The Writers' Studio Australia—Jess Black and Kelly Rigby; fiction fairies—Jayne, Suzie and Kaneana; and my many beautiful friends and family members who eagerly asked for updates and propped me up when my confidence waned. I am so grateful for all your suggestions, input and encouragement.

Cheers to Donna Barber, who let me slip fanciful words like 'crestfallen' into my Year Three creative writing stories; librarians and book-loving friends who championed my love for literature; and the fabulous tribe of authors I've met through Romance Writers of Australia for their encouragement and advice as I dipped my toes into the wonderful world of publishing. Big thanks to James and Kate for medical insights, Meagan for shearing shed stories and the eagle-eyed duo Samantha Kent and Claire Gatzen for their fantastic editorial assistance. All of my characters and settings are fictional and any mistakes are entirely mine.

Jason—thank you for your love, support and encouragement. This book would not have been written without you cheering me on in the background and bringing me endless cups of tea. Charlie, Amelia and Elizabeth—my three littlest fans with the biggest hearts. I love that you've been part of this journey all along, from helping brainstorm book titles and plot ideas to joining me as we happy-danced our way around the supermarket when the good news came through. And also for both my nannas—Pamela and Dareen—two strong yet gentle ladies who passed down their passion for books, baking and all things crafty.

Finally, a huge thanks to the lovely Annette Barlow and her enthusiastic and talented team at Allen & Unwin. I'm so grateful you took me under your wing and gave *Wildflower Ridge* the perfect home.

Bottlebrush Creek

Between managing a bustling beauty salon, hectic volunteer commitments and the lion's share of parenting three-year-old Claudia, Angie McIntyre is a busy woman. And with each passing month, she feels her relationship with fly-in, fly-out boyfriend Rob Jones slipping through her fingers. When Rob faces retrenchment, and the most fabulous fixer-upper comes onto the market, Angie knows it will be the perfect project to draw their little family together.

But it doesn't take long for rising tensions to set a wedge between the hard-working couple. Instead of drawing them closer together, Angie and Rob have to find out the hard way whether their grand design will be the very thing that tears them apart.

One

Angie McIntyre dusted her hands on her apron, opened the oven and groaned. Instead of a gush of hot air that normally sent her curls into ringlets, it was cold in the dark and silent cavity. *Not again.* She twisted the temperamental temperature dial left and right, but no matter how hard she willed it to work, the oven didn't so much as hum.

Angie slammed the door shut and surveyed the mess in front of her. Clearing the bench full of ingredients would be easy enough but the cake would be ruined if she didn't get it into a hot oven soon.

The peal of her mobile ringtone cut through the quiet kitchen. As she hunted for it on the benchtop, a pile of magazines slipped to the ground, the glossy pics of grand kitchens and elaborate bathrooms fanning out across the floor, mocking the cramped space.

A cold breeze followed Angie down the corridor as she went in search of her phone. No amount of gap-filler had yet fixed the endless draughts in the sixties brick veneer, and pigs would fly before the landlord would make good on his promises to bring their Eden Creek rental into the twenty-first century.

Two little feet poked out from beneath the king-sized bed. Angie could hear snatches of conversation.

'Claudia Isobel Jones. Do you have Mummy's phone?'

Claudia's pink socks retreated, quickly replaced by a shock of blonde curls and the cheekiest grin this side of the South Australian border. Angie raised her eyebrows. The little phone thief handed over the phone, adding a handful of fluff-covered sultanas into Angie's outstretched palm for good measure. Claudia ran down the hallway in a blur of sequins to escape a scolding.

'Rob?'

'Hey Ange, wondered how long it'd be till you realised she'd pinched your phone.'

'She gets that from you, cheeky thing.'

'Fat chance of cheekiness being allowed in the Jones family. Must be the McIntyre in her,' he laughed. 'So, fancy a drive this arvo?'

'A drive? You'll have been travelling since 4 a.m. What happened to our quiet night in when you get home?' Angie frowned. Her chances of pulling off this impromptu birthday party were getting slimmer by the minute.

Rob laughed again. 'Thought you'd like a surprise, so get the . . . ready . . . home . . .' His voice faded in and out before the reception failed altogether.

'Rob? Hello . . . ?' Angie stared at the beeping phone. *I'm the one planning the surprise around here . . .*

Back in the kitchen, she twisted the oven dial one last time. Still nothing. She hated the idea of letting Rob's birthday pass without a homemade cake and racked her brain for a Plan B.

'C'mon, Claud. Let's go next door and ask if we can borrow their oven again. Then it's tidying up time.' With the brimming cake tin in one hand, and Claudia's little fingers in the other, she glanced around the cramped rental. It was barely big enough for a couple, let alone a family, but if she gave the place a quick tidy while the cake baked and popped a few candles on, they'd have everything they needed to celebrate Rob's birthday.

The landscape of western Victoria whipped past the windscreen in a green blur. Freshly shorn sheep dotted the paddocks, their bright white wool catching the sunlight like coconut on a lamington, but Angie couldn't drag her eyes away from Rob Jones.

Rob's height was always more pronounced in her little hatchback. His dark hair almost touched the car roof and his legs were cramped underneath the steering wheel.

He'd barely stopped to take a breath since he'd pulled into the driveway, dumped his backpack on the porch, whisked them out to the car and pointed the car towards the coast.

'There's enough land to crop and run cattle. The bones of the place are sound. Owners upgraded the wiring a few years ago, so it's not a death trap like all the other houses we've looked at,' said Rob, his animated gaze switching between the road and her. 'Deadset winner!'

Angie couldn't help laughing. 'You've said that about every old place we've seen. Remember last time you were home? That dive in Macarthur? The real estate guy had to catch the front door when it fell off its hinges! And the floorboards in that "renovator's delight" in Allansford had more termites than timber.'

Angie smoothed the newspaper clipping. Rob had waved it around like a winning lottery ticket when he'd arrived home. With four bedrooms, two living areas and acreage, there'd be ample room, but by the look of the photograph, there was a lot of hard yakka required.

4

MAYA LINNELL

'They've used the phrase "fixer-upper" twice. That's code for downright awful.'

Rob took his large hand off the steering wheel to squeeze her knee. 'Wouldn't stay that way for long with the two of *us* on site.'

Small country towns blurred into one another as Rob took them down unfamiliar back roads and single-lane tracks. The ocean glimmered in the distance, and after two hour's driving they finally arrived in front of the weatherboard cottage. 'Perfect, or what?'

Angie felt a surge of excitement as she studied the building. It was even more derelict in the bright spring sunshine than the photograph had suggested, but the ornate latticework and wide verandah offered an air of elegance. Even in its state of disrepair, she could see the cottage had once been someone's pride and joy.

She looked back at the advertisement, feeling the need to balance Rob's excitement. *She* was normally the one who rushed into things, yet Rob looked like he was about to whip out his bank card and lay down a deposit as soon as she gave the nod.

'Better than the others we've seen,' she said cautiously. 'Probably miles outside our price range, though.'

Rob tapped his nose as he unbuckled Claudia from the back seat. 'Motivated seller, apparently.'

He grabbed Angie's hand, almost dragging her down the driveway. The smell of wisteria and jasmine wafted up from the neglected garden. Overgrown rose tendrils snagged Angie's jeans as she followed the path to the house. The newspaper photograph must have been taken years before, or strategically cropped so that the wild garden beds and piles of rubbish at the side of the yard were out of shot. The lawns had been given free rein, growing knee-high and creeping up onto the cement path around the cottage. Even so, just as she'd been drawn to the black-and-white photo in the ad, Angie found herself gravitating towards the old building.

'Here's the agent now,' said Rob. The real estate promo car pulled in behind their hatchback.

Angie stuck out her hand but the agent leaned in to kiss her on the cheek before slapping Rob on the back. 'Good to see you, Jonesy! And Angie, I've heard so much about you and this little cutie.' He tweaked Claudia's nose. 'What a great opportunity, hey?'

Angie lifted an eyebrow as the man shoved a key into the front door. Friendliest real estate agent she'd ever met. Rob took her hand and they headed inside.

They went from room to room. The high ceilings and generous windows made the cottage feel spacious, and even with furniture, there'd be oodles of room for hide-and-seek, plus enough floor space for those oversized jigsaw puzzles Claudia loved and maybe two sofas, instead of the two-seater they'd made do with in Eden Creek. Sunshine streamed in through dirty windows and dust motes danced. Angie swooned when she saw the ornate ceiling roses in the lounge room, and more in the smaller bedroom, which would be perfect for Claudia.

The real estate agent noticed Rob admiring the open fireplace and launched into his sales pitch. 'Winters snuggled up in front of the wood-fire, summers at the beach down the end of the lane. What more could you want? There's even a creek at the back of the property, if you fancy a bit of eel trapping,' he said.

Angie almost caught herself nodding, and strode out of the room. *The floral carpets in the bedrooms would need to go, and most of the bathroom fittings and cabinetry.*

Angie tried to remain impartial, willing herself to find fault with the pressed-tin kitchen ceiling, cracked foot-high skirting boards and worn floorboards. But after half an hour inside, the cottage had an undeniable hold on her. The features she loved steadily outweighed the cons. She could picture them here as a family. It felt like they'd found their new home.

Angie buckled a tired Claudia into the car seat, watching her daughter's eyelids close. She joined Rob and the real estate agent in a surreal conversation about timelines and deposit options, unable to believe that they may have finally found their dream cottage. Enough land to run a few cattle. Close to the ocean. With a little orchard. Room to plant a weeping cherry tree in memory of her mum, Annabel. The perfect place to turn Claudia into a little green thumb, and, maybe one day, expand their little family.

'Cooooeee.'

Angie swivelled towards the familiar voice. *No, it can't be . . .*

'Yoo hoo. Is that the birthday boy and his beautiful girls?'

It wasn't until Angie spotted Rosa Jones striding across the paddock that she noticed the black-and-white Friesian cows, and the thick bottlebrush hedges bordering the neighbouring property. She flashed Rob a look of disbelief and sucked in a sharp breath. *What is his mother doing here?*

Angie barely had time to comprehend the situation before she was squeezed in a vice-like hug, complete with back pats, murmurs of delight and the scent of roses.

'Oh Angie, isn't this great? I've barely slept a wink.'

Okay, how did Rosa know about this before me?

The real estate agent drove off with a toot and a wave. Rob strode over to his mum, his tall frame dwarfing Rosa as she gave him a tight squeeze. They shared the same black wavy hair and olive skin, but Rob's height was definitely from the Jones side of the family tree.

'What did you think? And where's my beautiful granddaughter?'

'Mum, she's aslee—'

Rosa yanked the back door open. A sharp cry escaped from the car. Angie and Rob both grimaced.

'Oops, Granny woke you up. Let's get you out of that seat, poppet.' Rosa fumbled with the five-point harness. 'I've got some beautiful new calves to show you.'

Claudia shook her head mutinously. Angie knew exactly how she felt.

'Here, Mum, let me.' Rob squeezed in and lifted Claudia out.

Rosa stepped in closer. 'Granny's missed you, poppet. And haven't you grown tall!'

Standing on tiptoe, Angie whispered to Rob. 'It's within walking distance of the dairy? How could you not mention that?'

'Would you've come?'

Angie groaned, now spying the Jones' dairy and farmhouse further down the road. Of all the fixer-uppers in the country, had she just fallen in love with the one right next door to his folks?